JOSEPHINE'S TEAR

A CRIMSON AND SHADOWS NOVEL

V.I. DAVIS

To my mother,

If I am even a fraction of the woman you are, then I am doing something right.

The vampire clans coveted beauty above all else, so it had only been a matter of time before I was sent as a Candidate to participate in the Selection. With golden-brown hair and hazel eyes, I looked like my mother. Her true beauty hadn't been in her appearance, though. It had shone from within, radiating warmth and brightening the world around her. That light had forever been extinguished two nights ago when I'd found her being drained by a vampire in our home. The creature had fled the scene with my mother's lifeless body before the scream lodged in my throat could claw its way out.

"Sophie?" my father asked, snapping me out of my thoughts. He must have knocked and walked in while I was lost in the horrible memory of that night—the worst, most devastating night of my life.

Pulling myself back to the present, I found my reflection in the vanity mirror. I'd always known this day would come. All my life, I'd been aware of the attention my features could garner. Now, the girl in the mirror looked haggard, her face gaunt and her mouth wan. My eyes were haunted, and I squeezed them shut, willing myself to wake up, but this was no nightmare. It was my reality. I felt numb—the cold feeling that had crept into my chest on the night of my mother's death and settled there, spreading to my entire body, chilling my insides.

"Are you ready?" my father asked.

When I turned around to face him, he looked defeated. Tension bracketed the corners of his mouth, and his blue-gray eyes were dull and smudged with purple beneath. My welling tears blurred his features, but there was no mistaking the devastation I saw on his face. Two nights ago, I'd lost my mother, but he'd lost the love of his life.

"I asked Madam St. Clair to reconsider in light of recent events, but she denied my request," my father said, hanging his head.

The way his shoulders slumped, and his voice broke halfway through the sentence, let me know that he was on the brink of falling apart. So was I. In the recesses of my mind, I knew that I hadn't yet begun to process my mother's death. That realization was there, looming over me, but I had neither the strength nor the courage to face it. Not yet. There was a more pressing issue at hand—the Selection. I had hoped to avoid it, but the Governess, Madam St. Clair, hadn't found my mother's death to be a valid reason to spare me from being sent as a tithe to our vampire overlords.

Everything inside me shriveled up at the thought of going to the Duval Estate and meeting the members of the ruling clan. I'd just lost my mother; I didn't want to lose a year of my life to be their vassal and blood donor. For all I knew, one of them could be the same monster who'd killed her. A shudder of trepidation rolled through me at the thought, and tears spilled, gliding down my cheeks.

"I'm sorry, Sophie," my father rasped, his own eyes glimmering with tears. "At least, if you're selected, you won't have to go far."

The Duval Estate was in New Haven, the capital of the

Eastern region, where we also resided, but knowing that brought little consolation. If I was selected, my childhood home might as well be thousands of miles away. For a year, my life would not be my own—it would belong to the Duvals.

"I'm ready," I lied, not recognizing my own voice. It was dead and cold. Resigned.

My father and I loaded into the carriage and spent the ride to the estate in somber silence. There was nothing either of us could say to alleviate the dreadful weight of the situation. My mind was empty, and my body didn't feel like my own. Anxiety replaced the emptiness as we got closer to the estate, and a feeling of hopelessness settled over me. At that moment, I was not in control of my life, and I didn't have the faintest idea what I could do to regain it. It was as if a chasm had opened under my feet on the night of my mother's death, and I'd been falling ever since, deeper and deeper into the oily abyss with no end in sight.

When the carriage rolled through the black and gold fence enclosing the estate, I instinctively curled into my father as if looking for his protection, but he couldn't shelter me from what was to come. A scratchy lump formed in my throat as tears threatened again, but I forced them down. It was too early to panic. There were always eleven Candidates, one from each town in the region—I might not get selected.

Taking a steadying breath, I pulled away from my father and peeked out the window at the sprawling estate I'd only ever seen from afar. Visits to the estate were not allowed, and any interaction with the ruling clan was prohibited. The Duvals had always kept themselves separate from the humans living in New Haven, conducting all their business through Madam St. Clair.

My heart stuttered and stopped when the carriage jerked to a halt in front of a magnificent three-story mansion with stained-glass windows and a set of double doors. Lit lampposts in front of the house bathed the dramatic facade in a yellow glow.

"The Candidate comes with me. You can wait here," said a

stern-looking servant as soon as my father and I exited the carriage.

My anxiety intensified as my stomach turned over.

"Will I have a chance to say goodbye?" I asked shakily.

The servant didn't respond as he turned on his heels, expecting me to follow. He strode toward the front doors, and after one last panicked look at my father, I hurried after him. We entered the mansion but didn't go far, stopping in the brightly lit foyer where I joined the other Candidates. Full of nervous energy, I picked a spot in the back, trying to attract as little attention as possible. Demurely clasping my hands to stop their trembling, I fixed my gaze on the Candidate's back before me.

"You," came an old woman's voice from the front of the crowd.

I was so focused on making myself invisible that I didn't realize the woman had referred to me until the other Candidates stepped aside. Lifting my gaze, I made eye contact with Madam St. Clair.

"Come to the front," she commanded, her voice husky and cold.

I was frozen in place. The foyer was eerily quiet as all the eyes were on me. When I didn't move, the Madam arched one perfectly groomed brow, making a sound of impatience. The other Candidates spurred into action, shoving me to the front, where I was left standing, feeling too exposed. The Governess scrunched up her wrinkled face in disapproval when she saw what I was wearing. The long-sleeve black dress was not reveal-ing, and I'd picked it for a reason—to avoid being noticed. The task had been made more difficult now because I was in the front row.

My palms were damp when I unclasped and wrung my hands as a hushed silence settled over the Candidates. The very air stilled as the Duvals entered the foyer. I'd seen many paintings of the ruling clan through the years but being in their presence was still deeply unsettling.

Over six feet tall, Henry Duval was a wall of coiled muscle, and there was no mistaking the violence his body was capable of. Despite his large size, he moved like a predator with quiet grace and fluidity, which made him even more intimidating.

His sister, Isabelle, moved in a similar manner, her dark brown eyes scanning the rows of the Candidates as if she were a huntress and we were her prey. I supposed that wasn't that far from the truth. My breath left me at the thought, and I clasped my hands again, lowering my eyes to the floor. The clan leader, Vincent Duval, was not here, which was strange but a relief. Perhaps only two people instead of three would be selected tonight, increasing my chances of leaving this situation unscathed.

Holding my breath, I waited as Henry and Isabelle began their selection, gliding through the room, looking for their next vassals.

Please, not me. You don't want me, I chanted in my head, counting down the seconds until this torture was over.

The vampires' light footsteps echoed in the otherwise quiet foyer, growing closer until a pair of polished black boots came into my line of vision, stopping before me.

"What is your name?" Henry Duval asked in a deep timbre.

Terror seized me as tiny tremors started in my hands and spread to my entire body. Slowly lifting my head, I met his deep-blue gaze and opened my mouth to speak, but no words came out. I was paralyzed by fear; every instinct in me screaming to run.

"Her name is Sophie Devereaux," Madam St. Clair said, coming to stand beside the Lord. "She lost her mother two days ago. Dark Witches took her. As you can see, she is still quite shaken up."

Henry's eyes widened at her words, and something I couldn't

quite decipher flickered across his features. It looked like pity, but that couldn't be right. Though they protected us, vampires were cold creatures, devoid of emotion, so I doubted the Lord felt empathy for me. There was something in the way he looked at me, though, but I wasn't sure what it was.

Did he somehow know my father and I had lied about my mother's death?

We'd hid the truth and said Dark Witches took her. Vampires were our protectors. They didn't kill humans; Dark Witches did, which made what I had seen that night unbelievable and bizarre.

When the Lord pinned me with a stare, I found myself unable to avert my gaze. His eyes were turning darker by the second, and my heart dropped when I saw bald hunger in them. He wanted me, was interested in me like a collector in the business of acquiring pretty things. Time seemed to slow and come to a halt as I waited for my fate to be sealed. Just when I thought the Lord was going to select me, he reluctantly dragged his gaze away from me, focusing his attention on a young woman to my left.

"What is your name?" he asked her, his eyes turning back to deep blue.

"Eleanor Dumont," the woman replied.

She didn't sound nervous or unsure. On the contrary, there were notes of excitement in her voice. Confused by her reaction, I glanced at her.

Like the rest of the Candidates, she was beautiful, with delicate features, glossy, blonde hair, and green eyes. Eleanor perked up when Henry looked at her, confidently meeting his gaze. The low-cut dress she was wearing left little to the imagination, and the way she stood, flaunting her curves, made it obvious she wanted to be selected.

Her wish was granted a moment later when Henry said, "I choose you as my vassal."

A rough exhale escaped me at the same time Eleanor gasped

with joy. All my tense muscles relaxed, and for a second, I thought I might actually collapse on the stone floor with relief. The torture was over—he'd chosen someone else.

My reaction didn't go unnoticed by the Lord, who stole a glance at me, his brows knitting. I assumed a neutral expression, fixing my gaze in front of me while Isabelle chose a vassal for herself, selecting a young man who looked terrified of being chosen. The two vassals remained in the foyer while the rest of the Candidates began filing out of the front doors.

A strange sense of awareness swept through me as I waited to flee this place, trying and failing to contain my excitement at not being selected. The back of my neck tingled as if I were being watched. About to step outside, I dared a glance behind me and saw Henry standing by the foot of the grand staircase. He was watching me, and our gazes locked and held as a second passed. Then another. There was a promise in his eyes, and I shuddered as a feeling of foreboding crept into my chest. It was as if a tiny voice whispered in my mind that I would see the Lord again. My lips parted on a sharp inhale, and I all but ran out the doors and into the cool night air, feeling like I was barely escaping with my life.

My father stood by the carriage, his expression guarded. He didn't know if I'd come out to say goodbye or if I was leaving with him.

I shook my head "no" as my lips curved into a smile. Potent relief washed over my father's face, smoothing out his taut features before he pulled me into a tight embrace.

"Let's go home," he murmured against the top of my head before helping me into the carriage.

The ride back to the house was quiet, but the mood was lighter now as if a weight had lifted from our shoulders. I couldn't believe I'd gone to the Selection and hadn't been chosen. Being in the carriage with my father, heading back home, felt surreal, and I wanted to pinch myself to make sure I wasn't dreaming.

When we returned to the house, I forgot that my mother was dead. Smiling, I hurried through the front door, excited to run into her arms and tell her about how I'd barely escaped the vampire's clutches. I made it all the way to her study before I caught myself. My hand on the study door, I paused as memories from the other night flooded my mind. It was as if I were reliving my mother's death all over again at that moment. Drawing in a shallow breath, I pushed open the door and took a tentative step into the study.

For a second, I expected to see what I'd witnessed that night—my mother's unseeing gaze and her frail, pale body. What greeted me was emptiness, with my mother's rosewater scent still lingering in the air. A solitary lamp atop the cluttered desk and silvery moonlight drifting through the window illuminated the room as I walked across it on shaking legs. I slowly turned around when I reached the far wall and sagged against it as the finality of my mother's death washed over me.

Dreading the Selection had helped numb the pain of my loss, but now that the Selection was behind me, I had to face this world without my mother in it. Never again would she pull me into a warm embrace, offer her advice, or a shoulder to cry on. I didn't stop the tears when they came this time. Instead, I let them stream down my cheeks as I slid down the wall all the way to the hard floor, my black dress pooling around me.

It felt like ages passed as I sat there, unmoving, my eyes fixed on the wooden floorboards. Perhaps I would just stay here forever, wrapped in my pain, until nothing was left of me but dust. Suddenly, my gaze snagged on one of the floorboards, and I tilted my head to the side. The board looked out of place as if the edges were not seamlessly fused with the rest.

The night of my mother's death flashed through my mind.

Vampires didn't kill humans.

Was it possible that the vampire who killed my mother was here for some other reason? What if he was looking for something?

Willing my numb limbs to move, I rose from the floor and rummaged through my mother's desk until I found a letter opener. Lowering back down, I used it to pry the floorboard free. As I'd suspected, there was a secret compartment underneath.

My breath caught because this felt like a moment of great significance. There was a feeling inside me that whatever I was about to discover would be life changing. With trembling hands, I reached inside and retrieved a single piece of paper stashed in the secret compartment. I carefully unfolded it, immediately recognizing my mother's handwriting. The first few lines were neatly written, but the last two were scribbled as if she'd been in a hurry.

My eyes widened in disbelief as I scanned the paper, and it took me a few seconds to comprehend what I was seeing. It was impossible. Yet, I'd never wanted to believe anything so much in my life. My heart stopped and then sped up as I lifted my eyes from the paper. My mother had believed there was a way to destroy the supernatural—an amulet called Josephine's Tear.

The note rustled in my shaking hands as I set it aside and reached back into the secret compartment. I felt around the shallow opening just to confirm what I already knew—it was empty. The amulet was not inside. My heart sank with disappointment. It was possible the vampire who'd killed my mother had taken it, but then why would he leave the note behind?

I lifted the paper back to my eyes, studying it closely. My mother had drawn a sketch of the amulet—a teardrop-shaped pendant—and scribbled "Vincent Duval" and "power of three" below it. I didn't know what the notes meant, but I decided right then and there that I would make it my mission to find out. I would find Josephine's Tear and destroy the supernatural, setting humanity free.

1

ONE YEAR LATER...

A smile tugged at my lips as I wove my way through the rows of the Candidates to assume a position in the very front. A year ago, I'd stood in this very spot, shaking with dread at the prospect of being chosen as a vassal. Now, I stood with confidence—no longer the timid creature I'd been at eighteen. The wooden dagger strapped to my thigh and hidden beneath the skirts of my gown helped me to feel more at ease. The long, slender blade was honed to a needle-like point intended to pierce through a vampire's heart. As I'd suspected, no one had searched me when I'd arrived at the estate. Since the clans were all that stood between us and the Dark Witches, no human would make an attempt on their lives.

Madam St. Clair stood before the grand staircase leading up to the second story of the mansion, her back to the wide stone steps. Her shrewd gray eyes narrowed when she noticed me in the front row, and I wondered if she could see the determination in the stubborn set of my jaw and the resolve in my hazel gaze. Squaring my shoulders, I lifted my chin, then lowered it slightly —I needed to appear eager, not defiant.

As the human Governess of New Haven, the Madam oversaw

the Selection for the Duvals every year. Convincing her to send me as a tithe again hadn't been difficult. While the Selection was an accepted reality in our world, people didn't usually volunteer to go as Candidates.

"Lord Duval would be pleased," her exact words had been when I'd asked. "He seemed interested in you last year."

Henry Duval had almost chosen me last year, and I hoped he would this time. I needed to stay on the Duval Estate as his vassal so I could search for Josephine's Tear, the amulet my mother had believed could destroy the supernatural. In a world ruled by vampires and threatened by witches, it could be humanity's only hope for salvation.

We'd lived in this world ever since the Red War over a century ago when Dark Witches had appeared in our land, terrorizing and sacrificing any humans they could get their claws on in an attempt to resurrect their Dark god. Our warriors had fought valiantly but had been outmatched against a powerful, wicked enemy we'd barely understood. When our future had seemed bleakest, vampires had emerged from the shadows and fought to defend humanity. They had been able to decimate the main force and drive the remainder out. But our salvation had not come without a price.

"The Selection will begin in a few minutes." Madam St. Clair's husky voice rang out in the foyer, snapping me out of my thoughts. "Remember, you are all here for a noble reason. If you are chosen, you will provide fresh, willing blood for the Duvals, our saviors and protectors. It is an honor and a privilege to be selected."

I grimaced at her words but quickly schooled my features.

Most didn't see being selected as an honor. Our subservience to the vampires was a necessary evil to keep our country safe. Dark Witches were still out there, roaming the Black Forest, a hungry and unnatural place even the vampires knew to tread with caution. After the vampires had prevailed in the Red War, they'd divided the country into seven regions, each ruled by a familial vampire clan, and constructed warded stone walls on the border with the Forest. Still, Dark Witches occasionally slipped through our defenses and stole away humans to sacrifice.

When a vampire had killed my mother a year ago, my father and I had lied and said Dark Witches took her. Who would believe the alternative? A vampire killing a human just to feed their thirst was unthinkable. Countless human lives had been lost during the Red War, and the vampire clans had established strict rules about bloodletting. In the Empire of Seven, preying on humans was forbidden. Instead, each town in a region was required to send a Candidate to the capital for the yearly Selection, where the vampires of the ruling clan chose vassals to live with them, providing access to fresh blood until the next Selection when someone new was chosen, and another cycle began. The Selection had been carried out every year since the Red War, and everyone believed in the system the clans had established. I'd believed in it as well until last year when everything had changed.

I had hunted in vain for any mention of Josephine's Tear after discovering my mother's note. I'd scoured high and low, even venturing into the other regions of the country, but my search had rendered no results.

I still didn't know what "power of three" signified, which left my mother's scrawled reference of "Vincent Duval" as my only lead on finding the Tear. Vincent had been the head of the Duval clan ruling over our region but had disappeared a year ago, around the same time my mother had died. The Selection was a perfect opportunity for me to gain access to the Duvals and their mansion. As a vassal, I also hoped to infiltrate the cloistered vampire society so I could search for my mother's killer. But first, I needed to be chosen.

Telling myself to focus, I glanced at the young man standing in the front row to my right. When he offered a small smile, one side of my mouth turned up in response. There was no harm in being friendly—he was not my competition. As far as I knew, Henry Duval always chose women, not men, as his vassals. The Candidate to my right was probably here for Henry's sister, Isabelle.

"You, come to the front," Madam St. Clair said a moment before a demure young lady joined me in the front to my left. She was a picture of innocence with big doe eyes and full, lush lips, and that made me nervous.

He will choose me, I told myself, taking a steadying breath.

As if I'd conjured him with my mind, Henry Duval stepped into the foyer. He looked just as I remembered, not having aged a day. As a vampire, he was forever frozen in time, a still life of eerie perfection. His thick, wavy black hair was swept back from his face, revealing his chiseled features—high and broad cheekbones, a straight nose, and a wide and full mouth. He was wearing black breeches and a white dress shirt that molded to his powerful body.

A few soft gasps escaped the other Candidates when the Lord walked in before a hushed silence settled over the room. Isabelle joined Henry a moment later. She was still utterly beautiful, with black, thickly curled hair and deep-brown skin. Her lips were painted a vibrant shade of red, matching her low-cut gown. The color reminded me of blood, and I suppressed a shudder, schooling my features and swallowing thickly to relieve my suddenly dry throat.

Henry strolled through the foyer, moving with fluid grace, and Isabelle followed close behind, her long gown clinging to her legs like liquid. The Lord glided down the first row of the Candidates, stopping abruptly before me. My pulse quickened as I met his stormy blue eyes.

"Sophie?" he asked, his voice as deep as I remembered. It had haunted my dreams for a few weeks after the Selection last year.

I sucked in a sharp breath, relieved yet unnerved that he

remembered me. This was my moment. Forcing my shoulders to relax, I curled my lips into a smile.

"My Lord," I breathed, inclining my head to gaze up at him from beneath my lashes.

The game of pretense did not come easily to me, but I was hopeful my behavior conveyed the message I was trying to send—choose me, I want to be yours.

A muscle flexed along Henry's jaw as he stared at me, his expression unreadable. Our gazes locked and held for what felt like a small eternity as I waited for what he would do next. So much hinged on me becoming his vassal. Human lives were on the line. It felt like what happened tonight would change the course of history.

That was why when the Lord broke eye contact and turned to the young woman next to me, my heart tumbled all the way to the pit of my stomach. He was losing interest. I had to do something—*anything*. In a desperate attempt to keep the Lord's attention, I grabbed his hand and immediately dropped it when my fingers brushed the cool skin. There was a question in his eyes when they darted back to mine, but I found myself at a loss for words. So, instead of speaking, I bit down on my lip, drawing Henry's attention to my mouth. His gaze dropped to my lips before moving lower.

My body tensed under his appraising stare, and I wanted to fidget but held myself still. The emerald-green dress I was wearing cut low across my chest, and my hair was pulled up with a few wispy strands left down to frame my face. My appearance was a calculated move, which I knew had worked when Henry's gaze lingered on my exposed neck. His features sharpened, becoming stark. A few moments passed before his eyes returned to mine. They were darker—almost black—with hunger that made my skin crawl.

"I choose you as my vassal," he said, his voice low and thick.

Relief snagged in my throat. My chest felt tight, my heart fluttering like a caged bird.

"And I choose you." Isabelle stopped before the young man to my right.

She breathed the words rather than said them, sensual and soft. It was as if everything about her meant to entice and seduce.

"My Lady," the young man purred. "May I?"

Isabelle inclined her head, and my brows knitted as I watched the man take her hand. He brought it to his mouth and skimmed his lips over her knuckles. If the coolness of her skin bothered him, he didn't show it.

"The Selection for this year is complete." Madam St. Clair's voice rang out in the foyer. "The vassals stay. Everyone else is dismissed."

There were a few sighs of relief and some of disappointment from the other Candidates as they began leaving the estate through the double front doors.

I looked at Henry and found him watching me, his eyes now back to deep blue.

"My father is right outside. Can I say goodbye?" I asked him, expecting to be shut down.

To my surprise, he nodded, and I turned around and walked toward the open doors.

A gust of cool night air washed over my skin when I stepped outside. My father looked dejected, standing by the carriage several feet away from the mansion. Two lamps by the driver's seat cast his face in a soft, warm glow as shadows crept across his features.

"Did you get selected?" he asked when I approached.

"I did," I replied.

His shoulders slumped, and he rubbed his forehead, briefly closing his eyes. I knew that what I had to do weighed heavily on him. He'd aged so much during the past year. His once blond hair had gone gray, and his face now had more wrinkles than smooth lines.

"You know why I'm doing this. This is the only way—" I cut myself off, not wanting to speak the words aloud in case we were overheard.

My father opened his mouth as if to argue but clamped it shut. He knew I was right.

"Do you still have it?" he asked instead, his gaze flicking to my thigh.

"I do," I said with a small nod, referring to the dagger.

"Good. That's good." He dragged a hand down his face with a heavy sigh. "Sophie—"

"Father," I interrupted. I couldn't handle a drawn-out good-bye. Emotions clogged my throat, making it difficult to breathe. My chest tight, I stared at my father's face, trying to commit all the sharp lines to memory. "I love you," was all I said, fighting back sudden tears.

"I love you, too," my father rasped, pulling me into a tight embrace.

I hugged him back, holding on for a few moments as if trying to cling to my old life and everything that I was.

"I think our time is up," he whispered all too soon.

Pulling away from him, I glanced over my shoulder and found Henry standing in the doorway of the mansion, watching our exchange.

Scowling, I turned back to my father and gave him a quick kiss on the cheek.

"Sophie, are you sure?" he asked, his worried gaze searching my face.

I wondered if, at that moment, he was not seeing me standing before him but my mother. He didn't want to lose me like he'd lost her. When I'd told him I'd made finding the Tear my mission, he'd been crestfallen. He'd lost the trust in the clans on the night of my mother's death as I had, but the desire for retribution hadn't enflamed his heart as it had mine. He'd wanted to keep our heads down, terrified of incurring the vampires' wrath if we'd exposed them. But I couldn't return back to my old life, knowing the truth.

"I am," I told him, looking within.

This felt like my destiny—my purpose. I would do this for my mother and for my people—for the world where humans wouldn't have to choose between two supernatural evils. It was time we stopped serving one blood-thirsty creature to protect us from another deadly threat. It was time we reclaimed our world.

2

Despite the initial surge of determination, it took everything in my power to turn away from my father and face the mansion. The short walk back to the house was the longest of my life. Each step took me farther away from the life that I knew but closer to my goal. Or so I hoped.

When I passed Madam St. Clair on the way back, she stopped and said, "Congratulations. Remember, there is no greater honor than being selected. Serve him well."

My jaw ached at how hard I was clenching my teeth, but I managed to keep my features relaxed as I gave a small nod and kept walking.

Henry's expression was grim when I stepped back inside the mansion, and he closed the doors behind me with a loud thud, sealing me away from my freedom. My heart lurched in my chest as I suddenly felt trapped, the need to burst through the doors and run as far away as my legs would carry me, gnawing at me.

Pull yourself together, I told myself, swallowing the lump in my throat. *You want to be here. You have a mission.*

"Isabelle and I have some business to attend to, but the

servants will show you to your rooms," the Lord said, drawing my attention to him.

Without a second look in my direction, he strolled away, and Isabelle followed, leaving me and her vassal alone in the foyer.

The young man turned to me. "Wren Lockhart."

"Sophie Devereaux," I introduced myself, shaking his warm hand.

He couldn't be more than a couple of years older than me, with shaggy blond hair and light stubble. His pale-blue eyes danced as he smiled at me.

"Nice to meet you, Sophie. Exciting night, isn't it?"

"Uh, yes, it is." My voice came out shaky and unsure as nervousness invaded my senses. I'd succeeded at becoming a vassal, but now I had to face the consequences of my actions, and I had no idea what my stay on the Duval Estate would bring.

Wren opened his mouth to say something else but stopped when two servants dressed in dark tunics walked into the foyer and approached us. Like all those who served the clans, they were human and appeared quite young, about fifteen or sixteen. With hair the same shade of mahogany brown and eyes the same shape with upswept corners, they looked like siblings.

"Fresh blood." The male servant rubbed his hands together as if in anticipation, a flicker of amusement on his face.

"Ezra, stop it." The female servant swatted him playfully on the arm before turning to me and Wren. "I'm Rory, this is Ezra. We will be at your service for the duration of your stay."

However long that would be.

My plan was to find the amulet or another clue leading to it as soon as possible and escape. I hoped that I would also find my mother's killer in the process, but if I didn't, I wouldn't risk my mission by lingering on the estate. In the end, even if I didn't get to look into my mother's killer's eyes as I drove a stake through his heart, he would still meet his demise when I found a way to activate the Tear.

"Let us show you two to your rooms." Rory smiled and turned, but before we could leave the foyer, Henry and Isabelle returned, and they were not alone.

I recognized the man and the woman who were with them—they were the vassals selected last year. Though I couldn't recall the man's name, I thought the woman's name was Eleanor.

The vampires and the former vassals stopped in the foyer, and a strange, tense silence settled over the room.

Isabelle broke it first by saying, "Goodbye, Archie."

"Goodbye, Isabelle." The man—Archie—gave a tight-lipped smile and shook her hand. The entire exchange felt very formal, as if they were concluding a business transaction.

The conversation unfolded differently when it was Eleanor's turn to say goodbye. Her red-rimmed eyes told me she'd been crying, and there was a look of resignation on her face. Our gazes locked for a second, and I frowned when I saw anger flash in her eyes. I looked around me in confusion, making sure she was, in fact, staring at me because I wasn't sure what had warranted such a strong reaction from her toward me. I solved that mystery a moment later when Eleanor turned to Henry, gripping his arms so tightly her knuckles turned white.

"You don't need her. I can still give you everything you want," she begged.

"Goodbye, Eleanor," the Lord said, his tone cold and final.

Eleanor bristled and clenched her jaw but didn't say anything else as Henry pried her fingers from his arm and turned her toward the front doors. Ezra hurried over and opened one of them, and with one final look of icy resentment in my direction, Eleanor walked out. Once she was gone, everyone in the foyer was silent for a few minutes, and I wondered if that was because they were as shocked by her outburst as I was.

Why was Eleanor so desperate to stay? Had she gotten so used to the life of luxury on the Duval Estate? Did she not want to go back to her old life where she had her freedom?

Rory cleared her throat, drawing my attention back to her.

"Please, follow us," she said and turned to leave.

Sensing that no one was going to acknowledge what had just transpired, I didn't voice any of the questions that had flashed through my mind. I glanced at Henry and found him staring at the door that had just closed behind Eleanor. He seemed to be lost in thought, his features taut. He appeared bothered by Eleanor's behavior but didn't say anything as he turned and left the foyer with a heavy sigh.

"After you." Wren motioned in the direction of a long hallway illuminated by wall sconces.

Rory was already halfway down it, patiently waiting for us to join her. When I reached her side, she resumed walking, with Ezra and Wren following close behind.

"Good riddance," Ezra murmured under his breath. "Eleanor was crazy."

"Ezra," Rory said quietly, shaking her head.

We passed by several closed doors before Rory stopped and smiled at me. "This is your room, Sophie."

"Yours is farther down the hall," Ezra said to Wren. "Follow me."

Wren gave me a nod, his eyes bright, before strolling off after the servant. My gaze followed them until they rounded the corner, disappearing from view. Wren seemed genuinely excited to be here, which was unusual. Perhaps he was from one of the remote towns of the region and saw being selected as a chance to escape poor living conditions for a year.

"Ready?" Rory asked, pulling me out of my thoughts.

Dragging my gaze away from the now-empty hallway, I turned to her and nodded.

She opened the door to my room, and I walked in, taking a sweeping look around.

The bedroom was much bigger than I'd expected, illuminated by two lamps sitting on top of the nightstands on either side of the wide bed. A chest, a dresser, and a vanity took up the rest of the large space. The furniture was dark, and the walls were deep teal, but the drawn cream-colored curtains and the fur rug of the same color brightened up the dimly lit room. My brows pinched as I wondered if this was where Eleanor had stayed or if each new vassal got their own room.

All of the surfaces were bare, with the exception of the dresser. The small bag I'd brought with me from home sat on top of it. Candidates were not expected to bring much to the Selection, and to be honest, I didn't have that many belongings. My father was a scholar, and my mother had been one as well before she'd died. I'd been taking on odd jobs here and there since I'd turned sixteen to help pay the bills. We were not poor but had to be frugal to live comfortably within our means.

"We'll go shopping tomorrow for clothes and anything else you might need. Lord Duval is very generous with his vassals. You will be able to shop to your heart's content," Rory said, clasping her hands in front of her.

She seemed excited about going shopping, and I wondered if she had any friends her age or if she felt lonely living in the mansion with the vampires.

"How old are you?" I asked her, curious.

"I'm fifteen, and Ezra is seventeen. He is my brother," Rory said, confirming what I'd suspected earlier. "I remember you, you know. From the Selection last year. You looked so frightened then," she added, her brown eyes searching my face.

"I had just lost my mother," I explained, surprising myself. It wasn't a secret, but I didn't like talking about it. I wasn't sure why I'd admitted what I had, but Rory seemed genuine and sweet, and it would be nice to have a friend in this place for however long I'd have to stay. "Dark Witches took her," I added hastily to curb further questions.

"I'm sorry to hear that." Rory's gaze softened before deep

sorrow filled her eyes. "Ezra and I lost our parents a year ago. That was when Master Henry took us in."

"He took you in?" I asked, confused.

"Yes." She smiled. "You see, Ezra and I are from Fairview, and the living conditions there are rough. When our parents died, the Lord hired us as his servants, so we didn't end up on the streets."

My eyes widened at her words.

"Don't look so shocked." Rory laughed softly.

"Well, I am shocked," I admitted. "I just wouldn't expect a cold creature like him to care enough to take you in."

Her expression turned serious then as she said, "The Duvals aren't that bad. You probably don't know what to expect from your stay here, but it could be worse. Trust me." Shadows crept across her delicate face. "At least the Duvals wait for their Candidates to turn eighteen before the Selection. One of the other clans takes children." My stomach knotted as I cringed in disgust. I'd heard stories but had hoped they weren't true. "There is also a clan that…doesn't always return their vassals alive."

Rory's already pale face became ashen. I felt all color drain from my face as well. That was not supposed to happen. Vassals served the clans for a year and then returned to their homes, alive and well. At least, that was what the clans wanted us to believe. I gritted my teeth so hard, my jaw hurt. I'd lost my belief in the system the clans had established the night of my mother's death, but Rory's words were another confirmation that the system was broken beyond repair. How long did the humans have before the vampires decided they wanted free rein? I needed to find Josephine's Tear and use it to destroy vampires and Dark Witches alike.

"I'm sorry, I didn't mean to upset you," Rory said, her tone apologetic. "I was just trying to show you that the Duvals aren't that bad."

"They're vampires, Rory. They're all evil," I said, my voice hollow. I had witnessed their monstrosity firsthand.

"Master Henry showed me and Ezra kindness," Rory countered, her dark brows knitting. "Besides, vampires protect us from the Dark Witches."

"In exchange for our servitude," I pointed out.

"That's how it has been since the Red War, and that's how it will always be," Rory stated, matter of fact.

What if it doesn't have to be that way, I thought to myself, knowing better than to say the words aloud. I had already said too much.

Turning away from Rory, I opened the bag I'd brought from home and rummaged through it until I found my necklace. My lips curved upward when I opened the locket holding a miniature portrait of my mother. Our resemblance was uncanny. My hazel eyes had the same warm green hue, and I had the same smattering of freckles on the bridge of my nose. If only I could talk to her again. I would tell her how much I loved and missed her, and then I would ask about the Tear. Where had the amulet come from? How had my mother known about it? I hoped finding the Tear would shed some light on what had truly happened on the night of my mother's death.

Closing the locket, I clasped the delicate chain behind my neck and took a deep breath. Wearing the necklace steadied me, reminding me of who I was and of my purpose.

"I can give you a tour of the house," Rory offered softly from behind me.

"Actually, I'm pretty tired." I faced her, mustering a small smile that she instantly returned. I needed to be alone as I explored the mansion, so I could search for the Tear.

"As a vassal, you are expected to maintain the same schedule as the Lord, which means sleeping during the day and being awake at night," Rory explained. "I would try to stay up tonight if I were you. Makes the adjustment easier."

No wonder she and Ezra were so pale. They must be adhering to the same schedule. Did they ever see the light of day?

I was about to ask her but got interrupted by a knock on the door.

After a moment, Henry strolled in. His stormy blue eyes warmed when they settled on Rory.

"Please give Sophie and me a few minutes in private," he told her, and I was thrown by his gentle tone.

"Of course, my Lord." Rory bowed her head before sweeping from the room.

The moment the door clicked shut behind her, all my senses went on high alert. I was in a confined space with a vampire, alone. Knowing the Lord could move incredibly fast, I watched him like a hawk. My hand came to rest on my right thigh, where I felt the outline of my wooden dagger through my dress.

"I hope the room is to your liking," Henry said, coming closer.

His gaze was fixed on my neck, and I instinctively backed away, running into the dresser. The Lord stopped his approach, his brows pinching.

"Was it Eleanor's old room?" I asked, trying to distract him.

"No, each vassal gets a different room from the last," Henry replied before his gaze dropped to the locket resting on my chest.

In the blink of an eye, he was right in front of me, towering over me. He was too close—the coldness emanating from his body chilling my skin. Sucking in a startled breath, I steeled myself, tracking his every movement. He lifted his right hand deliberately slowly, gently picking up the locket.

The moment his cool fingers brushed my skin, my instincts took over. Before I could think twice about what I was doing, the dagger was in my hand, poised at the Lord's heart. I imagined the look of shock on his face mirrored my own. My heart dropped— I'd made a huge mistake. I was supposed to play the role of a compliant vassal. I'd thought I was prepared to do whatever it took to accomplish my goal, but perhaps I'd been mistaken. Perhaps there were some lines I just couldn't cross.

"Don't touch me," I bit out, my chest rising and falling quickly.

The Lord smirked, oddly calm, considering there was a wooden dagger aimed at his heart. Unless, of course, he didn't see me as a threat. Why would he, I realized. I'd lost the element of surprise. He was so much faster and stronger than me. He could snap my neck before I could even think about thrusting the dagger into his heart.

"If I am not to touch you, then how am I supposed to feed from you?" Henry asked, one side of his mouth turning up.

"I don't want you to feed from me." The words left my mouth before I could stop them.

The Lord's half-smile disappeared. Foolish, I was so foolish. My chances of remaining on the estate were dwindling by the second. Henry was probably wondering if it was too late to send me away and choose another vassal. If he would even send me away. He might decide to kill me for threatening his life. My breath left me at the thought as the Lord grew incredibly still, staring down at me like a predator about to pounce.

Just when I thought he was going to rip out my throat, he said quietly, "Lower the dagger."

The underlying menace in his voice told me if I didn't do it, he'd do it for me. Slowly, I lowered the weapon, my hand trembling, but didn't let go of the handle, keeping it by my side.

Henry's eyes narrowed, and his lips thinned before he said, "If you don't want me to feed from you, I won't." When I arched my brow in disbelief, he explained, "The choice was once taken away from me. I will not do the same to you."

"A vampire with a conscience? Am I supposed to believe that?" I scoffed, surprised to find my voice steady.

"You can believe whatever you want," Henry said calmly. He sounded almost bored with this conversation.

"Did Eleanor have a choice?" I asked.

I wasn't sure why I was trying to provoke him. Except, I didn't believe a word he was saying and wanted to call him out on his lies.

"Yes. She didn't do anything against her wishes," the Lord replied.

"She didn't want to leave," I pointed out.

A muscle flexed in his jaw before he said, "She had to. Her year was up. Rules are rules. This country rests on a delicate balance. We all have to do our part."

"And what is *my* part exactly?"

I needed to know what was expected of me, if what he was saying was true, and he wasn't going to feed from me. It sounded like he was playing a game, and I needed to know the rules.

"You tell me. You clearly wanted me to choose you as my vassal. Yet, you don't want me to feed from you. Why are you really here?" Panic flared in my chest as Henry leaned in, bringing his face mere inches from mine. As I scrambled to come up with a response, his eyes searched mine as if looking for the truth there. After a moment, he frowned, looking confused, and shook his head before saying, "Are you running from something? Do you want to live in luxury for a year? I don't care. I will not feed from you, but I also have a reputation to uphold. I cannot appear weak, so no one can know about our little...arrangement. You are my vassal, and when we are in public, you are going to act as such. Do we have an agreement?" He extended his hand, but I hesitated.

"Are you going to feed from someone else if you don't feed from me?" I wouldn't forgive myself if someone else suffered.

Henry's eyes softened a fraction before he replied, "No. I will drink the blood we have stored in cold canisters in the cellar."

Of course.

Each vampire clan had a cellar like that, and every healthy adult in the country had to regularly donate blood to help keep those cellars well-stocked. The Selection was not even necessary. It was nothing more than a demonstration of the power vampires held over humans. They didn't need vassals to have access to blood, but they took them anyway as a token of good faith.

I narrowed my eyes at the Lord. A vampire who didn't feed from his vassal? I couldn't have asked for a better arrangement, but why would the Lord agree to that? Regardless of what drove his actions, I needed to stay on the estate so I could look for the amulet.

My mind made up, I quickly gathered up my skirt and sheathed the dagger at my thigh.

Henry's eyebrows lifted in surprise, and I was willing to bet that from now on, Candidates would be searched when they arrived for the Selection.

Swallowing, I shook the Lord's hand, trying not to flinch at the coolness of his touch.

"We have an agreement."

Henry nodded, releasing my hand and turning to leave.

"Keep the dagger," he threw over his shoulder. "Now that I know you have it, you will not be able to catch me off guard."

As soon as he left the room, exhaustion washed over me, nearly knocking me off my feet. All the muscles I hadn't even realized were tense, relaxed, and air whooshed out of my lungs as if I'd been holding my breath. I unstrapped the dagger from my thigh and pulled the weapon from the sheath before kicking off my shoes and stumbling over to the bed. A sigh escaped me as I sank into the soft mattress, barely managing to hide the dagger under the pillow before falling asleep.

3

____

The house was bathed in the yellow glow of the lamps when I walked in, glad to leave the blue-black darkness of the early hours of the night behind me. A decadent smell of birthday cake hung in the air. Smiling, I followed it to the kitchen, expecting to find my mother there. When I didn't, my brows knitted in confusion. A chocolate cake, which was my favorite, sat on top of the small kitchen table, but my mother was nowhere to be seen. I knew I'd stayed out later than usual, but I'd still expected her to wait up to celebrate with me. Besides, my father wasn't even home yet, and she'd always waited up for him.

My skin prickled with a strange sense of awareness as I walked out of the kitchen and into the short hallway in the middle of the house. Something told me not to call out for my mother like I normally would as I paused and listened. My childhood home was quiet as if it were a living thing holding its breath. An ugly feeling I couldn't quite place began to rise inside me. It started in the pit of my stomach, slowly bubbling up as my legs moved as if of their own accord, carrying me through the hushed space in the direction of my mother's study.

"Mom?" I wanted to say, but once again, some inner sense of self-preservation told me to be silent as I reached the study and pushed the *slightly ajar door open. My chest rose and fell with short breaths as the oily, dark feeling inside me reached my lungs, filling them with cold sludge. I knew. Somehow, I knew that my life was about to change. That this house full of bright childhood memories would turn into a place of my worst nightmares.*

At first, I couldn't comprehend what I was looking at when I fully opened the door to the study. There was a mass of blackness, of shadowy darkness, and in it was my mother. Except, she didn't look like herself. She looked like a shell of a person, utterly empty and lifeless. She was already dead. The ugly feeling inside filled me completely and over-flowed, spilling into the world around me. I opened my mouth to scream, but no sound came out. I just stood there, frozen, as my mother's killer gathered her in his arms and fled, his dark, cavernous eyes meeting mine for a brief second before he disappeared.

With a gasp, I bolted upright in the bed, looking frantically around the dimly lit room. My skin was slick with sweat, and my heart thrummed in my chest. Memories from the night when I'd found my mother dead didn't haunt my dreams as much as they'd used to, but once in a while, they still crept into my subconscious, filling me with dread.

Willing my racing heart to slow, I reached under the pillow and pulled out the dagger, instantly feeling more at ease. Then, Henry's words invaded my head, "Now that I know you have it, you will not be able to catch me off guard."

My cheeks heated with shame when I thought about last night. I couldn't believe I'd almost failed at my mission because I couldn't control my volatile emotions. No matter. I was still here, and it was a new day. At least, I thought it was day. The drawn cream-colored curtains were so thick they didn't let in even a sliver of light, which was to be expected in a place inhabited by vampires. They were creatures of the night and could not walk in daylight without decaying until nothing was left of them but ashes.

Setting the dagger on the bedside table, I left the bed and

walked toward the window. When I opened the heavy curtains, early morning light greeted me, and I squinted before my eyes adjusted to the brightness. The window was not stained glass like the ones on the front of the mansion, allowing me to see the outside clearly. The house sat on a hill overlooking the rest of New Haven, and my gaze grew distant as I conjured up images of the familiar city streets in my mind. I wondered if there had been another attack last night and if the members of the Order had been able to fight off the Ravager and save the life the vampire was trying to take.

The attacks had started shortly after my mother's death. We called them Ravagers—feral vampires driven by bloodlust to attack humans in the middle of the night. They were not like the refined vampires of the ruling clans. We didn't know where they came from or where they scurried off to if they managed to escape our wooden stakes. We hadn't been able to capture one for interrogation. Perfect predators, vampires were faster and stronger than humans. Always at a disadvantage, we had to act fast when we came across an attack—the element of surprise our only hope of prevailing. We also didn't dare ask the ruling clans about the Ravagers. After all, they had to be the ones turning them. Since vampires couldn't procreate, they had to be made. I wasn't sure who was making Ravagers and for what purpose, but the number of attacks had been increasing.

My friend Waylon had been the first to come across an attack. As one of the human guards on the border with the Black Forest, he was a skilled warrior and had been able to fight the Ravager off but couldn't save the poor soul who'd fallen prey to the vampire. If I'd found my purpose upon discovering the note about the Tear, Waylon had found his that night with the Ravager victim dying in his arms. Gathering a few of his closest friends, who were also guards, he'd created the Order of Light—a secret organization to patrol the streets at night in hopes of preventing the attacks or stopping them when they occurred. Once I'd become a confident fighter under Waylon's tutelage, I'd often joined him on the nights when it was his turn to patrol.

My heart thumped heavily in my chest as I shook my head to clear my thoughts. What I was doing here was important. I needed to focus on my mission and trust that the Order could take care of the horrors lurking in shadowed alleyways at night.

With a heavy sigh, I turned from the window and walked to the adjoining bathing chamber, my bare feet stepping softly over the cream-colored rug on the floor. My hand blindly grazed the wall until I found a switch and flipped it. Bright light filled the space, glimmering off a porcelain soaking tub. A shower sat in the corner, and a marble counter with a sink lined the wall immediately to my right. Turning on the water, I splashed some on my face. Born and raised in New Haven, I was used to electricity and running water, but the amenities became scarcer and more expensive the farther one traveled away from the capital.

As I stared at my reflection in the gilded mirror, the events of last night replayed in my head. My brows pinched as I once again wondered why Lord Duval had made that deal with me and let me keep the dagger. I was not going to question it, though, not when I was one step closer to finding the amulet.

Turning off the water, I gave my reflection a nod of encouragement before walking back into the bedroom, where I retrieved a change of clothes and a brush from the bag I'd brought from home. Donning a simple blue dress, I quickly dragged the brush through my hair, letting it fall in soft waves around my shoulders, and righted the locket on my chest. I then slipped into a pair of worn but practical shoes I'd brought with me and, last but not least, strapped the dagger to my thigh.

When I opened the bedroom door and poked my head out, the hallway was quiet. I tentatively stepped out of the room and waited, expecting someone to stop me. After another beat of silence when no one did, I closed the door behind me with a soft click and set out to explore the mansion.

For a while, I wandered the empty halls undisturbed, discovering an ornate ballroom, an extensive library, and a formal dining room. All rooms were spacious, had decorative ceilings and were filled with elegant mahogany furniture and lavish artwork. The dark wood paneling, velvet drapery, and gilded elements created a refined atmosphere, but the crimson-hued accents scattered throughout left a bad taste in my mouth because they reminded me of blood. The curtains were drawn throughout the entire house, and the soft glow of several lamps did little to banish the shadows from all the nooks and crevices of the estate. The mansion was the epitome of luxury and excess, highlighting the insurmountable gap between the ruling clans and the humans who lived in the Empire.

My steps faltered once in a while when I ran into servants, but they didn't acknowledge me, so I continued to roam the quiet house, wondering where Josephine's Tear might be hidden if it was on the estate. If it wasn't at the mansion…Well, I wasn't sure where I would go from here. I would have to find a way to search the other clans' estates. My throat dried at the thought.

One step at a time, I told myself as I continued exploring the mansion.

When I turned down yet another empty hallway on the first floor, I noticed a slightly ajar door leading into a study. I peered through the narrow opening, but the room appeared empty. Opening the door wider, I slipped inside and took a sweeping glance around.

The space was dominated by a large mahogany desk with a stately leather chair behind it. A low credenza lined the opposite wall with several crystal bottles half-full of amber liquor and some glasses sitting on top of it. I'd read before that vampires didn't eat human food but judging by the selection on the bar, they didn't shy away from human drink, unless the liquor was for the vassals.

My gaze glided over a map of the Empire on one of the deep

crimson walls to two crossed short swords hanging above the unlit fireplace. With blades honed to fatal sharpness, and sides serrated to cut through flesh and muscle, the swords were clearly for more than just decoration, and my fingers itched to reach for them. I wondered if this was Henry's study and if there would be repercussions if someone found me in here. Swallowing, I glanced at the door I'd shut behind me when I'd walked in, trying to listen for any footsteps outside in the hallway, but all was quiet. It was daytime, and the vampires were probably asleep, which meant less chance of being discovered. Slowly, I came around the oversized desk and looked down at the large piece of paper lying on top.

What I saw on it reminded me of the family tree I'd helped my father with when I'd been a little girl. We'd been able to trace my father's lineage all the way back to before the Red War, but my mother's side stopped at my Grandmother Celine, who'd died years ago before I'd been born. The design on the paper looked similar to a family tree, except it depicted the seven ruling clans and the relationships within each clan. Miniature portraits of the clan members with names and dates written underneath mapped out the vampire history.

I was familiar with the names and the faces, having poured over records similar to this one many times before in the past year, looking for the one who'd killed my mother. It had to be someone from the ruling clans because the vampire who'd killed her had not been lost in the frenzy of uncontrollable bloodlust like a Ravager. Though reliving my mother's death was always torture, I'd done so many times, focusing on every tiny detail. Still, my mind had been unsuccessful at conjuring up an image of the vampire I'd seen that night. All I remembered were the eyes, so dark and bottomless, and even that memory was hazy as if it were hiding behind a sheer vale—so close, yet out of my reach.

My gaze swept over the depiction of the Duval clan, and my brows knitted when I saw two additional members I'd forgotten about. One of them was a stunning female with thick, loose curls the color of red wine. The other one was a male with short dark hair and warm, beige skin. Rosalind and Gerard Duval. The female had been Vincent's wife, and Gerard had been Henry and Isabelle's brother. The two had perished during the Red War.

The dates written underneath the portraits were something I'd never seen before, and my eyes widened when I realized they must be dates of birth. All the ruling clans had been alive during the Red War one hundred years ago, but I hadn't known that some of the vampires were that ancient. According to the dates, Vincent Duval had been over three hundred years old when he'd disappeared a year ago. Henry was almost two hundred years old, while Isabelle was the youngest of the Duval clan—she was one hundred and fifty.

I lifted my gaze from the desk, lost in thought. It was difficult for me to fathom living for so long. No wonder vampires were so cold and detached. I thought I'd be jaded, too, if every day was nothing more than a drop in the ocean of eternity. How could anything truly matter to them when they'd been around for so long and would carry on for ages to come? My brows knitted at the thought. It was pointless to try to understand them. They were monsters, and if I succeeded at finding the Tear, they would be destroyed. Every last one of them. Provided we could figure out how the amulet worked. My mother hadn't left any instructions on how to use it once we found it.

One thing at a time, I reminded myself.

My heart was heavy when I turned away from the desk and faced the large oil painting on the wall behind me. It depicted the final battle of the Red War—the battle of New Haven. Similar renditions could be found at different establishments throughout the city. This version was by far the bloodiest and the most terrifying I'd ever seen. In it, Vincent Duval was portrayed standing on a hill, holding a severed witch's head in his clawed hand. His expression was not one of triumph as one would expect. On the contrary, deep sorrow was etched into his striking features.

Frowning, I searched the painting for the other Duvals. Henry was not difficult to find because of his staggering height and large frame. He was holding a witch by the throat; his fangs bared in an animalistic snarl. His hair disheveled and his eyes wild, he looked drastically different in the painting than in real life—a killer through and through. A shudder racked me when I remembered him towering over me last night. There was a part of me that found it difficult to comprehend how I was still alive. Swallowing to relieve my dry throat, I forced my gaze away from Henry and found Isabelle tearing out a witch's throat, blood spraying everywhere. I cringed at the violence but didn't look away. Instead, I picked out the Dark Witches scattered throughout the canvas.

With eyes entirely black and skin as pale as vampires' but marbled with dark veins, they were something straight from a nightmare, sending my pulse into a frantic pace. Like vampires, Dark Witches were creatures of the night. They could walk in daylight without turning to ashes but preferred nighttime for their nefarious acts, drawing power from the shadows. It was in the darkest hour of the night when they'd sneak through the border and snatch women and children to take back to the Black Forest for sacrificial rituals. Sometimes, they didn't make it past the border, settling for one of the border guards.

The painting was so realistic that I felt the urge to back away from it to escape the horrors it portrayed. With a heavy sigh, I turned away from it and noticed another smaller painting closer to the window. It was a portrait of Vincent Duval, I realized, recognizing the long blond hair and piercing amber eyes. Coming to stand before the painting, I studied it for a few moments as if it held the answer to the question of why my mother had written "Vincent Duval" on the note about the Tear.

"How are you connected to the amulet?" I murmured, searching the vampire's stoic features.

I tilted my head to the side, thinking. My father had a secret compartment in my mother's study, hidden behind her portrait. What if...I reached out and carefully lifted the portrait off the wall before peeking behind it. My pulse quickened when I saw a safe.

4

"Sophie?" came Wren's velvet voice from the entrance to the study, catching me off guard.

Startled, I let the painting drop against the wall with a loud thud and quickly turned to the young man.

"Good morning!" He beamed at me, walking deeper into the room and looking around.

"Good morning." I shakily smiled back, placing a hand over my racing heart, trying not to look too flustered. Had he seen me look behind the painting? And if he had, would he tell on me?

I focused on Wren's face as he came closer, looking for any indication that he'd seen me. His features were relaxed and carefree, so I willed the tension out of my body, deciding that he hadn't seen anything. Then, I noticed twin puncture wounds on Wren's neck. Isabelle hadn't wasted any time before feeding from him. He looked a bit pale, and I wondered how much blood she'd taken.

"Did you have a good night?" Wren asked, stopping in front of me. Before I could answer, he said, "Having a vampire feed from you is…well, I don't know what I expected, but I'd never experienced anything like it." His gaze landed on the right side of my neck, and I involuntarily lifted my hand up, running my fingers over the smooth skin there.

You are my vassal, and when we are in public, you are going to act as such, I remembered the deal I'd made with Henry. As I was scrambling for an explanation as to why I didn't have any puncture wounds, Wren said, "I see the Lord gave you his blood to heal the bite marks."

That's right. I'd read that vampires' blood had healing properties.

"Isabelle offered to do the same, but I declined. I want to wear them as a badge of honor," Wren added, pride in his voice.

I arched an eyebrow, staring at the young man.

"Where are you from?" I asked, curious.

He must be from one of the poorer towns. That would explain his eagerness to be here.

"Weldon Heights," Wren said, confirming my suspicion. "You?"

"New Haven," I replied, glancing at the large oil painting on the wall.

Wren followed my gaze.

"Ah, the battle of New Haven. That was the pivotal moment in the Red War when the vampires drove the Dark Witches away," he said, facing the painting.

I watched him closely as he took in all the tiny details. His features became more taut the longer he stared at the painting, and I could tell when he found Isabelle in it because his eyes widened with fear. Just like Henry, Isabelle looked nothing like she had yesterday during the Selection. All fangs and claws, she was truly terrifying, and I wondered if Wren had gotten a glimpse of that side of her when she'd fed from him last night.

"This painting is…I have no words," Wren said, his voice strained.

"I think it's an excellent depiction of the monsters that dwell underneath the beautiful facade," I said, unable to hide disdain from my voice.

Wren looked at me, his brows pinched.

Suddenly, Rory burst into the study with a fluffy duster in her hand, stopping short when she noticed Wren and me.

"What are you two doing up?" she asked, raising her delicate brows. She didn't ask what we were doing *here,* which led me to believe Wren and I were not in trouble for being in Henry's study. "You both should have stayed up last night to start getting on the same schedule as the Lord and the Lady."

I offered an apologetic shrug while Wren gave her a sheepish smile. Rory had a certain way about her that made you feel terrible for disappointing her.

"Alright, well. Since you are up, let me get Ezra, and the four of us can go shopping. Both of you need more clothes and outfits for tonight."

"What's tonight?" I asked, confused.

"The Vassal Ball," Rory replied, turning to leave.

"The Duvals host a ball every year after the Selection," Wren explained as we walked out of the study and strolled to the foyer, stopping before the front doors to wait for Rory and Ezra. "Isabelle told me about it last night. All the clans attend with their new vassals."

Unease settled heavily in the pit of my stomach, and I quickly pressed my hand to my right thigh, feeling the outline of the dagger. Tonight, the house would be teeming with vampires.

This is a good thing, I told myself, taking a steadying breath.

I'd wanted an opportunity to gain access to the vampire society, I just hadn't expected to be presented with one so soon. I wasn't sure what I would do if I came across my mother's killer tonight. Even if I did, there wasn't much I *could* do. I wouldn't be able to take my revenge on him because that would jeopardize my mission. Still, tonight was a unique opportunity to learn more about the clans. Perhaps I could glean some information that could help me find the amulet or another clue.

A fist pounding on the front door echoed through the foyer, pulling me from my thoughts. Wren and I exchanged a glance and waited for someone to answer the door. Several silent seconds passed when no one came, and the knock sounded again, louder than before. With a shrug and another quick glance in my direction, Wren opened one of the double doors, revealing Eleanor on the other side. She looked like she hadn't gotten any sleep since she'd left the estate. Dark shadows smudged the skin under her eyes, and her pale cheeks looked hollow. The maniacal gleam in her gaze stirred the tiny hairs along the nape of my neck, and all my muscles tensed.

"Get Master Henry," I heard Rory's hushed voice from somewhere behind me.

She and Ezra must have just walked into the foyer. I didn't dare to look at them, though. My attention zeroed in on Eleanor. Her feverish green eyes met mine, and a heartbeat later, she snapped into action, lurching through the front door, coming toward me. A knife glinted in her hand as she swiped it, trying to cut me, but I danced out of her reach. I saw Wren start to step forward, but he stopped himself when I gave a curt shake of my head—I didn't need his help.

Eleanor lunged at me again, slicing the blade through the air in an upward motion. I jumped back and then rushed her, gripping the arm holding the knife. Jamming my elbow into her chest, I pushed Eleanor backward and slammed her into the wall on the left side of the open front door. Her eyes were wild and frantic as the knife clattered to the floor, and I stepped into her, my arm pressing on her throat.

"Eleanor? What are you doing here?" Henry demanded in a raised voice as he strode into the foyer.

When I glanced at him, he drew up short, and I followed his gaze to the open front door. Ezra hurried over and shut it, sealing off the sunlight so the Lord could approach where I was holding Eleanor against the wall.

It was obvious he'd just gotten out of bed. His dark hair was tousled, tumbling over his forehead, and he was wearing a loose white shirt that exposed a part of his chest. My gaze snagged on a thin metal chain with a key hanging around his neck before I lifted my eyes to his.

Wry amusement settled into his chiseled features as he said, "Ezra woke me up by banging on my door. He said there was an emergency, but I can see that you have it under control."

I gave a small nod and turned back to Eleanor, finding her staring at Henry with a look of utter devotion on her drawn face.

"Please," she rasped when I lifted my arm to alleviate the pressure on her windpipe. "You have to take me back. I can't return to my old life."

Henry's expression turned severe. "You can, and you will. You have your freedom back."

"I don't want it!" Eleanor shouted, tears rolling down her sunken cheeks.

My brows climbed my forehead. I didn't know if she'd been this way before she'd become Henry's vassal or if staying with the Duvals for a year had warped her mind, but I couldn't help but feel sorry for her. Henry's expression was almost pained when I glanced at him.

"Let me talk to her," he said quietly, and I released Eleanor and slowly backed away.

Eleanor's face turned reverent when Henry stepped in front of her and leaned in.

"Go back to your old life, Eleanor, and be happy. Do not come back here," the Lord said low. His voice sounded even deeper somehow, like smoke and shadows, causing a wave of goosebumps to break out over my skin.

Eleanor's green eyes glazed over, and she seemed to have

stopped breathing as Henry abruptly moved away. He bent down and picked up the knife I'd knocked out of her hand.

"Ezra, please show her out," the Lord said to the servant.

He briefly glanced at me, his eyes and his jaw hard, before striding out of the foyer. The moment he was gone, Eleanor slumped against the wall as if all the fight had left her frail body. She didn't object when Ezra approached and grabbed her by the arm before leading her to the door like a rag doll. He left her right on the other side of the threshold before shutting the door behind her back.

Stunned silence hung in the foyer for a few moments before Ezra broke it by saying, "Well, it's been an eventful morning. Who's ready to go shopping?"

5

The atmosphere in the carriage was tense for several long minutes after the four of us had left the estate. A part of me had expected Eleanor to still be on the other side of the door when we'd walked out of the mansion, but she was gone. I hoped she would find happiness and put the last twelve months on the Duval Estate behind her.

Rory sat opposite me in the black and gold carriage as it bounced along the uneven cobblestones. What had transpired earlier had clearly made her uncomfortable because her gaze was cast down and fixed on her lap, where she nervously worried the material of her skirt.

"I told you Eleanor was crazy." Ezra gave a small shake of his head. "That's why Lord Duval now sleeps with his door locked."

My ears perked up at that tidbit of information. I planned to search Henry's bedroom for the Tear, which would be difficult if he locked it at all times.

"He sleeps with his door locked?" I asked, trying to sound nonchalant.

"Yes. Wears the key around his neck," Ezra said, and my mind flashed back to the key I'd seen on the Lord earlier. "He only started doing that after Eleanor snuck into his bedroom and tried to stake him in his sleep."

"She tried to stake him?" I asked, my brow furrowing. "But she seems so devoted to him."

"Too devoted." Ezra gave me a pointed look. "That's why she tried to kill him a few weeks before the Selection. Said that if she couldn't have him, then no one else would."

My eyebrows lifted in surprise. I would have never expected a human to become so attached to a vampire. From all the stories I'd heard, vassals usually couldn't wait for their year to be up so they could return to their old lives and try to put that period of their lives behind them.

"How were you able to disarm Eleanor?" Ezra asked, looking at me with curiosity on his pale face.

"I learned some self-defense after the Dark Witches took my mother," I lied.

Ezra's brown eyes softened at my words. "I see. Rory told me about what happened to her. I'm sorry."

He sounded genuine, and I wondered if there was an unspoken thing between all children who'd lost their parents. A shared pain that let them relate to each other because only the ones who'd experienced it could truly understand it.

"Your mother was taken by the Dark Witches?" Wren asked low, his eyes wide. "I'm sorry, Sophie."

He looked ashen, and there was a flicker of terror in his eyes, making me wonder if there was someone Wren had lost to the Witches.

Before I got a chance to ask, Rory said, "Let's just try to have a good day, okay? Despite how it has started." She looked at each one of us before peering through the window. "It's been a while since I was last out during the day," she mused, looking at the scenery rushing by.

I wondered if she found it difficult to keep the same schedule as the vampires.

"Do you like working for the Duvals?" I asked her.

"I do." She met my gaze. "I told you last night, it's really not that bad. The other clans are so much worse."

"You'll see tonight," Ezra chimed in. "When you meet them at the Vassal Ball."

It didn't go unnoticed by me that Wren looked as uneasy as I felt at Ezra's words, his throat working on a swallow.

"It will be okay. We'll get through it," Rory said, taking a steadying breath.

She seemed apprehensive about the ball as well, which didn't help my own anxiety. I wondered if her words of reassurance were as much for herself as for us.

As the carriage rolled through the city center, I glanced out the window, looking for the familiar sign of Baylor's Corner. The tavern was the usual gathering spot for the Order of Light's members, where they quietly planned out patrol schedules and routes. I wondered if Waylon was inside. A childhood friend, he'd always been by my side, and I trusted him with my life. It hadn't been the only thing I'd trusted him with when we'd found ourselves at the inn next to the tavern after a patrol one night a few months ago. I'd never let it go beyond the physical with him, though. I suspected he wanted more, but I couldn't afford to have feelings for him. Feelings were a distraction from my mission.

"We're here!" Rory clapped her hands excitedly, snapping me from my thoughts.

When we exited the carriage, I realized we were at Madam Claremont's—one of the oldest and most expensive clothing shops in New Haven. It was widely known that the Madam outfitted the Duvals, the Governess, and the few human noblemen and women. Needless to say, I'd never set foot here before. Rory was brimming with enthusiasm as the four of us walked through an ornate black door into a brightly lit anteroom.

When we entered, my gaze flicked up to the elaborate gold

chandelier before sweeping down to a decorative white desk with curved legs. A full bouquet of flowers sat atop it, infusing the air with a pleasant, sweet scent. Though I felt out of place and wished I was here under different circumstances, a spark of excitement invaded my senses as I looked around, noticing that the anteroom opened into a larger room to my left and another one to my right.

"You're coming with me," Ezra said to Wren before leading him into what looked like the men's section of the shop, judging by a variety of displayed shirts and breeches I could see from where I was standing.

"And you can follow me." Rory grinned at me before pulling me to the room on the left.

The women's section was bursting with gowns of different styles and colors, and I was fascinated and a little overwhelmed by the selection.

"What do you want to wear tonight for the ball?" Rory asked, looking around with bright eyes.

A smile tugged at my lips, brought on by her girly excitement.

"I've never been to a ball before," I told her, running my fingers over the fine satin fabric of one of the gowns. "But I can't bring myself to feel anything but dread about a ball thrown by vampires to show off their newly acquired pets," I confessed.

The spark of excitement I'd felt earlier fizzled out as I scrunched up my face at the thought.

"Don't make that face," Rory said, watching me. "I told you—"

"I know, I know. It could be worse," I interjected, waving my hand dismissively.

"So, what do you think?" Rory proceeded to point out a few gowns in different sections of the room.

When I thought about being in a house full of vampires tonight, all I wanted to do was cover myself up from head to toe, but I wasn't naive enough to think I could get away with it. So, I settled on a long, black, off-shoulder dress that hugged my hour-glass shape but wasn't too revealing.

"What about this one?"

"Excellent choice. I think Master Henry would approve." Rory smiled at me.

I grimaced at her words because I wasn't looking for his approval. In fact, what she'd said almost made me want to reconsider and pick another gown.

"Oh, there she is," Rory said, and I followed her gaze to an old woman hurrying toward us. "Madam Claremont, the shop owner," Rory explained before greeting the woman with a warm smile.

The shop owner was short, plump, and the complete opposite of what I'd expected her to look like.

"This is Sophie, Lord Henry's new vassal," Rory introduced me.

"Nice to meet you, Sophie." The old woman clasped my hands in greeting. "Let's find you some gowns to make all the other clans envious of Lord Henry's new vassal." She winked at me.

I had to suppress a shudder as an ugly emotion reared its head at her words. I'd tried all my life not to attract attention because of my looks. Still, the Governess had noticed me around my fourteenth birthday. She'd told me I would be a tithe to the clan one day. The next four years had been spent in nervous anticipation as I'd tried really hard not to feel like a commodity.

Tonight, I would be just that—I would be diminished to nothing more than a trophy on Henry Duval's arm. A trophy for winning the Red War a century ago and protecting humans from the Dark Witches ever since. It didn't matter, I tried to remind myself. What I would have to endure tonight was a small price to pay if I was able to find the amulet.

"Are you alright, dear?" Madam Claremont asked, pausing in her search of dresses.

"Yes." I smoothed the scowl from my face and forced a smile.

For the next few hours, I obediently followed Madam Claremont and Rory around the shop as they helped me pick out dresses. Whenever I couldn't decide between two gowns, Rory just added them both to the pile. By the time we were done, I had gowns to last me for months, though I hoped I wouldn't have to stay on the estate for that long. Rory also made sure I'd picked out casual dresses and clothes, toiletries, and some jewelry, even though I didn't plan on ever taking off the locket holding the picture of my mother.

"Lord Duval will cover the cost," Rory said to Madam Claremont when the three of us returned to the anteroom.

"Of course." The shop owner smiled at her.

A moment later, Ezra and Wren emerged from the men's section, and the four of us walked outside and loaded into the carriage.

"Everything will be sent in a separate carriage to the estate," Rory explained as she got settled in her seat opposite me.

My brows shot up in surprise. A separate carriage just for clothes? Wren must have gotten as much as I had. I gritted my teeth, thinking about how all that money could be spent on helping the poor. The Duvals should be using all the wealth they had accumulated to improve the living conditions in the region instead of spending it to maintain their lavish lifestyle. I couldn't wait to destroy vampires, erasing the clans from existence. All their wealth would then be redistributed among those in need.

"Well, that was fun. I love shopping," Rory said, and I focused on her.

"What do you want to do now?" I asked, meeting her gaze.

"What do you mean?" Her brows pinched in confusion.

"You said it had been a while since you were last out during the day. Would you like to do anything else before we head back?"

I was in no hurry to return to the mansion and spend the next few hours dreading the Vassal Ball.

Rory glanced at Ezra, who lifted his shoulders in a shrug.

"I suppose we could get some food and have a picnic?" she said hesitantly with a small smile.

"Great idea." I grinned at her. "We can go to the Mayfair Park. It's not far from here."

We stopped at the local market and bought a basket of food before heading to the park tucked away on the outskirts of the Garden District.

The Mayfair Park was my favorite place in New Haven. I liked that it was usually not as crowded as the Rosewood Park in the heart of the city. Today was no exception. When we arrived, only a handful of people were in the park despite it being a clear and sunny afternoon.

"This is lovely," Rory said, looking around as we strolled toward one of the weathered cast iron benches.

We picked the one close to the fishpond under the shade of a large viloria tree. Its twisted branches sprawled out over the bench and half the pond. Small delicate petals from its flowers blanketed the ground in a sea of white and floated in the calm water of the pond, providing cover for the colorful speckled fish leisurely swimming there.

Our little group perched on the long bench and shared a meal of meat, bread, and cheese. Everyone was relaxed, and the conversation flowed easily, almost making me forget that soon we would have to return to the house inhabited by vampires. After a while, when the conversation slowed, and everyone was just enjoying the weather, Wren took a hunk of leftover bread and went to feed the fish. Ezra rose from the bench as well and began strolling around the pond, lost in thought. Rory and I remained where we were, sitting in comfortable silence as a light breeze stirred the tree branches, shaking more white petals free and making them drift to the ground.

When the clouds shifted, drenching the bench in sunlight, Rory closed her eyes and lifted her face up, basking in the warm rays. Her smile was serene as the wind teased her topknot, loosening a few wispy strands of dark hair to rest against her pale cheeks. She looked so young then, and my heart squeezed. I didn't have any siblings, but it was easy to imagine Rory as my little sister and feel protective of her.

Facing forward, I looked around the park, my gaze sweeping over the lush greenery. Phantom images of me and my mother filled the place, appearing here and there as my mind conjured them up. I could see us sitting on a thin blanket on the grass and strolling around the pond. A faint smile appeared on my lips at the happy memories before it faded as my eyes pricked with tears.

"Sophie, are you okay?" Rory asked, and I realized she was watching me.

"Yes." I cleared my throat and wiped away a tear that had escaped. "My mother and I used to come here often."

"You two were close?"

I nodded. "She was my best friend. I told her everything."

Rory was silent for a moment, her big brown eyes searching my face.

"Does this place still bring you joy?" she finally asked.

My forehead creased as I thought about it. I wasn't sure what brought me joy anymore. I'd used to read a lot, curled up on the old settee in my mother's study, and that had brought me joy. Rainy days had been my favorite, especially when my mother had been there, working and, at times, absentmindedly humming to herself. I hadn't read a book since her death. Ever since that night, I'd been so preoccupied with finding the Tear I'd forgotten how to enjoy life. Truth be told, I wasn't sure I *could* enjoy it again until I'd completed my mission and destroyed Dark Witches and vampires.

I couldn't tell Rory all that, so I settled for, "I think so. What brings you joy?"

The corners of her mouth tilted upward in a soft smile.

"The sun, the breeze." She giggled. "Good company." She bumped my shoulder with her own. "Hope," she added quietly, her expression turning serious.

"What do you hope for?" I met her gaze.

"A bright future where I feel safe," she replied in a hushed voice, looking around the nearly empty park.

Her admission brought a frown to my face.

"You don't feel safe with the Duvals?"

The question sounded silly the moment it left my mouth. She was a fifteen-year-old girl living with vampires. Of course, she didn't feel safe. She was innocent and sweet, and I hoped the Duvals did not take advantage of that.

"I feel safer than most," Rory said, and I relaxed a bit. The Duvals seemed to be treating her well. Still, I wished that her circumstances were different. "But can anyone truly feel safe in this world where Dark Witches steal us for sacrifices, and vampires drink our blood in exchange for their protection?"

My brows lifted in surprise. I hadn't realized Rory had such a strong grasp of our reality. It made sense that she would. Since she lived with the Duvals, she'd glimpsed more of the vampire world than most. She knew how vampires truly were, even though she seemed to have a twisted perception that Henry Duval had shown her kindness. Even if he had, it wasn't guaranteed to last. When you lived with predators like she did, it was only a matter of time before nature prevailed and they turned on you. I hoped I was able to find the amulet before that happened.

"I want the same future," I told her vehemently. "For all of us."

My words sounded like a vow. I could give her that future if I was successful at finding the Tear.

We stayed at the park for a while. The way everyone behaved gave me the impression I wasn't the only one who dreaded returning to the mansion to prepare for the ball. When the sun began its descent toward the horizon, we couldn't fight it any longer. With one last longing-filled look around the green haven, Rory announced that it was time we headed back to the estate.

The ride back to the mansion was spent in idle chatter that eventually died out the closer we got to the Duval Estate. Everyone's unease was palpable by the time we arrived in front of the mansion.

After exchanging nervous glances, we climbed out of the carriage and set off toward the house. It was difficult to will my legs to move to walk inside. A small part of me wanted to turn around and run as far away from this place as I could. Reminding myself of my mission, I gritted my teeth with resolve and entered the foyer, which was humming with activity in preparation for the ball.

"I'll see you in a little bit to help you get ready," Rory said in a hollow voice as she forced a smile that didn't reach her eyes.

I couldn't bring myself to smile back, so I simply nodded before trudging to my room. Once there, I hunched over the vanity, planting my palms on the smooth wooden surface. My eyes were big as I stared at myself in the mirror.

There was no way to delay the inevitable. The Vassal Ball would soon be upon us.

6

Rory helped me change into the black off-shoulder gown I'd picked out earlier and bound my hair into a simple knot at the nape of my neck. We were both quiet as she helped me get ready, each of us lost in our own thoughts. Her delicate hands trembled slightly as she worked on my hair, betraying her nervousness about tonight.

"I'll let Master Henry know you're ready," she said, lowering her hands from my head and clasping them in front of her. The corners of her mouth were turned down when I faced her, meeting her worried gaze. She didn't try to feign a smile as she swallowed and said, "Ezra and I will be helping during dinner tonight, so I'll see you again soon."

Her words didn't bring me comfort. On the contrary, they made my heart turn over with dread. I had the strongest urge to hide the siblings away for the duration of the ball and make sure they didn't come near it.

With a heavy sigh, I nodded, and Rory slipped out of the door. I knew there was no way to avoid the ball, but I wasn't ready for it. I doubted anything could have prepared me for tonight. In an attempt to calm my nerves, I took a deep breath, finding my center. After regaining some composure, I put on my necklace, letting the locket fall to my chest, and strapped the dagger to my thigh, making sure it was concealed under the skirt of my dress. The silky material of the gown molded to my body, but the outline of the weapon was not visible, which was a relief. I would have had to choose a different dress before I would forgo bringing my dagger.

I wasn't foolish enough to think the weapon would do me any good in a room full of vampires. I knew I wouldn't be able to prevail. My hope was to at least put up a small fight before being torn to shreds by fatally sharp teeth and claws.

A shudder of trepidation rolled down my spine as I turned back to the mirror. My face had become ashen, and my lips were pressed into a thin line, their color almost white. I truly didn't know what to expect tonight, and the feeling was more than disconcerting.

A knock sounded on the door, and all my muscles tensed because I knew it was Henry here to collect me for the ball. The Lord walked in a moment later, and I turned from the mirror to face him. He was wearing all black; the color a striking contrast against his pale skin, making the deep blue of his eyes stand out. His dark hair was combed back from his face, and his features were taut as if the Lord was on edge. The line of his lips was firm like mine, making me wonder if he was not looking forward to the ball.

"Good evening, Sophie," Henry said in his deep voice, appraising me from head to toe.

His blue eyes were assessing as they roamed over me, flickering over the strands of hair left down to frame my face and lingering where the locket rested on my chest.

"Good evening," I managed to say.

Every sense I had honed over the last year heightened the moment the vampire stepped into the room. I couldn't forget for a second that I was in the presence of a predator.

"You look lovely," the Lord said low.

I cringed at his words and couldn't bring myself to thank him for the compliment.

Uncomfortable silence stretched for a few seconds until Henry asked, "Did you have a good day? Rory told me you went to the park."

"We did." I inclined my head. "I think everyone had a good day. Despite how it started."

Henry's brows knitted in a frown. "Yes. What happened this morning was…unfortunate. I'm glad you were able to hold your own against Eleanor and that no one got hurt."

"Do you think she will heed your advice and return to her old life?"

"I hope so," the Lord replied, shadows creeping into his eyes.

"Does it bother you? Eleanor's attachment to you?" I asked, recalling Henry's reaction to Eleanor's presence at the mansion earlier. He had seemed conflicted, and there had been something akin to sorrow in his eyes.

"What bothers me is that she was put in that situation. We pluck humans from their lives for a year and then expect them to go back as if nothing happened. It is harder for some than most."

The way the Lord spoke sounded almost as if he didn't approve of the concept of the Selection.

Puzzled by his answer, I tilted my head to the side, studying his face.

"You care about her?"

"Enough to only wish her the best. She served her purpose. There is no reason for her to still cling to this…life."

"What about Rory? Do you care about her, too? She said you took her and Ezra in?" I asked, curiosity getting the best of me. The Lord's actions and behavior were not what I had expected from a vampire.

"I do care about her and Ezra, and I did take them in. It seemed like the best decision at the time, but sometimes I find myself wondering if it truly was," Henry said, running a hand over his jaw as if lost in thought. "Sometimes I wonder if they would be safer with humans instead of living here."

"Especially on evenings like tonight?" I surmised, thinking about my own reservations about having the siblings at the ball.

"Yes," Henry admitted, once again surprising me with his candor. "About tonight..." His stormy blue eyes met mine. "I must apologize in advance for what you might witness or experience at the ball."

Swallowing the lump in my throat, I stared at the Lord. He was apologizing for tonight? He was not at all what I'd expected, but I knew better than to let my guard down. If he didn't condone the other clans' behavior at the ball, he could choose not to host it, and if he didn't agree with the Selection, he could change that, too. Or, at least, try to. Perhaps he was just saying these things to lull me into a false sense of security around him. My eyes narrowed with suspicion at the Lord before I noticed a flat, black box in his hand.

"This is for you," Henry said, following my gaze.

He opened the box to reveal a string of diamonds, and my breath caught. I'd never seen anything so beautiful, and I couldn't even imagine how much the necklace was worth.

"I am not taking off the locket," I stated, my tone flat.

My simple necklace did not go with my gown, but I couldn't bear the thought of parting with it. As silly as it sounded, I felt like it offered some kind of protection. As if by wearing it, I carried my mother's strength and wisdom with me.

Henry's jaw tightened as his gaze dropped to the locket.

"What is so special about it?" He sounded agitated, closing the jewelry box with a click and depositing it on top of my vanity.

"It holds a miniature portrait of my mother," I told him, seeing no reason to lie.

Sympathy filled his eyes as he said low, "I'm sorry about what happened to her."

My lips parted slightly, and it took me a moment to form a reply because I was so taken aback.

"I'm sorry about Vincent," I finally said. "I've heard he was like a father to you."

Everyone knew the Duvals were not related to each other by blood but had chosen to form a family-like bond. Vincent had been the father figure, while Henry and Isabelle were like brother and sister. I wasn't sure if vampires regarded familial ties with the same importance as humans did. Did they mourn their loved ones? Or did they carry on as if nothing happened because loss was just a part of their eternal life?

"I did consider him my father. Taking over the clan after his death has not been easy," Henry said. Not much was known about Vincent's disappearance. I knew he had gone missing around the same time my mother had died. He'd been presumed dead, and Henry had become the new leader of the Duval clan. "A year later, I still have to keep proving myself to the others," the Lord continued. "That is why it's so important that no one knows about our arrangement. I cannot show any weakness."

"I understand," I told him, turning back to the mirror.

My gaze landed on my neck, and a thought occurred to me.

Frowning, I glanced at Henry. "Will the others think it's odd that I don't have any bite marks?"

Henry's chin dipped, and his eyes turned darker as they fixed on my exposed neck.

I shivered at the intensity of his stare.

Quickly closing the distance between us, he came to stand behind me, a cool presence at my back.

"No. They will assume I give you my blood to heal the wounds. I don't have to give you bite marks," he paused, one side of his mouth turning up. "Unless, of course, you're curious."

His tone was almost teasing as he reached up as if to touch me.

Meeting his gaze in the vanity mirror, I scowled at him.

"I'm not," I assured him coldly.

He smirked but lowered his hand.

"I will have to touch you tonight," he pointed out. "You are my vassal. You will have to act as such." He arched one dark brow.

"So, act like you own me?" I snapped.

"In the eyes of the others, I do own you for a year," Henry said calmly.

I bristled at his words but then schooled my features. It was in my best interest to play the role tonight so I could remain on the estate.

"I understand," I said again, gritting my teeth.

I told myself I was committed to my mission and hoped I wouldn't do anything foolish to jeopardize it. I could not allow my emotions to get the best of me like I had last night.

"Ready?" Henry asked, stepping away from me.

A soft sigh of relief left me because there was now some distance between us. The Lord stopped on his way to the door and half turned as I took one small step toward him.

"Are you wearing your dagger?" he asked, his gaze dropping to my thigh.

His mouth was taut, and his eyes were wary when they met mine again.

"I am," I replied, unsure of what would happen next. If he asked me to take it off, I'd refuse.

"Good," he said, surprising me. "Try not to pull it out unless you absolutely have to."

"Will I have to?" I asked, my scowl increasing as unease curled its way down my spine.

"I don't think so, but it is good you have a weapon and know how to use it."

There was a faint note of approval in his tone, but I had to admit it was disheartening he was so relaxed about letting me have the dagger. Because that meant he truly didn't see me as a threat.

"Shall we?" Henry asked, and I hesitantly curled my arm around his.

The coolness emanating from him made my breath hitch and my skin prickle.

"Try to look more relaxed," he murmured as we left my bedroom and strolled to the ballroom. "The others need to believe you are comfortable around me."

"They need to believe that I let you feed from me," I clarified under my breath.

"Among other things," he said quietly, and I glanced at him, appalled.

Cheeks heating, I quickly looked away. The relationship between a vassal and a vampire was not expected to be sexual, but I'd heard most of them were. I'd also heard that having a vampire feed from you could be an intense experience. Wren had confirmed as much this morning. A tiny part of me was curious about it, but I was more terrified than intrigued.

Anxiety flooded my system the moment we entered the ballroom. The night had descended, and all the heavy curtains were open, revealing the darkness outside. Henry untucked my arm from his and placed his hand on the center of my back, guiding me deeper into the crowd that had already filled the large space. His touch bothered me, but I knew better than to pull away. I was just here to play a role. All I had to do was pretend for a few hours and act as his vassal.

My skin prickled with awareness as all the heads in the room turned to us. All conversation ceased for a brief moment before resuming again. I caught a few curious glances in our direction as Henry and I stopped in the middle of the ballroom, not far from Isabelle and Wren.

The other vassal looked dashing in a pale-blue shirt that matched his eyes. He appeared a bit nervous, but the smile he flashed me when he noticed me was easy, and I had to admire his composure. Isabelle also smiled at me, her fangs peeking through her crimson-painted lips. She wore a revealing gown made of ivory-hued silk that hugged her slender form, pooling by her feet on the floor. Her hair was twisted up, with a few tight curls framing her heart-shaped face.

When a servant came by with a tray of champagne glasses, Henry took one and offered it to me. Grateful for something to occupy my hands to conceal their trembling, I accepted the drink and took a sip, trying to be subtle as I looked around the room.

Distinguishing vampires from their vassals was easy. It wasn't just their preternatural stillness. They had a certain air of superiority about them. They knew they were apex predators and carried themselves as if they owned this world, and humans were nothing more than pets.

A wave of anger swept through me at the thought. My dagger scorched the skin of my thigh, begging me to reach for it. My hands spasmed around the champagne glass, and I gritted my teeth, fighting the pull of my weapon. I was in a room full of vampires. Was I going to go on a killing spree? I almost laughed at the absurdity of the idea.

"Are you alright?" Henry asked low, inclining his head closer to me.

I almost jerked away at his proximity but held myself still, willing the tense muscles of my shoulders and neck to relax.

Before I could reply, one of the vampires glided over to us. He was tall and thin, with a sheet of jet-black hair that fell below his shoulders to his trimmed waist. I'd seen his portrait before when researching the clans, but I couldn't recall his name.

"This must be your new vassal," the vampire said in a smooth, rich voice.

His features were arrogant and relaxed as he took a drink from his glass.

Henry stiffened beside me, and his hand flexed where it was resting on my back.

"Yes, this is Sophie," he said, his tone cold. "Sophie, this is Everett Stern, the clan leader in the Southern region."

I gave a curt nod as I met Stern's gaze. His eyes were so dark, they appeared bottomless, and I had to suppress a shudder as I stared into the twin pools of blackness. The Lord from the South smirked and began appraising me, tapping his index finger on his chin. My skin crawled as his fathomless eyes roamed over every inch of my body. When his perusal was finally over, those eerie eyes met mine again. The blackness in them was like thick, viscous liquid, pulling me in and drowning me, robbing me of my breath. I dared a peek at Henry, but his stoic, silent presence by my side only heightened my anxiety. He was clearly uneasy around Stern, and that was very unsettling.

"You are exquisite, Sophie," Stern purred, and I instantly hated how my name sounded on his lips.

"Thank you, my Lord," I murmured, my stomach twisting with revulsion.

He turned to Henry. "You have made an excellent choice. Perhaps we could trade."

My grip tightened on the delicate stem of the champagne glass in my hand. Did the vampires do that? Trade their vassals as if we were some kind of a commodity?

"No, thanks," Henry bit out, his tone openly hostile. "I am not interested in children."

So Stern was the one who took children as his vassals. Bile rose in my throat as a feeling of disgust slithered across my skin.

There was another smirk on Stern's well-formed mouth.

"My vassal is almost seventeen this time. However, I do prefer them to be much younger. It's as if you can taste the innocence in their blood."

All color drained from my face, and I thought I was going to be sick. When my eyes darted to Henry, the look of revulsion on his face mirrored my own.

"Do not give me that look." Stern chuckled. "If you want to get all judgmental, Moreau over there did not return his vassal again this year." The Lord nodded at another vampire in the room—a burly one with a rough-hewn face, sable hair, and brown eyes.

Cold to my very core, I drew in a shallow breath, my chest painfully tight. When I swayed on my feet, Henry held me in place with his hand still on my back. His upper lip curled at Stern's words, revealing one gleaming sharp fang.

"That is not supposed to happen," he bit out, pinning Moreau with a stare.

When Moreau noticed his glare, he smirked arrogantly and lifted his glass, demonstrating the behavior of someone who knew there would be little to no consequences for his actions. I clenched my teeth to prevent myself from doing something foolish, like trying to stake him.

"Yes, well. We are vampires. It is in our nature." Stern lifted a shoulder nonchalantly.

"This Empire is founded on a delicate balance," Henry repeated the words he'd spoken to me last night.

"It was founded on one, yes, but perhaps it is time for a change," the other Lord said.

"What change?" Henry narrowed his eyes as my breath got stuck in my throat.

"A change where we vampires take what we want."

7

Stern's words chilled my blood as my heart sank. Did he think that vampires should be able to hunt and feed like the predators that they were? Henry's eyes widened in dismay, and he opened his mouth to reply but was interrupted by Isabelle, who announced that it was time for the celebratory dinner. I was not sure what the clans were celebrating besides having the human population in their tight grip for another year.

My mind racing after what Stern had said, I all but stumbled on numb legs to the long rectangular table in the other part of the room. Henry took a seat at the head of the table while a servant pulled out a chair for me to his right. I'd expected Isabelle to sit close to Henry, and my heart dropped when Stern sat down opposite me, to Henry's left.

A young girl approached the table a moment later, dressed in a red satin dress that barely covered her thighs.

"This is Marie, my vassal," Stern drawled, and my stomach turned over.

Anger rose up again, and my fingers flexed on my thighs, knuckles turning white with how hard I was gripping the material of my skirt. Marie took a seat next to Stern, fixing her gaze on the empty table before her. It wasn't empty for long as servants began bringing out plates of food and pitchers of water and wine. I noticed Rory making her way down the length of the table in my direction, carrying a tray with cold cuts and cheese. She looked so small and fragile in this room full of monsters that the urge to hide her away almost had me rising from my chair. She looked nervous but gave a small smile as she neared and put the tray in the middle of the table before me.

"You grow more beautiful each time I see you," came Stern's smooth voice, and my eyes darted to him just in time to see the tips of his fangs drag over his bottom lip.

His gaze was fixed on Rory, and he stared at her like she was a meal.

"Leave her alone," I said through my teeth. "She's just a child."

Stern's sharp features contorted in condescension. His nostrils flared as his gaze shot to mine.

"And you are just a pet. Know your place."

A bitter taste pooled in the back of my mouth as I clamped it shut.

"Don't talk to my vassal like that," Henry snapped at the Lord, and my eyes flicked to him.

A muscle ticked in his cheek as if he were barely containing his anger. I did not expect him to have such a strong reaction to Stern being rude to me, but the way Henry glared at the Lord of the South gave me the impression that there was more to it.

"Well, look who has decided to grow some claws." Stern smirked, seemingly unbothered by Henry's icy tone. "I was worried after Vincent's disappearance. Thought I might have to take over the clan. Didn't know if you were up to the task."

"I would never let you take over my region," Henry bit out.

"And what would you have done to stop me?" Stern countered.

He looked as if he found the entire exchange amusing, but his hand on the table had balled into a fist, making it clear he was not as unaffected as he wanted to appear.

"Whatever it takes," Henry growled, baring his fangs.

His features became stark, and his fingernails elongated into sharp claws. I felt terrified but also a little thrilled by his outburst because I would give anything at that very moment to see him rip out Stern's throat.

Heavy silence settled over the table as the two vampires glared at each other. The tension was palpable, making me wonder how strained the relationships between the clans actually were.

"Boys, behave," a female vampire said from the other end of the table, her voice low and husky.

Her straight, shoulder-length hair was so blonde it was almost white, and her eyes were like two chips of ice. I recalled her name was Camilla, and she was the clan leader in the Northern region.

"Camilla," Stern purred, glancing in her direction. "Ever the diplomat." He looked back at Henry as a chilling smile broke across his face. "Let us relax and enjoy ourselves tonight. A drink to celebrate our truce?"

Henry's features hardened as he stiffened in his seat. In the next moment, I understood what had caused such a reaction when Stern reached for his vassal and brought her wrist to his mouth. The girl, Marie, flinched but didn't pull her hand away, her gaze remaining fixed on the table.

Henry cleared his throat, briefly glancing at me, but didn't reach for my hand. I felt frozen in place, all my muscles tense.

"Are you not going to join me?" Stern asked Henry, his brows raised, looking between me and the Lord.

My heart sank as understanding dawned on me. Stern was asking Henry to join him in feeding. Containing my emotions at that very moment was one of the hardest things I'd ever had to do. Slowly, I dragged my gaze to Henry's. There were shadows in his deep-blue eyes, and he looked almost apologetic. He couldn't hide his true nature for long, though, as sparks of excitement invaded his gaze.

Eyes fixed on me, he reached for my hand and brought my wrist to his mouth. His lips peeled back, revealing his sharp fangs. My instinct was to wince and turn away, but I forced myself to sit still and hold his gaze to avoid making it obvious that this was the first time he'd ever fed from me. I couldn't stifle a flinch and a sharp intake of my breath when his fangs broke the skin. The instant burning sensation and the cool touch of his lips sent a shiver through me as he pressed my wrist more fully to his mouth, drawing blood from the wounds his fangs had created. His eyes fluttered closed, and I wondered if, for a vampire, drinking fresh blood was like having a hot meal after eating nothing but cold meat for a while.

Having a vampire feed from you was…strange. The burning sensation that had started in my wrist spread throughout my entire body, warming the blood flowing through my veins. My breath hitched, and my brows knitted when the liquid warmth pooled in the pit of my stomach before moving lower. When a soft gasp left me, Henry abruptly let go of my wrist, running his tongue over his blood-smeared lips. My mind was hazy as I lowered my hand and covered my wrist with a napkin.

Stern let go of Marie's wrist a moment later. He then proceeded to bite his own wrist, offering it to the vassal. She hesitated for only a second before bringing it to her mouth and taking a few gulps. My eyes widened as I watched her.

"That is enough, pet," Stern said, taking back his wrist.

Marie's pupils dilated, and her cheeks pinkened as she ducked her chin, returning her eyes to the table, her thick blonde curls spilling across her forehead.

"Her skin is so pristine," Stern drawled, his gaze like an oily caress on my exposed neck and shoulders. "Do you not want to give her some of your blood to heal the bite marks?"

When Henry hesitated, the other Lord lifted his wrist up.

"I can offer her mine," he taunted, leaning across the table.

"No," Henry stopped him, his brows knitting.

He then bit his own wrist before holding it over my champagne glass that was half-full. A few drops of his blood glided down, mixing with the bubbly liquid. His eyes were still apologetic when they flicked to mine, but the sparks of excitement still danced in them as well, now burning brighter. He grabbed a napkin off the table and pressed it to his wrist. I watched in awe as he wiped away the blood, revealing the almost-healed bite marks.

He nodded at my champagne glass, and I slowly lifted it off the table and brought it to my mouth. I swallowed thickly before I took a sip, letting the drink coat my dry throat. A swirl of tingles erupted over my tongue, and a warmth similar to the one I'd experienced when Henry had fed from me invaded my body. I took a few minutes to finish the champagne, and by the time I sat the glass down, the bite marks on my wrist were nothing more than twin pink dots. I was amazed at the healing properties of vampire blood but also felt it was unfair that such monsters were blessed with such a gift.

Scowling, I stared at my empty plate as conversation at the table picked up and became a steady hum. Swallowing, I looked at the feast laid out before me. We never had a full spread like this at home. I doubted many human families did. The roasted meat and potatoes smelled delicious, but I had lost my appetite. My stomach churned as I sat at the table, unable to eat. I kept thinking about my mother and the Ravager victims. I felt like I'd betrayed them when I'd let Henry feed from me. Sitting here, doing nothing, also felt like a betrayal. I had to play the long game, though. I had to get through tonight if I wanted a chance at finding the Tear.

Henry kept stealing glances at me and, after a while, piled some food on my plate.

"Eat," he ordered in a low voice.

I reached for a fork and used it to spear a piece of meat on my plate. Taking a small bite, I chewed slowly, not really tasting the food as I dared a look around the table. Glasses and plates clinked, and laughter sounded as the vassals ate while the vampires drank wine and…blood.

My gaze wandered to the other end of the table where Camilla was feeding from her vassal—an attractive young man who seemed like he was enjoying it. Instantly regretting taking a bite of my food, I set the fork down and reached for my wine glass. I took a generous gulp as my eyes darted back to the vampire. She was drinking from her vassal's neck as a thin trail of blood glided down his olive skin. Uncomfortable, I shifted my gaze to Wren and Isabelle, but what I found wasn't much better. They were kissing, and she was biting his lower lip, drawing blood. Unable to suppress a shudder, I fixed my gaze on the wine glass in my hand.

The dinner lasted for a few hours, and wine and blood flowed freely. Henry kept stealing glances at me but didn't say anything as I sat there quietly, counting down the seconds until the night was over. Halfway through dinner, I told myself to focus and use this opportunity to learn more about the other clans. I took the time to discreetly study each and every one of the clan members, looking for my mother's killer. When I didn't find him in any of the near-perfect faces, I focused on the conversations the vampires were having.

Unfortunately, that did not provide much helpful information. The vampires talked about mundane things, like the weather and the latest fashion. I was surprised they didn't discuss the Dark Witches. From Waylon, I knew that it had been quiet on the border, coincidentally after my mother's death. Hearing less about the Witches' attacks, people had been growing more comfortable with being out after sundown, though most were still too terrified to be out on the streets at night. I was glad for it because that meant fewer potential Ravager victims.

The word about Ravagers had been spreading but most people were still unaware of the danger. I was beginning to wonder, though, if, at this point, vampires were more of a threat to humans than the Dark Witches. I also wondered if the clans knew Dark Witches were no longer a threat but chose not to disclose that to the humans. They needed us to think we still needed their protection so they could keep us in their clutches.

When the dinner was finally over, dancing ensued. Having been up since early morning, I was exhausted. With barely any food and a good amount of wine in my system, I felt dizzy when I rose from the table.

Henry's eyes were soft as he reached for me.

"One dance, and then you can leave," he said quietly before taking my hand and leading me away from the table.

We stopped in the middle of the ballroom, a few feet away from Isabelle and Wren, who were already dancing—if one could call it that. She was draped over him with hardly any space between their bodies, and I thought they belonged in the privacy of her bedroom instead of on the ballroom floor.

I focused my attention on Henry, who took my hand in his and placed the other one on my lower back. I propped my hand on his arm, and we began swaying to the soft instrumental music. When I looked up at the Lord, his features were taut, making me wonder if he was counting down the seconds until tonight was over like I was.

"I know what you are thinking," he said under his breath, lowering his head to meet my gaze.

"You have no idea what I'm thinking," I bit out, hot anger flashing through me.

I want to kill every last one of you, I thought, glancing around and picking out the vampires in the room.

"It's almost over," Henry said low as if talking to himself.

When my gaze darted to him, a look of misery briefly marred his features but was gone in the blink of an eye. His scowl smoothed out, and he assumed a neutral expression. It was as if a mask had slipped, and he'd righted it back on. Once again puzzled by him, I searched his face while we danced as if it would reveal an explanation for his behavior that was so contrary to what I'd expected from a vampire.

"What is it?" Henry asked, one side of his mouth turning up when he noticed me staring at him.

"You are not what I expected," I admitted.

His half smile faded.

"I would not be able to live with myself if I behaved as was expected of me."

It sounded almost as if he didn't like being a vampire. Confused, I frowned but didn't say anything else.

"Can I steal her away for a dance?" Stern asked, approaching us when the dance was over.

I had to try really hard not to recoil in his presence.

"Actually, Sophie was just leaving," Henry said, his tone cold and final.

A sigh of relief left me as I turned and headed for the door, feeling their eyes on my back. I forced myself to walk at a steady pace even though all I wanted to do was run.

Safely inside my room, I quickly closed the door and sagged against it, letting out a rough exhale. I was shocked by what I'd witnessed tonight, but my emotions were conflicting. On the one hand, I wished I could erase the ball from my mind, but I also wanted to remember tonight because it fueled my rage and made my desire for retribution so much stronger.

Nausea churned as a sticky residue of disgust and shame clung to my skin. I was disgusted by what I'd witnessed tonight and ashamed of what I'd let Henry do. Closing my eyes, I took a steadying breath. It was over now. I couldn't do anything about what I'd seen tonight, but if I was successful at finding the Tear, things like that would no longer happen.

Opening my eyes, I hurried to the bathing chamber, where I

quickly showered and changed into one of the new nightgowns I'd gotten earlier today. I put on a new silk robe that matched the nightgown and ran the brush through my hair, letting it fall around my shoulders. Exhausted but too wound up to sleep, I paced the room for a few minutes until a soft knock on the door stopped me in my tracks.

Slowly, I approached the door and cracked it just enough to peek through. Henry stood on the other side, holding a tray of food. He was still dressed in the clothes he'd worn to the ball.

I opened the door a bit wider, and our gazes locked and held until the Lord cleared his throat and said, "I noticed you didn't eat much during dinner, so I brought some food. May I come in?"

With a small nod, I let him in, and in two long strides, Henry crossed the bedroom and sat the tray on the dresser. I didn't move from where I stood by the door, lost in thought, my fingers skimming the wrist the Lord had bitten earlier.

"What happened during dinner bothers you," Henry stated, his gaze landing on my wrist.

"More than you know," I admitted.

There was regret in his blue eyes.

"I had to do it."

"I know," I told him. "Tonight was one of the worst nights of my life," I added low.

"It's not over yet," Henry said, his gaze flicking to the open door. "The clans usually spend the day here and travel back to their regions at sundown. I wouldn't leave this room if I were you."

Shuddering, I quickly closed the door, desperate to seal myself away from the monsters roaming on the other side. Doing so brought little comfort—there was still a monster right here with me in this room.

Henry's throat bobbed as he swallowed.

"You must know I don't condone it."

"You could do something about it," I challenged, my voice rising.

Henry's eyes widened in shock at my boldness before he spoke, his tone measured, "It's not that simple. I am not their king. I am one of them."

I scoffed and shook my head in disappointment. I wasn't sure why I'd expected a different answer. Like he'd just said, he was one of them—a vampire.

"I want to be alone now," I told him, suddenly feeling defeated.

Tonight had taken a lot out of me. I wasn't sure if I could sleep, but I was certain I didn't want to spend another second in the presence of a vampire.

"Very well," Henry said and started for the door. He paused before me, and I briefly met his piercing gaze. "Try to eat if you can. You did well tonight, Sophie."

He didn't wait for my reply before walking out of the room, shutting the door softly behind him.

It didn't feel like I'd done well tonight. It felt like I'd crossed some kind of a line by letting Henry feed from me and by consuming his blood. I felt strange, as if my body was not my own, and when I caught my reflection in the vanity mirror, I didn't recognize the girl staring back at me. My eyes were bright, and my cheeks were flushed from the effects of Henry's blood. I swore my tongue still tingled from the decadent taste. If only a few drops had such an effect, what could more of his blood do? While a small part of me was curious, I still hoped I'd never have to find out.

8

———————————

I woke up at dusk, surprisingly well-rested. It had taken me a while to fall asleep, but once I had, it had felt like floating. I'd been peaceful and content with no anxious thoughts interrupting my slumber. I wasn't sure if it had been because of Henry's blood, the wine, or the combination of both.

Unease was back, though, the moment I opened my eyes. I'd let Henry feed from me and had tasted his blood. I hadn't liked the way it had made me feel. Or, rather, I *had* liked it, and that was what was truly upsetting me, making me feel like a traitor, as if I'd betrayed myself and my beliefs. My chest tight, I heaved a heavy sigh and left the bed.

After washing my face, I rooted around the dresser until I found the green dress I'd personally selected yesterday at Madam Claremont's. It was shorter, so I pulled on a pair of thin leggings and then stepped into a pair of new brown boots. The new clothing paid for by the Duvals also made me feel like a traitor, but I hadn't brought much with me from home and needed something to wear. Scowling at my reflection in the mirror, I swept half of my hair up and pinned it away from my face, letting the other half cascade down my back. I took a deep, measured breath and left the bedroom, feeling a surge of determination. If last night had proven anything, it was that I needed to find the Tear as quickly as possible.

The house was quiet as I hurried through the long halls until I reached Henry's study. Unsure of how much time I had before the Lord was up for the night, I quickly slipped through the door, closing it softly behind me. Striding to the painting of Vincent Duval, I lifted it off the hooks before carefully setting it down on the floor to rest against the wall.

My mind raced as I stared at the safe. What could be the combination? I began to pace, tapping my chin, as I looked around the study in search of an answer. Rounding the desk, I hunched over it, my palms flat on the mahogany surface as I studied the paper depicting the clans. My gaze snagged on the name of Vincent Duval with his date of birth written underneath before gliding over the other objects on the desk. One of them was a small black frame holding a portrait of the Duval clan. It must have been painted before the Red War because Rosalind and Gerard were still in it, along with Vincent, Henry, and Isabelle. I studied the portrait for a few seconds. The Duvals looked happy in it. Their features were still cool and unnaturally flawless, but they looked like a real family.

Vincent was like a father to me, I remembered Henry's words.

A thought occurred to me then, and I walked back to the safe, my eyes dropping to the painting of Vincent sitting on the floor.

"Could it be that simple?" I murmured, lifting my hand to the dial on the safe to try Vincent's birth date as the combination.

My pulse quickened with every faint click, and by the time I turned the dial to the last number, my heart was hammering against my ribs. A shuddering breath left me when the safe unlocked. I couldn't believe the combination had worked. Swallowing, I opened the safe and peered inside. Disappointment washed over me, and I let out a rough exhale when all I found were banknotes and coins.

"It's not in there," came a male voice from the entrance to the study.

I whirled from the safe and saw Wren strolling in. He looked relaxed, walking toward me, one side of his mouth turning up.

"What?" I asked shakily, all color draining from my face.

Wren had just caught me breaking into Henry's safe, and I didn't know if he would turn me in.

"Josephine's Tear. It's not in the safe," he explained calmly, coming closer.

My eyes widened in disbelief.

"You know about the Tear?" I asked in a hushed tone, my gaze flicking to the door to make sure Wren had shut it behind him.

The young man nodded instead of replying and closed the safe before lifting the painting off the floor and hanging it back on the wall.

"I've searched the mansion," he said, facing me. "Everywhere, except for Henry's bedroom. He locks it even when he's not there."

I'd wondered about that…First things first.

"How do you know about the Tear?" I asked, folding my arms over my chest.

"From the Order of Light," Wren replied without skipping a beat.

My brows lifted. "You know about the Order?"

Another nod. "Ravagers have been terrorizing people all over the region, not just in New Haven. We heard about the Order Waylon had established here and created a similar one in Weldon Heights. I am a part of that Order."

I hadn't known that the other towns in the region experienced Ravager attacks, but I supposed it would be foolish to assume only New Haven was affected. Anger and desperation burned in my blood. The situation was so much worse than I had thought. I needed to find the Tear.

It was suspicious Wren knew about the amulet. My father and

I had only told Waylon about it. We had chosen to keep the information a secret from everyone else because the more people knew about it, the higher the risk that vampires or Dark Witches would learn about it.

"And the Order in your town knows about the Tear?" I pressed, narrowing my eyes at Wren.

"Yes, and they sent me to participate in the Selection. Well, I volunteered, hoping to gain access to the Duval Estate, so I could search for the amulet. I figured you were on the same mission when I caught you sneaking around Henry's study."

That could be possible, I reasoned with myself. My mother couldn't have been the only one who'd known about the Tear.

"What do you know about the amulet?" I asked. "The only clue I have is—"

"Vincent Duval," Wren finished my thought. "It's the only lead we have as well. That's why I'm here."

After a moment of hesitation, I let myself relax, deciding to believe Wren. I didn't know him well, but I couldn't think of a reason why he would lie. Besides, it would be nice to have an ally in this place. Now I understood why he had so eagerly embraced his role as a vassal. I also had to admire his dedication. He was much better at the game of pretense than I was.

"I am not truly Henry's vassal," I admitted. "He doesn't feed from me. I only act as his vassal in public."

"I figured," Wren said, surprising me. "You seemed very on edge yesterday when he drank from your wrist." His pale-blue eyes searched mine for a moment before he said, "Sophie, you need to get inside Henry's bedroom so you can search it."

"How do you suggest I do that? You said he locked it at all times."

Wren's eyes danced with amusement as a little smile played on his lips.

"The Lord selected you. He wants you. I'm sure you can convince him to let you inside his bedroom."

My cheeks heated at what he was implying. I knew that he was right, but I refused to admit it, even to myself, so I changed the subject.

"So, if you're in the Order of Light, it means you know how to fight, right?" I arched a brow.

"Yes," Wren said hesitantly, looking unsure.

"Do you know how to sword fight?" I asked, hopeful.

"Yes," Wren drew the word out, now looking worried.

My gaze snapped to the two short swords above the fireplace as the corners of my mouth lifted. Nervous energy buzzed through my veins, and I needed to expel it from my system. It was a combination of residual rage from what I'd witnessed last night at the ball and steadily increasing panic about what I would soon have to do to try and get into Henry's bedroom.

Grabbing one of the chairs by the credenza, I dragged it closer to the fireplace.

"What are you doing?" Wren's brows knitted.

I climbed on top of the chair and pulled the swords out of the hooks mounting them on the wall. When I tossed one of the swords to Wren, he caught it skillfully with a surprised look on his face. I jumped down from the chair and lifted my sword, making sure my legs were braced and my feet were shoulder width apart.

"Show me what you got," I challenged Wren in a playful manner, excitement tampering down my anxiety.

"I don't think this is a good idea, Sophie," Wren warned, his sword still lowered.

"Oh, come on," I whined with a breath of frustration. "I haven't practiced in a while. It'll be fun."

A hint of excitement crossed Wren's features as he prowled around me before facing me again and raising his sword.

"Protect yourself," he said, his eyes bright.

He attacked, but I deflected the blow, the metal of our swords clashing with a loud clink. For a moment, we just grinned at each other before I snapped into action, swinging my sword around. I was quick, but Wren was quick too, moving with the grace of a dancer. We exchanged blows for a while, our chests rising and falling rapidly until, suddenly, something flickered across Wren's features. He lunged at me with a look of determination on his face. I darted out of the way, narrowly avoiding his swipe.

"Wren—" I tried to get his attention, deflecting another blow, but he kept coming at me.

The next time he shot forward, thrusting his sword out, my foot slipped, and I lost my balance, stumbling backward. Hot, sharp pain sliced through my skin as the edge of Wren's sword nicked the outer side of my left arm. I dropped my sword and heard it clatter on the floor. Covering the wound with my right hand, I breathed through the pain as my warm blood seeped through my fingers.

"Shit! Sophie…" Wren paled, staring at me with wide eyes. He tossed his sword to the side and pulled his shirt over his head. "Here, we need to stop the bleeding."

He moved to come closer, but I instinctively backed away since he'd been the one who'd hurt me, even if not on purpose.

His jaw tightened as his eyes roamed my face. I didn't say anything as my gaze dropped to his bare torso covered in Isabelle's bite marks. Seeing them was a shock to my senses. Wren was willing to go to such lengths in order to obtain the amulet. I really didn't have the right to cower away from what I would have to do to gain access to Henry's bedroom. After all, it was a small price to pay if I could find the amulet or a clue in his room.

"I'm sorry," Wren rasped, trying to reach for me again, but before he could touch me, Henry stormed into the study, his nostrils flaring.

"Sophie! Why are you bleeding?" he growled, at my side in an instant.

"I…we were just sword fighting," I said meekly.

"What?" His eyes flashed in anger as he turned to Wren. "What did you do?!"

"It was an accident," Wren and I both said at the same time.

"Here, we need to put pressure on the wound," Wren added, offering his shirt again.

"I think you have done enough," Henry snarled at him. "Get out."

Wren's hand holding the shirt balled into a fist before he lowered it to his side. With one last look at me, his eyes apologetic, he turned and strode out of the study. As soon as the door closed behind him, Henry bared his fangs and bit into his wrist. I watched with wide eyes as deep-red blood began trailing down his forearm. My mind flashed back to the last time I'd tasted it, and panic flared in the pit of my stomach.

"I don't want—" Before I could finish the sentence, Henry pressed his torn wrist to my lips.

"Drink," he ordered, clasping the back of my neck, leaving me no choice but to comply.

Closing my mouth around the wound, I quickly swallowed a few gulps of his blood, feeling it coarse down my throat. Sooner than I'd expected, Henry let go of my neck, pulling his wrist away from my lips and wiping it on his loose white shirt. The second he let me go, I shoved at his chest.

"Don't ever do that again!" I seethed, wiping my mouth with the back of my hand.

"Don't do anything foolish again, and I won't have to," Henry snapped. "Sword fighting? What were you thinking?" he asked, his tone exasperated.

It took a few seconds for his question to sink in because my mind was becoming hazy from ingesting his blood.

"I was bored," I said, lifting a shoulder.

"You were..." He exhaled roughly, briefly closing his eyes and pinching the bridge of his nose. "Sophie, the clans are still here. You were bleeding in a house full of vampires."

Somehow, I had forgotten about that. Suddenly, I did feel very foolish for starting the sword fight.

Henry opened his eyes, and his gaze dropped to my arm, which I realized didn't hurt anymore. I looked at it and found the cut had healed, with only a pink mark remaining.

"You're welcome," the Lord said in a clipped tone, and I met his piercing gaze.

We stared at each other for a few minutes as my skin began to hum. My heartbeat quickened as liquid heat invaded my body, seeping into my muscles and pooling in my core. I sucked in a sharp breath as a throbbing ache settled between my thighs, so much more potent than what I'd felt last night at the ball. The longer I stared at Henry, the hotter I felt, my skin becoming flushed and sensitive. Wren's words floated up from the recesses of my mind, *The Lord wants you. I'm sure you can convince him to let you inside his bedroom.*

Swallowing to relieve my dry throat, I stepped closer to Henry, running my fingertips down his hard chest. He stilled, his lips parting on a soft inhale. The angles of his face became stark in the soft glow of the fireplace as his eyes turned several shades darker. My gaze flicked over his tousled hair, and I realized he must have just gotten out of bed. I intended to put him back in it.

"Sophie," Henry ground out as if in warning. "What are you doing?"

"What does it look like?" I whispered, arching my back to bring my chest flush with his powerful body.

The Lord swallowed thickly before he rasped, "You had my blood. It's making you not think clearly. The haze will pass, but you need to stop doing what you're doing."

"Why? Do you not like it?" I asked innocently, gazing up at him from beneath my lashes.

Henry's eyes fluttered closed for a second as if he were fighting an inner battle. When he opened them again, they were almost black.

"I do like it," he murmured, low and rough. "But you will not like yourself if we go through with what you are trying to initiate."

In the back of my mind, I knew he was right because I was at the same time in control of my body and not. I thought what I was doing was intentional, but a small part of me knew my actions were not entirely my own. They were guided by the pulsing desire ignited by Henry's blood. I was trying to use what I was experiencing to my advantage, hoping it would help me go through with what I didn't have the courage to do with a clear head.

"Take me to your bedroom," I whispered, gliding my lips over Henry's jaw, my hands fisting in his shirt.

His hands curled into fists at his sides as he stood unmoving, his muscles tense and coiled tight.

Just when I thought he would deny me, his chin dipped, and he lowered his head, his thick black hair spilling across his forehead. My breath caught as his dark lashes lowered. I felt his intense gaze on my mouth and my lips parted in anticipation.

My plan is working. He is going to kiss me, I thought to myself as he brought his mouth closer to mine. His cool breath coasted over my lips, eliciting a shiver from me. Any second now, he would claim my mouth. The pleasant ache between my thighs pulsed through me at the thought.

"No," he whispered against my lips, and my heart dropped. "You only think you want that. It's the blood." He gently pried my hands from his shirt and stepped away. "I suggest you go to your room until the effects of it wear off. You didn't drink much, so it shouldn't take long."

I swayed on my feet. It felt like a bucket of ice-cold water had been dumped on my head. My face turning several shades of red, I lowered my hands, balling them into fists at my sides. I'd only been trying to seduce the Lord so I could search his bedroom, but the rejection still stung. I also felt a hint of disappointment that he hadn't kissed me. Internally, I recoiled at the thought—I shouldn't feel disappointment, only relief.

My eyes pricked with tears as I turned and left the study, feeling very foolish. I followed Henry's advice and went to my room but didn't stay there long. After strapping my dagger to my thigh, I snuck out of the mansion, leaving the estate.

9

I wasn't sure what drove my actions as I hurried through the dark city streets in the cool night air. There was something exciting about sneaking out, reclaiming my freedom, if only for one night. I *was* free, I reminded myself. Coming to the Selection had been my decision, and I was only staying on the estate because I wanted to be there. Still, I wasn't truly free. I was bound by my duty, albeit the duty I had imposed upon myself.

In the back of my mind, I knew I was being incredibly reckless. Henry would not approve of me venturing into the city and might even be furious if he found out I'd snuck out. But right now, going against his wishes excited me. Anger surged as I thought about what had happened in the study, and my cheeks flushed with embarrassment all over again at my failed attempt at seducing the Lord.

Who would have thought a vampire would turn down a girl throwing herself at him? I scoffed. Henry continued to defy my expectations of him. Perhaps he hadn't taken me to his bedroom because he was suspicious of me. After all, I had drawn a dagger on him. I shook my head as disappointment in myself swelled in my chest. I should have been more subtle when I'd first arrived at the estate. If I'd played the role of a compliant vassal, I would have already been to his bedroom. Shivers skittered over my skin at the thought, and I scowled in confusion. I wasn't supposed to feel that way about the Lord but knowing that only made it more difficult for me to ignore my reaction. I needed a distraction.

My steps became more confident as I made up my mind about where I was heading. I couldn't go see my father because then I would have to admit that I was in the middle of jeopardizing my mission. My recklessness tonight could have consequences. Henry might decide to banish me from the estate for disobedience and choose another vassal. I stopped in my tracks and almost turned back at the thought, but that was when I realized I'd arrived at my destination.

I stood in front of Baylor's Corner. The tavern door was wide-open, allowing yellow light and hum of lively chatter to spill into the night. I quickly glanced behind my shoulder in the direction of the Duval Estate. I could turn back. Henry might never learn of my escape. Or I could go into the tavern and see if Waylon was inside. I wanted a distraction, and Waylon could provide that. He'd never turn me down like the Lord had. I cringed as another wave of anger swept through me. I'd made a fool out of myself earlier because Henry had forced me to drink his blood. If I was being reckless and impulsive tonight, it was entirely his fault. Cursing the Lord under my breath, I walked inside the tavern, shutting the heavy wooden door behind me with a loud thud.

The pungent odor of liquor and tobacco hung heavy in the air, and the establishment was half-full, mainly with guards from the border who'd just finished the day shift. They were the ones who usually stayed out late. Most people were already inside somewhere or hurrying to their homes since the night had descended. Trained and armed, the guards were among the few people who braved the city streets after dark. Of course, many didn't go far after leaving the tavern. They only walked several feet to the adjoining inn to spend the night in the arms of one of the women who charged coin for their company.

Casting aside my conflicting emotions about why I was here, I made my way deeper into the tavern, looking for Waylon. I spotted him in the middle of a card game at one of the tables. When my gaze landed on his handsome face, my throat dried as everything I'd felt earlier when I'd been with Henry rushed back in, flooding my body with heat.

Waylon didn't notice me at first, too absorbed in the game. His brows were pinched, and his gaze was intent on the cards he was holding. They must not have been good because after a second, he dragged a hand through his short, light-brown hair and laid the cards face down on the table with a heavy sigh. His gaze shot to me, and his forest-green eyes widened in shock.

I flashed him a smile and glided over to one of the empty tables in the corner. Taking a seat, I watched as Waylon excused himself from the card game and swaggered over to me. He wasn't wearing his guard leathers, which told me it wasn't his turn to patrol tonight. In a loose white shirt and buckskin breeches, he looked relaxed, matching the atmosphere in the tavern.

He slid into the seat opposite me and smiled, his round face lighting up with excitement and a bit of apprehension.

"Sophie. What are you doing here?" He still smiled when he asked the question, but I could pick up on the notes of concern in his tone. "I thought vassals weren't allowed to leave the estate."

"The Duvals don't know I'm here," I admitted.

His smile faded as his eyes dimmed.

"Is everything alright? Are you in trouble?" he asked, lowering his voice and leaning closer to me across the small wooden table.

I lifted my shoulders in a noncommittal gesture instead of responding.

"Have the streets been quiet? Has there been another attack?"

I changed the subject, keeping my voice down. Not many knew about the attacks, and it was important to keep the information contained. We couldn't expose the clans as monsters that they truly were. Not until we had the Tear as the means to destroy them.

Waylon eyed me for a moment before responding. I had a feeling he wanted to press for answers but chose not to.

With a heavy sigh, he said, "There was an attack last night." His eyes were haunted as he continued, "We were too late. The body was drained of blood, and it looked like the person was mauled by a wild animal."

My vision blurred, and it felt like shards of ice had filled the pit of my stomach.

"Anyone you knew?" I asked, my voice hollow.

Most Ravager victims had been border guards because they were the ones usually out on the streets after dark. It really didn't matter if the victim had been someone we knew. A human life had been lost.

Waylon gave a small shake of his head before reaching across the table to take my hand.

"Are you okay? How…" His throat bobbed before he continued, "How are the Duvals treating you?"

My mind flashed back to the Vassal Ball, and an involuntary shudder rolled through me before I could reply. Waylon's eyes shuttered, and his brows knitted.

"I swear to gods if they hurt you—"

"They didn't," I interjected. "Besides, you taught me well. I know how to take care of myself," I reminded him.

He looked as if he didn't believe me at first, but then his gaze dropped to my neck, and his features smoothed out when he didn't find any bite marks there.

One side of his mouth turned up.

"You were a very apt student. You have skills."

"I could be putting those skills to use right now. We should be patrolling the streets instead of sitting here."

Patrolling hadn't been on my mind when I'd come to the tavern, hoping to find Waylon here, but now that I knew there had been another attack, I had the strongest urge to get out on the streets. A small, twisted part of me even hoped that I would come across a Ravager, just so that I could take out my frustration by driving a stake through his heart.

Waylon's half-smile faded.

"Andre and Jared are patrolling tonight," he said. "Besides, don't you think you're already doing enough?" He gently tucked a lock of hair behind my ear.

"No," I replied without hesitation, thinking about the Vassal Ball.

Would those abused by the clans think I was doing enough?

Then, my mind shifted to the Ravager victim from last night. Would that person think I was doing enough? I shook my head, thinking that nothing would ever be enough until Dark Witches and vampires were destroyed.

"You don't have to carry the weight of the world on your shoulders." Waylon's eyes softened as he looked at me.

"Yes, I do."

I was the one who'd found my mother on the night of her death. I was also the one who'd discovered the note about the Tear. It was up to me to do something with the truth I now knew about our world. I wouldn't have it any other way. I'd never regretted my decision to take on that mission even though sometimes its weight threatened to pull me under. Like now, when it felt as if the walls of the tavern were caving in on me, making it difficult to breathe.

"Sophie—" Waylon started, his eyes flicking over my features and undoubtedly picking up on the nonverbal cues my face betrayed.

"Don't," I interrupted, even though I wasn't sure what he was going to say.

Probably that I wasn't on my own and to not put too much pressure on myself. But he hadn't been there the night of my mother's death, just like he hadn't been there last night at the Vassal Ball. He didn't know everything I knew. Speaking of which…

"Wren—the other vassal staying on the estate—said he's a part of the Order of Light in his hometown of Weldon Heights. Did you know that yours isn't the only Order of Light? Wren said Ravagers have been terrorizing other towns in the region and that Weldon Heights heard about your Order and created one of their own."

Waylon's brows shot up in surprise.

"No, I wasn't aware of that. You know we're as discreet about the Order as possible, but with the number of attacks increasing, I've been recruiting more men. It's possible the information got out."

"He even knows about…the Tear," I said barely above a whisper.

"Now, *that*," Waylon enunciated the last word, "I haven't disclosed to anyone."

"I know. I don't doubt you," I assured him. "I figured my mother couldn't have been the only one who knew about it."

"Well, does that Wren have any other information about the amulet?"

"No." I shook my head. "He had the same clue we did. That was why he volunteered for the Selection."

Waylon nodded in understanding.

"And I'm guessing neither of you have made any headway in finding the Tear?" he asked low.

"Not yet," I told him, swallowing thickly. I would have to find another way to search Henry's bedroom. "But we will. We have to," I added vehemently. "Waylon, things are so much worse than we thought."

I quickly told him about the Vassal Ball and how horrible some of the clans were. Waylon's face was ashen by the time I finished, and shadows crawled behind his eyes.

"I wish we could wipe out the clans. There are more humans than vampires. We should be ruling this country, not them," Waylon said fiercely. "But we need their protection," he added with a heavy sigh.

"Do we? Still need it?" I challenged. "You said there hasn't been a witch attack in months."

"I did say that, but what if we get rid of the clans and Dark Witches launch a full-scale assault like they did during the Red War? We'd be defenseless."

My gaze roamed over Waylon's taut features.

"Are they really that bad? The Dark Witches?"

He swallowed thickly, his throat bobbing before he replied, "They are. I've only been through one attack during my time on the border, but that was more than enough." He couldn't suppress a shudder that racked him. "I'm a good fighter, but I think I only survived because Lord Duval was there when it happened."

My brows flew up in surprise.

"Henry was there?"

I knew he didn't mean Vincent. I'd seen Waylon that night after the attack. He'd been white as a sheet and hadn't shared much about what had transpired, his eyes full of all-consuming terror.

"He was," Waylon confirmed. "He's been coming out to the border ever since Vincent disappeared. It was strange at first seeing him out and about like that, but now everyone is pretty used to seeing him out there."

"Just him? What about Isabelle?"

"Just him. I've never seen his sister step foot on the border. She didn't even come out when the witches attacked last time."

That wasn't surprising. The human guards were the first line of defense. The clans were tucked away behind the warded wall, ready to rush to our aid only if we needed them. Henry coming out and helping to keep watch was unusual—another thing to add to the list of behaviors I wouldn't expect from a vampire.

"The Lord seems…different from the others," I said for some reason. Thoughts like these did not need to be shared aloud. They were foolish and pointless. Perhaps I'd only uttered the words because I wanted Waylon to tell me I was wrong in my observation. A moment later, he did just that.

"He's a vampire. He still takes vassals and drinks human blood. He can't be that much different from the rest of them," Waylon said vehemently.

We sat in silence for a few minutes until Waylon ran his thumb over my knuckles, making me realize we were still holding hands. The rough calluses of his palm elicited a shiver, and my gaze dropped to our joined hands before darting back up to Waylon's face.

"As much as it pains me to say this, you should return to the Duval Estate," he said low. "Coming here was risky."

His words urged me to be responsible, but his eyes told a different story. He didn't want me to leave. Not yet. Still, I knew he'd always put my safety first before his own desires. Waylon cared too much about me, always had. My reasons for seeking him out tonight were selfish. He deserved better than this. But my pulse still thrummed with liquid warmth. It was fading—I could feel it—but I wasn't ready to let go of it yet.

"I know what I should do, but I'm not ready to go just yet," I said, my voice husky. Waylon's breath caught as if he were hanging on my every word, waiting to hear what I would say next. "Do you think they still have rooms available at the inn?"

His eyes flooded with heat as his throat worked on a swallow. He looked conflicted. He probably wanted to send me away because he knew I shouldn't be here. Several seconds passed as I waited, holding my breath, wondering if he'd turn me down like Henry had done. That would be a first.

Finally, he gave me a charming smile, his cheeks turning pink, and said, "There is only one way to find out."

We left the tavern, hand in hand, and walked over to the inn. They did have a room available, and for a few hours, I let myself get lost in the sensation of Waylon's body on mine, finally releasing the pent-up desire that Henry's blood had created.

10

It was the middle of the night when I said goodbye to Waylon and left the inn. He'd offered to escort me back to the estate, but I'd refused, not wanting to risk being found with him if Henry was out looking for me.

Under the silvery moonlight, I navigated the empty streets of New Haven, steadily making my way back to the mansion. I'd expected the city to be quiet at this time of night. Still, tiny bumps prickled my skin as I strode down the stone sidewalk, staying in the yellow glow of the streetlamps. Cool air caressed my cheeks as I walked fast, scanning the dark buildings, my footsteps the only sound in the eerie silence.

When I entered one of the many shadowy pathways that connected one city block to another, I saw a man standing there, garbed in a hooded, black cloak. Jerking back a step, I froze. I couldn't see his face, but I could feel his stare, and it raised the tiny hairs on the back of my neck. Every muscle in my body tensed as something told me not to run or make any sudden movements because I was in the presence of a predator.

The man stood motionless for a few moments before he cocked his head and let out a hiss. My heart dropped—it was a

Ravager. I saw a flash of fangs as the creature lurched toward me, quickly closing the distance between us. Slipping my hand under the skirt of my dress, I curled my fingers around the handle of my dagger.

The Ravager was on me in the blink of an eye, and I didn't hesitate as I shoved the dagger deep into his chest. I must have missed the heart because the vampire didn't die. Instead, he let out a screeching wail that made my blood run cold. With a curse, I jerked the dagger out of his chest to go for the heart, but before I could, the vampire sank his fangs into my forearm. A sharp cry tore from my throat as searing pain rippled across my skin. My fingers spasmed, and the dagger slipped out of my grip and onto the ground.

The Ravager latched on to my arm as his other hand came up and clamped down on my throat, squeezing and cutting off air. I slammed my fist into the arm holding me and kicked out, my booted foot connecting with his leg. My efforts were futile as I fought for my life, kicking and screaming. The Ravager stood unmoving as I thrashed in his hold, feeling his fangs tearing the flesh of my forearm. Despair took over—I was going to die.

Suddenly, Henry appeared behind the Ravager as if out of thin air. Wrapping one arm around the Ravager's torso like a vise, he brought his hand to the vampire's face, pressing his fingers into the skin under his jaw.

"Let go of her," the Lord snarled, pulling the Ravager's head back.

The vampire's jaw unclenched, and Henry jerked him away from me. The moment he did, my legs went out from under me, and I went to crumple to the ground. Before I could, Henry caught me, and I grabbed on to his arms, feeling lightheaded. A hiss from my right snapped my attention back to the Ravager, who bared his fangs before turning to flee.

In a matter of seconds, he was several feet away from us, on the other end of the street. Moving surprisingly fast, thanks to the adrenaline flooding my system, I scrambled out of Henry's hold and picked up the dagger, flipping it so I held it by its wooden blade. A heartbeat later, the weapon flew from my fingers, spinning through the air. I doubled over with a strangled cry of pain, clutching my injured forearm.

The blade struck true, embedding itself deep in the vampire's back, and piercing the heart. The creature froze in place and did not make a sound as his flesh instantly dried out, turning him into a husk before he caved into himself.

"Nice throw," I heard Henry's deep voice. When I turned, he was right in front of me, holding the dagger I hadn't even seen him retrieve. "However, I wanted him alive so I could question him," he pointed out, sounding agitated.

"I couldn't let him get away," I explained.

"I wouldn't have let him get away," he stated, matter of fact.

"I didn't see you trying to stop him," I snapped.

A muscle flexed along Henry's jaw, but he didn't snap back at me. Instead, he asked, "Are you okay?" Concern settled into his features as he looked down at my forearm.

I covered it with my hand, applying pressure to slow the bleeding. And I was bleeding a lot. My entire body shook as I stood on unsteady legs.

"Yes. I had it under control," I managed to say through my teeth, trying to conceal how much pain I was in.

"It didn't look like it to me. You're lucky I found you when I did," Henry said low.

"I can hold my own against a Ravager," I assured him, squaring my shoulder even as sweat beaded on my forehead.

"A what?" Henry asked, his brows knitting.

"The feral vampire who attacked me," I explained.

"You call them Ravagers?"

I nodded as something occurred to me. Henry didn't seem shocked that we'd just run into a rampant vampire in the streets of New Haven.

"You know about them?"

Shadows crept across his face as he cast his gaze at the ground.

"I do," he admitted, lifting his eyes back to mine. "One of them killed Rory and Ezra's parents."

So, that was why Henry had taken them in.

Briefly closing my eyes, I breathed out through my mouth. It helped to control the pain and my volatile emotions.

"They don't know, do they?" I asked, opening my eyes and staring at the Lord.

"No." He shook his head. "They think their parents died in a carriage accident. I would prefer it if they didn't find out." He gave me a pointed look.

"Was that why you took them in?" I narrowed my eyes at him. "To cover it up?"

"No." His jaw hardened as he denied my accusation. "I took them in because they had no one left. The attack on their parents was the first one I had learned about. I was just trying to make things right."

My eyes widened at his admission, and I found myself at a loss for words. He sounded convincing, but I still couldn't bring myself to believe him.

"You don't believe me," Henry stated with a hint of disappointment in his tone. "It matters not. Come. We need to get you back to the mansion."

We started down the now empty street as I cradled my arm to my chest, the warm blood soaking my gown. The bite was not clean and precise like the one Henry had given me when he'd bitten my wrist at the Ball. There was a tear in my arm rather than two puncture wounds. It looked as if I'd been attacked by a rabid dog.

"What do you know about...Ravagers?" Henry asked, breaking the tense silence.

"Not much," I admitted. "I don't know where they come from.

Only that they terrorize the streets at night, and the attacks are becoming more frequent."

Henry cursed under his breath.

"Do you have any idea who might be turning them?" I glanced at the Lord. For some reason, there was this feeling in my chest that he wasn't the one responsible for Ravagers.

"No," he replied, scowling. "But when I find out...there will be repercussions. It is forbidden to turn humans."

Another rule the clans had established when they'd founded the Empire of Seven. If a vampire wanted to turn someone, they had to get approval from the other clans. Not counting Ravagers, no new vampires had been made since the Red War. I wasn't sure if the vampires were just very selective about who could join the clans or if they simply didn't want to share their wealth among more members.

"How did you know where to find me?" I asked, changing the subject.

"Rory told me you were missing from your room. I have been looking for you for hours. I'm glad I found you when I did."

I scoffed. "Don't act like you care."

"As my vassal, you are my responsibility for a year," he pointed out.

"And if I'd died, you would have to explain what happened," I countered.

"You truly think the worst of me, don't you?" He didn't try to hide the disappointment in his voice this time as he shook his head.

"You're a vampire, so yes, I do." I didn't see any reason to lie. I was too drained to choose my words carefully.

"Even though I haven't done you any harm?"

"Your kind has just almost killed me!" I halted and whirled on him, my eyebrows and my voice raised.

"And I saved you!" Henry raised his voice as well.

"It doesn't matter. You're one of them. You've said so yourself before." I threw the words in his face before turning and stalking away, staying a few feet in front of him all the way to the estate.

The bleeding had slowed by the time we returned to the mansion, but the front of my gown was now covered in crimson.

"Follow me," Henry said the moment we stepped into the foyer.

"I need to change and clean the wound," I said to his back as he started to walk away, expecting me to follow.

He stopped mid-stride and blew out a breath of frustration.

I saw the muscles of his neck and back tense before he threw over his shoulder, "Can you just listen for a change, and do as you are told?"

Frowning, I pursed my lips but still followed him as he climbed the grand staircase to the second story. To my surprise, he led me to his bedroom. My eyes widened when he took the thin chain off his neck and used the key to unlock the door before walking inside. He stopped on the other side and gave me an expectant look that said he wanted me to follow. I hesitated only for a second before stepping inside. I'd wanted to get into his room, and now my wish was being granted.

Henry didn't go past the small anteroom that opened into a bedroom. The dimly lit space was not as stately as I'd expected from a vampire lord. Two chairs sat by the lit fireplace, and a dresser and a chest lined the opposite wall. I could see a wide bed from where I was standing, but only one nightstand. A heavy fur rug covered the floor in front of the bed. All the walls were bare and no trinkets or knick knacks decorated the space. Nothing to give a glimpse into who Henry was or into his past.

"How badly are you hurt?" the Lord asked, scanning me from head to toe.

There was genuine concern on his face.

"Just my arm," I replied, moving it away from my chest.

I winced when I looked at the jagged wound.

"Here." Henry bared his fangs, bringing his wrist to his mouth.

"No." I backed away, almost running into the chair.

The Lord looked confused before his gaze dropped to my forearm.

"Are you sure? It might scar," he said, his brows knitting.

"I'll take my chances," I bit out with resolve.

If the wound was properly cleaned and cared for, scarring was the only thing I had to worry about. I'd never been bitten by a Ravager before, but I knew there was no danger of turning into a vampire from one bite. I'd previously read that the process of turning was more like a ritual, though I didn't know the specifics.

A flicker of amusement crossed Henry's chiseled features illuminated by the glow of the fireplace.

"Are you concerned about what my blood makes you feel?" he asked, his blue eyes searching mine. "Or are you curious, and that is what concerns you?"

I swallowed the lump in my throat and said, "I need to clean the wound," instead of answering his question.

His expression turned serious.

"Stay here," he said before walking out the door.

The moment he was gone, I looked around the room again. I didn't know how much time I had before the Lord returned. My gaze darted to the dresser, and I stepped toward it, but before I could reach it, Henry was back.

"What are you doing?" he asked, his gaze flicking to the dresser.

"Just looking around," I said nonchalantly. "You don't have much in your room," I observed.

"I don't need much. Sit." He nodded to one of the chairs before the fireplace.

"You don't need much?" I scoffed in disbelief. "I find that hard to believe when you just spent a lot of money to buy me clothes at one of the most expensive shops in New Haven."

"It is customary for the clans to buy clothes for their vassals." Henry shrugged. "Now, sit."

"That money could have been better spent elsewhere," I said in a clipped tone.

"I couldn't agree more. Sit."

"You couldn't agree more?" I seethed, my brows climbing my forehead. "Then why don't you share some of your wealth with those in need?"

"How do you know I don't already do that?" Henry snapped, and I clamped my mouth shut. "Sit." The last word came out as a low growl, so I decided to stop pushing the Lord and my luck and perched on the chair before the fireplace.

I noticed Henry was holding a small bowl of water in one hand and bandages and what looked like an ointment in the other. A hand towel was draped over the crook of his arm.

"I didn't know the clan donated money to charity," I admitted quietly.

"The clan doesn't. I do," Henry said, pulling the other chair closer to me and taking a seat.

"Let me guess, Isabelle doesn't approve?" I narrowed my eyes.

"Isabelle has lost her way a little after Vincent's death," Henry said with a heavy sigh.

I didn't know what he meant. I thought vampires lost their way the moment they were turned because they lost their humanity.

"And you haven't...lost your way?"

"I hope not," Henry replied, setting the bowl and the other items on the floor by my feet.

He took the towel and dipped a small section of it into the water.

"Give me your arm," he said low, reaching for me.

Taken aback, I didn't protest as I slowly extended my arm, wincing when he began to clean the wound. His brows were drawn in concentration as he worked, gently dabbing the towel around the bite. I watched him closely. The sight and smell of blood didn't seem to bother him.

"You're good at this," I said, and Henry looked up from my arm and met my gaze.

"I was a doctor a long time ago," he said, looking down again as he finished cleaning the wound and reached for the ointment.

"Before you were turned?" I surmised.

He gave a small nod as he opened the jar and dipped his fingers in, scooping up some of the salve. A strong, minty smell climbed up my nostrils, making me scrunch up my nose.

"This might sting," Henry warned before bringing his fingers to the wound and gently applying the ointment.

I jerked at the coolness of the salve and his fingers, clenching my jaw when a burning sensation started.

"Vincent and I worked at the same infirmary," Henry said. "He worked the night shift. I didn't know he was a vampire until I contracted a deadly disease from one of the patients. I was dying, and Vincent was there, and he…" he swallowed thickly, "he thought he was saving me."

"You didn't want to be saved?" I asked low.

"I would not have chosen this life for myself. This life is not something I would ever choose for anyone."

Words failed me at his admission. Deep sorrow was etched into his expression, and I wondered if he'd go back and change the past if he could. If he'd choose death over eternal life. Something told me that he would. A strange feeling crept into my chest as I sat there while Henry bandaged my forearm. He'd been turned against his will. I'd never really thought about the fact that not all vampires had wanted to be turned. It was easy to forget they had been human before becoming monsters. The new revelation made me uneasy, and I shifted in my seat, thinking about Ravagers. They were as much victims as those they preyed upon.

"Why did you sneak out?" Henry asked low, pulling me from my thoughts. "You know the rules. Vassals don't leave the estate."

My cheeks heated when I thought about the real reason

behind my escape. I couldn't admit it to Henry, though, so I decided to lie.

"I needed a breath of fresh air. The Vassal Ball last night was intense."

"And was that the only reason?" Henry probed, securing the bandage and lifting his eyes from my forearm.

My face was on fire, but I forced myself to hold his gaze.

"Yes."

Henry smirked like he didn't believe me.

"Look, Sophie, about what happened earlier—"

"I don't want to talk about it." I cut him off.

Another smirk and a pause as if he were trying to decide if he should pursue the subject or let it go. Thankfully, he decided on the latter.

"Alright. We will change the bandages tomorrow night," he finally said.

I nodded and then forced the words out I'd never thought I would say to a vampire.

"Thank you."

Shock flickered across his face before he nodded.

"Sophie," he said when I went to rise from the chair.

I stayed put and looked at him. He stared back, looking as if he were pondering something.

"You know about Ravagers, know how to sword fight, and use a wooden dagger. Care to explain how all those things tie together?"

His question caught me off guard as I stared at him with wide eyes. He sounded more curious than angry. I couldn't tell him about the Tear, of course, but I wanted to provide some kind of an explanation. I didn't want him to begin suspecting that I'd had an ulterior motive for participating in the Selection a second time.

"I've been patrolling the streets at night to try and prevent

Ravager attacks or help stop them when they occur. That's why I know how to fight and have a wooden dagger," I said, making sure my voice didn't waver.

Shock flashed across Henry's features.

"Tell me you haven't been doing that alone?" he asked, looking at me in dismay.

"I won't say anything else on the subject," I said, my tone final, as I rose to my feet.

Henry stood up as well.

"Do you need anything else?" he asked, and I scowled.

His caring nature was beginning to make me uncomfortable, mainly because it defied everything I believed about vampires. A Ravager had almost killed me, but Henry had saved me and bandaged my wound.

Confused, I shook my head "no" and headed for the door. The adrenaline that had my blood pumping earlier had worn off, and I was suddenly exhausted.

"Goodnight, Henry," I said and slipped out of his room.

After I'd showered and settled in bed, it didn't take long for sleep to claim me. I was dreaming about the night of my mother's death again, but this time, the vampire killing her was the Ravager who'd attacked me. When I walked into the study, his head snapped in my direction, my mother's blood dripping from his fangs. In the blink of an eye, he was on me, and this time, his fangs sank into my neck instead of my forearm. I screamed, or at least I thought I did, as excruciating pain seized my body. I tried to fight, but it was pointless, and soon I went limp in the vampire's arms.

My eyes lifted to the ceiling as I waited for my death to come. I could feel my life slowly draining out of me with every gulp of my blood the Ravager drew from me. Suddenly, the vampire lifted his head from my savaged neck, and my eyes widened because I was looking at Henry, his lips smeared with my blood.

A wave of shock rolled through me as I stared into his dark eyes. A warning? A premonition? I shivered. Had I really thought he was different? I should have known better.

11

"I'm sorry I told Master Henry you weren't in your room last night. I was worried about you," Rory said, pouring tea into the blue-and-white cup on the table before me.

"It's okay," I assured her, setting down the biscuit I was eating and wiping my hands.

I didn't blame her for alerting the Lord about my absence. If anything, I should be thanking her for telling him. I hated to admit it, but he'd come to my rescue last night. I wasn't sure I would have been able to fight the Ravager off. Shuddering at the thought, I pulled the long sleeve of my dress down to make sure my bandaged forearm was covered. I didn't want Rory to notice it and ask questions. I watched the girl while she worked, cleaning up the kitchen we were in. Was it right that she didn't know the truth about her parents' death? Would it matter if she did? I didn't have the answers, so I decided not to tell her anything for the time being.

"Good morning," Wren greeted Rory and me as he strolled into the kitchen. "Or, rather, evening, I suppose."

I glanced out the kitchen window at the rapidly darkening sky outside. I'd slept all day and had only risen a short while back with a feeling of guilt. What I'd done last night was reckless and impulsive. I couldn't believe I'd once again almost compromised my stay here. Worse yet, my poor judgment had almost cost me my life. I wasn't sure if it had been Henry's blood in my system that had made me do such a foolish thing or my own carelessness.

Rory came up and drew the heavy curtains closed, blocking the sky outside from my view.

"Sorry." She gave a small, apologetic smile. "The Duvals will be up any minute. We can't risk the last rays of sunlight coming through," she explained before turning to Wren. "Good evening," she smiled at him as he took a seat opposite me at the kitchen table. "Please help yourself to some breakfast."

"I sure will. The biscuits smell delicious." Wren returned Rory's smile.

She poured him a cup of tea and slipped out of the kitchen.

"I'm sorry about what happened last night," Wren said, his gaze dropping to my arm where he'd nicked me with the sword.

"It's okay. You got a little carried away. It happens," I told him, taking a sip of my lukewarm tea.

He looked around before leaning in closer to me across the kitchen table.

"Were you able to get into the Lord's bedroom?" he asked in a soft whisper.

Vampires had supernatural hearing, so he was trying not to be overheard.

"No. Well, not exactly," I replied. I'd been able to get into Henry's bedroom. I just hadn't been able to search it.

Wren looked confused by my answer, but before he could ask any follow-up questions, Henry stepped into the kitchen. I flinched, not having heard his approach. He was dressed in black leather like the guards who worked on the border with the Black Forest. My brows lifted as I took him in, noticing the two sheaths at his sides for weapons. Was he going to the border tonight?

"Good evening, Sophie," Henry said to me, and I inclined my head in greeting.

"My Lord," Wren chimed in, his voice a bit unsteady.

Reluctantly, Henry shifted his attention to him and narrowed his eyes.

"I would like to speak with you in private." He turned back to me, ignoring the young man. "Walk with me."

I glanced at Wren and rose to my feet, following Henry out of the kitchen.

"You don't need to be so rude to him. The sword fight was my idea," I said, figuring Henry was still upset about Wren wounding me.

"I don't like him," the Lord replied but didn't provide any more explanation as we made our way upstairs to his bedroom.

My brows knitted when we approached his door, but then I realized he probably just wanted to help me change the bandage on my forearm. I wanted to tell him I didn't need his help, but I held my tongue. If he was getting more comfortable with letting me into his bedroom, I could use that to my advantage.

Fresh bandages and a bowl of water sat on the floor by the fireplace when we walked in, confirming my assumption about Henry's intentions behind bringing me here. I took a seat in the same chair I'd sat in last night, and Henry dragged the other chair closer, leaning in to work on my arm.

"Initiating that sword fight was incredibly foolish," he stated, carefully rolling up the sleeve of my dress.

So, we were back on that subject.

I lifted a shoulder. "I told you I was bored."

"Right." Henry blew out a breath of frustration. "And then you snuck out and almost got yourself killed."

"It was your kind that almost killed me," I said through my teeth, getting annoyed we were having this conversation.

His blue gaze lifted to mine.

"Still, yesterday proved you were prone to reckless decisions," he said, and I rolled my eyes. "And you don't like to sit idle."

"Your point?" I arched a brow.

If he'd brought me here just to chide me, I could change my own bandages from now on.

"I'm going to the border tonight, and you are coming with me," Henry said, and my eyebrows flew up.

"You're taking me to the border?"

"I am. If you are going to put yourself in danger, I'd rather you do it on my watch so I can come to your rescue."

"I don't need you to rescue me." I scoffed.

"The fact that I'm changing your bandages right now proves otherwise," he murmured, looking at my forearm. I lowered my gaze to it as well. "The wound is looking better. It might not scar too badly."

"It doesn't matter if it does," I said, momentarily lost in thought. "It will just serve as a reminder."

"A reminder of your recklessness?" Henry raised a dark brow.

"A reminder of how monstrous your kind is," I bit out, meeting his gaze.

His jaw flexed, but he didn't say anything else as he cleaned the wound and put more ointment on it. When he was done, we both rose to our feet.

"You need to change," he said, eyeing my long yellow dress. "We will leave as soon as you are ready."

"Will I get a weapon?" I asked, excitement sparking in my veins.

"We will get you a sword when we get to the border. You can bring your dagger, though."

He didn't need to mention the last part. I wouldn't go anywhere without my dagger. Especially after the Ravager attack last night.

Streaks of moonlight cut through the carriage windows as we traveled through the silent and dark city until we reached the border. Without waiting for help, I jumped out of the coach, now dressed in thick black leggings and a deep forest-green tunic long enough to conceal my dagger. Despite it being a warm night, I'd settled on long sleeves to hide my injured arm.

Eyeing the mountainous wall looming ahead, I reached up and bound my hair at the nape of my neck, using the thin leather strap I'd brought with me. The wall erected on the border with the Black Forest stretched for miles, separating the Empire of Seven from the other half of the continent, where Dark Witches and all sorts of other things roamed. New Haven and a part of the Southern region sat right on the border while the rest of the Empire was tucked away safely behind them.

"The guards go through rigorous training and are very dedicated to the safety of the people," Henry informed me as we set off for the wall several feet ahead of us.

I already knew all that from Waylon and from the other guards who were a part of the Order. Being a border guard paid well and was one of the most reputable occupations in New Haven. It was also the most dangerous. Dark Witches preferred women and children for their sacrifices but often snatched the guards to avoid going into the city. I had a lot of respect for those who were willing to give up their lives to protect the people and had even considered becoming a guard myself, but only men were recruited.

When Henry and I approached the border, dozens of torches greeted us, bathing the stone wall in an orange glow. Leather- and iron-clad guards patrolled the top and the bottom of the structure that rose several meters above the ground. Their postures were relaxed as they talked to each other, exchanging jokes and laughing. The atmosphere was not as tense as one would expect on the border with the Black Forest.

"It has been quiet on the border lately," Henry said by way of explanation, following my gaze.

"That doesn't mean they should let their guard down," I murmured, frowning.

"I agree," the Lord said, motioning for me to follow him as he began strolling along the bottom of the wall.

Falling into step next to him, I noticed Waylon stationed at one of the posts. His eyes widened slightly as our gazes locked. A smidgen of guilt settled in my chest. I'd used him last night to take the edge off, just like I'd done a few times in the past. I knew I could never give him what he truly wanted and using him for my own selfish reasons was unfair to him. He deserved better. My eyebrows slammed down as I made a decision—when my mission at the Duval Estate was over, I would tell Waylon we couldn't carry on like we had been in the past few months.

Waylon's jaw flexed as if he knew what I was thinking, and he stared at me and the Lord for several seconds before averting his gaze.

"You know that guard," Henry said as we passed by Waylon's post. "You smelled like him last night."

My steps faltered. He didn't sound upset, but I wasn't sure if Waylon's life was now on the line.

"I would appreciate it if you stayed away from him while you are my vassal," Henry said, briefly glancing at me. "Or anyone else, for that matter. I don't want to have to explain to the other clans why you smell like other men."

I grimaced at his words because they made me sound loose. I'd only ever been with Waylon.

"I understand. I wasn't in the right state of mind last night when I snuck out. It won't happen again," I assured him, watching him closely, trying to gauge if my words would placate him.

One side of his mouth turned up. "So, you admit you were impulsive last night?"

I rolled my eyes but couldn't fight a small smile. "You don't have to harp on that."

Henry smirked but didn't say anything else as he stopped before a set of worn stone steps leading up to the top of the wall. He quickly climbed them, and I followed.

Once we were on the very top, I stepped close to the raised ledge that came up to my waist, resting my hands on the cool gray stone.

Torches lined the other side of the border as well, but they didn't do much to penetrate the darkness of the Black Forest. Squinting, I peered into the pitch-black but was unable to make anything out. I thought I could see twisted shadows moving in the woods, but I couldn't be sure. Wrapping my arms around me, I suppressed a shudder. No one knew what horrors lurked in the Black Forest. I'd heard there were giant wolves and other creatures, all equipped with claws and teeth sharp enough to rip humans to shreds.

A wave of goosebumps spread over my skin as the Forest seemed to still. All of the sounds died out. I looked around me and down the length of the border. The guards still seemed relaxed, standing around in idle chatter. Henry was talking to one of them close to my right.

I faced the woods again just as the flame in one of the torches beyond the wall wavered as if stirred by the wind. There was no breeze tonight, so I bent slightly forward over the ledge, my brows knitting. Planting my palms back on the narrow ridge, I focused on the fire, refusing to blink. Nothing happened for a few seconds, but then I thought I saw movement out of the corner of my eye. I snapped my head to the left as the entire line of torches beyond the wall began to ripple wildly. Gripping the ledge, I leaned out more, my chest tight with pressure.

"What is it?" came Henry's deep voice to my right, startling me.

He was beside me now, looking in the same direction I was.

"I am not sure..." I murmured just as one of the torches went out.

The others were quickly snuffed out as well, plunging the area on the other side of the wall into sudden darkness.

My breath caught as eerie silence settled over the border. I glanced at Henry. His features were stark as he stared into the darkness to my left. His chin lifted a fraction, and his nostrils flared as if he were sniffing the air.

His eyes widened, and he cursed just as a strangled scream pierced the night several feet away to my left.

12

My heart slammed against my ribs as my head jerked toward the sound. Suddenly, Henry grabbed my arm and spun me around to face him. My wide eyes met his as he leaned in, bringing his face mere inches from mine.

"Get down and hide," he barked an order, his voice somehow even deeper than usual.

Letting go of me, he jumped on the narrow ridge with feline grace and took off in the direction of where the scream had come from.

He didn't seriously expect me to run and hide?

Another scream tore through the night, this time to my right.

"A witch!" someone down the wall shouted, and I whirled toward the sound, looking frantically around.

A shadow moved on the wall, taking out guards one by one, their mangled bodies dropping into the darkness on the other side of the border.

I heard a commotion on the ground moments before dozens of fiery arrows lit up the night sky, climbing high in the air above the stone wall. They slammed into the tall grass on the other side, starting a fire that quickly spread along the entire length of the border.

I could see the witch more clearly now. The creature would appear out of nowhere, wrapped in smoke and shadows. She would deliver a deadly blow before disappearing into the thin air as if being sucked into the void, only to reappear several feet away in front of the next victim.

Instinctively, I pulled out my dagger but then sheathed it a second later. It wouldn't do me any good. Henry had never gotten a chance to get me another weapon.

"Here!" a guard shouted from behind me, and when I spun, he threw a short sword my way.

I caught it and turned just in time to see another guard only a few feet away from me being torn to pieces by the witch.

The sight of the creature paralyzed me for a brief moment before my training kicked in. My muscles tensed as I assumed a fighting position, waiting for the witch to come for me. She didn't make me wait long, appearing right before me out of the darkness. A bolt of cold terror shot through me as I lifted my sword.

The witch looked as they did in the paintings depicting the last battle of New Haven. Pitch-black eyes and skin so white, it was nearly translucent, marbled by black-blue veins. Her fingers were elongated into sharp claws that were dripping blood from the previous victim. The witch drew her arm back, preparing to attack, and I gritted my teeth, bracing for the coming onslaught. Suddenly, the witch cocked her head to the side, the movement rigid and unnatural as she sniffed the air, similar to how Henry had done earlier. Releasing a high-pitched shriek, she backed away and slithered down the stone wall to the guards below.

I didn't have time to dwell on why the witch hadn't attacked as screams of pain and terror erupted from the ground. Snapping into action, I raced down the cracked, uneven stone steps.

Several guards, including Waylon, were huddled together close to the wall, trying to fight the witch. I doubted they stood a chance against the creature. Still, I only hesitated for a moment before joining them, my sword raised. Even if the chances of survival were slim, I couldn't stand by and do nothing. I especially couldn't run and hide as Henry had ordered me to. I would fight, even if I fought to the death. It might very well come to that, I realized as my gaze darted around, following the moving shadow of the Dark Witch. Any time it drew near, I swung my sword, but the blade sliced through thin air. It felt like fighting smoke and shadows. The witch was using the same strategy on the ground as she had done on the top of the wall, taking the guards out one by one.

The number of men around me diminished quickly until only Waylon and I remained. We brought our backs together, our swords raised, waiting for the ambush. Out of the corner of my eye, I saw an oily shadow dart toward us. The witch was coming. I braced myself, preparing for impact, but it never came because Henry appeared a few feet away from me. With a roar that raised the tiny hairs on my body, the Lord snatched the witch by the throat, yanking her out of the shadows. She hissed and clawed at his arm, but he didn't even flinch. Moving incredibly fast, he slammed her into the stone wall of the border, that entire section trembling from the impact. Dark, inky blood rapidly pooled under the witch's limp body, where Henry held her above the ground.

My stomach tumbled with relief, but it was short-lived as I saw another shadow rush out from the side, lurching toward Henry's exposed back. There was another witch. Not a witch, a warlock, I realized as I watched him step out of the shadows right behind Henry. Time seemed to slow as the warlock raised his clawed hand high above his head, and a black lightning bolt appeared there. Without thinking, I sprinted forward and thrust my sword into the warlock's back before jerking it out with a shout. The creature screeched and whirled on me, his cloak billowing out behind him.

Terror shot through me when I saw my reflection in the glossy black eyes. He was about to kill me. I knew it as sure as I knew my own name. If I died tonight, my only hope was that others would keep searching for the amulet because Dark Witches and vampires had to be destroyed. Gritting my teeth, I lifted my sword again, knowing full well it would do me no good. The warlock lunged at me, but before he could reach me, he jerked back as if being pulled by an invisible string. His mouth went slack, filling with black blood until it overflowed and spilled down his chin.

I was frozen in shock as my eyes slowly lowered to the warlock's chest. Henry's clawed hand was protruding from it, holding the warlock's black heart that was spewing dark blood.

Abruptly, Henry snatched his hand back through the gaping hole in the warlock's chest and tossed the creature's heart to the side. It landed with a wet smack at the same time the warlock's lifeless body dropped with a dull thud.

I stared at Henry with wide eyes. A movement behind him snagged my attention, and my mouth dropped open as I watched the other witch's body slide out of the deep indentation in the border wall and crumple to the ground.

Lifting my head, I checked the wall for any more shadows, listening for any screams of pain or terror. When heavy silence settled over the border, a shuddering breath left me—the attack was over.

Slowly, my gaze returned to Henry. He stood under a beam of moonlight, his chest rising and falling with heavy breaths. Dark blood smeared his defined features and matted his hair. One of his hands, the one that he'd used to rip out the warlock's heart, was completely covered in black. The front of his leathers had been clawed, and I could see dark red blood gushing from the wounds.

"I told you to hide," Henry growled, the sound deep and rough.

His stare was intense and unblinking as he looked at me. His eyes were so dark I could barely see any blue.

I swallowed hard, taking several steps back. The Lord looked a little crazed, like a Ravager lost in the frenzy of bloodlust. I wondered if fighting the witches had brought out that side of him—the wild, beastly side.

"Henry…" My voice shook as I uttered his name.

He stalked toward me, his chin lowered.

"You are so incredibly reckless. How am I supposed to keep you safe if you are bound and determined to put yourself in danger?" he seethed, quickly closing the short distance between us.

"Don't come any closer," I warned, even though I knew there was nothing I could do to stop him.

A growl of annoyance rumbled from Henry, jarring me into action. I turned to run but didn't make it far before he caught my arm and spun me around, yanking me forward. He brought me flush with him, and my breath caught as I jerked my head back to look up at the Lord. Little remained of the Henry I'd dealt with in the past few days. He looked feral, a predator through and through. His lips peeled back to reveal the sharp fangs as a low hiss escaped him.

The dream I'd had last night floated up to the surface of my subconscious. Henry was seconds away from sinking his fangs into my neck like he'd done in my dream. He would bite me, and he would drink from me until the very last drop. Just like in my dream, a wave of shock rolled through me. I'd known all along he could not be trusted. My breath left me as I stared into Henry's eyes—the eyes of a killer. Suddenly, a soft thud sounded, and Henry froze before letting go of me and slowly turning around. A knife protruded from his back, and when I peeked from behind him, I realized Waylon must have thrown it. He stood a few feet away, his eyes full of panic, but his features set in determination.

"You," Henry snarled, and I knew I only had a few seconds before he went for Waylon's throat.

I darted out from behind Henry and whirled around to face him, blocking Waylon from his view. Fisting his shirt, I hauled myself up to his hard, unyielding body and brought my face inches from his.

"Henry, please. You're not yourself," I begged, trying to draw his attention away from Waylon.

His black, bottomless eyes darted to me. We shared a breath before Henry grabbed my hair, where it was tied at the nape of my neck and jerked my head back and to the side. A sharp cry left me, and I squeezed my eyes shut, preparing for the bite. I knew it would come at any second, and it wouldn't be as clean and precise as the one on my wrist at the ball. It would be savage and overwhelming. Seconds ticked by, but the bite never came. Henry just held me there, his cool breath chilling my exposed neck. I heard him swallow and felt him shudder against me. What was he doing? Was he trying to tame his inner beast that had escaped?

With a rough exhale, he released me and backed away so suddenly I lost balance, nearly landing on the ground. Shame and sadness marked his features as the Lord stared at me. His eyes were slowly becoming bluer, letting me know he had regained some control. A significant amount of black still remained, and I realized he probably needed to feed after losing so much blood.

"Are you hurt?" Henry asked low, still looking at me.

"Do you mean, did you hurt me or the witches?" I snapped, unable to contain my simmering rage.

Even if he hadn't been himself, that didn't excuse his wild behavior. He could have hurt me or Waylon. He could've killed us because of his lack of self-control.

The Lord flinched at my words before saying, "I am sorry."

He spoke very low so only I would hear, but Waylon still

overheard. I glanced at him and saw his brows shoot up in shock. Henry, a vampire, had just apologized to me.

"I'm not hurt," I said quietly, looking back at the Lord. He seemed genuinely concerned, and I wanted to put him at ease even if he didn't deserve it.

"I came as fast as I could." Isabelle's voice rang out as she came striding to where we were standing. "I've heard there's been an attack."

"It's over now," Waylon said. "Lord Duval was able to fight them off."

"You are injured," Isabelle declared, quickly scanning Henry from head to toe.

"I need to feed," was all he said, turning to leave. "Make sure Sophie gets home safely," he threw over his shoulder before disappearing into the night.

13

"He should be feeding from you," Isabelle snapped when we loaded into the carriage. "I know about your little arrangement, and I disapprove of it," she seethed.

"You should have been there to help him fight the witches," I snapped back, hoping to shut her up. I was too shaken up and tired for this conversation.

Her upper lip curled in a snarl, but she didn't say anything else before turning to stare out the window.

We were quiet all the way to the mansion, the only sound coming from the carriage wheels rolling over cobblestones. Folding my trembling hands in my lap, I thought about what had transpired at the border. What I'd experienced tonight had been eye-opening. Eye-opening and utterly terrifying. I'd been so focused on vampires since my mother's death that Dark Witches had faded into the background. I knew they were out there, in the Black Forest and beyond, but I'd considered vampires the real enemy. Tonight had changed my way of thinking. I was now painfully aware of the real threat Dark Witches posed. I'd almost died...

Henry had fought for us tonight, for the people of New

Haven. For me and for Waylon. The realization made me uneasy as I struggled to reconcile my conflicting emotions about the Lord. I realized I didn't need to. Vampires were still an enemy, and Henry was no exception. His wild behavior earlier had demonstrated that his true monstrous nature dwelled just below the surface, always on the verge of breaking free to deliver misery to those around him. After tonight, I had a better grasp on the monstrosity of the Dark Witches as well, having witnessed it up close. I doubted I would ever forget tonight. Its horrors would haunt my dreams just like the night of my mother's death.

When the carriage pulled up to the mansion, I peered out the window, wondering if Henry was inside and had already fed. I hoped he'd used the blood stored in the cellar. I wasn't sure letting him stalk into the night earlier had been a good idea. He'd seemed to be more in control, but I still felt uneasy. I also wondered how badly he was hurt. My brows knitted when the thought crossed my mind, and I shook my head, swallowing thickly. There were several reasons why I didn't need to wonder about that. Henry was a vampire. He could sustain a lot more injuries than a mere human. I also didn't need to wonder if he was hurt because I didn't need to care. I couldn't. Not when I'd been actively searching for the amulet that would destroy him and his kind.

As soon as the carriage stopped, Isabelle swept out of it, too fast for me to track her movements. I exited the carriage as well and headed straight for the kitchen once I was inside the house.

Wren was there eating dinner, and his forehead creased when he took me in.

"Sophie, are you okay?" he asked, his pale-blue eyes searching my face.

I gave a small shake of my head as I opened the kitchen cabinet, rooting around it until I found the white medicine box. I was about to take a shower and would need to change the bandage on my arm. I doubted Henry would help me with that tonight.

"What happened?" Wren asked.

"I went to the border with Henry," I said with a heavy sigh, retrieving the medicine box from the cabinet and turning to face him.

"He took you to the border?" Wren sounded dismayed.

"Yes, and there was an attack," I said with a shuddering breath.

The medicine box rattled in my trembling hands, so I sat it on the kitchen table, not sure how long this conversation would last.

"I see," Wren said, his face growing ashen. "You look pretty shaken up."

"I am," I admitted. "I didn't realize Dark Witches were still such a threat."

Wren's eyes widened, and he looked at me as if I were a crazy person.

"You didn't think they were a threat?" he asked, his face contorting in what appeared to be barely contained rage. It was clear my words had struck a nerve.

"What happened to you?" I asked low, disturbed by his reaction.

"Something terrible," Wren whispered.

His eyes became glossy and unfocused as he stared into the space before him. I could tell he wasn't seeing the brightly lit kitchen. He was lost in memories. Terrible memories, judging by his taut features. Several seconds passed before Wren blinked a few times and refocused on me.

"But I survived," he said. "Because I was prepared to do anything to survive. So, tell me, Sophie. What are you prepared to do to find the Tear?"

The last sentence had been spoken barely above a whisper, and my lips parted as I sucked in a sharp breath. After what I'd seen tonight, I would do anything to find the amulet. I wasn't sure who was worse, vampires or Dark Witches, and it truly didn't matter. If I had the Tear, I could obliterate them all. I needed to search Henry's bedroom. I didn't care what I had to do.

He'd been injured earlier. His nature drove him to feed. Perhaps tonight, he wouldn't turn me down.

"Whatever it takes," I told Wren, grabbing the medicine box off the table before leaving the kitchen.

Half an hour later, I found myself staring at Henry's bedroom door. I felt foolish. What exactly was my plan? Even if I was able to seduce the Lord, then what? Wait until he was asleep and search his bedroom? He could hear a pin drop with his supernatural hearing, and he didn't strike me as someone who was a heavy sleeper. On the contrary, I doubted he was ever not on high alert.

With a soft sigh, I hung my head, giving up on the idea. I turned to leave, but that was when Henry opened the door, staring at me from inside the darkness of his room.

"Sophie? What are you doing here?" he asked, his brows knitting.

He smelled of soap, and his damp hair was slicked away from his face. His clean white shirt was unbuttoned at the top, exposing part of his chest where a gnarly looking wound was still healing.

"I..." I hesitated, self-consciously wrapping my silk robe around my thin, nearly translucent nightgown. I'd come here to seduce the Lord and had dressed for the occasion. Now, I felt overexposed.

Henry's gaze flickered over me before landing on my forearm.

"Do you need help changing your bandage?" His eyes lifted to mine.

"No," I replied. "I just came to check on you."

The moment the words left my mouth, I realized I wasn't exactly lying. I'd wanted to make sure he was okay.

The Lord was clearly taken aback and stood frozen in the doorway for a few seconds, staring at me.

"Can I come in?" I asked shakily, unsure of what I was doing.

With a nod, he let me in, closing the door behind me.

The room was dark and quiet when I walked in, the only light coming from the lit fireplace.

"Have a seat." Henry gestured to the chair I'd used in the past when he'd changed my bandages.

He walked to the other chair, and I noticed he was barefoot, his loose black pants dragging slightly on the floor. I lowered myself into the chair and watched the Lord do the same. He then leaned over one side of his chair and picked up a short, wide glass full of deep red liquid. The coppery smell I could pick up on told me it was blood. Relief washed over me as I realized Henry must have come straight here from the border to drink some of the blood from the cellar instead of finding a human to sink his fangs into in a dark alley.

The Lord took a few sips from the glass before turning to look at me.

"I am sorry about how I acted earlier," he said, his lips tinged with red. His eyes were back to stormy blue, and his features were relaxed. "Fighting the witches took a lot out of me. I was not myself."

I wasn't sure that was entirely true. Perhaps he'd been more himself then—when the monster that was usually contained had been out.

"Apology accepted," I told him. I was not about to excuse his behavior and tell him he didn't need to apologize.

Henry nodded and took another sip of the blood.

"Are you okay?" he asked, watching me from above the rim of his glass. "I know Dark Witches can be terrifying, especially if you have never encountered them before."

"They *were* terrifying," I agreed. "I'm sure I will have nightmares for many nights to come."

"I wish I hadn't brought you with me," Henry confessed with a heavy sigh, looking regretful. "The attacks have been rare during the last few months. I did not expect one tonight."

"I'm glad you took me with you," I told him, and I meant it.

Like the Vassal Ball, fighting the witches tonight had enflamed my heart and fueled my resolve to find Josephine's Tear. I didn't regret going with Henry to the border. "Isabelle should have been there," I pointed out, frowning.

Henry nodded in agreement.

"Her sense of self-preservation sometimes outweighs her sense of loyalty," he explained before his eyes settled on me. "Your sense of self-preservation, however, appears to be non-existent. Seriously, what were you thinking? I told you to run and hide."

"I was thinking that I couldn't run and hide when people around me were dying." I met his deep blue gaze.

A look of admiration flickered across his face before his features hardened.

"You cannot save everyone," he said with a heavy sigh. Little did he know I planned to do just that. "I speak from experience."

I opened my mouth to ask about that experience but then closed it. Asking about that felt like crossing into a very personal territory, and I didn't need to know Henry on that level.

We sat in silence for a few minutes as a myriad of other questions danced on the tip of my tongue. The Lord was almost two hundred years old and had a wealth of knowledge I was dying to tap into.

"Can you tell me about the Red War?" I finally asked, giving in to my curiosity.

Henry's fingers tightened around the glass, and I thought he would deny my request.

To my surprise, he opened his mouth and said, "It was carnage." Staring with unseeing eyes at the flickering fire, he continued, "What you saw tonight on the border was nothing in comparison. The battle of New Haven was one of the worst nights of my life. I lost my mother and my brother in that battle."

My brows lifted in shock.

"You mean Rosalind and Gerard Duval? I knew they perished

during the War, but I didn't realize it was during the battle of New Haven. They are not depicted in any of the paintings I've seen."

"That is because our history does little to honor the fallen," Henry said bitterly.

I was inclined to agree. White Witches had fought alongside the humans and the clans in the War. Yet, they were hardly ever mentioned in the stories. Perhaps it was because their entire population had been eradicated, and no one was left to carry on their legacy. Still, it made me sad they had been erased from existence and forgotten.

"Can you tell me about the White Witches?" I asked the Lord.

A little smile lit up his face as he seemed to be lost in a memory.

"They were good people," he finally said.

"They couldn't have been that good since they were the ones who got corrupted by the Dark god and turned into Dark Witches," I pointed out.

Our history did mention that. At first, there had only been White Witches, but the Dark god, Xanthus, had poisoned their hearts with promises of infinite power that could only be achieved through black magic. One by one, they had surrendered their souls to him, turning into the pale, wraith-looking beings that haunted our nightmares and stole humans for sacrifices. In order to fully resurrect Xanthus and unleash an era of pain and suffering, the Dark Witches needed a mass sacrifice of countless human souls. To achieve that, they had set off the Red War one hundred years ago. The vampires had come to our aid and had been able to prevail in the War, but not before the remaining White Witches had been slaughtered or turned dark.

The Lord's smile faded.

"The downfall of a few of them does not make them all evil."

I had a feeling he wasn't just talking about White Witches but also his kind. He confirmed as much when he gave me a pointed look I chose to ignore.

"What were they like?" I asked, propping my elbows on my knees and cupping my face with my hands.

"They had a profound connection to the world around them and drew their power from it. Very strong magic wielders."

"Not strong enough…" I trailed off.

They hadn't been strong enough to survive the Red War.

Shadows crept into Henry's features.

"I tried to save them, but I couldn't."

"Why do you think it's your responsibility to save everyone?" I wondered aloud.

"I could ask you the same thing." His gaze was fastened on mine. "What drives a nineteen-year-old girl to patrol the streets at night and help the border guards to fight off a witch attack?"

My brows pinched as I pondered his question. I'd never asked myself that before. It felt natural to do those things, like breathing. Never once had I hesitated before a patrol, just like I hadn't hesitated before I'd joined the guards who'd been fighting the witch. It had felt right.

"I think…" Emotions clogged my throat before I continued, "I think I do those things because I couldn't save my mother."

The moment the words were out, I realized it was the first time I'd admitted that, even to myself.

The Lord's eyes softened as he stared at me.

"It was not your responsibility to save her," he said low. "It was mine. Dark Witches took her, and I am the one entrusted with protecting the people of New Haven."

My mouth opened slightly at his words. I doubted the other clan vampires felt the same way. Take Isabelle, for example. It seemed she wanted all the perks of being our protector without any responsibilities that came with the title. Henry, on the other hand, seemed to take his role of a protector seriously. He seemed almost devoted to the cause.

"Why do you do it?" I asked, my gaze sweeping over his features. "The other vampires don't seem to be that invested in the people's safety."

Henry's eyes filled with impossible sadness as he swallowed thickly.

"Because I am trying to atone for all the lives I have taken."

I sat frozen for a moment as his words hung between us in the tense silence. The crackling fire was the only sound in the room.

"You've taken many lives?" I asked as a cold feeling crept into my chest.

The Lord looked tormented by his admission, the feeling of misery emanating from him and sweeping me under. I couldn't relate to him because I'd never taken innocent lives, but I imagined it was a heavy burden to carry.

Henry was quiet for several long minutes.

Just when I thought he wasn't going to respond, he said, "When a vampire is first turned, the bloodlust is nearly impossible to control. I had Vincent by my side to guide me through it, but he couldn't always be there to stop me when the hunger struck."

I sat there, feeling like I should say something, but words wouldn't come. What could I say? I'm sorry that happened to you? I couldn't bring myself to feel sorry for him. I only felt sorry for his victims.

Henry cleared his throat and drained his glass before rising to his feet.

"I need more blood, and you need to get some rest," he said, turning to me.

I also rose to my feet, my robe parting to expose my flimsy nightgown. The Lord stilled as his rapidly darkening eyes roamed every inch of my body.

This was my chance.

You can feed from me, the words were on the tip of my tongue.

Yet, I couldn't force them out. I felt...conflicted like I had earlier. A part of me knew that if he fed from me tonight, I would enjoy it. Just like I would enjoy what might come after the feeding. My eyes widened at the thought, and I took an involuntary step back but couldn't suppress a wave of shivers that erupted over my skin. Henry's nostrils flared as his eyes, now nearly black, returned to my face.

"What do you want, Sophie?" he whispered roughly, his gaze ensnaring mine.

"Nothing," I whispered back. The words came out shaky and unsure. "Nothing," I repeated louder, scowling. "I'm going to bed. Goodnight," I said and fled his bedroom like a coward.

14

"Coward," I murmured into my teacup, sitting in the kitchen the following night.

"What?" Rory asked, having overheard me when she'd walked in.

She was holding a wicker basket full of fresh linens at her hip. Her simple topknot had all but unraveled, and she looked flustered.

"Rory!" I heard Ezra call from the dining room.

"Coming!" she yelled back. "I swear he always needs my help when he's cleaning," she sighed.

I smirked, thinking about their sibling dynamic. Ezra was older than Rory, but she seemed more mature, always taking care of her brother. She also took it upon herself to ensure the Duval household ran smoothly. I wasn't sure if she enjoyed the responsibility or did it because she felt indebted to Henry. Either way, from the interactions that I'd witnessed, it was clear the Lord cared about Rory and Ezra and treated them well.

"I'll be back," Rory assured me as she sat the linen basket on the table before me and hurried out of the kitchen.

I lifted my eyes from the teacup and froze. Henry's bedroom

key sat on top of the linens, gleaming in the glow of the lamp. My breath hitched as my eyes flicked in the direction of the dining room, where I could hear Rory and Ezra moving around. I had to act fast. Swiftly rising to my feet, I snatched the key and all but ran out of the kitchen, the skirt of my teal dress snapping around the heels of my shoes. When I got to the foyer and found it empty, I set off into a sprint, running to the grand staircase and up the wide stone steps. I didn't stop running until I skidded to a halt before Henry's bedroom door.

Breathing shallowly, I lifted the key with shaking hands but froze with it halfway to the keyhole. It was possible that Henry was inside, but I doubted he would give Rory the key if he was in his room. Taking a deep breath to calm my nerves, I unlocked the door and paused on the threshold, listening. When all that greeted me was silence, I walked inside and quickly closed the door behind me. The fire was out, but the lamps were on, their light reflecting off the few pieces of furniture. Quickly throwing the chain with the key around my neck, I hurried over to the chest and began rummaging through Henry's clothes stored there. When my search rendered no results, I walked over to the tall dresser. Yanking open the top drawer that was at my eye level, I lifted on my tiptoes to peer inside.

"What are you doing in my room?" came Henry's deep voice from behind me.

All color drained from my face, and I froze for a moment before quietly closing the drawer and lowering down to the balls of my feet. Slowly, I turned around and found the Lord watching me with narrowed eyes. My gaze flicked to the closed door behind him as I tried to gauge if I could make an escape. Quickly giving up on the idea, I refocused on Henry.

"I was just looking for you," I lied, my voice unsteady.

He smirked, prowling toward me. I took a tiny step back, running into the dresser.

The Lord didn't say anything as his gaze lowered to his

bedroom key resting on my chest. I swallowed and held my breath as he slowly reached for it. He carefully untangled his necklace from the one holding the locket with the picture of my mother and pulled the thin chain up and over my head. After he hung it around his neck, his gaze returned to mine. He leaned in closer, staring into my eyes. What was he doing? Was he going to kiss me? Panic flared in my chest with a hint of something else I refused to acknowledge.

"What are you doing in my room?" Henry asked low.

"I wanted to see you," I lied again.

He backed away a few inches, his brow furrowing.

"How are you doing this?" he asked, confused.

"Doing what?" Now, *I* was confused.

"Resisting the compulsion?"

"The what?"

In the blink of an eye, he was even closer, his face mere inches from mine. The coolness radiating from his body chilled my skin as our gazes locked.

His eyes transfixed me, the pupil expanding and contracting as he said, "Tell me the truth. What are you doing in my room?"

"I already told you," I said, the words sluggish and difficult to get out.

"The truth, Sophie!" he shouted or maybe whispered. I wasn't sure as I got lost in his eyes, which seemed bottomless. Suddenly, I needed to tell him the truth. I had to.

"I was looking for Josephine's Tear."

With a gasp, I clamped my hand over my mouth. Why had I just told him that?

"What's Josephine's Tear?" Henry asked, his voice as soft as velvet, coaxing the truth out of me.

"It's an amulet—" The words began spilling out of me before I could think twice about what I was saying. *No! Fight it!* "—that can destroy the Dark Witches."

My throat burned from the partial lie I'd just told, and I

clenched my jaw to make sure no more words got out against my will.

Henry's eyes widened in shock as he abruptly backed away. The spell he'd had on me was broken; I could feel it.

"What did you do to me?!" I seethed, glaring at him.

"I used compulsion to make you tell me the truth."

"You forced the truth out of me!" I shouted, shoving at his hard chest. He didn't move an inch; it was like pushing at a wall. "I can't believe you did that!"

"Stop," he ordered, clasping my shoulders to hold me in place. He ducked his chin and looked into my eyes.

"Don't!" I jerked my head to the side.

"I am not trying to compel you," he bit out, exasperated. "Just tell me about the amulet. Can it really destroy the Dark Witches?"

He sounded doubtful but hopeful as if he really wanted to believe something but was too afraid to. His reaction surprised me and doused some of the anger. Slowly, I turned back to face him.

"Yes, it can destroy the Dark Witches," I said, tilting my head up to look at him.

"Why were you looking for it in my room?" Henry asked, his brows knitting.

"Do you not have it?" I asked low, even though I already knew the answer. The Lord had been genuinely shocked to learn about the Tear, or at least he'd appeared to be. My heart sank with disappointment.

"No, I don't have it," he said. "But I will help you find it."

"Why would you do that?" I asked, searching his face.

"If Dark Witches are destroyed, humans will no longer need the vampire clans," he explained quietly. "We can slink back into the shadows where we belong. Humans deserve to have their world to themselves."

I stared at him in utter disbelief. He sounded sincere, but I couldn't compel him to tell me the truth, so I had no way of knowing if he was lying. Granted, I hadn't told him the truth either, at least not the whole truth. In the end, vampires wouldn't slink back into the shadows because they would be destroyed together with the Dark Witches.

Henry had said he would help me find the Tear, but could I really trust him? I had no choice, I realized. He knew about the amulet now, and if he wasn't helping me look for it, then he would search for it on his own. I needed him by my side so I could know what he was doing.

"Okay," I said calmly.

"Okay." He slowly let go of me and lowered his hands by his sides. "Tell me what you know."

"It isn't much." I gave a small shake of my head. "When my mother died, I found a note from her with a sketch of an amulet. She called it Josephine's Tear and said it could destroy the Dark Witches. She scribbled "Vincent Duval" on the paper."

"Is that it?" Henry asked, eyeing me like he didn't quite believe I didn't have more information.

I hadn't told him about the other clue— "power of three"— deciding to keep it to myself.

"That's it."

"So, you came back as a Candidate again this year to gain access to the estate," Henry surmised, and I nodded.

"Do you have any idea why my mother wrote Vincent's name on the note about the amulet?"

"I am not sure," Henry replied, pondering my question. "Eloise was Vincent's vassal for a year when she turned eighteen. I know they kept in touch…" he trailed off as his eyes widened at my reaction to his words. "You didn't know?"

Disbelief surged through me, and I felt as if the ground had shifted under my feet.

My mother had been Vincent's vassal?

"You're lying," I said through my teeth.

"Why would I lie about that? Eloise was Vincent's vassal, and he cared about her."

I didn't say anything for a few minutes, my mind racing. Henry didn't have a reason to lie, and his claim was something I could easily confirm. My eyes fluttered closed as I took a deep breath to regain my composure. When I opened them, the look on Henry's face was one of compassion.

"When you say Vincent cared about her and they kept in touch, you don't mean…?" I forced myself to ask the question even though I wasn't prepared to hear the answer.

"No," Henry said, his tone final. "Eloise had a special place in Vincent's heart, but she was in love and happy with your father."

A breath of relief left me as I leaned against the dresser, my shoulders sagging.

"I can't believe she didn't tell me," I murmured. My chest was tight with disappointment. "I thought we told each other everything," I added as if to myself. "Obviously, I was mistaken. She also didn't tell me about the amulet."

"She was probably just trying to protect you. Vincent didn't tell me about the amulet, either. If he even knew about it," Henry said, his face taking on a contemplative look as he was trying to process all the information. "He probably *did* know about it and was helping your mother search for it," he concluded before meeting my gaze again. "The question is, did they ever find it, and if they did, what happened to it? Perhaps Dark Witches took it when they took Eloise. That would explain why Vincent went to the Dark Witches after they had taken her. He wanted to try and bring her and the amulet back."

My heart sank at his words as a lump rose in my throat. Vincent had disappeared right around my mother's death…

"He went to the Dark Witches? To try and rescue her?" I asked, my voice strained.

"Yes," Henry replied.

His gaze latched on to mine as he waited for what I would say next. I knew I didn't have to tell him the truth, but something urged me to. He deserved to know.

"Dark Witches didn't take my mother," I admitted, barely above a whisper.

"What?" Henry asked just as quietly.

I swallowed to relieve my dry throat, averting my gaze.

I couldn't bring myself to look at him as I confessed, "My father and I lied and said she was taken. The truth is…a vampire killed her."

For a few moments, I wasn't even sure he'd heard me as silence stretched between us. Slowly, I lifted my gaze, but before I could look at him, a fist slammed into the dresser, inches away from my face, splintering the dark wood. I jerked my head to the side and winced, squeezing my eyes shut for a brief second before opening them again. I knew Henry had used only a fraction of his strength when he'd punched the dresser. Otherwise, the piece of furniture would have been demolished.

"So, Vincent went to the Dark Witches and died for nothing?" Henry growled, his cool breath stirring the fine hairs on my temple.

I whipped my head to look at him, refusing to cower before him, but my eyes pricked with tears.

"I'm sorry," I managed to get out, but my voice shook.

Vincent had been a vampire, but I still felt regret for lying about my mother's death. When my father and I had lied, we'd sentenced the head of the Duval clan to sure death at the hands of the Dark Witches.

When I met Henry's blue eyes, they were full of anguish, leaving no doubt in my mind that he'd truly loved Vincent. His nostrils flared as he bared his fangs in a snarl. For a brief moment, I thought he might go for my throat, but instead, he hit the dresser again, rattling the drawers, and promptly stepped away, turning his back to me and running his hands through his hair.

A shuddering exhale left him as I watched the taut muscle of his back move and shift under his shirt. His shoulders slumped as he hung his head. He looked so very human at that moment that I had to fight the urge to comfort him. My hand lifted to reach for him, but I brought it down, my fingers curling into a fist at my side.

"Why did you lie?" Henry suddenly asked softly. His menacing tone told me that if I didn't have a good enough reason, I wouldn't leave this room alive.

"We didn't think anyone would believe us if we'd told the truth. That a vampire killed her," I explained quickly. "We hadn't yet known about Ravagers then."

Henry's head lifted, and he looked at me over his shoulder.

"Was it a Ravager?" he asked.

"No." I shook my head. "It had to be a vampire from one of the clans."

"What makes you say that?" Henry faced me fully then, his brow furrowed.

I wasn't foolish enough to think he'd gotten over his rage that quickly. It seemed he'd pushed it aside for now, and I had no doubt he would unleash it on me later.

"I was the one who found her," I said, my gaze growing distant as my mind flashed back to that night. "I returned home before my father," I continued as an icy chill crept into my chest. I knew my mind was just playing tricks on me, but I swore I could smell the birthday cake my mother had made and had left sitting on the kitchen table. "I walked into my mother's study and," I paused, swallowing thickly, "and saw them. She was already dead. He held her in his arms…"

I blinked rapidly and met Henry's gaze. Only then did I realize that my cheeks were wet with tears.

Henry's eyes softened a fraction, and I thought I saw his hand twitch as if he wanted to reach for me.

He must have thought better of it because his eyes became hard again as he asked, "Did you see who killed her?"

"No," I replied, quickly wiping away my tears. "I'm not sure if I blocked it from my mind, but all I remember are eyes so dark they were like oily pools of blackness. But I don't think it was a Ravager. That vampire was in control, and—"

"Not driven by bloodlust like a Ravager," Henry finished for me, and I nodded.

He dragged a hand over his face with a heavy sigh.

"So, we really have nothing to help us find the killer…"

"I wish I could remember more—"

"That was a traumatic experience," Henry cut me off. "It's possible you were compelled. Don't blame yourself for not remembering."

I *did* blame myself as tears threatened again. I felt like a failure. I'd really hoped to find the Tear or another clue on the estate, and now I didn't know where to go from here.

"I'd like to see my father," I said, swallowing hard and lifting my eyes to the ceiling to keep the tears at bay.

Henry didn't immediately respond, but I could feel his gaze on me, heavy and accusing.

Finally, he sighed and said, "Okay, but I'm coming with you."

Henry and I were quiet on the carriage ride to my house. Tension rolled off the Lord in waves as I sat across from him, dumbfounded by what I'd learned about my mother. She'd been Vincent's vassal and then kept in touch with him. Henry even believed they'd been looking for the amulet together. Vincent had cared enough about my mother to try to rescue her from the Dark Witches. Tonight's revelations had made it clear I hadn't known my mother as well as I'd thought.

My chest ached, but I refused to let my emotions take over. Instead, I dared a peek at Henry, who was staring out the window, his eyes shuttered and his jaw hard. He'd told me before that Vincent was like a father to him, and now he was dead because of the lie my father and I had told. My heart turned over heavily in my chest at the realization that what my father and I had done was causing Henry's anguish. The Lord must have felt me looking at him because he turned from the window and met my gaze. We stared at each other for a few minutes without saying a word.

I broke the silence first when I cleared my throat and said, "I'd understand if what you said earlier about helping me find the Tear has changed."

"It hasn't. I will still help you look for it," Henry said before turning back to the window. "That's what Vincent would have wanted."

When the carriage stopped before my house, I took a deep breath, preparing to explain myself to my father. Henry stepped out first before turning around and extending his hand to help me out. My brows lifted in surprise as I lowered my foot to the carriage step and placed my hand in his. I hadn't expected him to still be civil with me after what I'd revealed. I wasn't sure I would be able to show the same grace if the situations were reversed. The Lord dropped my hand the moment I was out of the carriage, turning to face the weathered front of my childhood home.

I rapped my knuckles on the old wooden door and waited, taking another steadying breath.

My father's eyes widened in shock when he opened the door.

"What is the meaning of this?" he asked, looking between Henry and me, his tone guarded.

"It's okay, father. I can explain once we're inside," I said calmly, trying to put him at ease.

He stared at me for a moment as if waiting for a sign that I was under duress. When I gave none, he opened the door wider and let us in.

"Henry, this is my father, Thomas Devereaux," I said after we'd stepped inside.

The house did not have a foyer, so we were standing in the small but cozy living room illuminated by two lamps and the glow from the fireplace.

"Lord Duval." My father inclined his head in a half-bow, giving Henry a wary look from beneath his gray eyebrows.

I could tell he was on edge in the vampire's presence, and I didn't blame him. I hated bringing Henry here and putting my father through this, but the Lord had been adamant about not letting me out of his sight.

Henry gave a curt nod, his features sharpening, and I wondered if he was considering ripping out my father's throat for lying about my mother's death.

"I'd like to speak with my father in private," I told Henry, coming to stand in front of him in an attempt to block my father from his view.

Henry looked around the living room.

"Where do you expect me to go?"

"Actually, you can stay here. My father and I will talk in the study."

"Whatever you have to say to him, I'm sure I need to hear it as well," Henry insisted.

He clearly didn't want to leave me and my father in private because he didn't trust me. I didn't trust him either.

"I just want to talk to him about my mother," I said low, looking into the Lord's eyes, pleading with him to understand. "Please."

Henry's gaze softened even as a muscle flexed along his jaw.

"Okay, just don't take long," he conceded.

With a nod, I turned from Henry and walked with my father to my mother's old study. I had mixed feelings about this room. Some days, I couldn't bring myself to step foot into this space where I'd found my mother dead in the arms of a vampire. On other days, this room brought me comfort. After all, I'd spent most of my childhood here. Even now, I could picture my mother hunched over her desk as she worked while I played or read, sharing in on the comfortable, silent companionship.

My father had taken over the study after my mother's death and had been spending most of his time here ever since. He needed the space to work, but I also wondered if being in this room made him feel closer to her somehow. A few weeks after her death, I'd helped him sort through and organize her things.

Now, a year later, the study looked as cluttered as when my mother had used it. Copious books sat stacked precariously on the desk while various maps, papers, and notes littered the floor.

"Sophie, what's going on? Why did you bring the Lord here?" my father whispered as soon as he closed the study door behind us.

"I..." I paused, looking around the cramped space.

Only a few days had passed since I'd last stepped foot in the study, but it had felt like years. With everything I'd seen and experienced, I felt like a different person. My gaze landed on the portrait of my mother on the wall, her hazel eyes so much like mine, watching me as if waiting to see what I would do next. My heart squeezed in my chest. I didn't blame her for having secrets from me. I couldn't. I had to trust she had her reasons.

"Did you know that Mother was Vincent Duval's vassal when she was eighteen?" I asked, strolling to the cluttered desk.

I realized then that it didn't matter what my father would say. Even if he had known and hadn't told me, it wouldn't change anything. It wouldn't change the past, just like it didn't affect the future.

"Sophie..." my father said from behind me, his voice hoarse.

I closed my eyes and took a breath—he'd known.

"Why didn't you tell me?" I asked as calmly as I could, opening my eyes and moving some papers around on the desk until I found a blank sheet.

I picked up a pen and began writing.

"Your mother and I...we tried to protect you from that world as much as possible. And when she died...well, I didn't think it really mattered anymore. And I think...I think I was still trying to protect you even though you hadn't needed my protection for a while now," my father said, coming to stand beside me by the desk.

The Tear is not on the Duval Estate, I wrote on the paper.

"It's okay, father," I said as I put the pen's tip on the note and moved it across the desk toward my father.

When he looked down and read it, his brows lifted in shock.

The Lord said he'd help me look for it, I wrote next.

"Why would he—" my father started, but I brought my index finger to my lips and then tapped it to my ear.

He has his reasons. He thinks it only destroys the Dark Witches, I wrote. *I don't trust him, but I'm staying on the estate to figure out the next move.*

My father gave a nod of understanding before staring at me with a look of awe on his wrinkled face.

"I'm…" He cleared his throat as his eyes glimmered with tears. "I'm just so proud of you," he rasped, pulling me into a tight embrace.

I found that being in his arms still grounded me. He'd withheld the information about my mother being Vincent's vassal from me, but I didn't hold it against him. I could understand why he'd done it as much as I could understand doing something to protect your child without having any children of my own. I still loved him and always would. Just like I didn't love my mother any less for hiding things from me when I'd thought we'd told each other everything.

A knock drew my attention to the study door as I pulled away from my father.

"Come in," I said, glancing at the note on the table.

My father promptly picked it up and shoved it in his pant pocket.

Henry walked in a moment later.

"I'm sorry to interrupt. I was just wondering if…" His gaze fastened on mine. "If I could see where it happened."

I swallowed to relieve the tightness in my throat as my father gave me a questioning look.

"Henry knows what really happened that night," I explained.

A look of terror rippled across my father's features as his eyes darted to the Lord. He widened his stance as if preparing to fight.

"Relax, Thomas. If I were a threat to you, you'd be dead already," Henry stated calmly.

He didn't sound arrogant, just confident. The words were spoken with the self-assurance of an apex predator, causing a shiver to curl down my spine. What was it like to be that powerful?

"It happened here," I said low. "In the study."

I told Henry about the night of my mother's death again in every painful detail, showing him where the killer had stood and where I'd found the note.

"I want to see it," Henry said, looking at me.

I tensed, my mind racing. The note was right here with us, in the safe hidden behind my mother's portrait, but I couldn't let the Lord see it because it would reveal I'd lied to him and that the Tear could also kill vampires.

"We destroyed it," my father said hastily next to me.

Henry glanced at him before his gaze returned to me, and I wondered if he knew that we were lying. I stared back at him, waiting for him to confront me.

"Are you ready to go?" he said instead, turning to leave.

I quickly said goodbye to my father and followed the Lord out into the night. The scent of rain hung heavy in the air as we loaded into the carriage.

As we traveled back to the mansion, the moonlight seeping through the carriage window caressed Henry's cheekbones and brow, making his profile flawless and severe. I wondered what he was thinking as the steady hum of rain filled the air outside the carriage.

"I'm sorry you had to witness your mother's death," the Lord said after a while, catching me by surprise.

I gave a small nod, unable to admit out loud that night would forever haunt my dreams.

"I'm sorry about Vincent. If I could go back and not tell that lie, I would," I said quietly.

Henry scoffed and shook his head. "Do us both a favor, and do not lie to me now. Vincent was a vampire. With him dead, it is now one less of us. You wouldn't go back and change that," he said bitterly. "You hate us. At least now I know why."

I opened my mouth to deny his allegations but then clamped it shut. I wasn't sure he was entirely wrong in his assumption.

We spent the next few minutes in uncomfortable silence.

I finally broke it by asking, "Compulsion. How does it work?"

"It is a special power some vampires have," Henry replied. "We can bend a human's will to ours."

Another advantage vampires bore over humans. I gritted my teeth, thinking about how outmatched we truly were.

"You said some vampires. So, not all of you can do it?"

"It is a skill that takes practice. Usually, older vampires can do it, and the older they are, the better they are at it. Ravagers wouldn't know how to compel."

That was a relief. Still, the fact that some vampires could compel was wrong on so many levels. If someone like Stern could do it, there was no doubt in my mind that he often abused that power.

"You used compulsion on Eleanor when she showed up at the mansion?" I asked, recalling her strange behavior after Henry had talked to her.

"I did."

"Have you ever used it on me before tonight?" I asked and held my breath, not entirely sure what I would do if he said "yes". I couldn't go back and change the past if the Lord had compelled me before to do something against my will. I would just have to live with the knowledge that had happened. I thought I still wanted to know, though.

"No. I don't like resorting to compulsion. It feels...wrong. Like a violation."

A breath of relief left me, and I realized I wasn't all that surprised to hear Henry say he didn't like to use compulsion. I really should be counting my blessings that I'd ended up as his vassal and not someone like Stern or Moreau.

"It is incredibly invasive," I agreed. "Can you promise not to use it on me again?"

I knew I didn't have the right to ask Henry that in light of recent events and didn't expect him to make that promise.

"Yes," he said, surprising me.

"Thank you," I said, and I meant it. I had no guarantee he would keep his word, but for some reason, I wanted to believe him. "Do you have any idea where we go from here?" I asked, hopeful the Lord had something in mind.

Vincent Duval had been my only link to the Tear besides the "power of three", and now that I knew the amulet was not on the Duval Estate, I wasn't sure what my next step should be.

"Yes," Henry said hesitantly, briefly closing his eyes and pinching the bridge of his nose.

"Yes?" I asked, sitting up straighter on the edge of my seat.

"I think Stern might have been involved with what happened to your mother."

16

"Stern?" I asked as the carriage jerked to a stop back at the mansion.

I looked out the window and saw that the rain had let up to a light sprinkle.

"Yes. He hated Vincent and had a strange obsession with your mother, probably because she and Vincent were close. I caught him sniffing around the estate right after Vincent's disappearance," Henry explained before he opened the carriage door and jumped out.

He helped me out of the coach, and together, we walked hurriedly toward the house, trying to get inside in case the rain intensified again.

Once we were in the foyer, the Lord kept walking in the direction of his study, and I had to practically run to keep up with him. Raindrops clung to his hair and clothes as he seemed to be lost in thought. I wondered if he was trying to piece together everything he'd learned tonight. By the time I walked through the study door and shut it behind me, Henry was by the credenza pouring amber liquor into two glasses. He handed one of them to me when I approached.

"Do you think he was looking for the amulet?" I asked, taking a sip of the drink. It burned going down, but I welcomed the warmth it created once it settled in my stomach.

"Perhaps," Henry said, emptying his glass in one smooth motion. "Maybe he was the one who attacked your mother and compelled her to tell him where the amulet was. Perhaps Vincent had it here, on the estate."

Molten rage filled the pit of my stomach where warmth had started a moment ago.

My face must have betrayed my volatile emotions because Henry's eyes widened before he added, "We don't know anything for certain at this point."

Taking a steadying breath, I reined in my feelings and finished my drink. Henry was right—we had to be smart about this.

"What do you suggest we do?" I asked, setting the empty glass on the credenza.

"Firstly, we need to tell Isabelle."

"Tell me what?" came Isabelle's voice from the entrance to the study, and Henry and I both whipped our heads toward the sound.

Isabelle's delicate brows pinched as she looked between us.

"Am I interrupting something? I heard you return, and I needed to speak with you," she told Henry.

The Lord turned his head back to me. There was a question in his eyes.

Our gazes locked and held as I asked, "Do you think we can trust her?"

"Yes," he replied without hesitation.

It was risky. I didn't trust Henry, but he'd gotten the information about the Tear out of me, and there was no going back. That didn't mean I wanted to share the information about the amulet with yet another vampire. But I didn't have a choice. If Henry wanted to tell Isabelle, I couldn't stop him. There wasn't much I *could* do at this point. If Stern had been involved in my mother's death and now had the Tear, it was in my best interest to work with the Duvals.

Perhaps the Lord had spoken the truth when he'd said he wanted humans to have their world back. A dream from the other night rose to the surface in my mind again. The one where Henry had been killing me, but I squelched the thought. I couldn't afford to doubt his motivations now. I needed his help to find the Tear.

"Okay." I gave in with a small nod. "We can tell her."

"What is going on?" Isabelle asked, gently closing the door behind her before approaching us.

"There is an amulet that can destroy Dark Witches," Henry said without further ado, and Isabelle's brows shot up. "Sophie is searching for it. Her mother left a note about it, and it had Vincent's name written on it."

Isabelle's big brown eyes darted to me as she mulled over what Henry had just disclosed.

"An amulet that can destroy Dark Witches?" she said slowly, and I could see her mind working, trying to piece it all together. "Your mother was taken by Dark Witches, right?" she asked me, and I stilled, quickly glancing at Henry.

His jaw flexed as he met my gaze, and a moment passed before he said, "Dark Witches didn't take Eloise. A vampire killed her. Sophie and her father hid the truth."

"What?" Isabelle gave a small shake of her head, making her dark curls bounce around her heart-shaped face. "But Vincent left to go after her. He…"

I could tell when the realization about what had really happened hit her because she froze and seemed to have stopped breathing. The next thing I knew, she lunged at me with a hiss, her nails growing longer and shaper as she pulled her hand back, preparing to attack.

I didn't have time to react, and I didn't need to because Henry was in front of me, shielding me from his sister.

"Isabelle," he said in a warning tone as I stared at his broad back. He was blocking me from her view. Swallowing, I wondered how he found it in himself to stop Isabelle from ripping out my throat when he, undoubtedly, wanted to do the same. "Calm down. I understand how you feel, but violence will not help solve anything."

"Why are you protecting her? It was because of her that Vincent went to the Dark Witches. He would be alive if it wasn't for her and her father," Isabelle seethed, and her voice sounded guttural and animalistic.

I cringed at her words because she was right.

"I know you are hurting, but we can't change the past. Sophie and her father did what they thought was best at the time. They didn't know Vincent would go after Eloise. Breathe, calm down," Henry tried to reason with her.

He was the only thing between me and the sure death at the hands of his sister, and I found I couldn't move as I waited for my fate to be sealed. I knew I wouldn't be able to do much if Henry decided to let Isabelle get to me.

My heart pounded in the silence that followed.

Finally, after several long minutes, the taut muscles in Henry's back relaxed and shifted. I realized he was embracing Isabelle, holding her close while she sobbed.

"You know he was the only father I ever knew," she rasped through the tears.

I could hear the heartbreak in her voice.

"I know," Henry said low.

Heavy remorse filled me as I stood there. I wanted to curl into myself and disappear. What Henry had said was the truth. My father and I had made the best decision at the time. We hadn't known that our lie would lead to Vincent going to the Dark Witches. Still, that didn't change the fact that it was our fault Vincent was dead.

I stepped out from behind Henry, folding my arms over my

chest and curling my shoulders in as if trying to ward off a chill. I was cold on the inside, my chest tight. I dared a peek at Isabelle when she lifted her head from Henry's chest. Anger flashed in her red-rimmed eyes as she looked at me, wiping away her tears.

"Why did you tell me all that?" She looked at Henry.

He let go of her then and stepped to the credenza to pour her a drink.

"Because we need to help Sophie find the amulet so she can destroy the Dark Witches," he told her, handing her the glass.

I noticed he positioned himself in such a way that I was still partly hidden behind him, as if he didn't trust his sister not to lunge at me again.

"Henry, if the Dark Witches are destroyed, why would humans let us rule over them?" Isabelle asked him, confused, taking the glass from his hand.

"They wouldn't," Henry told her, and a look of shock marked her striking features. "Things would go back to how they used to be before the Red War."

"So, we would go back into hiding? Live in secrecy in a tiny part of the human world we carve out for ourselves?" Isabelle asked, searching his face as if trying to see if he had gone insane.

"You know that's how it should really be," Henry said low. "It's not our world, Isabelle. It belongs to the humans."

Tilting her head to the side, Isabelle cast her gaze down, fixing it on a spot on the floor.

"No, no, no," she chanted as if refusing to believe Henry's words. "I don't want to go back to that. We rule this world, Henry."

She lifted her eyes back to his, and I could see they were pleading.

"You know what the right thing to do is," Henry said calmly, meeting her gaze.

Isabelle's brown eyes glimmered with tears as her throat

worked on a swallow. Silence reigned for a few minutes before she released a heavy sigh.

"Sometimes I curse the day you and Vincent took me into the clan," Isabelle said as her gaze grew distant, as if she were lost in a memory. "You made me find my humanity again. In a way, things were easier when I didn't have to be concerned with right or wrong."

Henry hung his head at her words as if it pained him to hear her say them.

"But then I wouldn't know what a family truly is," Isabelle added, a faint smile gracing her lips.

Henry lifted his head then and looked at her. Tension eased from his taut features as his eyes lit up with hope.

"Are you going to help then?" he asked.

I had a feeling he would have still helped me find the amulet, but he didn't want to go against his sister.

"Yes," Isabelle said softly, and I heard Henry's breath of relief. "That's what Vincent would have wanted," she added, repeating the same words Henry had said earlier.

I was touched by their loyalty to their father and to each other.

"Where do we begin?" Isabelle asked Henry, taking a sip from her glass.

She was avoiding looking at me, which I understood. She probably didn't trust herself not to kill me at the moment.

"I think Stern is involved. He might have even been the one who killed Eloise. Do you remember him lurking around the estate right after Vincent disappeared?"

"Fucking Stern. I wouldn't be surprised if he was involved. I even suspect that he might be behind the—" Isabelle glanced at me, "The situation we have been dealing with."

"Sophie knows about the turned," Henry told her.

"What? How?" Isabelle narrowed her eyes at me.

"I've come across them before." I lifted a shoulder, guessing they were talking about Ravagers.

"She's hiding something." Isabelle looked back at Henry.

"I know. I will find out what it is, but right now, we need to focus on Stern," Henry said calmly.

I stared at him in dismay, my brows lifted. He didn't seem overly concerned about me hiding something and seemed confident he would discover what it was. That was a problem for another day, I told myself, focusing on the situation at hand.

"What are you thinking?" Isabelle asked Henry.

"We could search Stern's estate," I suggested, and Isabelle reluctantly shifted her gaze to me. "If Vincent had the Tear, perhaps Stern stole it and is now hiding it."

"That would make sense. He wouldn't want for it to come out that there was a way to destroy Dark Witches. He wouldn't want to lose the leverage of having that threat, so the clans could remain in power over humans," Henry said, thinking out loud.

"Can't really blame him," Isabelle muttered under her breath.

I scowled. I hoped Henry had been right about trusting her.

"Don't give me that look," Isabelle snapped at me. "I'm still going to do what's right, but it doesn't mean I have to like it." She turned to Henry. "What if Stern destroyed the amulet?"

My heart dropped at her words as my head swung to Henry. If Stern had destroyed the Tear, then all would be lost. Pressure clamped down on my chest as I waited for what Henry would say.

He seemed to think it over before he shook his head.

"Stern is no fool. He wouldn't destroy such a powerful weapon. We prevailed in the Red War, but Dark Witches have had one hundred years to grow more powerful. He would want to have a way to destroy them if there was another war."

Isabelle nodded in agreement, but the pressure on my chest hadn't lifted. What if Stern knew the Tear could also kill vampires? Would he have destroyed it then? Or would he have kept it because that way he could establish dominance over the other clans?

"So, we need to search Stern's estate," Henry said as I took a deep breath, telling myself to focus. "We will need to draw the clan out."

"Let's throw another ball." Isabelle shrugged. "Invite all the clans. You can search the estate while I provide a distraction."

I had to admit it was a good plan.

"I'll go with you to search the Stern Estate." I looked at Henry.

"No." He gave a small shake of his head. "Santoria, where the Sterns reside, is a two-night trip on horseback. I can be there and back in a few hours while the clan is at the ball."

I gritted my teeth but nodded my head. What the Lord had said made sense even if I didn't like it. I had no assurance that Henry wouldn't take the Tear for himself.

"I know what you're thinking," Henry said, studying my face. "You're just going to have to trust me."

Trust him…as if it were that easy. I clenched my jaw and nodded again, pretending I hadn't just agreed to trust one of my most hated enemies.

17

A week later, I stood before my vanity mirror, wrapped in yellow silk. The neckline of my gown plunged low, exposing too much skin, but I'd selected a revealing dress on purpose. The ball was tonight, and I wanted to serve as a distraction for Stern while Henry left to search his estate.

We hadn't wanted to raise suspicion by hosting the ball at too short notice, so we'd settled on tonight, a week after we'd devised the plan to lure Stern and his clan out.

The past few days had been filled with anxiety and anticipation on my part. Tonight, Henry might find the amulet. Then, I would steal it from him and escape. I swallowed as uncertainty crept in. I wasn't sure how I would get the Tear from Henry, but I had to believe that I would find a way.

"Done!" Rory peeked from behind my shoulder, meeting my gaze in the mirror.

She'd made thin braids on either side of my face, intertwining and pinning them on the back of my head.

"Thank you." I gave her a warm smile that she instantly returned.

Henry hadn't told Rory I'd taken the key she'd left in the

kitchen. When she'd realized it was gone, the Lord had told her he'd taken it. He'd told me he didn't want Rory to be upset with me if she found out. I appreciated his thoughtful gesture and tried not to dwell on the fact that he'd still found it in his heart to do that after he'd learned the truth about my mother's death.

Henry had kept me close by his side in the past week, taking me to the border almost every night. Still, Wren had managed to catch me alone one morning in the early hours of dawn after Henry had gone to bed. I'd told him the Lord knew about the amulet and explained our plan to search the Stern Estate. Wren had agreed it was a good plan. He felt uneasy about trusting Henry with the Tear as I did but realized we had no choice. He'd promised to help me get the amulet from the Lord if he was successful at finding it.

When I hadn't been with Henry, I'd spent time with Rory, bonding over our mutual love of books. With little to do but anxiously wait for the ball, I'd often found myself in the library in the past week, long after sunrise, when the vampires and most of the servants were asleep. On one such morning, I'd found Rory there, nose buried in a book. That was how we'd discovered we both liked to read. Our tastes were different, though. While I liked adventure-filled novels, Rory liked love stories and hoped to meet her own Prince Charming one day.

I was in awe of her positive attitude and yearning for life. Despite her misfortunes, she had a bright spark inside of her. She had hopes and dreams and believed in a better future. Her passion for life was contagious, and being around her made me believe that a better future was possible. Seeing how hopeful she was made me hopeful as well—hopeful that Henry would find the Tear, and then I would get it from him and find a way to activate it.

I'd decided that if I was successful, I would take Rory and Ezra under my wing. They could live with me and my father. The four of us, together, could make a new life for ourselves in the new world—the human world where the supernatural no longer existed.

"You look beautiful," Rory said, pulling me from my thoughts.

"Thank you." I smiled weakly, turning to face her.

I didn't want to look beautiful or attract attention tonight, but I would do it. I would do it to keep Stern focused on me instead of asking questions about where Henry was.

When I looked at Rory, my smile fell. She wore black leggings and a crimson tunic to match the other servants working the ball tonight. I really wished she didn't have to be there.

"I finished the book you recommended," Rory said, clasping her hands in front of her. "It was really good." A small smile graced her lips. "The ending made me a bit nervous, but at the last minute, the hero showed up and saved the princess. It was so very romantic." Her face took on a dreamy expression, and I couldn't help but laugh.

"See, that's the difference between you and me. I don't want some knight in shining armor to save me. I'd rather save myself," I pointed out.

"That's because you're brave and courageous. I can't believe you've been going to the border with Master Henry. I would be terrified." Rory placed one delicate hand on her chest.

There hadn't been another witch attack, but I would be lying if I said that trepidation didn't curl down my spine every time I was on the border of the Black Forest.

"It's not that I'm not terrified," I admitted. "It's just...I know how to fight, and if I can help...I'll do it in spite of the fear."

"I admire you, Sophie. Truly," Rory said, her eyes shining with the admiration she'd just mentioned.

"And I, you." I smiled at her. "Your relentless optimism and hopeful nature."

"You are too kind." Her cheeks reddened as she cast her gaze down before lifting it to my forearm. "You never told me what happened."

I looked down at the pink scar. The night of the Ravager attack flashed through my mind, and I shuddered.

"It wasn't Master Henry, was it?" Rory asked low, her wide eyes taking up most of her pale face.

"What?" I frowned. "No!"

My frown deepened at how fast I'd defended the Lord. It wasn't that I didn't think he was capable of such things; I knew he was, but I'd grown more comfortable around him in the past week. It was difficult to imagine Henry doing me any harm. I shook my head at the thought. I could not let my guard down around him despite how he'd been treating me.

As if I'd conjured him with my mind, Henry walked in a moment later after rapping his knuckles on my bedroom door.

He drew up short when he saw me, and I noticed Rory duck her chin with a small smile before she slipped out of my room. The Lord and I stared at each other for a few minutes without saying a word. I had to admit he looked debonair and handsome in his black trousers and a snug-fitting jacket.

Henry broke the strangely tense silence first.

"Sophie, you look…" he said, his brows knitting as he appraised me.

It was hard to read him. I wasn't sure if he didn't like the dress or liked it too much. I got my answer when he reluctantly met my gaze, and I saw the hunger in his dark eyes.

My throat went dry, and I swallowed, shifting my weight from foot to foot.

"Stern seemed interested in me at the Vassal Ball. I wanted to look…appealing to him so he would focus his attention on me tonight," I explained.

"Good idea. I'm sure it will work. You look…ravishing," Henry said, his voice low and thick.

My fingers spasmed at my side, brushing the hilt of the dagger through the fabric of my dress. I wasn't scared of Henry.

Rather, I was disgusted when I pictured Stern's bottomless eyes roaming over every inch of my body.

Henry's nostrils flared as his gaze dropped to my thigh.

"You can't bring the dagger, Sophie," he said in a measured tone.

"What? Why not?" I scowled at him.

"I can smell the Ravager's blood on it. The others will, too."

I cursed under my breath—he was right. When I'd used the dagger to kill the Ravager, the vampire's blood had stained the blade, seeping into the wood.

With a heavy sigh, I lifted the skirt of my gown and unstrapped the dagger from my thigh. Letting go of the delicate fabric, I watched it glide down my leg, molding to it like liquid.

I put the sheath and the dagger on the vanity and met Henry's piercing gaze. His stare was so potent it felt like a caress, and I saw the hints of his fangs peeking through his slightly parted lips.

Suppressing a shiver, I cleared my throat and asked, "Ready?"

Henry shook his head as if to clear his thoughts and nodded, offering me his arm.

"I will make an appearance but leave shortly after on the pretenses of trouble at the border," he said as I wove my arm through his.

"The others won't offer to go with you to help?" I asked as we walked out of my bedroom.

Henry laughed, but there was no humor to the sound.

"You overestimate their dedication to the cause," he said bitterly. "They will not offer to help unless I ask."

I glanced at the Lord as we made our way down the hall and toward the ballroom.

I'd seen his dedication to protecting the people of New Haven firsthand. He was at the border almost every night. He took his role of a protector seriously, and I couldn't help but admire that.

You know you don't have to carry the weight of the world on your shoulders? Waylon had said to me the last time I'd seen him.

I wanted to say the same to Henry now. He had this air of heaviness about him. It was as if he carried a burden he thought he deserved.

"So, it really is every vampire for himself?" I asked, looking at him.

"For the most part. Vincent and my mother were different and tried to instill their values in me and my siblings."

"I wish I had a chance to meet Vincent," I mused. "If he and my mother were close, she must have trusted him."

"Something you find very hard to believe, I am sure," Henry said, raising one dark brow.

"Yes," I admitted. I wasn't telling him anything he didn't already know. "You know I don't trust you, and I know you don't trust me. That's why you've kept me close this past week."

"That wasn't the only reason," the Lord said, one side of his mouth turning up. "I like your company."

My eyebrows flew up in surprise. I had to admit I liked his company, too. I enjoyed the stories about his long life, but I couldn't let myself get too close. After all, I planned to kill him.

"Do you think you'll find it tonight?" I asked, changing the subject.

"I hope so. The real question is, what will you do if I find it?"

My heart turned over in my chest. Did he suspect I was planning to steal the amulet from him?

"What I mean by that is do you know how to activate it?" Henry asked, and I exhaled softly with relief.

"No, I don't, but I'll figure it out. First, we need to find it. One step at a time."

Henry nodded and led me inside the ornate ballroom. Wren and Isabelle were already there. The other clans and their vassals started to arrive shortly after. I froze when Stern walked in. Red-hot, burning hatred filled my chest as I stared at him. Was he the one who'd killed my mother? I wished I could remember more about that night. I remembered black, fathomless eyes, but all vampires had black eyes when they were in the throes of blood-lust. Even if Stern hadn't killed my mother, he still deserved to die. They all did.

One step at a time, I repeated the words I'd said to Henry in my head.

Taking a deep breath, I found my center and plastered on a smile that I knew didn't reach my eyes.

18

"*S*ophie, you look absolutely stunning," Stern drawled as he approached.

He was dressed in white, and his jet-black hair was bound at his nape, highlighting his sharp and angular features.

His gaze slithered over me agonizingly slowly, just like I'd known it would. I willed myself to stand still and take his perusal with a soft smile while I was screaming with revulsion on the inside. My fingers brushed the silk on my thigh, looking for the familiar outline of the dagger, and my heart sank when I remembered I didn't have my weapon. I felt Henry move closer to me on my left, his proximity bringing unexpected comfort.

"Another ball so soon? What's the occasion?" Stern asked Henry, shifting his attention to him.

"Do we need an occasion?" Isabelle purred as she neared. "You know better than anyone, Everett, we vampires, love lavish parties almost as much as blood and sex."

I cringed at her words but instantly forced my facial expression to smooth out.

"You are right about that," Stern murmured, clearly distracted.

He was looking behind me, his black eyes full of bald hunger. When I glanced over my shoulder, I saw Rory standing there, holding a tray of fruit and cheese for the vassals. My blood turned to ice as I jerked my head back to Stern. He looked like a predator that had sighted his prey. Molten rage bubbled up, melting the ice in my veins as my lip curled in a snarl.

"Dance with me," Henry said low, his cool touch on my back snapping my attention to him. It wasn't a request but a demand, so I knew better than to resist as he led me to the center of the room and away from Stern.

"Breathe," the Lord murmured as we began swaying to the slow music.

I tried to do as he'd instructed but couldn't get a full breath in, my chest tight with pressure.

I will kill him, I wanted to say but knew better than to voice my intent in a room full of vampires. So, I kept my mouth shut as I focused on Henry's deep-blue gaze. He must have read the words in my eyes because his jaw hardened as he stared at me. He pulled me closer to him and brought his mouth to my right ear.

"Get ahold of yourself," he whispered, his cool breath tickling my cheek.

I inhaled, holding my breath until I felt my racing heart slow.

Henry pulled away and looked at me. Suddenly, his features became stark, and I felt his muscles tense under my hand on his arm. I glanced around us, noticing the other dancing couples—vampires with their vassals. They weren't just dancing. Many were also feeding, the coppery smell of blood filling the air.

Lifting on my tiptoes, I brought my mouth to Henry's ear and whispered, "Get ahold of yourself."

The Lord laughed, the sound nice and deep as it rumbled through him.

"Your dress choice tonight is making it quite difficult," he murmured as I pulled away.

I couldn't fight a small smile at his comment. One side of his mouth turned up as well.

We danced for a while in silence, and my smile slowly faded as anxiety flared and swelled. So much hinged on tonight. If Stern didn't have the Tear, we would be back to square one. Something told me we were close to finding the amulet, though. It was as if I could feel it.

When the dance was over, Henry leaned in and murmured, "I'm leaving. Keep an eye on Stern."

I nodded, taking a sweeping glance around the ballroom.

"Where *is* Stern?" I asked low, my brows knitting. "And where is Rory?"

Henry's face fell, and he frantically looked around the room before his gaze returned to me. My heart dropped when I saw panic and fear flash in his eyes. I knew. I didn't know how, but I knew.

I didn't realize I was running until I burst out of the ballroom, heading in the direction of the kitchen.

No, please, no, I begged as my feet carried me to the white paneled door.

My mind flashed back to the night of my mother's death as I pushed it open, feeling like I was opening the door to my mother's study.

Everything stopped. My heart, my breath, the world. All the noises died as I stared at my mother's lifeless body in the arms of a monster. Except, it wasn't my mother before me. It was Rory in Stern's arms, limp and motionless. Sweet, innocent Rory, who had hopes and dreams and knew how to find happiness in the little things. Her wide brown eyes were on me, but the stare was unseeing as her head lolled to the side.

Stern's head jerked in my direction, and our gazes locked.

He was the one who'd killed my mother. There was no longer a doubt in my mind. It was as if the sheer veil that had been hiding my memories from that night had lifted, and I could see clearly now.

"You!" I wanted to scream, but just like on the night of my mother's death, the sound got stuck in my throat, choking me.

I reached for my dagger but then remembered I didn't have it. A ragged cry, full of fury and pain, tore from me as I lunged at Stern. He lifted his arm to block my attack, tossing me aside as if I were nothing more than a helpless pup. I hit a wall, my teeth rattling at the impact before I crumpled to the floor. Through my blurry vision, I saw Henry storm into the kitchen. When his blue eyes darted to me, I was already getting up, using the wall for support.

"I got a little carried away." Stern smirked, his lips smeared with Rory's blood.

When he released his grip on her body, I rushed to her, but Henry got there first, not letting her drop to the floor.

"Get out," he growled, and Stern swept out of the room much like he'd done on the night of my mother's death. Only this time, he didn't take the body with him.

Swaying on my feet, I approached where Henry gently laid Rory on the floor.

"You're bleeding," he said, his nostrils flaring as I carefully lowered to my knees next to him.

My fingers came away bloody when I gently prodded the back of my head. I wasn't feeling the pain, though. I was too concerned about Rory, who was still on the floor. Too still.

I pulled her head into my lap and looked at Henry.

"Give her your blood."

"Sophie..." the Lord said, and the deep sorrow I saw in his eyes shattered my heart.

"Please," I begged as my eyes filled with tears.

"My blood won't help her," Henry said gently as if talking to a child.

"Your blood heals, she's injured," I said low. I couldn't believe I had to explain the obvious.

"She's…" He swallowed thickly. "She's dying, Sophie. My blood won't help her."

"Isn't there anything you can do?" I asked, my voice breaking.

"I would have to turn her to save her, and I—"

"Do it!" I shouted, grasping at the tiny glimmer of hope that sparked in my chest. "Please," I added barely above a whisper.

Henry's jaw ticked as he stared at me. Several seconds passed. Precious seconds that took Rory further into the void.

"I will not do it," the Lord finally said, and a strangled cry left me.

"Yes, you will!" I seethed, fisting my hands in his shirt and getting in his face. "You will save her!"

"Sophie," Henry said calmly and quietly as he brought his hands to my wrists. "It is forbidden."

Forbidden? Someone had been making Ravagers, and he was worried about breaking the rules and turning Rory?

My face contorted in rage, and I was about to spit the words out, when Henry added, "Even if it wasn't…Do you really think Rory would want that?"

I opened my mouth, but no words came out. He was right. Rory wouldn't want to be turned; to spend the rest of her everlasting nights craving human blood.

The fight went out of me as my arms went limp. I let go of Henry's shirt, and he held my wrists gently for a moment before lowering them to rest on either side of Rory. I looked down at her pale face as my tears spilled, landing on her sunken cheeks and her delicate neck, where some blood still oozed out of the two puncture wounds.

I jerked when Henry put his hand on my back, but then I curled into him, welcoming the coolness of his body. After all, it was nothing compared to the icy chill in my heart. He held me while I cried as Rory took her last breath.

In light of the attack, our plan to search the Stern Estate was put on hold, and we buried Rory three days later in the local cemetery. Ezra didn't shed any tears, but his anguish was palpable, as if he projected it onto the world around him. He stayed by Rory's grave long after the last servant had paid their respects and left. I wasn't ready to leave yet, either, but I felt like I didn't have the right to stay by Ezra's side. He'd lost his sister and the only family he'd had. I'd barely known Rory, although the pain of her loss cut deep. From the moment I'd met her, I'd felt protective of her, but I'd failed to keep her safe. Another innocent life had been snuffed out at the hands of a vampire. The same vampire who had killed my mother. I couldn't help but feel like it had been my fault. Perhaps if I'd recognized Stern when I'd first met him, Rory's death could have been avoided.

I wasn't ready to return to the mansion after the funeral, but I also wanted to give Ezra space to grieve, so I walked a considerable distance away and perched on a small hill overlooking the cemetery. I could see Rory's grave from here and Ezra's hunched figure by it. As I sat on the cool ground, my black skirts pooling around me, I didn't feel the cold, only the death. Rory's death, my mother's death, and the deaths of all those we hadn't been able to save from Ravagers. The deaths of the vassals who hadn't returned after serving Moreau for a year, and the deaths of all those I didn't even know about. Death surrounded me, clinging to my skin and suffocating me with its darkness.

"May I?" came Henry's deep voice to my right, pulling me from my thoughts.

I briefly looked up at him and nodded.

He joined me on the ground, staring at the horizon.

"It's almost sunrise. We have to go," he said low.

He had spoken gently as if he didn't want to upset me.

"Do you miss it? Sunrises? Daylight?" I glanced at the Lord as my heart squeezed. Rory wouldn't see another sunrise or bathe her face in the sun.

"I do. I miss being human," Henry admitted, his features cast in shadows.

"Do you even remember what it's like?" I whispered. He was almost two hundred years old, which was a long time to hold on to one's humanity.

"I do. And it is those memories I cling to most of all," he whispered back, and I could feel his piercing gaze on me in the darkness.

I wondered what those memories were. They must be very special to help him keep his inner monster at bay most of the time and set him apart from the rest of the vampires. I didn't ask him, though—it felt too personal.

"What are we going to do about Stern?" I asked instead, trying to keep my voice even.

I knew what I *wanted* to do. I wanted to stake him to the ground next to Rory's grave and watch him burn in the first rays of the rising sun. But I knew we couldn't kill him. Not yet. He might be the only one who knew where Josephine's Tear was.

"We still need to search his estate. Now that you are sure he was the one who killed your mother, I am even more certain that he might have the amulet or know where it is."

I nodded in agreement.

"I will go with you," I stated.

"Not a good idea." He gave a small shake of his head.

A few dark locks fell forward on his forehead. His hair had been swept away from his face at the beginning of the funeral but now looked disheveled as if he'd run his hands through it too many times. I wondered how much Rory's death really affected him. He'd seemed composed through it all, except for the occasional deep shadows crawling in his eyes.

"I *have* to go," I said low. "I have to do…something."

My voice broke as tears threatened.

Henry was silent for a few seconds until I heard his rough exhale.

"Alright. We will leave tomorrow night."

19

I met Henry the following night at the stables shortly after the sun had lowered below the horizon. Several oil lamps scattered throughout the place cast a golden glow on the Lord, who seemed to be lost in thought, standing between two saddled horses. He was dressed in black breeches and a deep-blue tunic, the color almost matching his eyes. A hooded, black cloak was draped over his shoulders, but I doubted it would do much to conceal him. People might not recognize who he was, but they would notice him—it would be impossible not to.

I was also dressed comfortably for the road, wearing my deep forest-green tunic and black leggings. I'd almost left my dark-brown cloak behind but was glad I'd brought it with me. It was a good idea to shield my face while we traveled. Especially once we reached Santoria, where the Sterns resided.

"Good evening," Henry said, coming to stand closer to the massive, black horse to his left. His eyes were wary when he looked at me. "It's not too late to change your mind," he said, but his tone wasn't, in the very least, hopeful.

"I'm going with you," I declared, reaching up to lightly rub the side of the horse's nose. "What's his name?" I asked the Lord.

"Onyx," Henry replied, scratching the horse behind the ear. The stallion neighed softly, shaking his glossy, black mane.

"How fitting," I murmured. "He's beautiful."

"Can you ride?" Henry asked, and I nodded. A look of surprise flickered across his features before he said with a heavy sigh, "In that case, you will need a horse." He stepped closer to the brown mare to his right. "This is Annabelle. She is intuitive and sweet."

"Hello, Annabelle." I smiled at her, stroking the fine hairs of the mare's neck.

"We will ride through the night," Henry said as he finished strapping down the saddlebags on his steed. "I have packed some food and water for you. We should reach Avalon by sunrise. We will sleep there and then finish our journey at sundown."

I nodded, checking the straps on the saddle. Avalon was the middle point between here and Santoria, so Henry's travel plans made sense. Annabelle didn't protest as I led her out of the stables into the cool night air. Henry and Onyx joined us a moment later. Placing my foot in the stirrup, I hoisted myself up onto my horse while Henry mounted his steed in one fluid motion. Under the shroud of darkness, we left the estate, setting off at a trot through the quiet streets of New Haven.

"How did you learn to ride a horse?" Henry asked as we rode through the city center.

The truth was, Waylon and I had spent a few months traveling around the country, looking for the Tear. He had insisted on that, hoping we'd find the amulet somewhere else, so I wouldn't have to participate in the Selection again to get on the Duval Estate.

I didn't want to tell Henry all that, so I settled on a partial truth.

"I had to learn so I could travel through the country, looking for the Tear," I said, my eyes trained on the road.

"Where did you look for it, exactly? Your mother didn't leave much information," Henry pointed out.

I shrugged. "I tried shadow markets and rare amulet collectors. All I had was a sketch of the amulet, so I would show it to people and ask around. Never saying what the amulet was, of course."

"Of course," Henry murmured. I felt his gaze on me as he said, "You know I don't believe you destroyed your mother's note with the sketch of the Tear."

My head swung to him, and several seconds passed as I held his piercing gaze, waiting for what he would say next.

"I understand why you lied. You probably thought I wouldn't need you if I knew what the amulet looked like," he continued, and I swallowed thickly. "I am okay with you keeping that knowledge to yourself. I trust you."

He wouldn't trust me if he knew the real reason why I hadn't shown him the note, I thought as I turned my head, fixing my gaze straight ahead.

"Where do you think it came from?" Henry asked, also facing forward.

"I don't know," I admitted. "It would have to be a magical object, powerful enough to destroy Dark Witches. Perhaps White Witches made it."

"Perhaps," Henry said, lost in thought. "If they did, I don't understand why they wouldn't use it during the War."

"Me either." I shook my head.

So many things were still a mystery, including how my mother had known about the amulet. Had she ever been in the possession of it? If she had, why hadn't she used it to destroy Dark Witches and vampires alike?

We rode in silence for a few minutes as I looked around me at the familiar shops that were closed for the night. When we passed by Baylor's Corner, my mind wandered to Waylon. I'd seen him at the border during the past week, but we hadn't spoken since the night the Dark Witches attacked. I'd often caught him looking at Henry and me with a hard expression on his face as if he didn't like seeing me next to the Lord. I wished I'd had a chance to tell him I was one step closer to finding the Tear.

"So, are you ready to tell me about the Order of Light?" Henry asked, and my head whipped in his direction. One side of his mouth turned up as he looked at me. "I did a bit of investigating after you'd told me you had been patrolling the streets. I was relieved to learn you hadn't been doing it alone."

I searched Henry's face with wide eyes. He didn't seem upset, only amused by my reaction.

I swallowed and decided to go with the truth since the Lord knew most of it already.

"Waylon created the Order when the Ravager attacks started. He also taught me how to fight."

"Is he the guard from the border?" Henry asked, and I nodded. "Your lover?" There was curiosity in his tone.

"No." I shook my head, and the Lord gave me a skeptical look. "Not a lover...a friend who's always wanted to be more. I've taken advantage of his feelings for me in the past, but I've decided I would no longer do that."

I wasn't sure why I'd shared what I had. Perhaps saying the words out loud made my decision to end things with Waylon more real, as if I were setting it in stone.

"How mature of you," Henry teased, and I rolled my eyes.

Thankfully, we didn't continue talking about my personal life because the Lord changed the subject.

"So, you traveled the country searching for the amulet, learned how to fight, and patrolled the streets, trying to prevent Ravager attacks. You had a busy year."

He sounded impressed, and I couldn't fight a small smile that pulled at my lips.

"I prefer it that way," I said, my smile fading. "If I'm busy, then

I don't have time to dwell on the past or the things that are out of my control," I admitted.

Henry's eyes softened. "I understand. That's why I spend so much time at the border."

We stared at each other in silence for a moment. We were more alike than I'd realized.

The thought made me uncomfortable, and I cleared my throat before asking, "What's the plan once we get to the Stern Estate?"

"I'll compel the staff so we can search the mansion," Henry replied.

"Will the clan be away?" I asked, frowning. Surely, he had thought the whole thing through.

"Yes." Henry nodded. "They will be away in the Northern region. I've asked Camilla to provide a distraction."

"What?" I jerked on the reins, making Annabelle stop and turn toward Onyx. Henry stopped his steed as well. "You told Camilla about the amulet?" I asked him, dismayed. It was bad enough that he and Isabelle knew.

"I didn't tell her about the Tear. I told her I needed the Sterns away from the estate. She agreed to provide a distraction," Henry explained.

"Do you think you can trust her?" I demanded.

"Yes," he said confidently. "She has been a friend of the family for centuries."

A low growl of frustration left me as I steered Annabelle toward the outskirts of the city and resumed our faster pace.

"You are upset with me," Henry said, quickly catching up with me on my right. It wasn't a question but a statement.

"I am more upset with myself for not asking what the plan was until now." I scowled.

"It's not the best plan, but it's the only one we've got," the Lord replied.

"What if we don't find it?" I voiced one of my greatest fears as despair threatened to pull me under.

"Then we will figure out the next step," Henry said calmly. "One step at a time, remember?"

His confidence and composure soothed my nerves, and my breaths became more even.

"Tell me more about your life," I asked, looking for a distraction, willing my tense muscles to relax as we rode out of New Haven.

The Lord agreed to entertain me with his stories, and the next few hours were spent in conversation or amicable silence until we reached Avalon—a smaller city on the coast of the Starling Sea. It sat on the border with the Southern region and was one of my favorite places in the Empire. Waylon and I had visited it during our search for the Tear last year, and I'd fallen in love with the dazzling blue waters and the white beaches. Looking at the horizon where the sky met the Sea had made me feel limitless, as if there was a world of possibilities out there in the vast expanse of the blue waters. This time, I wouldn't get to see the coastline in the light of day, and that made me a little sad. I needed to experience that feeling again, to reignite the spark of hope that had been doused by grief after Rory's death.

When we arrived in Avalon, Henry pulled up the hood of his cloak to shield his face, and I did the same, noticing people still milling around despite it being the late hours of the night. The city was located some distance away from the border, and I assumed people here were not as concerned about being snatched up by Dark Witches, having the freedom to stay out even at night.

"Follow me," Henry said, turning into an alleyway branching off the main city street.

We stopped at a medium-sized inn nestled between two taverns not far from the beach. I longingly glanced at the water glistening in the silvery moonlight as we walked to the entrance after leaving the horses at the stables.

"Two adjoining rooms if you have them," Henry said, pulling some money from his cloak pocket. "Only for a day."

The small foyer of the inn was mostly cast in shadows, the only light coming from a lone oil lamp on the front desk. The innkeeper nodded and grabbed the money, giving Henry two keys in exchange. He looked uneasy, eyeing the Lord as if trying to peer into the darkness hiding his face. Henry towered over him, his broad form taking up most of the foyer. I wondered if some inherent instinct was telling the innkeeper to be wary, that he was in the presence of something supernatural and inhuman.

Henry and I exchanged "goodnights" and retreated to our adjoining rooms. There was no running water, so I washed up the best I could using the lukewarm water that had been sent to my room. When I settled in the bed, sleep wouldn't come. I lay there for several long minutes, my eyes peeled and staring at the wall. I had barely gotten any sleep since Rory's death four days ago, and it looked like tonight would be yet another sleepless night. With a sigh, I rolled onto my back and stared at the ceiling for a few more minutes before giving up and leaving the bed.

Forgoing bringing my cloak, I slipped out of the inn and headed for the beach, dressed in the simple cotton tunic and thin leggings I'd brought with me to change into. A smile tugged at my lips as the balmy sea air clung to my skin, and the breeze stirred my unbound hair. I liked being here, close to the water and far from New Haven, where the horrors of my past lay. My steps faltered when I saw a tall figure standing by the water.

"You should be trying to get some rest," Henry said when I approached.

He didn't look at me. His eyes were trained on the murky waters sparkling in the light of the moon.

"So should you," I countered, coming to stand next to him on the shore, my booted feet sinking into the sand.

"Sleep has eluded me since Rory's death," the Lord admitted, and my heart squeezed.

"Me, too," I said low. "I keep thinking there was something I could've done to prevent what happened," I confessed as my eyes pricked with tears.

"Her death is not on you; it is on me," Henry said vehemently, turning to me. "I was the one who'd brought her into this life."

"You thought you were saving her," I pointed out, my brows knitting.

"Vincent thought he was saving me," Henry said bitterly. "Perhaps I am even more like my father than I realized. We both made poor decisions that cost lives."

The last sentence confused me. Was he referring to Vincent turning him? Did he think his life was over the moment he became a vampire?

"You are still here," I said, my eyes searching his face.

"Living a life I never wanted," Henry bit out.

I was at a loss for words for a few seconds until I found the ones that felt right.

"I didn't know Vincent, but from what you've told me, he had strong values and always wanted to do the right thing. If anything, you should be comparing yourself to him in *that* regard."

The Lord stared at me in shock for a moment. He seemed genuinely astonished. I could see it in his widened eyes and slightly parted lips.

"I think this is the first time you have ever said anything nice to me," he said as a flicker of amusement crossed his striking features.

My cheeks heated as I averted my gaze.

"Don't get used to it," I said, trying to sound firm, but I couldn't fight a small smile as it graced my lips.

20

$\mathcal{I}$ was able to get a few hours of sleep before we resumed our journey at sundown. We left the inn as soon as the night had descended on Avalon. The innkeeper looked relieved to see us go, and I wondered if he suspected who Henry was. The Lord seemed unaffected by the innkeeper's palpable unease as he strolled out of the foyer and into the cool night air. We retrieved our horses from the stables and set out toward Santoria, the capital of the Southern region.

A thought occurred to me as I snacked on the dried fruit Henry had brought with us.

"How often do you need to feed?" I turned my head to look at him as Annabelle trotted next to Onyx along the outskirts of the city.

I figured he couldn't bring any blood with him because he had no way to keep it cold.

"I can go days without feeding unless I am injured," Henry replied, and a breath of relief escaped my lips. I wouldn't want to be on the road with a hungry vampire.

"Was that really a concern of yours?" Henry asked as one of

his dark brows lifted. "I told you I wouldn't feed from you, and I have kept my word."

He was right, and a kernel of guilt settled in my chest for doubting him. Still, I could never truly let my guard down around him in case his true nature decided to break free.

"Thank you for that," I said quietly, and the Lord nodded before fixing his gaze on the horizon.

"We will be there in a few hours," he informed me.

My heart skipped a beat as anxiety surfaced. I was so close to my goal; I could almost taste it. Unless, of course, the Tear was not on the Stern Estate. A wave of panic threatened to take over, but I pushed it down. I couldn't give in to it until I knew for sure the amulet was not on the estate.

"Will you tell me more about the Red War?" I asked Henry, looking for a distraction from my frantic thoughts. "You're a good storyteller, and it will make the time pass by faster," I explained my request.

A mild smile lit up his face.

"This is the second nice thing you have said to me," he murmured, and I rolled my eyes, fighting a smile. "But I think it is your turn to tell a story."

My forehead creased. I doubted he would find anything I had to say interesting after having lived for almost two hundred years.

"Tell me about your mother," Henry said, meeting my gaze.

My heart dropped as breathing became difficult.

"You knew my mother," I told the Lord.

Talking about her felt very personal, and I didn't want to open up to Henry like that.

"I knew her when she was eighteen. Tell me about the Eloise that you knew," he prompted gently.

Turning to look ahead of me, I took a deep breath through my nose and let it out slowly through my mouth, gathering my thoughts.

It took a few minutes to force the words out, but once I did, they spilled out of me like a river ebbing and flowing, weaving childhood memories and stories about my mother into an intricate and beautiful tapestry of everything that she was to me. Henry's eyes were on me the entire time, and he looked as if he were hanging on every word, chuckling low when I said something funny or offering words of encouragement when I stumbled on particularly sensitive memories that tugged at my heart.

By the time I was done, tears were gliding down my cheeks, and I wiped them away with a startled laugh. What I'd shared with Henry was bitter sweet, but the memories didn't make me sad. They filled my chest with warmth as I thought about my mother. I'd lost her too early, but I was happy she'd been with me for as long as she had. She was still with me, in my heart, where she would forever remain.

"You and Eloise had a special bond," Henry mused, compassion filling his deep-blue eyes.

My cheeks heated at the intensity of his stare. He was looking at me as if he could see me—*all* of me—and I fidgeted in my saddle, suddenly feeling very exposed. I didn't regret telling him about my mother. I was grateful he'd asked because talking about her had made breathing easier, as if sharing what I had was healing my heart broken by loss. It hadn't been the first time I'd talked about my mother, of course, but those moments were rare. I didn't often allow myself to reminisce about the past.

"I miss her," I rasped, casting my gaze down and focusing on Annabelle's glossy mane.

"I miss my mother, too, and Vincent," Henry said, his voice hoarse with emotion. "And everyone I lost through the years."

"I'm sorry," I said low.

I'd wondered before if vampires experienced loss like humans did, and now there was no doubt in my mind that they did. At least, I knew for sure Henry did. I could see it in the deep shadows that settled into his features and in the nearly concealed glimmer of tears in his eyes.

The sound of hooves pounding off cobblestones filled the silence as neither of us spoke for a few moments until Henry cleared his throat and said, "I believe it is my turn to tell you a story. You wanted to hear more about the War?"

"Actually, tell me about your mother," I asked softly, feeling like I wanted to repay him for listening to me talk about my mother.

I caught a brief glimpse of appreciation in his gaze before his face lit up, chasing away some of the shadows.

"I will tell you about Rosalind. She was like a mother to me. She and Vincent were already together when he turned me. And they had Gerard. All three of them welcomed me into their family, helping me make sense of my new life and who I had become. Of what Vincent had made me." The emotions on Henry's face were conflicting as he said the last part.

"I still don't understand why Vincent turned you," I said because I'd wondered that before. "I know that you were ill, but even so...he doesn't strike me as someone who would make a decision like that lightly."

"He didn't. I am the only one he'd ever turned," Henry paused as if he weren't sure he wanted to continue. "He said he'd seen the good in me. He said...he thought the world needed more people like me. That I could do so much good." He cast his gaze down as if he didn't agree or didn't believe it himself. The heaviness that usually surrounded him began pouring out of him, prickling my skin. I wanted to pull him out of this state, to alleviate the weight on his shoulders.

"What about your life before you were turned? You've never told me about your human family."

The heaviness around him intensified, the shadows rolling off him growing darker. My attempt to lighten the mood had clearly had the opposite effect. Silence ensued as I frantically racked my brain for something else to say but I was afraid of making the situation even worse, so I kept my mouth shut. After a few seconds, Henry seemed to have regained some control over his volatile emotions. The darkness around him receded, and he forced a faint smile.

"That might be a story for another time," he finally said, not looking at me. "So, let me tell you about Rosalind."

He began a story that had started centuries ago, and I immediately got lost in Henry's memories, my imagination taking me to people and places that had existed long before I'd been born.

The Stern Estate loomed ahead of us sooner than I'd expected. The mansion was a sprawling structure of stone and glass and looked ominous, rising high into the night sky.

"Ready?" Henry asked as we approached the horse stables.

My heart pounded loudly in my chest as I nodded. This was it —the moment of truth.

We left the horses at the stables, with Henry compelling the stable hand to take a break, forgetting we were there. He then snuck inside the house, moving with supernatural speed, while I made my way to the wrought-iron front door. I stood before it for a few minutes, wondering if the Sterns were, in fact, away from the estate, and if Camilla had provided the distraction as she'd promised.

Several minutes later, Henry opened the door to let me in.

"I have compelled the servants to look the other way," he said low.

A breath of relief left me. So far, everything was going according to plan.

"I'll check the first floor if you can search the second story and up," I told the Lord, knowing he would be done much faster than I.

"Okay. Let's meet in Stern's study when we are done. It is down the hall and to the left," Henry said before he swept out of the room.

The second he was gone, I snapped into action, efficiently and methodically making my way through the rooms on the first floor. I checked the living room, the formal dining room, the kitchen, and the extensive library that occupied the first story of the mansion. The layout was similar to the Duval Estate, but the house felt more stifling and oppressive. I ran into servants here and there as I searched, but they quite literally looked the other way or acted as if they did not see me.

The longer my search rendered no results, the lower my heart sank and the higher my anxiety climbed up in my chest until it was threatening to choke me. Taking a steadying breath to pull myself together, I headed to Stern's study, hoping that Henry had been more successful in his search.

"It's not here," the Lord said with a heavy sigh when I walked in.

My heart dropped to the pit of my stomach as despair invaded my senses.

"Are you sure?" I asked shakily as I approached.

Henry stood in front of a wall lined with bookshelves, his arms folded over his broad chest.

"I wonder…" he said, his face taking on a contemplative expression.

"Sophie? What are you doing here?" came a female's voice from the entrance to the study.

Henry and I both whipped our heads to find Stern's vassal Marie standing there. My breath caught as I stared at her. She reminded me so much of Rory. Petite and delicate, she had the same air of innocence about her. Right now, she looked frightened, her wide eyes on me and the Lord.

Henry cursed under his breath and moved to go to her, but I stopped him with a hand on his arm.

"Wait," I said when he gave me a questioning look. I turned to the vassal. "Marie, we're looking for something. Does Stern have a safe or a secret compartment anywhere?"

The girl swallowed audibly as her eyes widened even more, taking up most of her pale, round face.

Silence reigned for a few minutes until Marie opened her mouth as if to say something but then closed it. She shook her head, sending blonde curls tumbling over her forehead. My hand still on Henry's arm, I could feel the Lord tense as if he were running out of patience. I stared at Marie, my eyes pleading. A few more seconds passed before she lifted her trembling hand and pointed at one of the bookshelves lining the wall.

Letting go of Henry, I strode to it. Turning my head to watch Marie's face, I reached for the shelf at my waist level. When the girl gave a small shake of her head, I lifted my hand higher to the shelf at my chest level. Marie's lips were in a thin line and almost white in color, but she did nod slightly. I brought my finger to the first title on the shelf and moved it down the row of books until Marie nodded again. I turned away from her and saw that my finger pointed at one of the titles bound in black and gold cover.

Holding my breath, I hooked the top edge of the book's spine with my index finger and tilted it toward me, feeling like a character in one of the adventure books I'd read before. With a faint click, the middle part of the bookshelf separated from the wall, sliding to the side. Pulse pounding, I came to stand next to Henry as we both peered into what appeared to be a secret passage. Lit torches lined the uneven walls of a steep and narrow stairwell.

Henry and I exchanged a look before I turned back to Marie.

"Thank you," I whispered.

Her face turned panicked.

"Please, take me with you. Don't leave me here. He's so cruel," she begged, her big eyes filling with tears.

My heart broke as emotion clogged my throat.

"I will come back for you. I promise," I rasped.

Suddenly, Marie lunged at me, her fingers digging into my forearm.

"No, please," she begged louder.

My eyes widened as I pried her fingers away from me. If she got any louder, she would draw attention to us.

"Marie, listen," I tried to reason with her through my teeth, keeping my voice low.

Henry clasped her shoulders and forcefully turned her to face him.

"Keep quiet. Go to your room, and don't tell anyone you saw us," he said urgently, his gaze locked on hers. He was compelling her. "Have hope," he added quietly before he let her go.

Marie stood frozen in place for a few seconds, her eyes glossy and unseeing. Then, she slowly blinked and turned on her heels toward the door.

"I *will* come back for her," I told the Lord, feeling a surge of determination. "I won't let what happened to Rory happen to her."

His expression was understanding as he looked at me, his gaze soft.

"We need to find the amulet. Then, her life will not be the only one you save."

He had no idea how many lives I would truly save once Dark Witches and vampires were no more.

I nodded and slipped inside the secret passage. Henry joined me a second later, a cool presence at my back, and the bookshelf slid back into place behind us with a soft click. Bracing a hand on the pale, rough wall, I began my descent, eyes trained downward to avoid a slip. I knew the Lord could make it down in no time, but he stayed right behind me, patiently waiting as I worked my way down. Having him here with me was comforting because I figured he'd catch me if I fell. At least, I hoped he would. For several long minutes, the sound of my breathing and scuffing steps filled the narrow space of the passage until it opened into a large, cavernous room illuminated by dozens of candles.

"What is this place?" I asked under my breath, walking deeper into the room and looking around.

A gasp of horror left me when I faced one of the walls. Sucking in a sharp breath, I stumbled backward, running into Henry. He clasped my shoulders to steady me as I stared at the wall before me, refusing to believe what I was seeing. There were shelves carved into the stone, and on them sat human skulls of different shapes and sizes. I couldn't move. I could barely breathe as bile rose in my throat, and my legs threatened to go out from under me. Squeezing my eyes shut, I turned away from the wall and took a deep breath.

"We are in Stern's lair," I heard Henry say in front of me, his voice hollow.

When I opened my eyes and looked at him, his jaw was hard as he stared at the wall behind me. He looked even paler than usual as deep shadows filled his eyes. I wondered if he was thinking the same thing I was. Would Rory's skull be on that wall if I hadn't walked in on Stern and her in the kitchen? Then, another thought invaded my mind. Was my mother's skull a part of the collection? I swayed on my feet, feeling lightheaded, and Henry clasped my shoulders again, his gaze focusing on me.

"Breathe," he said, and I did as he'd instructed.

Swallowing the lump that had climbed up my throat, I said, "We need to look for the amulet and leave this place."

The Lord nodded, and once he'd made sure I wouldn't faint, he let go of my shoulders and walked past me to search the part of the room containing the wall of skulls. I moved to the opposite wall and began rummaging through the ancient books and scrolls piled up in the nooks and crevices carved out in the stone.

"I found something," came Henry's voice from behind me a few minutes later.

My heart thumped in my chest as a spark of hope ignited. Trying to rein in my anxiety, I turned to Henry and found him holding a medium-sized chest. It was locked but didn't stay that way for long because Henry ripped the padlock off the hinges. He turned the chest toward him and opened the lid to look inside. I held my breath as I watched his eyes widen.

"Is it in there?" I asked in a hushed tone.

Henry didn't reply as he reached inside and pulled something out before dropping the chest on the ground with a thud. I winced as the sound echoed through the cavernous space. I would have preferred we'd stayed quiet, but Henry didn't seem to think he needed to be careful and not make any noise. Another advantage of being an apex predator, I supposed.

"I don't know what the amulet looks like," he said as I approached. "Is this it?"

He held up a teardrop-shaped amulet on a silver chain with a pale blue crystal in the middle. A soft gasp left me, and I brought my hand to my mouth, my eyes filling with tears.

"Yes," I breathed, my vision getting blurry.

I heard Henry's rough exhale of relief before he chuckled low.

"I can't believe we've found it," I rasped through the tears. I quickly wiped them away and smiled, wanting to pinch myself to make sure I wasn't dreaming.

I reached for the amulet, but before I could touch it, a faint noise drew my attention to the other end of the room, opposite where Henry and I had entered from Stern's study.

I peered into the shadows, making out an outline of another entrance or exit.

"Where do you think it leads?" I asked Henry, who was looking in the same direction.

His features sharpened as he became impossibly still— listening.

He must have heard something because he said low, "Ready your dagger."

Swallowing hard, I reached for the weapon strapped to my thigh under the cloak and unsheathed it without taking my eyes off the shadowy entrance. A moment later, a Ravager emerged from it, lurching toward Henry and me. She moved too fast for my eyes to track, but Henry stopped her with his clawed hand on her throat. He snatched her out of thin air, and I didn't hesitate as I thrust the dagger deep into the Ravager's chest, piercing the heart. With a shriek, the vampire shriveled up and caved into herself. Henry's head jerked toward where the Ravager had come from.

"She is not alone," the Lord growled. He turned back to me and pulled the Tear out of his cloak pocket. I hadn't even noticed him putting it there earlier. "Leave. Now," Henry said, hanging the amulet around my neck.

"What about you?" I asked, frowning.

I'd seen Henry prevail when he'd fought the witches on the border, but I didn't know how many Ravagers he could take on by himself.

"I will be fine," he replied, facing the shadowy entrance, his muscles turning taut under his clothes. He was preparing to fight.

"I can help," I said, surprising myself.

This was my moment. I had the amulet around my neck and a chance to leave Henry behind. A chance to escape with the Tear. Yet, I hesitated.

"I need you to leave so I don't have to worry about ensuring your survival," the Lord snapped, glancing at me. "Go!"

I heard them then. Light footsteps and snarls coming from the shadows. They were growing louder by the second, raising the tiny hairs all over my body. With one last look at Henry, I turned on my heels and ran out of the cavernous room.

My breath coming in short, rapid pants, I climbed up the steep stairwell until I reached the door that opened into Stern's study. Except, it was still closed. I frantically looked around the entrance, searching for a way to get back inside. Screeches and wails floated up from below, and my pulse quickened as I reached out and ran my hands over the wall around the door, looking for anything that could grant me access back into the study. My palm brushed over an indentation in the wall on the right side of the door, and I rose on my tiptoes and looked inside. There was a square-shaped hole carved into the wall. I felt around it with my hand, pushing and prodding.

The stone on the bottom gave way, and I kept pressing down on it until the door in front of me groaned and opened into the study, bathing me in the yellow glow of the lamps inside. Relief washed over me just as I heard Henry's roar from below. It was a sound of rage rather than pain, and hope flared in my chest that he was winning the fight against the Ravagers. Hesitating yet again, I glanced down the steep stairwell but forced myself to turn back to the door and walk through it.

Once I was inside the study, I set off into a sprint, running out of the room just as I heard the bookshelf slide back into place to conceal the secret passage. Quickly crossing the large foyer, I burst through the front door, trying not to dwell on the fact that I was leaving Henry behind. There was no point in worrying about the Lord, I told myself as I kept running, the amulet thumping against my chest with every step. If he didn't die tonight, he would die together with his kind when I found a way to activate the Tear.

Finally making it to the stables, I was relieved to find them empty. Annabelle neighed in greeting when I approached her, my chest rising and falling quickly. I swore Onyx gave me a questioning look when he didn't see Henry with me, and my heart fell. With a rough exhale, I took Annabelle's reins to lead her out of the stables, but before I could, a burst of pain in the back of my head plunged me into darkness.

21

The sound of crackling fire greeted me when I came to, my mind hazy and my head throbbing. I was lying on my side, my clothes and cloak the only barrier between me and the hard ground. Bracing my hand by my side for support, I sat up slowly, wincing at the ache in my stiff muscles. Memories rushed in, and I realized what had happened. Someone had hit me on the back of my head in the stables, rendering me unconscious.

Someone, who was now seated across from me, his face lit up by the flickering glow of the fire. Wren.

"You did it, Sophie," he said low. "You found the Tear."

All color drained from my face as my hand flew to my chest. The amulet was missing.

"What is the meaning of this?" I asked hoarsely, noticing he wasn't wearing the amulet around his neck.

Where was it? I quickly looked around, my vision swimming from the dull ache in the back of my head. I noticed Annabelle a few feet away, grazing in the moonlight.

"I wanted to take the black one, but he put up a fight," Wren explained, and I jerked my head back to him, hoping Onyx was okay.

"Where are we?" I asked even though I already suspected the answer. I could feel the wrongness in my bones. Like I wasn't supposed to be here, in these woods. Death and decay hung heavy in the air, chilling my blood.

"The Black Forest," Wren replied, and I sucked in a sharp breath.

"Are you out of your mind?" I hissed, my gaze darting to the fire burning on the ground between us.

It was bad enough that we were in the Black Forest; the fire would attract predators that lurked in these woods.

"It's okay. Nothing will touch us," Wren said. When I pinned him with a stare, my brows raised in question, he said with a heavy sigh, "I am under the protection of the Dark Witches."

My heart stopped and then sped up as I tried to piece it all together.

"You work for the witches?"

"Yes." There was another heavy sigh. Wren didn't seem proud of the fact. If anything, he sounded tired and defeated. "I came to New Haven a year ago to become a guard on the border. Went through the training. Thought my dream was coming true. Except, my first night patrolling the wall, a witch snatched me." He shook his head and chuckled low and without humor. "She took me to their stronghold in the Black Forest to sacrifice me to the Dark god. I begged them to spare my life, and they did."

I recalled how he'd told me before about his close brush with death and how he'd been prepared to do whatever it took to survive.

"But they asked you to do something in return," I surmised, and Wren nodded.

"They knew about the Tear and sent me back to New Haven to search for it. They suspected it was with the Duvals."

"How did they know about the Tear?" I asked, my brows knitting.

"I don't know. They don't tell me much," Wren replied, his expression serious.

"You didn't have to do their bidding," I bit out. "Once you were free—"

"Ah, but see, they didn't truly free me," Wren said bitterly, deep shadows dancing in his pale-blue eyes. "They put a spell on me so they could track me and another one that would kill me on the spot if I strayed from my mission of finding the amulet."

My heart turned over in my chest. What had happened to Wren was unfortunate, but I couldn't bring myself to feel sorry for him. I thought if I had been in his place, I would have chosen death if the alternative was working for the witches.

"You have the Tear now," I seethed. "Why am *I* here?"

I wanted to be here, of course. Well, not in the Black Forest, but where the amulet was, so I could try to get it back. But first, I needed to learn more about my current situation so I could devise a plan to get myself out of it. I couldn't help but feel like I didn't have all the pieces of the puzzle.

"My mission was not only to find the Tear but also you and bring both back," Wren explained.

"Why?" I narrowed my eyes at him as a cold feeling crept into my chest. Something told me that what I was about to hear would change my life. I took a deep breath, preparing for what Wren would say next.

Looking uncomfortable, he swallowed thickly, his throat bobbing before he replied, "They think it's your blood that activates the Tear."

"What?" I whispered, dumbfounded.

I hadn't expected that answer; just like I didn't expect what came next.

"The witches don't tell me much," Wren went on. "But they did tell me that you were a descendant of a White Witch."

My mouth dropped open as my mind worked on overdrive to put all the pieces together. I didn't know anything about my great-grandmother, and my grandmother had died before I'd been born. Had my great-grandmother been a White Witch?

My mother wrote "power of three" on the note about the Tear. Had she meant the power of three generations of White Witches?

If what Wren had said was true, and my blood could activate the Tear…

"Wren, listen to me," I tried to reason with him. "If my blood truly is the key, let's activate the Tear now. We can wipe out the supernatural. Dark Witches will no longer have power over you if they're destroyed."

Wren shook his head, his expression grave.

"Are you sure that it's going to work? You don't know anything about the amulet or how to wield it. Dark Witches believe its power can be manipulated. That the one controlling it can decide what species to destroy. They plan to use it to defeat the clans."

Disbelief surged through me as I stared at Wren over the dwindling fire. I wasn't seeing him, though. I was seeing thousands of humans being slaughtered in a sacrifice to the Dark god if the clans were destroyed. The people of the Empire would be left without protection. I couldn't let that happen. My eyes burned with tears, and I blinked to keep them at bay as my gaze landed on a short sword next to Wren. It looked like the one in Henry's study. He must have taken it before he'd followed me and the Lord to the Stern Estate.

My gaze zeroed in on Wren again, sweeping over his drawn features. He was staring into the fire, unblinking, as if lost in thought. I brushed my hand over my thigh, and my pulse quickened when I found my dagger still strapped there.

"Alright," Wren cleared his throat and rose to his feet. "There is no point in delaying the inevitable," he sighed, looking up at the starry night sky. "We need to keep moving." His gaze returned to me as he said, "I don't have to drug you if you promise to cooperate."

He planned to drug me? That would explain why he hadn't taken the dagger from me. He expected me to be unconscious while we traveled to our destination. My eyes trained on him, I nodded and slowly rose to my feet. Wren's expression was wary as he put out the fire and picked up the short sword off the ground.

"Give me your dagger," he asked, approaching me.

Panic flared in my chest. I didn't want to give up my only weapon. My gaze was locked on Wren's as I slowly unsheathed the dagger.

He must have seen the resolve on my face because his eyes widened as he warned, "Don't—"

I swiped the dagger, making him take a step back.

"Sophie," he growled, trying to grab me.

I dipped under his arm before kicking him in the back of his legs. His knees buckled, and he went down, catching himself with a hand on the ground. He was back up in an instant, thrusting out with the short sword. I danced out of his reach and whirled to my right, gauging the distance between me and Annabelle. Wren grabbed my arm, but I twisted around, slamming my elbow into his face. I heard a loud crack as Wren's head jerked back, and blood started rushing from his nose.

I set off toward Annabelle, but Wren grabbed my braided hair and pulled hard, sharply yanking me back. The movement caught me off guard, and I almost went down but managed to stay on my feet. I needed to end this, get the amulet, and escape. With a shout, I thrust my dagger into his midsection. A sharp gasp tore from Wren's lips as he released the sword, and it fell with a heavy thump against the ground. He let go of my hair and yelped in pain when I jerked the dagger out of his torso and sheathed it at my thigh.

"Bitch!" he snarled, his eyes wide, as he tried to grab me again.

Spinning out of his reach, I sprinted toward Annabelle. I could hear Wren's labored breathing behind me as I reached the horse and rummaged through the saddlebags until I found what I was looking for—the Tear. Potent relief washed over me, and I hung the amulet around my neck before hoisting myself into the saddle.

"Sophie, wait," Wren rasped, trudging toward me, one hand on the bleeding wound in his torso. "You won't survive the Black Forest," he said, blood trickling from the corner of his mouth.

"I'll take my chances," I threw at him and galloped away.

Annabelle was flying like an arrow through the woods as twisted branches whipped my face and snagged my clothes. Once we'd traveled a considerable distance away from where I'd left Wren, I slowed the horse down to a walk and then eventually stopped her altogether when we reached a clearing.

Taking a steadying breath, I looked around, trying to figure out which direction to head to find a way out of the Black Forest. A wall of dark trees encircled the clearing, and goose bumps prickled my skin as I tried to peer into the night, unable to make anything out in the pitch-black. The sky above me was clear, letting in the soft glow of moonlight, but the rest of the Forest was swallowed by darkness.

Annabelle's palpable unease mirrored my own as she pranced nervously, huffing and shaking her mane.

"I know," I whispered, placing my hand on her neck, trying to calm her.

Trepidation washed over me as I realized I didn't have any good options. I would have to blindly pick a direction and hope it would lead me back to Santoria. Then, I would make my way back to New Haven. If I survived tonight.

Just as the thought flashed through my mind, a rumbling growl came from the woods straight ahead of me. The sound raised the tiny hairs on my body and kicked my instinct into overdrive as Annabelle reared, nearly throwing me from my seat.

I tried to shush her as I held on to the reins, but the terrified mare was bound and determined to throw me off. Her movements became jerkier and more panicked until she eventually rose up, throwing me from the saddle, before taking off in the opposite direction of where the growling was coming from.

I landed on my hip, gritting my teeth through the sharp pain before I quickly scrambled to my feet and pulled out my dagger. I doubted it would do me any good against anything that lurked in the woods, but I refused to go out without a fight. The Forest grew quiet as if holding its breath as I watched the trees in front of me, refusing to blink or look away.

Terror shot through me as a black shadow separated from the tree line as if the darkness itself was bleeding from the woods. The shadow leaped into the air, and I didn't manage to stifle the scream that had climbed into my throat. It tore through the clearing just as a huge wolf slammed down on the ground several feet away from me. The creature crouched, claws digging into the earth, and bared long, sharp teeth in a vicious growl.

I was going to die. There was no doubt in my mind as I stood, frozen, my eyes locked with the red glowing ones of the beast. The wolf reared back and then launched into the air, sleek and fast. I didn't turn to run, deciding to meet my death head-on. I just hoped it would be quick as despair and regret rose up, suffocating me. Would the wolf swallow me whole with the amulet around my neck? That was my only concern in the last seconds of my life—that the amulet would be lost forever, and with it, humanity's hope for a future without the supernatural. A future where humans were safe.

The beast's wide-open maw was growing closer as it flew

through the air toward me. I gritted my teeth, preparing for the agony and pain that would undoubtedly come as the wolf tore me apart. I wanted to squeeze my eyes shut but forced myself to keep them open as the time seemed to slow. Any second now, the wolf would be on me. I could see the red glowing eyes and the glistening sharp teeth growing closer.

To my surprise, the wolf didn't make it to me. Henry grabbed it by the midsection, throwing it to the side. A gasp of shock and relief left me as I stared at the Lord in disbelief. His cloak was gone, and his shirt and breeches were covered in blood, but he was alive. He didn't look at me, though, too focused on the wolf, and for a good reason. The beast flipped in the air and landed on its legs, dipping its head and baring its fangs. Henry did the same, looking more animal than man.

The next thing I knew, the two supernatural creatures collided, becoming a blur of fangs and claws, moving too fast for my eyes to track. I frantically looked around, feeling like I should do something, *anything*, but what, I had no idea. All I could do was stand there and watch as Henry fought the beast, hoping that he would prevail. Their battle was short but also seemed to last for hours until everything slowed, and I saw Henry had the wolf in a chokehold. With a roar, he jerked the beast's head to the side, breaking the neck with a crunch that echoed through the clearing.

My breath left me in a ragged exhale as I stared at Henry in the silence that followed. I couldn't believe the wolf was dead and I was alive. I was alive because the Lord had come for me. Henry's chest was rising and falling heavily. He took a step toward me but went down on one knee, bracing his hand on the ground for support. I wanted to go to him but hesitated. I remembered all too well the crazed state he'd been in after his fight with the witches. Henry seemed himself, though, and I thought his eyes were blue instead of black when he looked up at me from beneath the thick, dark lashes.

"Are you okay?" he rasped, and that was all the confirmation I needed.

I sheathed my dagger and ran to him, dropping to my knees in front of him.

"I'm okay. Are you okay?" I asked in a hushed tone, looking around us to make sure nothing else came out of the shadows.

"Yes, but we need to get out of here. The dawn is fast approaching," he said quietly, his voice strained.

I nodded, scanning him for injuries. His shirt and breeches were torn, and there were four deep gashes on his chest, left there by the wolf's claws.

"Can you walk?" I asked, and the Lord nodded.

I rose to my feet, and, with a grunt, Henry did, too. He swayed where he stood, and when I offered my shoulder for support, my hand accidentally brushed the wound on his chest, making him wince in pain

"Sorry," I murmured as the two of us slowly began making our way toward the trees.

The Lord's steps were heavy, and his breathing labored. My mind raced, and my heart hammered in my chest as I tried to find a way out of the situation we were in. Henry was injured, and we needed his strength to survive in these woods. In the back of my mind, I knew what I had to do, but I refused to accept it until we neared the tree line, and I heard blood-curdling screeches and wails coming from deep within the Forest.

"Wait." I gently stopped Henry with my hand on his side. His head swung to me, and he gave me a questioning look. "You need to feed," I said quietly, the words difficult to get out. "You can feed from me."

Henry went impossibly still, staring at me in shock. His eyes had widened, his pupils dilating.

"You don't want that," he finally rasped, his gaze searching my face. "The idea terrifies you. I can smell your fear."

My throat closed up, and I cleared it before I said with determination I didn't truly feel, "It doesn't matter what I want. We won't survive if we go inside those woods with you in this condition. The idea of you feeding from me terrifies me, yes. But what lurks in the Forest terrifies me more."

Blue-black eyes roamed my face, and I thought he would turn me down, but after a few seconds, he conceded.

22

I was both relieved and terrified that Henry had decided to accept my offer. My legs were weak as we backtracked a few steps away from the tree line and lowered to our knees. With trembling hands, I took off the Tear, then my cloak, and put both on the ground beside me. I hesitated when my fingers brushed the locket holding the picture of my mother.

Henry didn't rush me, but his intent gaze was on me, tracking my every movement. His expression was wary as if he were waiting for me to change my mind. Taking a steadying breath, I reached behind my neck and unclasped the delicate chain, catching the locket in my hand when it glided down my chest. My emotions were conflicting. I felt like I was betraying my mother by taking off the locket so Henry could…feed. A shudder of trepidation rolled through me at the thought, and the Lord noticed.

"You don't have to do this," he managed to say, but he sounded weak, and the wound on his chest was still gnarly and bleeding. I would think it should have begun healing by now. Henry's breathing was labored, reinforcing my belief that he was in dire need of blood.

"You need to feed," was all I said.

I needed Henry's protection in the Black Forest, but a part of me also felt indebted to him for saving my life. Letting him feed from me was my way of repaying him.

We stared at each other in silence for a few minutes, and Henry's features were impossible to read. He was so eerily still that when he finally moved toward me, I instinctively jerked away.

"Sorry," I muttered, willing myself to sit still.

His lashes swept down, shielding his eyes as his jaw tightened. For a moment, I thought he might pull away, changing his mind, but then his gaze dropped to my neck. His face became sharper, and I could now see the all-consuming hunger in his eyes. His lips parted slightly, revealing the hints of his fangs.

My heart was pounding in my chest as he reached for me. Wrapping my braid around his fist, he gently tugged on it to move my head to the side.

"Are you sure?" he whispered, his cool breath caressing my exposed neck, making me shiver.

"Yes," I barely breathed before he struck.

I clenched my teeth through the burning pain when his fangs pierced my skin. My fingers curled inward to form a fist around the locket I was holding, nails digging into the palm of my hand. I held on to it as if it were a lifeline to my mother and everything I believed and stood for.

The discomfort of the bite was brief and was quickly replaced by something else entirely. The sensation flared to life in tiny sparks, growing in intensity the longer Henry's mouth remained sealed to my neck. Soon, I felt every deep, hungry pull in the space between my thighs, in my very core.

Henry's arm came around my waist to bring me flush with his hard chest. I gripped his shoulders…to pull him closer or to push him away…in that moment, I wasn't sure as I was lost in the sensation of his mouth tugging on my throat. A moan escaped me, and when it did, Henry ripped his mouth from my neck and backed away. Breathing shallowly, he stared at me with wide eyes. His lips were smeared with my blood, and I had to fight the sudden urge to kiss them, to taste myself on his tongue. Scowling, I lifted my trembling hand and pressed it to my neck.

Henry closed his eyes, running his tongue over his lips as his breathing became more even.

"You can have some of my blood to heal the bite marks," he offered, opening his eyes again.

I shook my head, not trusting myself to take him up on his offer. The wounds his fangs had inflicted stung, but I felt sparks of desire slowly flickering out, and I didn't want to reinforce them by ingesting his blood. We stared at each other for a moment longer until I swallowed and averted my gaze. I was stunned by the intensity of what I'd just experienced. Pulling my hand away from my neck, I looked down at my fingers, sticky and red with my blood. Only then did I notice the locket I'd dropped on the ground. Suddenly, I was desperate to put it back on as if it would ward me against everything I was feeling and bring me back to myself.

My fingers were numb as I clasped the chain behind my neck, letting the locket settle on my chest. I felt better the moment I put it on, but then I noticed it was smeared with my blood. My eyes pricked with tears as I quickly cleaned the blood off the best I could. My frown deepened as I stared at the locket, feeling like I'd forever tarnished it somehow. An ugly emotion similar to the one I'd experienced on the night of the Vassal Ball rose up, filling me with shame. I felt like a traitor again, and this time, the feeling was ten times stronger, threatening to pull me under before crushing me under its weight.

"Are you okay?" Henry asked when a shuddering breath left me.

I nodded as he carefully wrapped my cloak around my shoulders, fastening it below my throat. It did nothing to protect me from the chill that flared in my chest. A tremor coursed through me as the cold feeling spread through my entire body, coating my insides with ice.

I couldn't bring myself to look at Henry as he hung the amulet around my neck. It was hard to will my numb limbs to move when he offered his hand after swiftly rising to his feet. I placed my hand in his, and when he pulled me up, my knees buckled, and I almost went down again. He caught me with his arm around my waist, hauling me to his hard chest. My breath hitched as my gaze dropped to his red-stained lips. I forced my eyes up and found Henry watching me with a concerned look on his face.

"I might have taken too much," he muttered, but there was no mistaking the hunger I still saw in his eyes as they darted to the two bite marks on my neck.

"I'm fine," I assured him as I pulled away and looked at his chest.

A breath of relief left me when I saw the wound was beginning to heal.

"We need to find shelter before sunrise," Henry said, looking up at the night sky before lowering his gaze to me. "Can you walk, or do you need me to carry you?"

"I can walk," I said quickly. I didn't want to be in his arms again when my skin still hummed from the effects of him feeding from me.

He eyed me for a moment as if he didn't trust I was okay, and something akin to remorse flickered across his features.

"Where are we going to find shelter?" I asked, trying to distract myself from the cold feeling inside me.

"I remember this area of the Forest," Henry said, still looking at me with worry in his eyes that were gradually turning from black to deep blue. "There was a White Witches settlement here during the Red War. I'm hoping some of the cabins are still standing so we can stay there until sundown."

"Lead the way," I said, turning toward the woods.

Henry nodded but didn't move in front of me to lead the way. Instead, he gently placed a hand on my back to steer me in the direction he wanted to go before falling in step behind me. I held my breath as we entered the woods, only letting it out slowly when nothing jumped out at us to try and tear us apart. Dark, twisted shadows moved all around us, slithering through the trees with low hisses and occasional screeches and wails.

"We are surrounded by predators," I whispered as Henry and I slowly made our way through the forest. "Why aren't they attacking?"

"Because I am the biggest predator in here," the Lord said low.

He *was* the biggest predator, and I'd just let him feed from me. Willingly. A shudder rolled through me, and I felt Henry's fingers flex on my back.

"It's normal, you know," he said, keeping us moving deeper into the woods.

"What is?" I glanced at him.

He swallowed, his throat bobbing, but didn't meet my gaze.

"What you felt when I was feeding from you."

A flashback of his mouth on my neck instantly filled my mind, and I stumbled, nearly falling. Henry caught me, and I was in his arms again.

"Your body reacts that way to provide a false sense of security. It doesn't mean anything," he said, staring down at me.

"Okay." I scowled, stepping away from him.

I'd preferred it if he hadn't acknowledged how my body had reacted to him.

"How did you find me?" I asked him, resuming walking.

I didn't know where I was going, but I needed to keep moving, if only to avoid the uncomfortable conversation. Henry immediately fell in step next to me, for which I was grateful because I could feel dozens of eyes watching me from the darkness of the forest. My chest filled with dread when I thought about what would have happened if Henry hadn't found me when he had.

"I followed your scent...and Wren's," Henry replied, frowning.

"He followed us to the Stern Estate," I explained. "After we got separated, he knocked me out and brought me to the Black Forest."

Henry snarled with rage.

"Did he hurt you?" he demanded, grasping my elbow to stop me in my tracks.

"No," I said low, facing him. "I hurt *him*. I stabbed him with my dagger and escaped."

"Good," Henry growled in approval. His eyes shone with admiration as he stared at me. "Why did he bring you here?" he asked, his voice returning to normal as he regained his composure.

I swallowed, trying to decide how much information I wanted to divulge to the Lord.

"He is working for the Dark Witches. They sent him to New Haven to retrieve the amulet."

"And you?" Henry asked, and I grimaced. I should have known better than to hope he wouldn't pick up on that.

"He said the witches think my blood activates the amulet," I admitted.

"Because you're part White Witch?" the Lord asked.

"How did you know?" I breathed as my eyes widened in shock.

"I could taste it in your blood," he explained, swallowing thickly.

I stared at him in disbelief.

"Why didn't you tell me?"

"I only knew your blood tasted different. I didn't know why. I'd never tasted a White Witch's blood, so I wasn't sure what it was."

"Do you think my mother was a White Witch?" I asked him as we continued walking.

"It would make sense. If Vincent had fed from her when she was his vassal, he would have been able to tell. That would explain why they worked together, looking for the amulet. Unless…" he trailed off. When I glanced at him, he seemed to be lost in thought. "Unless your mother wasn't looking for the amulet," he finally said. "Perhaps she made it."

I nodded because I was wondering the same thing. Especially if the "power of three" meant the power of three generations of White Witches.

"That would explain why it's my blood that activates the amulet," I mused, my eyes trained on the dark forest floor.

"Do you want to activate it now?" Henry asked, glancing at the Tear on my chest.

"No." I shook my head, carefully stepping over thick, gnarled roots protruding from the ground.

Something that Wren had said earlier had stuck with me. I didn't know how the amulet worked. I didn't want to risk killing Henry and being left in the Black Forest without his protection. Would the amulet also wipe out all the supernatural creatures lurking in the woods? I didn't have the answer to that, and I didn't want to make the wrong move. There were too many unknowns.

"We don't know how the amulet works. I want to get out of the Forest and return to New Haven before we attempt to activate it," I explained, hoping Henry wouldn't push the issue.

Thankfully, he agreed with my line of thinking.

"We will spend the day in the Forest and then head back to New Haven at sundown," he said, and I nodded.

We walked for a while, and I was beginning to worry we wouldn't find a shelter in time, but that was when we came across another clearing. A cabin sat there, old and decrepit but still intact. Henry walked in first to make sure it was safe, but I followed close behind, refusing to leave the Lord's side and remain outside, surrounded by creatures that all wanted a bite of me.

The soft light of the moon streaming through the broken windows illuminated the small space as we moved through it. Thick spiderwebs covered all the surfaces, blanketing the place in gauzy white, and I could hear small rodents scurry around as I followed Henry to one of the rooms in the back of the house.

"I need to borrow your cloak," the Lord said, stepping into the small space and looking around.

I didn't feel as chilled anymore because the ice coating my insides was beginning to thaw, so I didn't mind parting with the cloak. When I unfastened it from below my throat and handed it to Henry, he hung it over the single small window, plunging the room into total darkness.

Momentarily disoriented, I just stood there, waiting for my eyes to adjust. Henry brushed my arm, and I jerked, not expecting his touch.

"We can sit down there," he said quietly, gently grabbing my arm and leading me to the right.

I was beginning to make out the objects in the room and realized we'd walked to the wall farthest away from the window. Henry lowered to the floor, resting his back against the wall and stretching his long legs out in front of him. With a heavy sigh, I assumed the same position next to him, hoping rodents would stay away from the Lord and, by extension, me, just like the creatures in the woods had done earlier.

"What happened at the Stern Estate?" I asked Henry, now able to make out his features in the darkness.

He rested his head against the wall, his eyes closed and his mouth a firm line.

"I did what I had to do," he said low.

He killed them all, I thought to myself, studying his face with wide eyes.

"How many were there?" I whispered.

"About a dozen or so." He sounded sad, like what he'd done weighed heavily on him.

My chest was tight as I faced forward, sitting silently for a few minutes. There was no doubt in my mind those Ravagers had to be killed, but my heart broke for Henry because of what he'd had to do. I wondered if he was going to add their lives to the list of the ones he was trying to atone for.

"Why didn't you take me as your vassal when I turned eighteen?" I asked suddenly, surprising myself. I'd wondered that for a while, and now seemed as good a time as any to ask that question.

Henry didn't say anything for a long time, making me wonder if he'd fallen asleep. My eyes began to drift close when he finally spoke, breaking the silence, "You didn't want me to take you."

My eyes flew open at his words.

"Not everyone wants to be taken. Yet, the clans take them anyway," I pointed out.

"You were grieving. Your misery was palpable. I had just lost my father, so I knew what you were going through. I was not about to tear you away from your father and the life that you knew."

His words rendered me speechless as my mind flashed back to our conversation on the night of the Selection.

"A vampire with a conscience? Am I supposed to believe that?" I'd scoffed then.

"You can believe whatever you want," he'd replied.

Right now, that notion wasn't so hard to believe. I felt a pang in my chest at the thought that I was planning to kill him.

"But when you came back the following year and so obviously wanted to be selected," Henry continued. "I was curious...and suspicious. I wondered what reason you might have for coming back. I knew Vincent had gone to the Dark Witches to try and save your mother. I hoped if I selected you, you would help shed light on my father's disappearance."

"Do you think Vincent is really dead?"

I didn't know why I'd asked that question. I'd seen firsthand what the Dark Witches were capable of, and Vincent had gone to face them alone. I doubted that, even as a vampire, he could have survived, but a tiny part of me still wondered if there was a chance, if ever so small. Perhaps I only wished there was a chance because I wanted the burden of his death off my shoulders. The burden of the lie I'd told that cost Henry his father.

"There is no doubt in my mind that he's dead," Henry rasped. "I just pray his death was swift."

"I'm sorry," I whispered, turning my head to look at him. "I truly am."

Henry met my gaze in the darkness.

"Thank you," he said low. "And thank you for letting me feed from you."

"Thank you for saving my life." I'd spoken the words softly as if my hushed tone would change the fact that one of my worst enemies had saved my life...thrice if I counted the Ravager attack.

A faint smile curved Henry's lips.

"Let's not make it a habit, okay?"

"Okay." I smiled back.

The Lord closed his eyes and rested his head against the wall.

"Try to get some sleep. I won't let anything happen to you," he murmured.

For the first time, I believed him, feeling safe next to him as exhaustion pulled me under, and I drifted off to sleep.

was dreaming about my mother, seeing flashes of my childhood memories. In the first one, I was a small child, playing with wooden puzzles on the floor in my mother's study. Dust danced in the sunlight pouring through the window above my mother's desk as I played while she worked. The day was bright and peaceful, filling me with warmth and joy. At one point, I looked up from the puzzle and found my mother hunched over her desk. Her gaze was cast down, and she was saying words I didn't understand. They sounded beautiful but foreign, and I didn't think I'd ever heard them before. My mother was saying them repeatedly in almost a singsong tone, and I tilted my head to the side as I listened, lulled by the musical lilt of her voice.

After a while, she stopped saying the strange words. Briefly closing her eyes, she rubbed the back of her neck with a long exhale. She then rose to her feet and picked something up from the desk before stepping away from it. I watched her lower to her knees on the floor, not far from where I was sitting. She pried one of the floorboards out and placed the object she'd grabbed from the desk inside before jamming the board back into place.

Once she made sure the board was seamlessly fused with the rest, she rose to her feet and came over to me.

"Come here, baby girl." She smiled, reaching for me. "Your father will be home soon."

The next thing I knew, I was in her arms, engulfed in her rosewater scent and her warmth. I could feel her unconditional love for me pouring out of her, and I squeezed her tight, basking in it. I couldn't hold on to her for long as the memory began to dissipate, receding into my subconscious.

Another memory surfaced. I was older in it, coming home early one day after school. I walked through the empty house until I reached my mother's study. She was saying the strange words again, over and over, but stopped abruptly when I pushed open the study door. She leaned over the desk as if hiding something from my view as she smiled at me.

"You're home early," she said. "Go start the fire in the hearth. You can help me make dinner. I'll be right there."

I smiled back and turned to leave. On my way to the kitchen, I thought it was odd my mother hadn't risen up from her desk to hug me as she usually did when I got home.

My brows knitted as the memory faded, and another one took its place. It was just my mother's face, her hazel eyes staring at me.

"Wake up, Sophie," she urged, her tone worried. "Wake up!"

My eyes flew open, and it took a few seconds for my vision to adjust to the darkness. I was still on the floor, propped against the wall, but Henry's cool presence wasn't by my side. Shadowy figures surrounded me, towering over me where I sat. I sucked in a sharp breath when I saw their pale faces that were an eerie contrast to the pitch-black of the room. Dark Witches surrounded me. I didn't have time to react as one of them muttered a spell, and I slipped into unconsciousness.

When my eyes fluttered open, I was lying flat on my back, staring up at the stone ceiling. It took me a few seconds to figure out what I was looking at. There was a mural on the ceiling, etched into the rough, beige stone. It depicted a monster with scaly black skin and dark, bottomless eyes. Two horns protruded from the creature's head, and its mouth was gaping, revealing two rows of long, sharp teeth.

Sheer terror climbed and swelled with the realization of where I was slowly sinking in.

"You are awake," I heard a voice to my left.

Bolting upright, I whipped my head in the direction of where the sound had come from.

A Dark Witch stood there, garbed in a hooded, black cloak and wreathed in wafting shadows. The churning tendrils pulsed around her as if they were a part of her, and she was a part of them. They licked her body and her face, which was a ghastly pale shade and marbled with black veins slithering under her skin.

"Welcome to the Shadow Temple," the witch said, her black eyes fixed on me. Her voice...I'd never heard such a sound before. It was an eerie mix between a hiss and a whisper.

I took a sweeping glance around the large, circular chamber illuminated by hundreds of thick, waxy candles. Looking down and around me, I realized I sat on top of a slab of stone—a sacrificial altar. A shudder rolled through me as tiny bumps erupted all over my skin.

"I am Antaris, the head priestess," the witch introduced herself. "You can get off the altar. We just put you on there until you woke up," she explained.

My heart pounding, I slid off the cool stone, standing on legs I didn't feel. Forcing myself to breathe, I stared at the priestess before my gaze stretched to the back of the chamber, where I could make out shadowy forms of other witches.

"Sophie Devereaux," Antaris hissed, and I returned my gaze to her pale face. "Daughter of Eloise, granddaughter of Celine," she paused. "Great granddaughter of Josephine."

Disbelief surged through me as my breath hitched. My great-grandmother's name was Josephine? That could not be a coincidence. Was the amulet named after her?

The dream I'd had before the witches had taken me rose to the surface, triggered by Antaris's words. It had been a kaleidoscope of memories about my mother...working on the Tear. She hadn't been searching for it; she'd been creating it as I'd been growing up. The power of three. The power of three generations of White Witches. My grandmother, my mother, and me.

"Where is Henry?" I asked, my throat dry and scratchy.

Terror shot through me at the thought that they'd killed him. Panic threatened, but I shut it down, refusing to give in to it until I knew for sure he was dead.

"The vampire fled the moment we came for you," the priestess replied.

Relief washed over me that Henry was alive, but it was short-lived as my heart dropped with shock and disappointment. The Lord had promised to keep me safe but had fled the moment the Dark Witches had come for me. I should have known better than to trust a vampire. In the end, Henry was just like the rest of them. I shook my head as my eyes burned with tears. I'd been so foolish.

"Fitting you would be working with a Duval, just like your mother and grandmother did," Antaris went on.

My brows flew up at her words. I knew about my mother working with Vincent, but my grandmother? Was my grandmother the one who'd started creating the amulet, and then my mother had finished it?

"We knew your grandmother was trying to create an amulet that could destroy us," Antaris said, confirming what I'd just pieced together. "But when we took her, we could not find it."

"You took my grandmother?" I rasped, a lump rising in my throat.

My grandmother had died years before I'd been born, and my mother had never told me what had happened to her.

Antaris nodded.

"We wanted to turn her. To have her join our ranks in servitude to Xanthus," the priestess said, reverently lifting her eyes to the mural on the ceiling. "But she refused, killing herself before the transformation was complete."

I swallowed the lump in my throat. I didn't know my grandmother, but what Antaris had just told me made Celine my hero. She'd chosen death over turning Dark. She'd sacrificed her life so she wouldn't lose her soul and join the Dark Witches. I should be thinking about doing the same thing—sacrificing myself before the Dark Witches could use me to activate the Tear.

It's too late, I realized with a sinking heart. I should have done that before they'd gotten their hands on me. Even if I killed myself now, they would still have my body and a way to activate the Tear and use it against the clans.

My hand flew up to my chest, but the amulet was no longer around my neck. It was in Antaris's hand as she approached me, gliding through the chamber much like a vampire.

"We did not know your grandmother worked with Vincent Duval," Antaris said, and my eyes widened. "She had given him the amulet before we stole her away, and your mother finished it years later," she explained. "Do you think the vampire knew they were working on a weapon that could kill his kind?" Antaris asked, cocking her head to the side, the movement jerky and unnatural. "What a treat it was when Vincent showed up here, looking for your mother," she hissed, her mouth stretching in a deranged smile that revealed two rows of sharp, pointy teeth, reminding me of Xanthus depicted above us on the ceiling. "His death was slow and painful. And now it is time to kill them all and take what belongs to us."

"Humans do not belong to you," I seethed, my face contorting in rage.

"You are right," Antaris said, "They belong to Xanthus."

Fast as a viper, she lashed out, grabbing my forearm right above the scar from the Ravager attack. Her claws dug into my skin as she brought her other hand up and sliced my wrist open with one deadly sharp nail. A shocked gasp left me as my blood welled and began dripping on the stone floor. Antaris didn't waste any time, placing the Tear under my wrist. I watched in horror as several drops of my blood splashed on the pale-blue crystal in the middle of the amulet. Deep sorrow filled my heart. I'd failed. I should have activated the Tear in the Forest last night and destroyed the Dark Witches. I'd hesitated, and now all would be lost.

Seconds turned into minutes as the priestess and I stared down at the amulet in her hand. It was now covered in my blood, and Antaris dropped my arm, lifting the Tear to her face. The moment she let go of me, I clamped my hand on my wrist, cradling it to my chest. My gaze was fastened on the amulet in the witch's hand as I held my breath. Several more minutes passed. Nothing happened. Relief blossomed in my chest, and a startled laugh almost left me. My blood didn't work. Then, a thought occurred to me, and my relief crumbled, quickly replaced by dread. If my blood didn't activate the Tear, that meant the witches couldn't use it to destroy the clans. But that also meant I couldn't use it against the witches.

Panic sank its claws into me as I realized something else. Since the witches didn't need my blood, they could now turn me into one of them. I wouldn't let them, I thought with resolve. I would not go down without a fight. I would kill myself rather than become one of the Dark ones.

Antaris made a sound deep in her throat that raised the tiny hairs on my body. She brought the amulet mere inches from her face, narrowing her eyes and staring at it intently. It looked as if she were trying to will the Tear to activate with her mind. When it didn't, her features mottled and twisted with rage. Her eyes were two oily pools of blackness as she looked at me, curling her clawed fingers around the amulet and lowering her hand down by her side.

"Your blood does not activate the amulet," she hissed. "But worry not, you will still serve Xanthus by becoming one of his devout followers."

No, I won't, I thought to myself, frantically looking around the chamber for something I could use to end my life. I wasn't delusional to think I could escape this place.

Suddenly, the heavy door to the Temple flew off the hinges, and screams of pain filled the large space. I could make out two robed figures moving through the chamber with the speed my eyes couldn't track, taking out the witches one by one.

Antaris's black, fathomless eyes grew big, and she opened her mouth unnaturally wide, releasing a high-pitched wail. The next thing happened too fast but also as if in slow motion. The priestess drew her arm back and struck, sinking her claws into my chest. With wide eyes, I watched the dark magic crackle down her arm and into me, filling my chest with burning pain that spread to my entire body. Screams of agony tore through the Temple, and it took me a moment to realize they were coming from me. A deafening roar came from my right as one of the hooded figures rushed Antaris. With a screech, the witch let go of me and swept out of the room in a whirl of dark shadows.

I was on fire. My body burned from the inside out, and the next breath I took scorched my throat. I went to crumple to the floor, but two strong arms held me up. I found myself staring at Henry. I couldn't speak, couldn't scream as the flames that no one else could see burned me alive from the inside.

"You'll be okay," Henry said, his voice hoarse.

No, I won't. Not this time, I wanted to say, but I couldn't make a sound, lost in the excruciating pain as it consumed me, shortening each breath I took.

"It's not looking good," came a familiar voice from my left. A second later, Isabelle's face came into view next to Henry. "She is going to need your blood and lots of it," she said, her gaze landing on my chest where it felt like a gaping hole had opened up, its edges smoking as it slowly expanded, burning my skin and flesh, eating up my entire body.

"Then I will give her what she needs," Henry replied, scooping me into his arms.

My eyes fluttered closed, and I felt weightless, finally giving in to the never-ending pain.

24

I was floating. The agonizing flames eating up my insides were gone and had been replaced by a different kind of burning as the liquid heat of potent desire invaded my blood. I came to with a sharp gasp, my hands fisting in the sheets as I writhed on the bed, my back arching from the throbbing ache settling between my thighs.

"Sophie, are you okay?" I recognized Henry's deep voice and saw him hovering over me, his features drawn, and his eyes panicked.

I couldn't focus on anything else but the curling sensation in my very core as I stared up at the Lord, his perfect face mere inches from mine. Driven to the brink of madness with desire, I fisted one hand in his shirt and another one in his hair. His eyes widened as I pulled him to me, sealing my mouth to his. He sucked in a breath, his lips parting, and I took advantage, deepening the kiss. A moan escaped me when our tongues touched, but Henry abruptly broke the kiss, throwing himself off me and into the nearby chair.

My lips tingling, I lifted off the bed on my elbows, pinning the

Lord with a stare. He stared back, both of us breathing heavily. I didn't understand why he'd broken the kiss and was desperate to get his mouth back on mine.

"I know it's difficult, but you need to control yourself," Henry said, briefly closing his eyes and running a hand through his hair.

I didn't want to control myself. My mind was hazy with desire, and I didn't want to come back to reality.

When Henry met my gaze again, his eyes were several shades darker. He swallowed thickly, his throat bobbing, making me wonder if I was not the only one who wasn't in control.

"It's just the effects of my blood. You had a lot of it. It will pass," he explained. "I can leave to make it easier," he rasped, rising to his feet.

"No, stay." I grabbed his hand, the cool touch eliciting a pleasurable shiver from me.

He looked unsure, his gaze darting to the door before returning to me.

"Only if you promise to behave," he said with a heavy sigh.

"I promise," I said quickly.

Henry shot me a skeptical look but sat down on the edge of the bed.

"How are you feeling?" he asked, his eyes searching my face.

I felt fine, not taking into account the pulsing ache between my legs.

"I'm alive," I stated the obvious.

"I thought we weren't going to make a habit out of me saving you," Henry said with a soft smile.

"I thought you left me," I admitted.

He frowned as regret flared in his eyes.

"I'm sorry you thought that. I did leave when the Dark Witches came for you, because I didn't think I could take on so many by myself. I went to New Haven and got Isabelle. She helped me break into the temple and save you."

Looking down at my chest, I found I was wearing a clean

white tunic and black leggings. Memories of what had transpired in the temple rushed in, and a shudder rolled through me as I remembered the excruciating pain. I swore I could still feel the remnants of it as tiny tremors racked my entire body. The memories overwhelmed me, threatening to pull me under, but I forced myself to breathe through the panic attack, willing my heart to slow. I knew the gaping hole in my chest had healed—I could feel it. Just like I could feel the burning shards of ice that coated my insides because I had failed.

"My blood doesn't activate the amulet," I said quietly, meeting Henry's gaze.

"I know. I heard the witch say so when Isabelle and I broke into the temple."

"And you still saved me?"

I didn't know why I found that so shocking. I'd seen Henry in a different light during the past week, but he was still a vampire. Once he'd learned my blood didn't activate the Tear, he hadn't needed to risk his life to try and save me. He could have gotten the amulet and fled. Yet, he'd saved me and given me his blood to heal my wound. Perhaps he was better than me because even after everything we'd been through together, I still planned to kill him.

"Of course I saved you. Was I supposed to let you die?" Henry said, his eyebrows pinched and his tone affronted. He dipped his chin and chuckled low but without humor. "I am not a monster, Sophie. Even if I look like one."

"You don't," I whispered, and his gaze snapped to mine.

He didn't look like a monster.

Quite the opposite, I thought as my gaze glided over his chiseled features, snagging on his well-formed mouth before moving lower to his broad shoulders and hard chest.

A shiver skated over my skin as I imagined what it would be like to feel the weight of his powerful body on mine.

"Sophie," Henry warned, his nostrils flaring.

"Can you do something for me?" I breathed, my voice low and husky. Henry's eyes fluttered closed as I reached up and skimmed my fingertips down his cheek. "Don't push me away," I whispered, my mouth so close to his, we shared a breath.

The Lord grew incredibly still and seemed to have stopped breathing as I brushed my lips over his, shivering at the soft contact. My next inhale got caught in my throat as everything slowed, and my attention zeroed in on his mouth. I angled my head and brought my lips to his again. A heartbeat later, Henry kissed me back, his lips cool and firm as they moved against mine. His sharp fangs grazed my lower lip, eliciting a gasp from me, and I opened up for him as a thrilling sensation invaded my blood. I flicked my tongue over his, and Henry groaned, his hand coming up to cradle the back of my head as he kissed me slowly and thoroughly, ratcheting up my desire. By the time he pulled away, I was breathless and wanting more. *Needing* more.

Fisting my hands in his shirt, I pulled him on me as my back hit the mattress. A low, rough sound came from Henry as he brought his mouth to mine again. He hovered over me, holding himself up on his elbow as he kissed me. I felt each stroke of his tongue in every part of me, wishing he would press his body fully down on mine, leaving no space between us. He kept his distance, but his hand lifted to caress my cheek before moving lower, gliding over my chest to my stomach before settling between my thighs. A raw moan escaped me as his fingers brushed over the very center of me, touching me where I ached. They settled over the throbbing point at the apex of my thighs and began moving in slow, steady circles. I rolled my hips into his touch, desperate to increase the pressure. The thin material of my leggings provided little barrier between his fingers and my flesh, but I wished there was nothing between us. I wanted to feel his cool touch on my flushed skin. I *craved* it.

The strokes of my tongue against his became more forceful,

more demanding as I threaded my fingers through his hair, tugging on the silky strands, urging him to do more, make me *feel* more. A deep, rumbling sound left him as he dragged his hand up, sliding it under my tunic. His cool fingers brushed the skin along my lower stomach, right above the band of my leggings, making me shiver as desire pulsed between my thighs.

My own hands started to explore, gliding over Henry's powerful body until one dove under his shirt while the other one brushed over the rigid length straining through his pants. His body jerked, and he made that rough sound again, sending a ripple of arousal straight through me. Suddenly, he broke the kiss and pulled away, quickly putting distance between us, leaving me alone on the bed. He stood by the door now, breathing hard, his pupils dilated so much there was hardly any blue left in his eyes. I knew the hunger in his gaze should terrify me, but instead, I felt another wave of intense desire roll through me.

"I should go," he rasped.

What?

"No, please." I sat up in the bed.

Henry let out a ragged exhale, closing his eyes and shaking his head.

"You have no idea how much I want to stay," he ground out.

"Then stay," I said, or maybe begged; I wasn't sure. I would give anything at that moment to make him not leave this room.

His eyes were more blue when he looked at me again.

"You are not yourself. You will regret it if I stay."

When he turned and opened the door, panic set in as I realized he was going to leave me like this, aroused and desperate for release.

"Don't leave me like this," I whispered.

His expression was pained as he walked out.

"Get some rest," he said with a heavy sigh, closing the door behind him.

With a grunt of frustration, I threw myself back on the bed and waited, hoping he'd come back to finish what we'd started. Several long minutes passed until I realized he wasn't coming back. I would have to take care of the pent-up desire myself, wishing it was Henry's touch on my body instead of my own.

25

*H*enry was back in the room when I woke up.

"You're an asshole," I grumbled, grabbing the flat pillow from under my head and hurling it at him.

He caught it with a low chuckle.

"I see you are back to being yourself."

I didn't say anything as I sat up in the bed. Henry rose from the chair he was sitting in and strolled over to me.

"How are you feeling?" he asked, propping the pillow behind my back so I could rest against it.

"Fine," I said quietly.

My cheeks heated as my mind flashed back to what I'd done right before I'd drifted off to sleep. What I *had* to do in order to get rid of the burning desire elicited by Henry's blood.

One side of Henry's mouth turned up as if he knew what I was thinking, and he dipped his head and smirked under his breath, walking back to the chair.

"Thank you," I said low as the Lord returned to his seat. "For not taking advantage of me. I wasn't myself."

"I know," Henry said, his expression growing serious.

His gaze dropped to my mouth and lingered there. My heart

skipped a beat and my chest felt inexplicably tight as I wondered if he was thinking the same thing I was. Now that I knew how his lips felt on mine, what was I supposed to do with that knowledge?

Dragging my gaze away from Henry, I shifted it to the exposed wooden beams of the ceiling before lowering it to the rustic bed I was in and the small table beside it. An oil lamp sat on top of it, casting a soft, yellow glow around the room.

"Where are we?" I asked Henry.

The Lord settled in the chair, deep shadows creeping into his eyes.

"I couldn't take you back to New Haven after Isabelle and I saved you from the Dark Witches. There was no time," he paused and swallowed thickly, his throat bobbing.

A cold feeling invaded my chest—I'd come so close to dying.

"I took you as far from the temple as I could before I didn't think I had another second to spare before giving you my blood," he paused and added with a shuddering breath. "You were dying."

Without thinking, I brought my hand up, rubbing the spot on my chest where Antaris's claws had dug in when she'd attacked me.

"We were in the middle of the Black Forest, and I was giving you my blood while Isabelle kept watch, and the most amazing thing happened," Henry said, his lips curling upward.

My eyes widened as I hung on every word, sitting up straight on the bed and crossing my legs.

"They came to our aid," he said quietly, resting his elbows on his knees and leaning forward.

"Who?" I whispered.

"White Witches," he said, and my heart sped up in my chest. "Not all of them perished during the Red War. Some survived and went into hiding." A look of awe and relief settled into his features as he shook his head and chuckled as if he couldn't quite believe it himself. "They let me bring you here while you healed," he said, looking around the small bedroom. "Isabelle went back to New Haven."

I was at a loss for words. I was a descendant of White Witches, and I'd just learned that my people had not all been eradicated. Perhaps the ones that had survived could help shed light on my heritage.

A soft knock drew my attention to the door.

"It's Celeste," Henry said, his eyes darting toward the sound. "The White Witch who lives here. Are you feeling up to speaking with her?"

"Yes." I nodded, my breath catching in anticipation.

Henry rose to his feet and walked to the door. When he opened it, an old woman stepped inside the room, holding an oil lamp in her hand. Her eyes were a striking cerulean blue, the color a startling contrast to her warm, beige skin and long, white hair.

"Sophie, this is Celeste," Henry introduced her. "Celeste, this is Sophie."

"It's so nice to meet you," I said, scrambling to get off the bed. When I stood up, Henry was by my side in an instant, his hand on my elbow for support. "I'm okay, I can stand," I told him, touched by the gesture.

"It's a pleasure to meet you, Sophie," Celeste said with a slight accent. The musical lilt of her voice reminded me of my mother. "You must be hungry." She smiled at me, but the smile didn't quite reach her eyes, which were wary as she appraised me from head to toe.

"Starving," I said, realizing that I indeed was.

"Follow me," Celeste said, leaving the bedroom.

I fell in step behind her, my gaze landing on the colorful woven shawl wrapped around her shoulders. Henry followed close behind, a cool and comforting presence at my back. When we walked into the small, cozy kitchen, my stomach grumbled at the smell of roasted meat and potatoes.

"I made dinner, but we can start with some tea if you'd like," Celeste said, placing the oil lamp she'd been holding on the kitchen table.

"Tea sounds wonderful," I told her, as I wasn't sure I could handle anything heavy.

Henry pulled out a chair for me, and I sat down at the rectangular table that took up most of the kitchen. When the Lord took a seat to my right, I glanced past him at the window. The curtains were drawn, but a thin gap in between let in a sliver of moonlight, letting me know it was nighttime.

An herbal aroma filled the small space as Celeste poured three cups of tea out of the weathered green teapot and took a seat across from Henry and me. The Lord took a sip from his cup, and I wondered if he actually liked tea or was just trying to be polite.

Cradling my cup, I let the warmth seep into my hands as I took a steadying breath.

"Celeste, did you know my mother or my grandmother?" I asked her, hopeful.

Her bright blue eyes were shrewd as they searched mine.

"I never met them," she said, and my face fell in disappointment. "But I know of your lineage," she continued, and my ears perked up as I scooted to the edge of my seat. "Your great-grandmother Josephine was a White Witch. She had a daughter, Celine…"

"My grandmother," I interjected, and Celeste nodded.

"When Dark Witches were hunting us during the Red War, Josephine hid Celine in New Haven and sacrificed herself to save her daughter's life."

My breath left me as I stared at Celeste, guessing that the amulet was called Josephine's Tear to honor my great-grandmother's sacrifice.

"Do you know about the amulet?" I whispered, unable to bring myself to talk about it in anything but a hushed tone.

"I do. I have heard Celine was the one who began creating it. She called it Josephine's Tear in honor of her mother."

"She didn't finish it," I surmised. "Because the Dark Witches took her."

Sorrow filled Celeste's voice as she said, "Yes. We tried to save her, but she was already gone by the time we got to the temple."

When she said "we", I remembered that Henry had said there was more than one White Witch who'd come to his aid in the woods.

"How many White Witches are left?"

Sharp blue eyes flicked to Henry before returning to me.

"A few." Celeste hesitated before continuing, "Our survival depends on our ability to stay hidden. That's why no one in the Empire knows about our existence."

My brows knitted as my eyes searched hers.

"White Witches could help us fight the Dark ones—" I started.

"We tried that during the Red War," Celeste interjected. "We lost and got nearly eradicated," she said.

Her tone told me to drop the subject, so I did, shaking my head as I lowered my gaze to my teacup. Even if the White Witches didn't want to help us fight the Dark ones, humanity still had hope. Just because my blood didn't activate the Tear didn't mean the amulet didn't work.

"Do you know how to activate the Tear?" I lifted my hopeful gaze to Celeste.

"I always thought it was Josephine's bloodline that would activate it. We all did," she said, and my heart dropped.

"My blood didn't work," I said, my voice hollow.

I couldn't help but feel like I'd let everyone down.

"That's what the Lord said." Celeste glanced at Henry. "Did your mother leave any clues about the Tear? I assume she was the one who finished it."

"I think she did, too. The only other clue I have is…she wrote "power of three" on the note about the amulet." Henry's head swung to me, but I ignored his questioning look. "Do you know what it could mean?"

Celeste pondered what I'd told her for a few minutes until she shook her head and said with a heavy sigh, "I'd think it meant the power of three generations of White Witches."

"That's what I thought as well," I admitted, hanging my head. I lifted it as a thought occurred to me. "What if I need to tap into my magic to activate it? If I am a descendant of a White Witch, I should have magical powers, right?"

Celeste studied me for a moment as if looking for signs of magic in my features before she replied, "Yes, you have the magic in your blood. It is possible that you need to bring it forth before your blood can activate the Tear."

"Perhaps examining the amulet could help answer that question," Henry said nonchalantly, pulling the Tear from his pant pocket.

I stared at the Lord with wide eyes.

"How did you get it?" I asked in disbelief.

"I snatched it from the Dark Witch before she fled the temple," he said, handing me the amulet. "Take it. It belongs to you."

I stared at him in awe. He'd broken into the witches' temple, saved my life, and managed to retrieve the Tear in the process.

"Thank you," I breathed, trying to convey with my eyes the gratitude I felt.

"You're welcome," Henry replied with a small smile.

"Would you like to examine the amulet?" I asked Celeste, turning back to her.

When she nodded, I handed her the Tear. She placed it in her palm and covered it with her other hand, closing her eyes in concentration. I took a sip of my cooling tea to relieve the sudden dryness in my throat. A few minutes passed before Celeste opened her eyes and looked between Henry and me.

"He doesn't know, does he?" she asked.

I flinched at her words. Somehow, I immediately knew what she meant.

"No," I replied, feeling Henry's stare boring into me. I refused to meet his gaze.

"You need to tell him," Celeste said, surprising me.

"Why?" I asked, my eyebrows slamming down. She needed to give me a good reason to reveal to Henry that the Tear could also kill vampires.

"I have a feeling he needs to know," the witch replied.

"You have a feeling?" I gave her a dubious look.

Celeste shrugged. "As White Witches, we have a strong connection to the world around us. Sometimes, the world whispers things to us, and we choose to listen."

26

My heart was in my throat as I turned to Henry. He was looking at me with a wary expression. Suddenly, I wanted to be anywhere else but here, doing anything else but this. How was I supposed to tell him the truth after everything he'd done for me?

"The Tear doesn't just kill the Dark Witches," I started, the words difficult to get out. Henry's face fell, and I could tell he knew where this was going. "My mother wrote it could destroy all supernatural beings," I finished, my heart sinking to the bottom of my stomach.

The next breath I took went nowhere as I waited for Henry to say something, *anything*. He didn't for a long time.

"You lied to me," he finally said, barely above a whisper.

My eyes pricked with tears as pressure tightened my chest. Henry closed his eyes and rubbed his forehead, a look of utter disappointment on his face.

"I thought that you wouldn't want to help me look for the amulet if you knew the truth," I explained.

Henry opened his eyes and looked at me. It was hard to hold his gaze.

"I understand why you did it," he said, but I didn't feel relief at his words because I knew there was more. "Tell me, if you can find a way to activate the amulet, do you still plan to wipe out vampires along with the Dark Witches?"

I opened my mouth, then clamped it shut. I didn't want to lie to him again.

"I'm sorry," I whispered.

I was beginning to believe he didn't have to die, but I didn't know how the Tear worked. I doubted I would be able to choose who died and who didn't.

Henry chuckled low, shaking his head as if he couldn't believe this was happening. Then, he focused on Celeste.

"What about the White Witches? If the Tear is meant to defeat all supernatural forces, how do you know you'll survive?"

My heart sank—I hadn't thought about that. To rid this world of evil, I might have to give up my own life in the process.

"I doubt Celine would have created an amulet that would require her to forfeit her own life to defeat her enemy," Celeste said. "On the other hand, such powerful magic rarely comes without a price."

I suppressed a shudder. My ancestors had paid their share. My great-grandmother had sacrificed herself to save her daughter's life. My grandmother had ended her life to protect the Tear from the Dark Witches. And my mother had died in the arms of a vampire. Now, it was my turn to sacrifice. I didn't know yet in what way, but a feeling of foreboding invaded my chest.

"Can you cast a spell over the amulet that will show you how it works?" Henry asked Celeste.

"Not exactly," the witch replied, drawing my attention to her. She then looked down at the Tear in her hand as if contemplating something. "There is a spell I can use that will show us the amulet's memories."

"Its...memories?" I asked, frowning in confusion.

"Yes. Each object has memories, so the amulet does as well. I should be able to go as far back as the day its creation was completed."

Henry and I exchanged a look. That could shed some light on my mother's death.

"Do it," I said low.

Celeste nodded and clasped the Tear with both hands. Closing her eyes again, she began to chant, and my skin prickled with goosebumps. Her chanting reminded me of what my mother had done in my dream. The witch chanted for several minutes while Henry and I watched her in silence. Tension rolled off the Lord in waves as a myriad of unspoken things hung in the air between us.

Celeste stopped chanting abruptly, and my breath caught. Her eyes were moving under the eyelids, and I wondered if she was seeing the amulet's memories she'd spoken about. When she opened her eyes, her features softened as she looked at me.

"Would you like to see?" she asked me.

Surprisingly, I hesitated. I'd always thought I'd give anything to see what really happened in the last few hours leading up to my mother's death. Now, I wasn't sure I wanted to know. I didn't want to tarnish my memories of my mother with what I might see.

"Will I see my mother's death?" I asked, bracing myself.

"No," Celeste replied. "The amulet wasn't with your mother when she died."

Henry and I had suspected as much. It must have been with Vincent.

"Okay," I said, taking a steadying breath. "I'm ready."

In the end, I had to know what had truly happened on the night of my mother's death. Too many things were shrouded in shadows of the unknown. I was ready to shed some light on them, to reveal more pieces of the puzzle that was my legacy.

Celeste nodded and lowered the hand holding the amulet to rest on the table between us.

"Give me your hand," she said. When I reached out, she took my hand and covered the amulet with it. "Close your eyes."

The moment I did as she'd instructed, images appeared in my mind, similar to a dream, and I watched them play out in my head. A soft gasp left me when I saw my mother's face. She was alive and seeing her like this filled my heart with deep sorrow but also with glowing warmth. Tears threatened as I watched her work on the amulet, hunched over the desk in her study. She was wearing a long floral dress, which told me I was seeing the night of her death. She was chanting a spell over the amulet, and after the last few words left her lips, she smiled softly, releasing a shuddering breath. Scooping the Tear off the desk, she stared at it in awe, her eyes wide in disbelief. A white glow pulsed three times in the pale-blue crystal in the heart of the amulet before fading away.

"I did it," my mother murmured. "I can't believe I did it."

A startled laugh burst from me. I could feel her elation at finishing the amulet as if it were my own. Hope and pride swelled in my chest just as they did in my mother's when she realized what she'd accomplished. Suddenly, her smile fell, and her head snapped up to the window above the desk. She quickly stood up and drew the curtains, blocking out the late evening light coming from outside. With trembling hands, she hung the amulet around her neck, hiding it under the collar of her dress, and left the study and then the house altogether.

I had a feeling I knew where she was headed as I watched her hurry through the streets of New Haven. The night had descended by the time she arrived at the Duval Estate. A servant I didn't recognize opened the front door and let her in. She strode through the foyer in the direction of Henry's study. Back then, it had been Vincent's study, I realized when she rattled her knuckles on the door and walked in.

"I did it," my mother whispered, quickly closing the door with a soft click. "It's complete."

She drew up short when she turned around and saw Vincent wasn't alone. Stern stood by his desk, a dark and malevolent presence.

"Eloise," he purred, his pitch-black, fathomless gaze roaming over every inch of her body.

All color drained from my mother's face.

"I'll come back later," she said, turning to leave.

"No." Vincent stopped her, his voice rich and deep. "Stern was just leaving." He gave the Lord a pointed look, letting him know it was a demand, not a request.

"You and your favorite pet are up to something," Stern drawled, looking between Vincent and my mother.

"She is not a pet," Vincent said through his teeth, his tone icy and cold. "Get out," he ordered Stern. "But remember what we discussed. The Selection is in two days, and you will *not* choose another child."

"We'll see." Stern shrugged. "My region, my rules," he added nonchalantly.

"The rules are the same for everybody," Vincent bit out.

"Then, perhaps it's time we changed the rules," Stern said, a maniacal gleam in his eyes.

"You are a psychopath," Vincent said, a look of disgust on his face.

"And you are delusional if you think everyone is content to live like this. We rule this world, Vincent. It's time we started acting like it."

In the blink of an eye, he was right in front of my mother, his face mottling in a mockery of a smile, revealing his deadly sharp fangs.

"Eloise," he purred my mother's name again before sweeping out of the room.

"He's such a monster," my mother said, visibly shaken-up.

"That he is," Vincent said, approaching her in a few long strides. "Is it truly complete?" he whispered.

The portraits I'd seen of Vincent did not do him justice. He was stunningly beautiful, with flawless, chiseled features and piercing amber eyes.

My mother nodded and pulled the amulet out from under the collar of her dress. She then took it off from around her neck before handing it to Vincent.

His slender fingers folded around the Tear, and he stared at it in shock for a moment before lifting his captivating gaze to my mother's.

"I need you to hold on to it," she said low. "I will talk to Thomas and Sophie tonight and explain everything," she paused, swallowing thickly. "We will activate it soon."

Vincent stared at her for a few moments in silence.

"There is no rush," he finally said softly.

"Yes, there is," my mother answered shakily.

"Eloise—"

"Don't...It has to be done. It's the only way." Fear and determination shone in my mother's eyes. Was she scared the Tear wouldn't work? Why did Vincent seem hesitant? Was it because she was going to destroy all supernatural beings, including vampires and White Witches?

"Okay." The Lord nodded. "Henry is away in Fairview, but he should be back before the Selection. I would like to speak with him and Isabelle before we do anything."

"I understand," my mother said. "Vincent, about the Selection...Madam St. Clair is sending Sophie..."

"Say no more. She will not be chosen."

"Thank you." My mother pressed his arm in a gesture of appreciation.

"Be careful," Vincent told her, his eyes searching her face. "I can't believe you did it," he added with a short burst of laughter.

My mother smiled, genuine and warm, and my heart squeezed. I remembered what it had been like to be on the receiving end of those smiles. It had always felt like being kissed by the sun.

"I can't believe that soon we will be able to defeat the Dark Witches and give the humans their world back," my mother said, her eyes glimmering with tears.

Vincent seemed to be at a loss for words as he looked down at the amulet again and shook his head in disbelief.

"I will see you soon," he told my mother, his own smile bright and sincere.

"Goodbye for now, my friend," my mother said before she slipped out the door, leaving the amulet with Vincent.

"I always knew you could do it," he whispered fondly, staring at the door for a few seconds after it had closed behind my mother.

He chuckled and wiped a few tears from his eyes before turning away from the door.

The setup of the study was almost identical to how Henry had it, but instead of Vincent's portrait on the wall covering the safe, it was Henry's striking features.

Vincent walked over to the portrait, stopping before it.

"I can't wait to tell you," he murmured, staring at it. I could see the love for his son shining through on his handsome face. "You will be so happy. Your heart has always been in the right place, and I am so proud of you," he added, getting choked up.

My heart cracked open, and deep sorrow spilled out, filling my chest. Henry had never gotten to hear those words because my father and I had lied about what had truly happened to my mother.

Vincent cleared his throat and took the portrait off the hooks, placing it on the floor, resting against the wall. He then proceeded to open the safe, using Henry's birth date as the combination. The Lord placed the Tear in the safe, and his gaze lingered on it for a moment before he closed the door, plunging the world around the amulet into darkness.

The next time the safe door opened, it was Stern's face on the other side. His black eyes darted around the secret compartment until his gaze landed on the amulet, and his brows knitted. He grabbed the Tear and closed the safe with a faint thud. The amulet was in Stern's pocket all the way to his estate as the vampire crossed the distance between New Haven and Santoria with supernatural speed.

Once he was at the mansion, he descended to his underground lair and took the Tear out of his pocket. Standing in the middle of the cavernous room, bathed in the flickering light of the dozens of candles, he just stared at the amulet for a few minutes as if trying to figure out what he was looking at. With a smirk, he lifted his eyes from the Tear and moved to the shelf of skulls that would forever be etched in my mind.

"I don't know how you were able to resist the compulsion, but I will find out what this amulet is," Stern said to one of the skulls —a gleaming white one that looked fresh.

I breathed through the nausea as bile rose up in my throat. Somehow, I managed not to faint or vomit as I realized the skull was my mother's. My heart was a heavy stone in the pit of my stomach as I watched Stern root around his lair until he found a medium-sized chest. He dropped the amulet inside it and shut the lid. The next time the lid opened, it was Henry reaching for the Tear. Knowing what happened next, I opened my eyes and took my hand off the amulet. Tears were rolling down my cheeks, and I quickly wiped them away.

The amulet's memories hadn't showed what had happened to my mother, but it wasn't difficult to fill in the blanks. My mother had gone home, where she'd waited for my father and me. Perhaps she'd sensed she was in danger. Celeste had said the world whispered things to the White Witches sometimes. Perhaps the world had whispered to my mother that something was coming.

I imagined her finding a blank sheet of paper on her desk and drawing a sketch of the Tear. She'd then found a pen and written: *Josephine's Tear is an amulet that can destroy the supernatural.* Maybe she'd heard a noise then and gotten spooked. She'd hurriedly scribbled *Vincent Duval* and *power of three* on the paper and hid it beneath the floorboard just before Stern had shown up. He'd tried to interrogate her, but she'd been able to resist his compulsion just as I had done when Henry had tried to compel me. Stern had bitten her then, intending to frighten her, but got carried away as he had with Rory. He'd ended up killing my mother. My father and I had lied and said Dark Witches took her, and Vincent had gone to the Black Forest to try and save her. After he'd left, Stern snuck onto the Duval Estate, broken into Vincent's safe, and stolen the Tear.

I inhaled deeply, finding my center before releasing a shuddering breath.

"You need to see this." I glanced at Henry, who was watching me, his expression unreadable.

"Here." Celeste dropped the amulet into the palm of my hand. "Show him."

"Me?" I frowned in confusion.

"Yes. The spell I have cast is still in effect and will draw on the magic inside you," she explained.

Hesitantly, I turned to Henry, extending my hand to him. His jaw was hard as he eyed the amulet in my palm. I wondered if he was as unsure about looking into the past as I had been.

"Trust me," I said and immediately regretted it. "Not the best choice of words," I admitted, as he gave me a look that said, "You think?"

"You won't regret it. I promise," I tried to reassure him.

Another moment passed before he let out a rough exhale, giving in. His large hand swallowed mine as he closed his eyes, his brows pinched in concentration. I knew he started seeing the memories when his brows lifted before slamming back down again. While he watched the memories, I watched him, my gaze gliding over his face bathed in the soft glow of the oil lamp. His features were not as refined as Vincent's, but he was still beautiful. I'd never truly let myself acknowledge that before, too blinded by my hatred for his kind. The planes and angles of his face were near perfect, and I had to fight the urge to reach up and trace the high and wide cheekbones and the firm square jaw with my fingertips. I knew when Henry was seeing the last of the memories because his expression became pained, and his throat bobbed as he swallowed thickly. Tears glistened in his eyes when he opened them, looking at me from beneath the thick black lashes.

"Thank you for showing me," he said, his voice hoarse with emotion.

I nodded, placing my other hand on top of his resting on the amulet. His gaze softened as he stared at me, and I momentarily got lost in the deep blue of his eyes.

I snapped back to reality when Celeste sucked in a sharp breath, bracing her hands on the kitchen table. Dropping Henry's hand, I turned to the witch. The Lord did the same, briefly flexing the hand I'd just held.

"What's wrong?" I asked Celeste.

Her cerulean eyes seemed to glow as she tilted her head as if listening to her surroundings. I wondered if the world was whispering to her, and if so, what was it saying?

"You need to leave," she finally said, and Henry and I exchanged a glance.

"Leave?" I asked, confused. "We need to figure out how to activate the amulet."

"There is no time. You can leave the Tear here with me if you want, and I will work on it, but you two need to return to New Haven and prepare."

"Prepare for what?" Henry asked.

"War," Celeste replied, and my heart sank.

27

"*W*ar?" I asked as disbelief surged through me.

"Yes," Celeste replied, rising to her feet. "Dark Witches have been growing stronger over the last hundred years, and now that they know you don't have a way to activate the amulet, they are going to attack."

"When?" Henry asked, his voice steady despite the gravity of the situation. In one fluid motion, he rose from the table. I scrambled to my feet as well.

"I do not know for certain." Celeste shook her head. "But you need to leave to prepare."

"Will the White Witches help us fight?" I asked, hopeful.

Celeste pursed her lips.

"I cannot answer that," she said in a clipped tone. "I will need to speak with the others."

I looked down at the Tear in my hand. I didn't want to part with it, but the White Witches had a better chance at figuring out how to activate it than I did.

"Here. Take it." I handed the amulet to Celeste. "See if you can find a way to activate it."

"I will see what I can do," she said, taking the amulet and

hanging it around her neck. My fingers curled into a fist as my hand suddenly felt empty without the Tear. "You can take your horse to travel back," Celeste said, looking at me.

"My horse?" My brows shot up in surprise. "Annabelle survived the Black Forest?" My gaze darted to Henry, and he nodded, one side of his mouth turning up.

"Yes. She is out back. Follow me." Celeste grabbed the oil lamp off the kitchen table and walked through the house, illuminating the way as she went.

Henry and I followed her outside, where Annabelle grazed a few feet away from the house.

"Hey, girl," I said in greeting, rubbing Annabelle's nose. She nudged my hand, and I brushed the side of her neck with a low chuckle. "It's good to see you, too." I couldn't believe she was alive and unharmed.

"We will have to ride together," Henry said, snapping my attention to him.

I froze in place as the Lord came up to Annabelle and checked the saddle. My heart skipped over itself with a mix of conflicting emotions.

"Is that going to be a problem?" Henry asked, looking at me. I thought his mouth twitched barely before he schooled his features.

"No," I assured him, but my gaze dropped to his mouth, and I was momentarily distracted, remembering how his lips had felt on mine.

"Here's some bread and cheese," Celeste said as she approached.

I shook my head to clear my thoughts as Henry packed the food in one of the saddlebags.

"If you find a way to activate the Tear," I said, turning to Celeste.

"I will find a way to let you know," she assured me, clasping her hands in front of her.

My gaze lingered on the amulet on her chest. My mother's creation. I'd always felt like I was a part of something bigger, and now I knew what it was. I was part White Witch and wanted to do something with my legacy.

"When this is all over, I want to learn more about the magic in my blood." I looked at Celeste expectantly.

She nodded. "Survive the war, and I will teach you," she said calmly, as if surviving the war was not an impossible task.

Perhaps she had more faith in me than I currently did in myself. I wasn't going to give up prematurely, of course. I would fight against the Dark Witches. I would fight for my life and for the lives of others, but I wasn't a fool. I knew what we were up against. Celeste did, too. She hadn't said "win the war" because that wouldn't be up to me or any other human. Prevailing in the war was the clans' task. The humans just had to survive.

"Thank you for everything," I told the witch, and she nodded again. "I hope you join our fight," I added, looking into her luminous blue eyes that seemed to glow in the dark.

"I cannot make that decision on my own," she said, her tone final. "Remember, don't tell anyone that the White Witches still exist," she added, looking between Henry and me.

"We won't," Henry assured her, coming to stand beside me. "Thank you for your help."

"You're welcome. Be safe." Without another word, Celeste turned and walked back into the house.

"Ready?" Henry asked, and I folded my arms around myself, suddenly feeling nervous.

"Yes," I said with determination I didn't feel. We had bigger problems than me and my conflicting emotions when it came to the Lord.

Henry helped me mount the horse and then settled in the saddle behind me. Little space separated our bodies, and I sat up straight, trying to avoid touching him as we left the witch's cottage and started our track toward New Haven.

"Will we need to find shelter at sunrise?" I asked Henry, trying desperately to ignore his cool presence at my back.

"No. We are actually not that far from New Haven. We should make it back to the estate before dawn."

A breath of relief left me. I wanted to get back as soon as possible so I could warn my father and the Order about the impending war. Perhaps I could convince my father to go up north, as far away from the border as possible. Anxiety surfaced and swelled. If Celeste was right and the Dark Witches were going to attack, there would be so many casualties. So many people would die all because I'd failed to accomplish the one thing I'd thought I was destined to do. I'd failed to activate the amulet.

"Are you doing okay?" Henry asked, his cool breath dancing over my cheek.

Somehow, when I'd been lost in thought, I'd ended up closer to him, my back nearly pressing into his hard chest and my hips cradled by his thighs. I cleared my throat and sat up straighter, moving away from him.

"I'm okay," I lied and gritted my teeth. I really didn't want to lie to Henry anymore or to myself. "I'm not okay. I feel like I failed," I confessed, my words a soft whisper.

"You didn't fail," Henry said, leaning down to speak to me.

"It was supposed to be my blood that activated the amulet, and it didn't work," I rasped, my vision blurry with tears.

"You don't know for sure it was supposed to be your blood," Henry pointed out.

"It only makes sense that it was. My grandmother had started creating the Tear. My mother finished it. It was my destiny to activate it, and I failed because there is something wrong with me." I wasn't sure where the words were coming from, but I couldn't stop them from spilling into the darkness around us.

"There is nothing wrong with you," Henry said vehemently, curling his arm around my waist and shifting closer to peer at my face. I refused to meet his gaze, staring straight ahead. His other arm slid down to my hip, and I drew in a shallow breath, feeling his cool touch through my clothes. "We will find another way to activate it," he said low.

I could feel him staring at me intently. I half-turned my head and glanced at him.

"And what if we don't?"

"Then I will fight." He didn't hesitate. "Like I did in the Red War."

"I will fight, too," I said, and Henry's lips pressed into a firm, unyielding line.

"No, you will not. When we get back, I want you to travel up north, as far away from the border as possible."

I whipped my head to face him fully then, twisting at the waist. He was closer than I'd expected, and my breath caught before I forced myself to focus.

"What?! You can't possibly expect me to do that!" I exclaimed, my voice ringing out in the night air.

"You know you can't fight alongside me," he tried to reason with me.

His tone wasn't condescending. He was simply stating a fact, and I hated it. I hated that I was so weak because I was human. It was deeply unfair that the fate of my people was in the hands of supernatural creatures. Our lives were not our own, and it went against my every instinct. I wanted to be in control of my life and my destiny. Suddenly, a solution presented itself, but I squelched it immediately. The thought I'd just had rendered me shocked and speechless as I felt all color drain from my face. Knots of dread formed in my stomach as I faced forward, my breath coming in short, rapid breaths.

"What is it?" Henry asked softly.

I could still feel his gaze on me.

"Do you think we can win?" I whispered, refusing to acknowledge what I was really thinking.

Henry averted his gaze, looking straight ahead. He was silent for several long minutes, which told me everything I needed to know. I appreciated that he didn't lie to me even though anxiety resurfaced, speeding up my heartbeat. I began trembling as trepidation washed over me. It felt as if when I'd failed to activate the Tear, a countdown had begun. A countdown to our inevitable demise. Henry's arm around my waist tightened as if he could feel my unease.

"I do not know the answer to that," he finally said. "The clans will fight like we did in the Red War. I hope we can prevail and save as many lives as we can."

*Prevail and save as many lives as we can...*the words stuck with me, sinking into my heart. I should be a part of that battle. I should fight for my future and the future of my people. I knew of a way I could join the fight even if I wasn't ready to accept it yet.

28

My mind was made up by the time we reached New Haven. I'd spent the hours of our trek contemplating my life, everything that I was, and what I'd failed to be—my people's liberator. Perhaps I could be their protector instead.

I could feel the sunrise in the air by the time we reached the mansion. My legs were numb and a little sore from riding for so long. When we arrived at the stables, Henry dismounted first and reached for me to help me down. I swung one leg over the saddle and let him lower me to the ground as if I weighed nothing. His hands lingered on my waist as our gazes locked and held. My cheeks flushed as I remembered how his hands had roamed my body on the bed at the witch's cottage. Henry's nostrils flared, and his eyes darkened as he held me, his fingers flexing on my waist. I didn't realize I'd leaned in until Henry dipped his chin, bringing his face closer to mine. His gaze was fastened on my lips, and I dropped mine to his well-formed mouth.

"You're back," came Isabelle's voice to our left.

She stood several feet away from us, undoubtedly having gotten here from the house so fast using her supernatural speed.

Startled, I pulled away, looking anywhere but at Henry.

Reluctantly, he let go of me and turned to his sister.

"You need to get inside," Isabelle told him. "It is nearly sunrise."

Henry nodded and led Annabelle inside the stables, where he passed her to the stable hand. I peeked inside the stables, too, and a sigh of relief left me when I saw Onyx in there, alive and well.

"Thank you for helping Henry rescue me," I told Isabelle as the three of us started toward the house.

"I only helped him because I thought your blood would activate the amulet," she explained without looking at me. "I wanted to leave you for dead once I heard the Dark Witch say it didn't work."

"Isabelle!" Henry threw over his shoulder, walking a little ahead of us.

"What? It is the truth." She shrugged.

Henry gave me an apologetic look before facing forward. I wondered if he'd, too, only come for me because he'd thought he needed me to activate the Tear. It didn't matter, I decided. Even after he'd learned that my blood didn't work, he'd still saved me.

"Henry told me about Wren," Isabelle said, glancing at me. "I should have suspected something. He was a perfect vassal. Too perfect." Her brown eyes narrowed.

I realized I had forgotten about Wren. Now, I found myself wondering if he'd survived the wound I had inflicted. I wasn't sure if I wanted him to live or die. I could never excuse his decision to work for the Dark Witches just to save his own skin, but I did feel sorry for him.

When Henry entered the house and crossed the foyer, heading toward his study, Isabelle and I followed.

The Lord poured himself a drink and quickly threw it back before turning to us.

"We need to have an urgent meeting with the clan leaders," he told Isabelle.

She eyed the heavy crimson curtains that were already drawn in preparation for daybreak.

"I don't have time to round them up before sunrise, but I will after sunset," she said, her gaze returning to Henry. "Do you want to tell me what's going on?"

Henry's eyes flicked to me, and he swallowed thickly before he said, "War is coming."

Isabelle staggered back, her hands curling into fists at her sides.

"Dark Witches?" she asked.

"Yes," Henry replied, his tone grave. "They will attack now that they know we don't have a way to activate the amulet. I don't know when, but we need to start preparing."

"They had a century to grow stronger," Isabelle said. "Henry, what if this time we—"

"Isabelle," Henry interrupted. His tone was gentle but firm. "Drink some blood from the cellar and try to get some rest. We will talk at sunset."

He hadn't lied and said it would be okay, and I admired his honesty even if despair threatened to take root inside my chest and spread.

I expected Isabelle to argue, but to my surprise, she nodded.

"Okay. I'll round up the clan leaders at sundown," she said and swept out of the room.

Once she was gone, Henry focused on me.

"You need to go to Waylon and ask him and the Order to help prepare the people of New Haven to travel up north," he said, meeting my gaze.

When I didn't move, he gave me a questioning look.

"Sophie?" he asked, coming to stand before me, his eyes searching mine.

I opened my mouth, but the words wouldn't come. I needed to say them, though. I'd already accepted my fate. No, I'd *chosen* my fate, and now I needed to follow through and make it happen.

"I want you to turn me," I forced the words out. They scorched my throat and broke my heart.

Henry took a step back as his eyes widened in shock.

"What?" he said so low I could barely hear him.

Emotion clogged my throat, and I cleared it before I said louder, "I want you to turn me."

Henry shook his head and chuckled without humor. "I knew you were too quiet on the ride here." His expression grew serious when he looked at me again. "You are not thinking clearly. I know you're scared—"

"I'm terrified," I interjected, my voice rising almost to a shout. "Of war and Dark Witches, but most of all, I'm terrified of not being able to do anything about it."

"You *will* be doing something about it." Henry's voice rose to match mine. "You will be taking the people up north where they will be safe."

"Safe?" I scoffed. "They will no longer be safe if New Haven falls."

Henry clenched his jaw, his eyes boring into mine. He couldn't tell me New Haven wouldn't fall. He knew he couldn't promise me that.

"I want to join the fight," I told him, my voice steady and my tone final.

"You don't know what you're asking for," he growled, turning away from me.

I grabbed his arm to stop him. "It's my choice."

His face contorted in rage. "It's my choice, too. And I choose not to grant your request."

With a gasp, I backed away as if he'd delivered a physical blow. Then, anger crowded out the shock.

"How dare you?" I seethed, my hands fisting in his shirt as I brought my face inches away from his. "You told me before that the choice was taken away from you. And now you're doing the same thing to me!"

Henry bristled as his expression turned pained.

"Do not make me do it," he begged low.

His reaction doused the anger, and I let go of his shirt.

"I want you to be the one to do it," I said, looking into his eyes. "I…trust you."

He grimaced at my words. "I wanted your trust. But now I wish I didn't have it."

"I *will* fight alongside you in the war, whether I am a vampire or not," I stated. "It's up to you whether or not you'll give me a fighting chance."

"You are not being fair," he said, sounding tired and defeated.

"I don't care about being fair. I only care about protecting my people," I said calmly.

"And I am trying to protect you!" Henry raised his voice again as if that would make me hear reason. He looked exasperated, running a hand through his thick hair.

"I'm sorry," I whispered. I truly was. I didn't want to force him to turn me, but I also saw no other way.

He stared past me for a moment as if he couldn't bear looking at me.

"Sophie," he finally said, clasping my shoulders and looking into my eyes. I met his gaze, preparing for what he was about to say. He was going to try to make me change my mind. I could see the intent in his blue eyes. "I know you think you failed because your blood didn't activate the Tear, but that doesn't mean you have to forfeit your life and become something you hate."

His words made me flinch.

"You're right. I do hate vampires," I told him, seeing no reason to lie. "But I love my people more."

Understanding crept across Henry's face, quickly followed by a glimpse of awe in his eyes. He hung his head, taking a deep breath. I thought he'd finally given up on trying to convince me to change my mind until he looked at me again.

"Before you make your decision, go talk to your father," he

said, and my throat instantly dried and closed up. Now, he wasn't being fair. The resolve I saw in his features told me I wouldn't be able to fight him on this. So, I conceded.

"I will go see him right now."

There was no reason to delay the inevitable, and if Henry thought that seeing my father would make me change my mind, he was sorely mistaken.

29

"Sophie?" my father said when he opened the door.

His face lit up when he saw me, and I heard his rough exhale as he scanned me from head to toe. He was relieved I was alive and well, but the feeling wouldn't last long because of what I'd come here to tell him.

"We need to talk," I said, cringing at my unusually cold tone toward him.

The truth was, I didn't want to be here, and I didn't want to drag this out. Henry had known exactly what he was doing when he'd told me to talk to my father. His plan wouldn't work, though. I wasn't going to change my mind.

"Okay…" My father's expression turned guarded in the early morning light. "Come in." He opened the door wider.

I was immediately overcome with emotion when I stepped inside my childhood home. This place had been my safe haven for nineteen years. Even after my mother's death, it was still my sanctuary. This house was where I'd been born, had taken my first steps, and had become the person I was today. Soon, I would become someone different. Some*thing* different.

Would I still be me? I hoped I would retain the values that

my parents had instilled in me. If I didn't, then it would all be for nothing. I hoped I didn't lose my humanity when I turned. Henry hadn't lost his. That was why I wanted him to turn me. I needed him to be my guiding light through the transformation, to remind me of my purpose and not let me succumb to the darkness that becoming a vampire would bring with it.

"Is everything alright?" my father asked, watching me with wary eyes.

I realized I stood unmoving, lost in thought, in the middle of the small living room.

"Yes," I told him, but my voice shook. "It will be," I assured him. "Father, war is coming."

He didn't say anything as he paled, grabbing the nearby chair for support. The rickety piece of furniture groaned under the pressure of how hard his fingers dug into the wood.

"Dark Witches know about the Tear," I began, looking at my father's weathered face. "They've known about it all along. Henry and I found it, but then I was snatched with the amulet and brought to the witches' stronghold in the Black Forest. They tried to activate the Tear with my blood. Their plan was to use it to kill the vampire clans…"

My father's face was becoming more ashen by the second. He looked as if he were going to be sick. I knew he was shocked to hear about what had happened to me, but I wished he would pull himself together. I couldn't handle him being emotional right now. I'd turned my own emotions off before I got here. I knew that was the only way to get through this.

"Why did they think your blood would activate the Tear?" my father asked, his voice hoarse and his brows pinched in confusion.

There was no way to prepare him for what would come next. Just like there was no way to prepare him for what I would have to tell him before I left here today.

"Because Mother came from a line of White Witches," I told him and waited.

His mouth opened in shock as his eyes grew distant. I wondered if the years of his life with my mother were replaying in his head. Hints at who she truly was had always been there. We'd missed them because we hadn't been looking.

"But my blood didn't work," I continued. I needed to get this over with as quickly as possible. Being in this house and seeing my father was already affecting me, pulling at my heart. "But now that the Dark Witches know we don't have a way to activate the amulet, they're going to attack."

"When?" my father asked, shuddering with trepidation.

"I don't know when," I told him. "But I need you to prepare to travel up north."

"And you?" he asked low.

I thought he already knew the answer because shadows crept into his face. Impossible sadness filled his eyes as he stared at me —his only daughter and the only family he had left.

"I will stay and fight," I told him, making sure my voice didn't waver.

"Then I will stay and fight with you," he said, defiantly lifting his chin.

I stared at him in shock. My father was not a fighter. I'd used to think I'd inherited that part of me from my mother, but perhaps it was from both of them. Perhaps he'd never embraced that part of him because he'd wanted to keep me safe. Now, it was my turn to keep *him* safe.

"No. I need you as far away from the border as possible."

"Sophie—" he protested, scowling.

"I have a plan," I interrupted.

He stilled, listening.

Silence ensued. I couldn't bring myself to say the words as if saying them would make what would happen more real. What if I didn't say them? It would be so easy to head up north with my father, leaving the fight to Henry and the vampire clans. But fleeing was not in my blood. My mother hadn't left the fate of the people in someone else's hands. She'd used the magic in her blood to create the Tear. The magic in my blood wasn't enough to activate it, but I could still do my part by joining the fight.

"I've asked Henry to turn me."

The words rang out in the otherwise quiet house. They had sounded louder, somehow, as if I'd shouted them.

My father looked like he'd stopped breathing. Slowly, he lowered himself into the chair he'd used for support and released a shuddering breath.

He propped his elbows on his knees and leaned forward, burying his face in his hands. He sat unmoving for a few minutes without making a sound. When he finally pulled his hands away and lifted his head up, his eyes were glistening with tears.

"There is no talking about it, is there?" he rasped, looking at me.

His reaction brought tears to my eyes. He knew me well enough to know I'd made my decision. He didn't demand I change my mind or take the choice away from me by forcing me to leave with him. He trusted me, and I couldn't have asked for anything more.

"I've made my decision," I told him. "I will become a vampire and help the clans fight the Dark Witches."

My father rose to his feet then and approached me. He pulled me into a tight embrace, holding me for what felt like hours. I was falling apart on the inside, squeezing my eyes shut to stop the tears from falling. A few escaped anyway as I held onto my father, letting this moment sink into my heart so I could pull from it later when I needed something to remind me of who I was. All too soon, my father pulled away and wiped the tears from his face.

"When?" was all he asked.

"As soon as possible. Henry will be holding a meeting with the clan leaders after sunset..." I paused, realizing there was something else I needed to tell him. "Father...I know who killed her."

He didn't say anything for a few minutes, his eyes searching mine. He didn't look relieved to learn that I'd found my mother's killer. I wondered if it didn't really matter to him anymore. Not in light of everything I'd just revealed and everything that was to come.

It still mattered to me, though. Now, even more so because Stern hadn't just taken my mother's life. Rory had died at his hands and countless others because he was the one who'd been turning people into Ravagers.

"What are you going to do about it?" my father finally asked.

I didn't hesitate before I replied, "I'm going to make him pay."

After I left my childhood home, I stopped by Waylon's place and told him about the impending war. I didn't tell him about what I'd asked Henry to do. Emotionally drained from telling my father, I didn't have it in me to go through that again.

When I returned to the Duval Estate, a strange feeling washed over me as I walked into the foyer of the mansion. My mind flashed back to the night of the Selection, which now seemed like ages ago. I'd been so hopeful then that I would find the Tear. Little had I known that finding it would not bring about our salvation but instead lead to our possible demise. My heart was heavy as I trudged to my room, where I undressed and took a shower, washing away the past two days, wishing I could wash away the feeling of failure that clung to my skin. Soon, I would have a chance to make it right, to redeem myself after not being able to do the one thing that I'd been born to do.

Sleep eluded me for hours as I lay in the dark room, thinking back on my life, trying to figure out where I'd gone wrong.

There is nothing wrong with you, Henry had said to me, but I couldn't stop thinking that there was. Otherwise, I would have figured out a way to activate the amulet.

My brows pinched as I stared up at the ceiling. White Witches listened to the world around them, and sometimes it whispered things. What if I listened and paid attention? Would the world around me whisper and reveal a way to activate the Tear?

Willing my mind to quiet, I let my breathing slow as I lay there, listening. Nothing happened for several long minutes, and I almost gave up, feeling foolish, when I heard them. Hushed voices, hundreds of them at once. The sound was faint, coming and going, amplifying at times and going nearly silent at others. The voices were all around me, and I could feel them almost like a physical touch brushing against my skin.

"Or I'm losing my mind," I grumbled, trying to discern what the voices were saying.

It was a cacophony of sounds, and I couldn't make anything out. I wondered if it took years of practice or if I needed help from the other White Witches to be able to tune into the world around me. With a heavy sigh, I gave up on trying to figure out what the voices were saying, and they died out the second I stopped concentrating. Frustrated, I threw the covers off me and got out of bed.

I grabbed my robe and left the room, unsure of where I was going. I roamed the quiet house for a while without a destination in mind, alone with my frantic thoughts, until I found myself in front of Henry's bedroom door.

Tightening the sash of the robe on my waist, I knocked and waited. A moment later, the Lord opened the door. He didn't look tired like a human would, but I could tell he hadn't gotten any sleep. He didn't look surprised to see me, though, and let me in without saying a word.

Slowly, I walked in, closing the door behind me with a soft click. When I turned around, I found Henry on top of the covers on his bed, propped up against the pillows. A glass half-full of blood sat on the bedside table, and the Lord took a sip out of it before setting it back down. My gaze focused on the red liquid, and I had to try hard to suppress a shudder at the thought that soon, that would be my sustenance.

When Henry looked at me expectantly, I tore my gaze away from the glass and crossed the room before awkwardly perching on the side of the bed close to where he was sitting. He was barefoot and wore casual black pants and a wrinkled white shirt that exposed a part of his chest. He appeared relaxed, but I knew he was anything but, as his hard gaze fastened on mine.

"Did you speak with your father?" he asked, his features bathed in the soft, warm glow of the bedside lamp.

His tone was measured but guarded, as if he were preparing to be either relieved or disappointed by my response. He watched me intently.

"Yes," I said, and Henry's jaw tightened.

"And?" he prompted, looking wary.

"He knows what I've asked you to do," was all I said.

My face must have betrayed that I hadn't changed my mind because Henry exclaimed, "And he's okay with it?!"

"He knows it's my choice, and he accepts it," I said calmly, refusing to let my emotions rise to the surface to mirror the Lord's.

Henry made a frustrated sound as he dragged his fingers through his hair, looking away and to the side.

"So, please," I breathed. "I need you to accept it, too."

I didn't realize I had reached up to touch his chest until my fingers brushed the cool skin where his shirt parted.

My hushed tone forced Henry's gaze back to mine. Moving faster than my eyes could track, he clasped the back of my neck, sitting up straight in the bed and bringing our faces inches apart.

"Or I could compel you," he whispered harshly. "Make you go up north with your father."

Fear flared in my chest at his threat, but the feeling dimmed just as quickly as it had appeared.

"You wouldn't do that to me," I said, bringing my other hand to rest on the taut muscles of the arm that held me.

Seconds turned into minutes as we sat there, unmoving, staring at each other. I knew I'd won when Henry's eyes shuttered, and he gave me a look full of anguish. He covered my hand on his chest with his own and rested his forehead against mine.

"I have done some terrible things in my life," he said, swallowing thickly. "But turning you, by far, will be the worst."

A shuddering breath left me as I had the urge to comfort him. I wished I could end his suffering by telling him he didn't have to do it. But I couldn't. I had to go through with it.

"I know what I am asking of you is a lot," I whispered. "I wish it didn't have to be this way." Letting go of my neck, he pulled away and looked at me. His jaw clenched as if he wanted to argue but didn't. "Thank you for respecting my decision," I added.

I wanted him to say something to alleviate this pressure in my chest, but he didn't. Instead, he pried my hand from his chest and lowered it to rest on the bed between us. My heart shattered as his expression hardened. He looked like he wanted me to leave, but I wasn't ready to go just yet.

"How does it work?" I asked, clasping my hands in my lap to conceal their trembling. "What will you have to do to turn me?"

Henry bristled at my question and didn't speak for a very long time.

"I will have to bring you to the brink of death," he finally said, looking anywhere else in the room but at me. My heart thumped heavily in my chest. "I will have to drain you until only a few drops of your blood remain in your body and then give you my blood. Lots of it."

He looked at me then, and his eyes were pleading.

Don't make me do it, his expression said even though he didn't utter a single word.

My heart was a bruised, battered mess at this point because of what I was asking him to do, but I didn't acknowledge the look he was giving me. I just sat there, quietly waiting for him to continue.

"When your transformation is complete, you will not be yourself at first," he said, swallowing thickly. "Too lost in the frenzy of bloodlust, much like a Ravager. Without proper training and guidance—"

"You will be there to guide me," I interjected.

"Still, there might not be enough time before the Dark Witches attack to get you ready to fight them," he explained.

"Then we need to do it soon…tonight."

"Tonight?!" His eyes widened in panic.

I didn't feel panic, though, only resolve. Still, my legs were shaky as I rose from the bed and headed for the door.

"Tonight," I said firmly and left Henry's bedroom.

30

Sunset arrived too soon and not soon enough. I'd tried to get some sleep—I'd given it my best effort—but in the end, I had been unable to quiet my racing thoughts. So, I washed my face and got dressed in a thin, sleeveless gown that hugged my lithe form. The dress was the color of champagne and parted on my right thigh, granting easy access to the dagger I'd strapped there. The gown was a statement. The clan leaders would soon arrive at the estate, and I didn't want to cover myself up in their presence. I wanted to look confident—to show them that I could be one of them.

I will *be one of them,* I thought, staring at myself in the vanity mirror.

My chest constricted as anxiety threatened to swell. I quickly tamped it down. My mind was made up. Dwelling on what was to come served no purpose.

A soft knock sounded on my door, and I was grateful for it because it pulled me from my thoughts. Henry walked in a moment later and froze mid-step, his eyes shamelessly roaming over my body. When I arched a brow, he cleared his throat, averting his gaze. Suppressing a smile tugging at my lips, I quickly dragged the brush through my hair, deciding to leave it down.

"The clan leaders will be here soon. I assumed you would want to come to the meeting, and seeing how you are already dressed and ready, my assumption was correct," Henry said.

"Yes, I want to be there," I told him, my fingers brushing the outline of the dagger.

"I also need to get the clans' permission to turn you," Henry said, his voice almost breaking on the last part.

"Right." I swallowed thickly.

"Sophie—" the Lord started.

"Let's go then," I cut him off, hooking my arm around his. I would not have another discussion about him turning me. I couldn't.

"You look nice," Henry murmured as we left my room and strolled down the long hallway.

A strange flutter stirred in my chest at his words. Things felt different between us now, ever since what had happened at the witch's cottage.

"Thank you," I replied, staring straight ahead as we entered the foyer on the way to the study.

Henry stopped suddenly, his brows pinching, as his gaze flicked to the front door. A second later, a knock sounded, echoing in the large, open space.

Henry's eyes darted to me as he said, "Someone is here to see you," just as Ezra entered the foyer and hurried to the front door. He promptly opened it, revealing Waylon on the other side.

My brows lifted in surprise as Waylon walked in, halting abruptly when he noticed Henry and me.

"Lord Duval." He gave a curt nod. "I'd like to speak with Sophie," he said in a clipped tone, sounding agitated.

"It is up to Sophie if she will speak with you," Henry replied, his voice laced with ice.

Frowning at his tone toward Waylon, I said, "I will speak with him. I'll see you in the study."

Henry's jaw tightened, but he didn't say anything else as he nodded and walked off.

"Follow me," I told Waylon, turning back toward the hallway leading to my room.

He didn't look at me as we walked, tension rolling off him in waves.

"So, this is where you've been staying," he said, taking a sweeping glance around my bedroom once we were inside.

"Yes," I replied. "What are you doing here?" I asked without further ado.

I suspected I knew the reason why he was here and wanted to get through this as quickly as possible.

"Your father told me about what you were planning to do," Waylon said, confirming my suspicion. "Or, rather, what you were planning to have done *to* you," he bit out, anger flashing in his eyes.

I gritted my teeth. "It's my choice."

"And it's the wrong one!" Waylon shouted, startling me.

I'd always known he had a rough side to him, but I'd never seen it directed at me before.

"My father accepted my decision, and that's all that matters to me," I declared, and Waylon bristled at my words.

I hated hurting him, but what I'd said was the truth. Waylon was a friend, and I cared about him, but in the end, it didn't matter what he thought.

"You hate vampires," he seethed, rage mottling his features. "And now you're willing to become one of them?"

"I'll still be me." The words tumbled out of my mouth before I could stop them.

I didn't know if I would still be myself. Henry had said I wouldn't be at first, but I hoped I would find a way back to what made me who I was and quickly so I could help him fight the witches.

"You don't know that!" Waylon snapped.

"You're right, I don't," I conceded. "But I do know that I have to do this. I have to try to save my people."

Waylon's face fell as he stared at me. It was clear his anger had deflated.

"Why is it your task to save everyone?" he asked quietly.

"Because it's my destiny," I said without hesitation.

I knew it was the truth. I could feel it in my heart. Perhaps I did have a connection to the world around me because of my White Witch blood. Maybe that was why I had this knowledge deep inside me that I was meant to do it—to make that sacrifice.

Waylon's eyes glistened as he dragged a hand down his face.

"I will never accept this," he said, exhaling roughly.

"I can live with that," I proclaimed, surprised to find my voice steady.

Waylon looked at me as if he didn't know me, and perhaps he didn't, not truly.

"You should leave," I threw over my shoulder as I left the room.

The six clan leaders were already gathered in Henry's study when I walked in.

"What is *she* doing here?" Moreau hissed as I strode deeper into the crowded room.

All the vampires were standing, and their tension and unease saturated the air, letting me know Henry had already told them about the impending war.

"She has a reason for being here," Henry said as I came to stand by his side.

"And what might that reason be?" Stern challenged, standing a few feet away to my left.

"I'm sure we will find out soon enough," Camilla interjected from my right. "One thing I don't understand," she said, looking at Henry. "Why would the Dark Witches attack now?"

Henry looked at me, and I met his deep blue gaze. He side-glanced at Stern before his eyes returned to me. There was a silent question in them, and I gave a slight nod, letting him know I was prepared for what would happen next.

"They bided their time because they thought we had a means to destroy them," Henry explained, turning back to Camilla.

A murmur swept through the room at his words. I saw Stern grow incredibly still, and all my muscles tensed as I watched him.

"My mother created an amulet that could destroy the Dark Witches," I said, not taking my eyes away from Stern. I was talking to him as I said, "I know what you did."

"You little bitch," he snarled, lunging at me.

A heartbeat later, his eyes froze in shock as I thrust my dagger into his chest, piercing the heart. The room faded to black as I stared into the twin pools of darkness, seeing my own reflection. I also saw my mother, Rory, and countless others who'd died at Stern's hands or at the hands of his minions. Stern opened his mouth as if to say something, but the only sound that came out was a low hiss as his features became sunken, his flesh drying out on his bones. Another second, and he was gone, caving into himself. The moment was over quickly, and I was glad for it because I realized that no amount of suffering I could have inflicted on Stern would bring back my mother or Rory. I didn't revel in his death like I'd thought I would, though I did feel relief that I'd rid the world of such evil. My hand trembled slightly as I lowered the dagger and sheathed it at my thigh.

"What have you done?!" Moreau exclaimed, baring his fangs.

Henry growled next to me and moved to block me from the Lord of the West, but I stopped him with a hand on his arm.

"Stern killed my mother," I said, looking around the room at the remaining five clan leaders. "And he was the one turning people into rampant vampires terrorizing the cities at night."

"It's true," Henry chimed in. "He had tunnels under his estate that the turned used to move between the regions."

Another murmur swept through the room.

"Are the turned still on the loose?" Camilla asked.

"No." Henry shook his head. "I think I killed them all."

With his voice deeply sad and his eyes haunted, he didn't sound proud of the fact. What he'd done weighed heavily on him, and I had to fight the urge to reach for him to offer a comforting touch.

"I think we can all agree that Stern deserved to die," Camilla said casually, looking around the room. "But couldn't it have waited until after the war?" Her gaze landed on me. "Now, it is one less of us to fight the Dark Witches."

When Henry stiffened next to me, I glanced at him, but he didn't meet my gaze.

"I will take his place," I said, and all the heads in the room swung to Henry.

Tension bracketed the corners of his mouth as he said, his voice rough, "I will turn her," he paused, looking at the clan leaders, "with your permission."

Camilla chuckled low. "Such a Duval thing to do—to follow the rules despite everything." She gave me an assessing look. "You will have to get her acclimated fast if we want her to join our ranks in the war."

"I am aware," Henry said calmly. "And I am willing to do it."

He did look at me then, and I gave him an appreciative smile. He didn't smile back, but his eyes softened just a fraction.

"I vote yes," Camilla said, her voice ringing out in the study.

"I vote no," Moreau spit out. "I don't trust her. I don't want to have to watch my back if she is turned."

Henry smirked bitterly. "You will have to watch your back even if she is not turned. I know you and Stern were close and that you agreed with his line of thinking on how the Empire should be run. Don't think I have forgotten."

Moreau's eyes widened in shock, and he took a step back as if trying to put more distance between himself and the Lord. Excitement sparked in my veins as I glanced at Henry. He could be quite intimidating when he wanted to be. Trying to hide the look of admiration on my face, I squared my shoulders and waited for the rest of the clan leaders to vote.

"I know she will be a new vampire, but having one more in our midst could make a difference," said one of the clan leaders—a tall and slim female with a golden-brown complexion and wide-set, amber eyes. "So, I vote yes."

The two remaining clan leaders—a petite female with creamy skin and copper locks and an older male with silver hair—nodded in agreement and voted yes as well.

My breath caught as the realization sank in that now my fate had officially been sealed.

Moreau scoffed, throwing his hands up in the air with frustration, but the rest ignored his outburst.

"Everyone should send their humans to my domain in the North," Camilla said, looking at the other vampires. "When will you turn her?" she asked, her ice blue eyes on Henry.

"Tonight," the Lord replied, his voice strained.

Camilla's gaze flicked to me as a strange smile touched her lips.

"We'll leave you to it, then," she said, her voice deep and smoky.

"We'll be in touch," the golden-eyed vampire said before sweeping from the room with supernatural speed.

The others bid their farewell as well before leaving the study in the same manner.

Silence stretched between Henry and me as we both seemed lost in our thoughts for a few minutes.

Snapping out of it before my emotions could rise and sweep me under, I turned to the Lord and said, "I'm ready."

31

Henry reluctantly met my gaze, releasing a shuddering breath. He nodded, and I followed him out of the study and to his bedroom upstairs.

My limbs began to tremble the closer we got to his room, and I had to grit my teeth and will my legs to move to put one foot in front of the other to make it all the way to his bedroom door. When we walked in, Henry whirled on me.

"We should wait," he said vehemently, and I scowled. "Sunrise is in a few hours," he explained.

"And?" I asked, confused, not sure why we had to wait.

"Don't you want to watch it?" he whispered. "Your last sunrise?"

My skin chilled as my heart squeezed in my chest. I didn't think Henry was trying to get me to change my mind again. There was tenderness in his eyes and something akin to regret in his voice. I wondered if he wished he'd gotten a chance to watch his last sunrise before he'd been turned. Then I wondered if it would've been better not to know what was coming. Because knowing it was my last sunrise made the moment poignant and heart-wrenching.

Still, I nodded, wanting to go with what the Lord had suggested, hoping it would make him feel more at ease. I knew I was asking so much of Henry. I hadn't been fair when I'd asked him not to take the choice away from me because I was taking away *his* choice by making him turn me. But he seemed to have accepted my decision, and I felt grateful beyond words. I wondered if I would ever be able to express the gratitude I felt.

Neither of us spoke as we sat in his dimly lit room, waiting for dawn. Strangely enough, there was no fear in my heart. I felt myself go numb as I sat close to Henry, his presence grounding me somehow. I trusted him, and I trusted myself. I believed in my decision and hoped that it would all work out in the end. But if it didn't…

"I need you to promise me something." I looked at Henry sitting by my side on the floor.

Our backs were propped against the side of his bed, our shoulders touching.

The look he gave me was tortured. I knew I was already asking so much of him, but there was one more thing I needed him to do. I swallowed the lump in my throat and forced the words out before fear took over, silencing me.

"When I turn," I said, and Henry grew incredibly still. "If you can't bring me back to my humanity, I need you to kill me."

I didn't need to explain my request. He knew by now I wouldn't forgive myself if I hurt innocent people.

Henry's already pale face became leached of all color.

Heavy silence stretched. Henry stared at me with what almost looked like hatred in his eyes. I wondered if he was cursing the night I'd walked into his life.

"I cannot promise you that," he finally said, his voice thick. "But I can promise you one thing. I will pull you out of bloodlust or die trying. I will not give up on you."

All words left me as I sat there, overcome with emotion.

Someone who I'd thought a monster was willing to go to such extremes for me.

"Why would you do that?" I whispered.

"Because Vincent didn't give up on me," he said, averting his gaze. "And if I was worthy of saving, then so are you."

My heart burst with gratitude to Vincent. He'd lost his life because of the lie I'd told. Even dead, he was still inadvertently saving my life because of the legacy he'd left behind.

A few hours later, Henry pulled open the curtains, revealing the night sky outside.

He stepped to the side and leaned against the wall next to the window, watching me as I rose to my feet and walked closer. I swallowed thickly as the night receded, and the sun crested the horizon, the first rays spilling over the sprawling estate, casting it in a soft pink glow. My eyes watered at the beauty as I imagined the sunlight slowly crawling up the walls of my childhood home and the streets of New Haven.

Feeling Henry's gaze on me, I turned my head to look at him.

He stared at me intently, his lips slightly parted, and I wondered if he was trying to live vicariously through me at that moment. I turned back to the window.

My last sunrise. The last time I got to watch the world light up with the colors of a new day and feel the sun on my face. Soon, I would be like Henry, forever hiding in shadows.

A tear rolled down my cheek at the thought, and Henry's hand twitched at his side as if he wanted to reach for me. He couldn't, of course, not when I stood before the window, bathed in the early morning light.

"You're crying," he rasped, his eyes searching my face. "You don't want to do this."

I smiled softly as I looked at him.

"I am willing to give up all my sunrises to give my people a chance."

Sadness was mixed with awe as he studied my features.

"I know," he said. "I just wish you didn't have to give up anything at all."

I wished the same thing, but wishing wouldn't make it so.

Pulling the curtains closed, I turned to Henry. His gaze was fastened on mine as I took off the locket holding the portrait of my mother and set it on the bedside table. With a rough exhale, he loosened the collar of his black shirt and ran a hand through his hair, disheveling it in the process.

"Lay down," he said low, and my breath caught when the blue in his eyes began to recede, overtaken by black.

I turned around and lowered myself on top of the covers.

Slowly, Henry approached and sat down on the edge of the bed, close to where I was lying. Leaning over, he gently brushed my hair away from the right side of my neck, his touch eliciting a shiver from me. His eyes were almost entirely black when he met my gaze again. He didn't say I still had time to change my mind, and I was grateful for that. He did hesitate, though, looking into my eyes as if trying to convince me not to do it without actually compelling me. I stared back at him, my breath surprisingly even as I waited. If he needed another moment to come to terms with what he was about to do, I could give it to him even if every second was torture.

It felt like I was standing on a precipice, one foot hanging over the abyss of uncertainty that was my future. I was ready to take the plunge, feeling like my next breath would not come until I went through with it. Finally, Henry's lashes lowered, and his lips parted, revealing the hints of his fangs. Another shiver rolled through me as my breathing sped up along with my heart. Anxiety surfaced, but with it was a hint of excitement; a feeling I tried not to dwell on as I released a measured breath.

"Do it," I whispered.

I expected Henry to strike fast, but instead, he lowered his head to my neck painstakingly slowly. My pulse quickened as his mouth hovered over my throat, his breath cooling my suddenly flushed skin. Holding myself still, waiting for the bite, went against my every instinct, but I didn't move, didn't breathe until a startled gasp left me when his cool lips brushed my neck. It was the only warning I got before he bit me, sinking his fangs deep into where my pulse hummed just below the surface of my skin. A spike of pain shot through me, and I jerked, but the discomfort was fleeting.

Henry began drinking from me, each draw of his mouth on my neck making me sink more into the mattress. My limbs began to relax, becoming heavy with liquid heat that warmed my blood and coursed through me, settling between my thighs. Bolts of pleasure darted through me, making my body arch off the bed. Henry's left arm encircled my waist as his right hand threaded through my hair. His hold on me tightened as he brought me flush with him, drinking as if he were starved. The contact sent shivers through me as I clung to him, finding myself willing to give him everything he wanted and more. He could have it all— my blood, my body—I didn't care as pleasure built until I was lost in what I was feeling.

It could have been hours or minutes, I wasn't sure, but suddenly, pleasure gave way to pain when the burn in my blood turned from warm to icy cold. Panic flared in my chest as my body began to ache and not in the pleasant way I'd been experiencing until now. Henry was taking too much—I could feel it. I was losing too much blood and, with it, everything that I was. My essence was seeping out of my body, leaving behind an empty shell. I couldn't let that happen.

Gritting my teeth, I tried to push Henry off me, but I was weak, and his hold on me was strong. In the back of my hazy mind, I knew this was supposed to be happening. Henry had told me he'd have to bring me to the brink of death, almost drain me entirely of my blood, but laying here and not fighting it was nearly impossible. I began to wonder if Henry was in control and if he would stop before he killed me. I hoped he wasn't lost in the frenzy of bloodlust and would stop before he took everything until there was not a drop of my blood left.

I trusted him, I reminded myself as I lay there powerless and completely at his mercy, feeling my heartbeat slowing in my chest. Teetering on the edge of oblivion, I felt his draws on my neck slow as I heard a soft "I'm sorry" in my ear before I tasted blood in my mouth, warm and thick. It coursed down my throat as I finally succumbed to darkness…in more ways than one.

32

When my eyes fluttered open, I was lying on soft grass, looking up at the starry night sky.

How did I end up outside?

The pain was gone, but so was everything else. I didn't feel anything as I lay there, empty. I was like a void waiting to be filled, but with what, I wasn't sure.

Suddenly, the world around me came alive, bright, and overwhelming, enveloping me in sounds, smells, and sensations overpowering with their intensity. Millions of blades of grass tickled my oversensitive skin, and my ears picked up hundreds of sounds. A light breeze stirred the individual strands of my hair that seemed to tingle, brushing my bare shoulders. Scents surrounded me with the most tantalizing one teasing me from somewhere up close.

"Sophie?" came Henry's deep voice from my left.

When I turned my head, I found him lying beside me. The silvery glow from the stars above poured over his near-perfect features, and I'd never seen anything so beautiful. He was stunning, and suddenly, I didn't feel empty anymore as intense lust rolled through me. I wanted him, and I was going to take what I wanted. In the blink of an eye, I was on top of him, having moved faster than I ever had before. My dress rode up as I straddled him, ripping his shirt before dragging my fingers down his bare chest.

"Sophie..." he warned in a strained voice.

I didn't heed his warning as my hands glided over his body, tracing the defined lines of his stomach to his hips and then lower still until I freed him from his pants. A harsh groan left him, and his body jerked when my fingers brushed the thick hardness. His head fell back against the grass as I tightened my grip before drawing my hand up and down his length. The rush of power I felt at being in control was thrilling. I reveled in it, in awe of how much my touch affected him as his large body shook underneath me. I wanted to keep touching him, but I was *starved* for him. Eyes drifting halfway closed, I lifted my hips and lowered myself on him, feeling him easing through my wetness...

I came to with a sharp gasp, my chest rising and falling rapidly as my eyes flew open, darting around the room. I found Henry's deep-blue gaze almost immediately, and my breathing evened out as I stared at him.

Just a dream, I thought as my racing heart and pulse began to slow.

I wasn't outside under the stars. I was still in Henry's bedroom, in his bed, and he was sitting in the chair, watching me, his eyes haunted.

"How are you feeling?" he asked low, and there was so much sorrow in his voice.

He was slumped in the chair, looking dejected as if he'd done something terrible. His dark hair was disheveled, tumbling across his forehead as tension bracketed the corners of his mouth.

"Thirsty," I breathed, my throat so parched it felt like I'd swallowed knives.

My entire body felt dry and achy, as if I were missing something essential, something I needed to survive. There was a gnawing, painful hollowness inside me.

Henry pulled out a bag of blood from the small ice chest sitting by the chair, and the moment my gaze latched on to it, I bared my fangs with a hiss.

My fangs? Lifting a shaking hand to my mouth, I ran my fingertips over the sharp points and winced. My fangs ached, too. They *throbbed* as the overwhelming urge to sink them into something rose, riding me hard.

"Here," Henry said quietly, coming to sit on the edge of the bed and handing me the bag.

I immediately ripped it open, pouring its contents into my mouth. The blood spilled down my chest, running down my chin as I took a few generous gulps. It helped to soothe my dry throat, but the relief was fleeting, and, with a snarl, I tossed the half-empty bag to the side, splashing the bed and the floor with crimson. That was not what I needed. It was blood, yes, but it was cold and stale. I needed warm, fresh blood. I would do *anything* for it.

"I need…" I whimpered, unsure how to put this primal urge inside me into words.

"I know," Henry said gently, and his eyes softened as he looked at me.

When he bared his fangs, lifting his wrist to his mouth, I stopped him with a hand on his arm.

"I need…" I tried again, my words rough and guttural.

I needed to be the one to bite him, to sink my fangs into his wrist, breaking the skin and spilling the blood.

Understanding washed over Henry's features, and with a small nod, he brought his wrist to my lips. Our gazes locked, and a heartbeat later, my fangs pierced his skin. My eyes fluttered closed as a low, rumbling sound came from deep within my throat. Nothing had ever felt so good, so right. Clutching his wrist with my hands, I closed my mouth over the wounds my fangs had created and drew in some of his blood, moaning as it hit my tongue. I shuddered at the sweet taste as instinct took over, urging me to take long, hungry pulls, filling myself with the rich, lush essence.

My body was coming alive with each deep draw as liquid fire rushed through my veins, making me hunger for more than just blood. Desire surged, overriding everything else as a wave of intense arousal rolled through me. My eyes snapped open, meeting Henry's deep-blue gaze. His pupils were expanding as he stared at me, and his lips parted on a sharp inhale when I pressed his wrist more fully to my mouth. Still drinking greedily, I planted one hand on his chest and pushed with shocking strength until his back hit the mattress.

"Sophie," he rasped, tensing as I climbed on top of him.

Straddling him, I tilted my hips until I felt him hard against my core. A raw moan escaped me, muffled by his wrist.

"Sophie," he said roughly. "You need to stop."

Stop? I wasn't going to stop. I was going to take what I wanted, just like I had in my dream.

I rolled my hips against him, and we both groaned as his hardness pressed into my softness.

"That's enough," Henry growled, his hand fisting in my hair.

He went to pull me away from his wrist, but I held on tight, refusing to give up the blood. He pulled harder, and with a snarl, I let go, but I wasn't finished with him yet.

Sitting up, I ripped open his shirt, dragging my fingers down his chest, much like I had in my dream. My breath caught when I reached the hardness straining through his pants.

"Don't," Henry grunted, catching my wrists. "Please. You are not yourself," he begged.

He *begged*, and that did something to me. Even through the lust-infused haze of my mind, I suddenly knew what I was doing was wrong. He didn't want this, and I was forcing myself on him. Terrified, I scrambled off him, throwing myself to the other end of the bed. I wasn't trying to get away from him, but from the feral version of myself that had just been on top of him, thinking she could just take what she wanted. A sorrowful, whimpering sound escaped me as I looked down at myself. I was covered in blood, and my nails had elongated into sharp, pointed claws.

"I'm a monster," I rasped, bringing my trembling hands up to clasp my head.

Henry hesitated for only a moment before he swiftly sat up, moving closer to me on the bed. He gathered me in his lap, cradling me against his chest, which didn't feel cool to my touch anymore.

"It's okay," he whispered as a ragged sob escaped me. "I've got you."

At first, there was pain—the kind that made you wish you were dead. It flared in the pit of my stomach before spreading like wildfire to the rest of my body, saturating my every pore through the ends of my hair and to the tips of my fingers and toes. Then, came the hunger. Or maybe the hunger was first. I wasn't sure as I lay there in the pool of darkness. It enveloped me in velvet blackness, lapping at my skin until it rose enough to swallow me whole, submerging me in the waters of unending thirst.

"You know what you need to do to make it stop," the darkness whispered. "Give in."

*Give in...*I couldn't give in, not yet. There was something important I needed to do. It niggled in the back of my mind, but I couldn't focus on anything else besides the roar of hunger in my ears.

I smelled it then. Blood. It was the most tantalizing scent, and my heart sped up in my chest. The blood smelled divine, but it was mixed with something else, fresh and woodsy. I felt my brows knit, the muscles of my face stiff and difficult to manipulate, as I tried to open my eyes. I needed to wake up so I could find the source of the alluring scent. My eyelids felt heavy as I slowly pried my lashes apart. My nostrils flared, and I twisted my head to the source of the smell, immediately zeroing in on it. On him. A man sat in the chair next to where I lay. He looked tired, rubbing his eyes with a heavy sigh. His hand stilled on his face before he lowered it slowly, his deep-blue gaze locking on mine.

"Sophie?" he asked in a deep voice that sent a ripple of shivers through me.

Sophie? The name sounded familiar, and I tried to focus on it to figure out what it meant, but I couldn't concentrate long enough as a painful wave of hunger rolled through me.

A groan left me as my muscles spasmed, arching me off the bed. Everything hurt, bringing tears to my eyes. I'd never known pain like this. I would give anything to make it stop. Panting, I focused on the man in the chair, who looked concerned but also wary. My vision sharpened on him, dropping to his neck, where I could see his pulse thrumming just below the surface of his skin.

I didn't know I'd moved until the man's eyes widened, and I realized I was crouched on the bed, my legs tucked under me, my dress pooling around me.

The man leaned forward, gripping the arms of the chair, but before he could rise to his feet, I shot off the bed, launching myself at him. He was fast, catching my wrists and slamming me back down on the mattress.

"Sophie," he rasped, getting in my face.

That name again. I didn't know what it meant. All I knew was hunger as it stretched my skin over my flesh and bones, threatening to tear me apart. My lips peeled back, and I bared my fangs before snapping at the man's throat, trying to get to the blood. He backed away but didn't let go of my wrists. I pushed up, trying to throw him off me. He grunted but didn't budge. Several minutes passed as I thrashed under him until finally giving up.

"It hurts," I whispered, my voice sounding foreign to my ears.

The man's eyes softened.

"I know," he said low. "I will give you some blood. It's in the chest by the chair, but I need you to lay still and don't move, okay?"

I nodded, swallowing thickly.

The man eyed me warily as he slowly pulled away. I didn't move a muscle as I lay there, waiting for him to release me. The moment he let go of my wrists, I bolted upright, my mouth stretching wide as I went for his throat.

The man cursed, clasping my head. He swiftly twisted my neck, and a loud crack echoed before everything went dark.

The sound of my name pulled me from the darkness. I was on my back, and Henry was hovering over me, staring down at me, his brows pinched. His features were taut as his eyes searched mine.

"Sophie?" he whispered.

I swallowed and realized his hand was pressing on my throat. Slowly, I brought my hands up and wrapped them around his wrist, pulling on it gently. He alleviated the pressure but didn't let go of me completely.

"Do you know who you are and what you're doing here? Do you remember why I turned you?" he asked.

Turn me? So, he was the one responsible for the sinister hunger, for turning me into *this*.

A low growl rumbled from deep within my throat as my nails elongated into claws, digging into Henry's wrist. His grip on my throat tightened.

"Calm down," he said in a warning tone.

It was in my best interest to comply, I realized, as a pang of hunger ripped through me. I needed to feed, and he could give me what I needed.

My eyes locked on his, I forced my muscles to relax as my claws retracted, and I let go of his wrist.

"Good," he said low, visibly impressed by my display of control. "I will let go of your throat and get the blood from the cooler," he paused as if to let what he'd just said sink in. "Don't. Move," he added, enunciating each word.

When I nodded, he let go of my throat but didn't move his hand away, letting it hover above my neck in case I decided to lash out. Several seconds later, when I didn't, he pulled away and rose from the bed.

Turning away from me, he walked to the chest, bending down to retrieve a bag of blood. The moment I saw the red liquid, the hunger seized me, and my body moved of its own accord. In an instant, I was crouched on the bed, my fangs bared. Henry tensed with his back still to me before slowly turning around.

"Do you remember what happened last time?" he asked, and I winced at the phantom pain in my neck—he'd broken it when I'd tried to bite him. "I will give you this blood," he said, holding up the bag in one hand. "But you have to behave." His eyes were soft as he whispered, "Please, I don't want to have to hurt you again."

Hurt me? I won't let him hurt me, I will hurt him, I thought as my body jerked.

I leaned forward as if pulled by an invisible string toward him. The desire to rip out his throat, spilling the blood, overwhelmed me, terrifying in its intensity.

You're a monster, the thought flashed through my mind.

With a snarl, I backed away, scrambling off the bed and tucking myself in the other corner of the room. Tears glided down my cheeks as I slid to the floor, curling into a ball. I couldn't live with myself, with what I had become, but I couldn't run away from it, either. This was my new reality. I felt utterly alone, trapped in this body that didn't feel like my own, with darkness whispering things in my head.

Suddenly, I was scooped up and pulled to Henry's hard chest.

He held me close, one hand on my knees and the other one stroking my hair.

I focused on the beating of his heart as sobs racked me for what felt like forever until they eventually slowed down.

"Here," Henry whispered, opening the bag of blood and bringing it to my lips.

It didn't smell as pleasant as the blood flowing through his veins, but it was blood nonetheless, so I closed my mouth around the opening and took a few gulps. A sigh of contentment left me as I drank, my eyes drifting closed. Suddenly, they snapped open and darted to the bedroom door as the darkness reared its head.

Escape, it whispered. *You can escape him and this room and find humans to sink your fangs into.*

As if he knew what I was thinking, Henry tensed next to me, his hand clasping the back of my neck.

"Don't even think about it," he said roughly, following my gaze to the door. "Please," he whispered against my temple, "I need you to fight the bloodlust."

Tears blurred my vision as I dragged my gaze from the door and turned to him.

"Help me," I begged, my voice hoarse.

I'd never felt this weak in my life. The darkness inside me was winning; I could feel it. I couldn't stop it from spreading, eating up my insides until it filled my heart.

A rough exhale left Henry as his hold on the back of my neck relaxed. He cupped my cheek with his other hand as a soft smile touched his lips.

"Let me tell you a story," he said, "about a girl who was so brave she chose to become something she loathed for a chance to save her people."

33

I rapped my knuckles on the weathered-wood surface and waited. My father's face was drawn and guarded when he opened the door to let me in. Two weeks had passed since I'd been turned. It had taken my father nearly all that time to be able to look me in the eye. Deep sorrow and regret were still etched into his wrinkled features every time he looked at me, but it was getting better. I wondered if every time he saw me, he felt like he had failed. I'd tried to comfort him once before by telling him the failure was not his but my own. I was the one who carried magic in my blood and hadn't been able to use it to activate the amulet. Still, I knew what I'd chosen to become weighed heavily on him. I understood his struggle and wished I could take away his suffering, but I couldn't. It would take time. My only hope was that we would get more time together to overcome that chasm that had opened up between us when I'd turned.

Tonight was the first time Henry had let me go visit my father without him by my side. He'd been too worried I'd succumb to bloodlust in the presence of my father without him there to stop me. He knew I would never forgive myself if I hurt him.

"I trust you to go by yourself," the Lord had told me earlier. "You have been doing extremely well. You are in control."

I felt in control—of my bloodlust and of my destiny. I finally felt like my life was my own. I felt stronger than I ever had before, both physically and mentally. It had taken me three days to overcome the bloodlust. It had sunk its claws into me when I'd first turned, but I had fought my way out, dragging myself from the abyss of endless hunger that had threatened to strip me of my humanity. The hunger was still there, of course, as it always would be for the rest of my life, but it was more manageable now, not as all-consuming as it had been at first.

Henry had been with me every step of the way, never leaving my side in the past two weeks. He'd been with me through it all. On the first night, that seemed endless as hunger lashed at my insides, making me feel like I was dying. And on the second night, when I'd begun gaining control over my insatiable thirst. My humanity had sparked back to life in tiny bursts of light, slowly banishing the shadows of bloodlust. Henry had noticed those faint glimpses and latched on to them, coaxing them out and making them burn brighter. He'd held me in his arms, stroking my hair as he talked to me about my past, my parents, and who I was, until the darkness of bloodlust had receded enough for me to gain purchase on my new reality.

By the third day, the pangs of unforgiving hunger had gone from tidal waves that crashed into me, sweeping me under, to a low, steady current of thirst in my blood. It had felt like I'd been able to take my first breath on that day as the red-hued shadows clouding my mind had lifted, and I felt more like myself again.

Henry was thoroughly impressed it had taken me only three days even though to me, it had felt like years. He'd told me it had taken him weeks to gain control when Vincent had turned him. Henry believed that I'd been able to find my way back to myself so quickly because I was part White Witch, but I knew that wasn't the only reason. I owed most of it to him—he was the one who'd pulled me out of the thick, deep-crimson darkness of bloodlust.

Potent emotions swelled in my chest every time I thought about what Henry had done for me. I was forever grateful to him. Forever…I tried not to dwell on the fact that I would live for a very long time if my life didn't get cut short in the upcoming war. I also tried not to imagine what it would be like decades later when everyone I knew was gone. When I did inadvertently picture those days, I wondered if Henry would still be by my side. More often than not, I found myself wishing he would be.

"Are you ready?" I asked my father, forcing myself out of my reverie.

"I think so." He sighed, looking around the dark, empty house.

He'd stayed in New Haven way longer than I'd wanted him to, helping everyone else gather their belongings to head up north. He was leaving tonight, though, so the pressure on my chest would alleviate just a fraction because he would be far away from the border when the Dark Witches attacked.

"I hope this house still stands when I come back," he said low, his voice hoarse.

"I hope so, too," I told him.

I loved my childhood home even though I knew I could never live here again. I'd changed too much; everything had. I belonged at the Duval Estate now or somewhere in the wild like other predators, but not here, where phantom images of me as a little girl still roamed the small and dated rooms.

"Waylon decided to stay and fight," my father informed me, and I nodded.

I hadn't expected anything else from him. I hadn't seen Waylon since the night I'd been turned, and I preferred it that way. Just like I didn't belong in this house, I didn't belong with him.

"What do you think they are waiting for?" my father asked, referring to the Dark Witches. "Why haven't they attacked yet?"

"Henry thinks they might still be trying to find a way to activate the Tear to wipe out the vampire clans."

"But they no longer have the Tear, right?" my father asked, even though he already knew the answer. I'd told him before that the White Witches had it.

"They don't," I reassured him. "We are not sure why the Dark Witches haven't attacked, and it doesn't matter. All that matters is that we will be prepared when they do. Which means you need to leave. Are you ready?"

When he nodded, I reached for his bags sitting by the door on the other side of the threshold. I lifted them as if they weighed nothing and loaded them onto the horse waiting patiently by the house, bathed in the bright, silvery light. The moon was full tonight, and I was glad for it—it would illuminate my father's path as he journeyed out of New Haven. When my father locked the front door and approached his steed, I reached for him to help him into the saddle, but he waved me away.

"I am not helpless," he grumbled, and I stifled a laugh. He wasn't helpless, I knew that. I was just exceptionally strong now and always felt the need to use that strength to help others.

My father turned away from me and put his hands on the saddle to hoist himself up. He stopped and spun back around, pulling me into a tight embrace. I stiffened in his arms, knowing that the coolness of my skin was seeping through his clothes, but he held onto me, and eventually, I relaxed, hugging him back. My heart squeezed as emotion clogged my throat. He'd accepted my decision to turn into a vampire before, but now it felt like he was accepting *me*, the new me that I'd become.

Tears glistened in his eyes as he pulled away and mounted his horse.

"You truly are magnificent," he told me, looking at me from atop his saddle. "You have vampire strength, but your heart is still human, and there is magic in your blood. You can do such great things in this world. I just hope to live long enough to see it."

Speechless, I stared at him. He *would* live long enough to see it. I would do anything in my power to make it happen or die trying.

"Goodbye, Father," I told him, my voice strained. "I love you."

"Goodbye, Sophie. I love you, too," he said and turned his horse to head up north.

Something my father had said stayed with me, nagging in the back of my mind as I quickly returned to the mansion.

"What if…" I murmured, walking into the house and heading straight for Henry's study.

When I strolled in, a dagger whooshed, embedding itself in the doorframe not far from my head. A big smile broke across my face—Henry was training. He'd been training nearly every night in preparation for war, and most of the time, I'd joined him. I needed to hone my new supernatural abilities, and I liked training with Henry because it was fun and thrilling, especially after the first few times when he'd figured out he didn't need to go easy on me.

"Can I join you?" I asked, walking deeper into the study.

My dark-blue tunic and black leggings weren't the best fit for a training session, but I would make do. My unbound hair was also not ideal—I would have to make sure not to let Henry get ahold of it to use it against me.

"I don't know, can you?" the Lord teased, one side of his mouth turning up.

I approached him and assumed a fighting position, making sure my legs were braced and my feet were planted shoulder width apart. With a smirk, Henry prowled around me, eyeing my stance. When he faced me again, I got momentarily distracted by his bare chest and torso. The chiseled muscles glistened with a fine sheen of sweat as my gaze glided over them all the way down to the band of his tight, black breeches. My throat dried as I forced my eyes back up to his face. I found him watching me, the black from his pupils slowly bleeding into the blue of his irises.

"Like what you see?" he asked low, his voice rough.

My muscles tensing, I ducked my chin and threw a punch instead of responding.

He blocked it with his forearm, chuckling under his breath. "Nice try."

Trying to distract him, I stepped back with my right foot as if preparing to kick. As I'd hoped, he dropped his guard, and I used the opening to slam my fist into his stomach, grinning when I heard a soft grunt.

Henry went to throw a punch in retaliation, but I ducked out of the way, swiftly coming up to deliver a blow to his side. I wasn't able to follow through because he grabbed my arm and spun me around, hauling me to his hard chest. With my back to him, I kicked, going for his shin, but he moved his leg out of the way. I threw my head back then, the crown connecting with his jaw. The move bought me time to twist out of his hold and run to the door, where the dagger was still embedded in the doorframe. Just as I pulled it out, a stir of air at my back let me know Henry was right behind me. I whirled on him, thrusting the dagger into his chest. Our gazes locked as my lips curled into a savage smile. The blade was iron, not wood, so I knew it wouldn't hurt him. Or rather, it wouldn't hurt him *much*.

His eyes widened as an odd look settled into his features. It was shock mixed with awe and a whole lot of hunger. I'd been on the receiving end of that look a few times in the past two weeks, and it excited me more than I was willing to admit. Slowly, Henry looked down at the dagger protruding from his chest. He stared at it for a moment before his lashes swept back up. His pupils were more dilated now, making his eyes more black than blue.

"You better run," he growled.

My pulse thrummed as I spun and ran out of the study. I started for the front door but skidded to a stop when Henry appeared right in front of me. He shook his head "no", one side of his mouth turning up. His blue-black eyes flashed, daring and challenging, as if he couldn't wait to see what I would do next.

I whirled to the right, but he jumped to block me, so I darted to the left instead. He caught my elbow before I could get away, but I twisted under his arm, slipping out of his hold. I then moved behind him, dipping low and kicking out. When I swept his legs out from under him, he threw his hands out to stop the fall, cursing under his breath.

I took off for the stairs but didn't make it far before an arm came around my waist, hauling me back against a hard wall of muscle. Henry's breath stirred the wisps of hair at my temple a moment before he spun me around, slamming me into the stone floor by the grand staircase. He pinned my arms by my sides and pressed in, his body caging mine.

I knew he'd only used a fraction of his strength when he'd brought me down because I wasn't hurt. There was barely a crack in the stone where my head had hit instead of a me-shaped hole in the floor several inches deep. A growl of irritation tore from me because he'd held back. If the past two weeks had proven anything, it was that I was more than capable of taking everything the Lord could throw at me. As a new vampire, I wasn't a match for him yet, but it was only a matter of time; he'd said so himself.

"You held back," I bit out, pushing up against him, trying to throw him off me, but he didn't budge.

"You stabbed me," he growled, his face inches away from mine. The deep sound rumbled through me, all the way to the tips of my toes.

"I knew you could take it," I countered, but my gaze still dropped to his chest to make sure the wound I'd inflicted was already closing.

"I have a feeling you'd wanted to do that for a while," Henry ground out above me.

When I looked up, his lips stretched into a teasing smile,

taunting me. The sight made my heart skip a beat as I stared up at him, lost in the perfect planes and angles of his face.

"Maybe," I breathed, dragging my fangs over my bottom lip.

Henry's smile faded as his gaze dropped and fastened on my mouth. His features became sharper as he tilted his head, sending a tumble of dark locks over his forehead. He was on me, his body close to flush with mine, and I could feel him—*all* of him. My lips parted as intense lust rolled through me, sending hot shivers over my skin. Henry's lips parted, too, revealing the hints of his fangs as he lifted his gaze back to mine. My breath caught at what I saw in his eyes. They were nearly black with a hunger that ignited my blood.

Eyes still on me, Henry lifted his hand to my face and brushed his fingertips over the curve of cheek, making my skin hum from the contact. His lashes swept down as his gaze returned to my lips, and he leaned in. Tensing with anticipation, I sucked in a sharp breath as he lowered his head, his mouth hovering over mine. He was going to kiss me. I'd never forgotten how his lips had felt on mine weeks ago, but this kiss would be different. I hadn't been myself back then, still under the effects of Henry's blood after he'd saved me. But I was myself now, and I wanted this. I wanted *him.*

34

My eyes drifted closed, and my heartbeat danced in my chest as I waited for Henry to kiss me. To my surprise, his lips didn't brush mine. They glided over my cheek and my jaw, eliciting a shiver from me. I didn't move, didn't breathe, as a pleasant curling sensation stirred in my lower stomach. My lips parted as I waited for him to claim my mouth. Growing impatient, I was about to sink my fingers into his hair and seal my mouth to his when a knock sounded on the front door.

My eyes flew open, and Henry jerked his head back, stiffening above me. We both turned toward the entrance, catching the scent of who was on the other side of the door. For a long moment, Henry didn't move, but then he shifted off me, rising to his feet. He reached down, and I placed my hand in his, letting him pull me up even though I didn't need his help. He didn't let go of my hand once I was on my feet, and I threaded my fingers through his as we walked to the door.

Celeste stood on the other side, under the bright glow of the moon. She looked calm and collected as she said, "Dark Witches are preparing to attack."

My breath left me as my heart stuttered and stopped before speeding up in my chest.

"How much time do we have?" Henry asked as his hand tightened around mine.

"A couple of hours at best," Celeste replied. Her gaze dropped to our joined hands before darting to me. Her luminous blue eyes were curious as she stared at me. "I see you have changed," was all she said. She didn't sound judgmental, but it wouldn't have mattered even if she did.

"I have." I lifted my chin.

I wasn't ashamed of becoming a vampire. I was proud that I'd had the courage and the strength to do it. To become something I'd loathed so I could try to save my people. Even though I was now different from them, humans were still *my* people. They always would be.

"Here." Celeste handed me the amulet. "We haven't found a way to activate it."

My heart dropped as I let go of Henry's hand and took the Tear, hanging it around my neck. All this time, I'd still held out hope that the White Witches would find a way and we would be able to avoid a war.

"Thank you for trying," I said, my voice hoarse.

"We didn't find a way to activate the amulet, but we will help you fight in the war," Celeste said, and Henry and I exchanged a look.

Having the White Witches fight alongside us didn't guarantee a victory, but it was still a big relief to have them join us.

"Thank you," Henry said with sincerity, echoing what I felt in my heart, and Celeste nodded.

"I am going back to the border to prepare. We will see you there," she said before walking away.

Closing the door behind her, Henry turned to me. My heart pounded in the silence that followed. There was so much to say, but suddenly, it felt like words would never be enough.

"So, it is finally here," Isabelle said, appearing in the foyer.

Henry reluctantly dragged his gaze away from me and turned to her.

"Finally?" he asked, raising one dark brow.

"Yes, finally." Isabelle exhaled. "I swear it felt like I'd been holding my breath for two weeks, waiting for the Dark Witches to attack. Now, the wait is over. I might die tonight, but at least I won't have to endure any more dread and uncertainty."

I found I agreed with her on that. Tonight, it would all be resolved—one way or another.

"I'm going to gather the clans," Isabelle said, and Henry nodded.

"I will change and then go to the border. Sophie will come with me," he told her.

"Take your time," Isabelle said low, looking between Henry and me. Her mouth twitched as if she were fighting a smile before she disappeared through the front door, stirring my unbound hair on her way out.

I looked at Henry, and our gazes locked again and held, the air between us becoming strangely charged. His features were impossible to read as he stared at me. My gaze dropped to his mouth, and I found myself wishing we could somehow recapture the moment we'd shared before Celeste had shown up. I knew we wouldn't, though, when Henry's face sharpened, becoming harsher and more unyielding. I knew at that moment that he had put what had happened between us behind, focusing on the issue at hand.

"We need to get ready and head to the border," he said, his voice rough and thick. "I will come to get you after I change," he added, turning to head upstairs to his bedroom.

I opened my mouth to say something, but I wasn't sure what, so I clamped it shut and stalked out of the foyer. Once I was in my bedroom, I stopped before the vanity mirror, stalling. I knew I needed to change, but I couldn't bring myself to move as I stared at my reflection, illuminated by the soft glow of the lamp on the bedside table. The room was dim, but I could see clearly as if it were brightly lit because of my new abilities. My hazel eyes were big with fear, and my lips were almost white, pressed in a thin line. I looked beautiful, as all vampires did, my already attractive features brought to nearly flawless perfection when I'd turned. I still felt flawed, though, as my gaze dropped to the amulet resting on my chest.

If only my blood had worked. All this could have been avoided. There would be no Dark Witches or war. There would be no vampires, I realized with a pang in my chest as my gaze lifted to the ceiling, where I could hear Henry moving around in his bedroom. I'd come to care about him deeply, and the thought scared me as much as it excited me. Perhaps everything happened for a reason, and our story was supposed to unfold this way.

Not all was lost.

Not yet, I hoped as I lowered my gaze back to my reflection. My hands trembled as I untangled the delicate chain of the amulet from the necklace holding the locket with the picture of my mother. Opening the locket, I looked at the miniature portrait stored inside. I loved my mother so much. Everything I'd done had been for her, my father, and others like them—my people. I knew my father was proud of me, and I had a feeling my mother would be, too, if she were still alive. Closing the locket with a heavy sigh, I took it off my neck and set it on the vanity. When I looked at the Tear still hanging on my chest, my father's words from earlier floated up in my mind. *You have vampire strength, but your heart is still human, and there is magic in your blood.*

"What if..." I murmured, reaching up to unclasp the chain holding the amulet from my neck. I halted when I heard Henry right outside my door.

Holding my breath, I waited. He seemed to be waiting, too. For what, I wasn't sure. I could hear him standing there for a moment before he exhaled roughly, resting his forehead on my door with a soft thud.

My heart turned over in my chest. What *were* we waiting for? We were wasting precious time. We might not survive tonight, and there was so much to say, to do, to…*feel.*

"Sophie," Henry breathed when I opened my bedroom door.

He was still shirtless and wearing the same black breeches, making me wonder if he'd spent all that time upstairs trying to find the courage to come talk to me.

When our gazes locked, everything stopped, and I was falling, swimming in the deep blue waters of his eyes.

I wanted to tell him how grateful I was for everything he'd done for me. How I'd never seen him as a monster, not truly. How thrilled I was to be like him now, so we didn't have to part. All those words rushed to the surface, dancing on the tip of my tongue, but none of them came out.

"I want you," was all I said.

The moment I uttered the words, panic set in. What if he didn't feel the same way about me? But then I saw raw emotion etched into his striking features, and that almost brought me to my knees.

He moved then, and his mouth was on mine. He kissed me deeply, desperately as if he'd waited for ages, and now that his restraint broke, there was no holding back. I didn't want to hold back, either, instantly lost in an all-consuming rush of desire. The world faded away as his tongue slid over mine, leaving only him and me in this moment.

35

He kissed me hard, his hand fisting in my hair, and I responded in kind, my fingers digging into the corded muscles of his arms. When I pressed against his chest, wanting to be closer, a rumble came from deep within his throat, eliciting a wave of shivers. Without warning, he broke the kiss, resting his forehead against mine. We were both breathless, our chests rising and falling heavily.

"We have terrible timing." He chucked low and without humor.

He was right. The timing *was* terrible, but it didn't matter. What mattered was here and now. We would have to face the witches soon, and there was a possibility that we would not survive, but we were alive now, right here in this room. And I wanted to be alive with him, to experience what I had in my dreams. They'd continued long after he'd turned me, growing in their intensity, driving me mad with desire. When I'd told him I was dreaming about him, he'd said it was because he was the one who'd turned me. He'd said it was his blood making me dream about him. But it wasn't his blood. It was him, *all* of him. I knew that now, without a doubt.

"Henry," I breathed, and he must have heard the desperate need in my voice because his eyes flooded with molten heat.

His features sharpened with raw lust a moment before he leaned in. I expected him to claim my mouth again and kiss me wildly, but instead, he brushed his lips over mine painstakingly slowly. My breath caught as I held still, reveling in the sensation as tiny sparks hit every part of my body. The tenderness of the kiss brought tears to my eyes as emotions rose and swelled in my chest. He was drinking from my lips, taking his time as if he would be content to do just that—kiss me for all eternity. Then Henry tilted his head, and everything changed.

The kiss became more—so much more. He tugged on my bottom lip with his fangs, and a soft gasp left me as I opened up for him. He increased the pressure, every fierce stroke of his tongue resonating in every part of my body as desire pulsed between my thighs. The kiss became urgent and demanding. He devoured me, and I responded in kind, our fangs clashing and our tongues mingling. I melted into him, as the throbbing ache between my thighs intensified.

Only kissing him was no longer enough, so I abruptly broke the kiss, reaching for the hem of my tunic. I pulled it over my head, casting it aside. Henry went still and seemed to have stopped breathing as his gaze dropped to the hardened tips of my breasts. He reached up, almost reverently, and brushed his knuckles on the underside of my breasts, stirring the amulet still resting between them.

"Beautiful," he breathed, running his thumbs over the sensitive peaks.

The fleeting touch sent a ripple of pleasure through me, and I gasped, arching into him. Dark, hungry eyes darted to mine as a deep, raw sound escaped Henry's lips. In a heartbeat, I was on the edge of the bed, and he stood beside it, pulling off my boots, then my leggings and undergarments.

"Sophie," he rasped as he towered over me, drinking in my naked form.

His eyes roamed over every inch of my body before settling on the throbbing space between my thighs.

Slowly, he reached for me, and all my attention zeroed in on his hand as his fingers glided through my wetness, eliciting a breathy moan from me. I knew we didn't have time to take this slow, to worship each other as we explored all the unexpected hidden places that made our breaths hitch. Even if we did, I didn't think I would be able to drag this out. I was desperate for him—my dreams making me feel like I'd been waiting forever to feel his touch on my heated flesh, to unleash the unspent desire humming just below the surface of my skin.

Sitting up on the edge of the bed, I reached for him, tearing at the buttons of his breeches. My throat dried as I freed him from his pants. I went to curl my hand around him, desperate to touch him, but before I could, he gripped my waist and lifted me off the bed. He turned us around and sat on the edge before lowering me down to straddle him. My knees fell to either side of his hips, and I shuddered when I felt him hard at my core. He groaned, tensing under me, and his eyes drifted closed as I glided my hands over his chest to his shoulders.

I wrapped my arms around his neck and tenderly kissed his brow before brushing my lips over his cheekbone and the firm line of his jaw. I loved touching him, feeling his smooth skin under my lips and my hands, and he seemed to be reveling in my touch, trembling slightly. His arms encircled my waist, pulling me tightly against him, leaving no space between us as he claimed my mouth again. My skin hummed from the contact, and my lips tingled from his kisses as I lost myself in the feel of him.

"Sophie," he whispered against my lips. "I have been dreaming about you, too."

My eyes pricked with tears and my chest became tight as I

pulled away to look into his eyes, which were nearly black with hunger. I knew it wasn't just hunger for blood but for *me*. Nothing mattered then. There was no past and no future, only this moment.

Suddenly, it felt like we had all the time in the world, but I wasn't going to wait any longer. I couldn't. Lifting up, I tilted my hips until I felt him where I ached, pressing into me. Henry shuddered, holding himself still as I slowly lowered myself, moaning at the exquisite sensation. Another harsh groan left him as I sank down on his length, taking all of him in. His fingers threaded through my hair, and he clasped the back of my neck, drawing my mouth back to his. I kissed him as I lifted my hips, trembling slightly before lowering myself once more. A ragged cry tore from my lips at the sharp wave of pleasure as Henry moaned, rough and deep. The sound spurred me into action as I began moving slowly but steadily, chasing that sound again and my own building pleasure.

"This," Henry rasped against my lips, "is so much better than the dreams."

He was right. My dreams didn't even come close to the feeling of having him inside me. I began to move faster, rocking against him, my breathing coming in quick, short pants. He clasped my thighs, his fingers digging in, as he helped me move on him, lifting me up before pulling me down again, harder each time. I gasped with pleasure as another need invaded my senses.

"I need..." I breathed, lowering my head, my fangs grazing the pulse at his throat.

"Yes," he rasped. "Take what you need. I am yours."

My fangs pierced the skin, eliciting a rough sound from him, and I moaned as his blood, rich and thick, filled my mouth. I had him—all of him—and the feeling was pure ecstasy.

After I swallowed a few gulps of his essence, my head fell back, and my eyes closed as pleasure climbed higher inside me. His breath coasted over my breast before I felt the wet glide of his tongue as his mouth closed over the hardened tip. I cried out as he sucked deep and long. The graze of his fangs over my nipple told me what he wanted, what he *needed,* as his hips flexed and thrust upward, harder and deeper than before.

Bringing my mouth to his ear, I whispered, "Do it."

I wanted him to bite me, to take from me like I'd taken from him.

Henry pulled my head back, exposing my throat, and every part of me trembled as his fangs scraped my skin. Under me, he moved his powerful body at a punishing rhythm, each thrust of his hips bringing me closer to the edge. When his fangs sank in, I shattered with a sharp cry, release crashing through me in waves. Henry followed me over the edge, his large body shaking, and the sound he made against my neck heated my blood, intensifying my pleasure.

I collapsed on him, limp and boneless, resting my head on his shoulder. He held me tightly to his chest, his hand still tangled in my hair, as we sat there, waiting for our breathing to slow. Still trembling slightly, I lifted my head and met his gaze, which was growing more blue and less black by the second. Suddenly, my heart was bursting with want and need and something else I wasn't quite ready to acknowledge. His eyes were full of awe and wonder as he stared at me. Lifting his hand from my hair, he pressed the tips of his fingers gently against my cheek, drawing in a shallow breath.

"That was—" he began saying but stopped, his dark lashes sweeping down as he lowered his gaze to my chest. "The amulet…it's glowing."

36

My hand trembled as I lifted the Tear off my chest and looked at it with wide eyes. It was smeared with my blood from when Henry had bitten me, and the pale blue crystal in the middle pulsed with white light.

"Power of three," I whispered in disbelief. "Human, witch, and vampire."

"Which are now all in your blood," Henry whispered, understanding washing over his face.

Celeste had said before that the powerful magic of the amulet couldn't have had come without a price. I now knew what the price was. My mother had planned to turn into a vampire so she could wield the Tear. Vincent was going to turn her. That was the ultimate sacrifice.

"Do you know what this means?" I asked Henry in a hushed tone, lifting my gaze to his.

I thought I knew what it meant, but I wanted to hear it from him. I felt a spark of hope in my chest, but I didn't want to give life to it, too terrified the hope was false.

"I do," he said with a soft smile as he cupped my face.

He kissed me then, and I shuddered as a wave of tears reached my eyes. I couldn't believe I was here with him—in this moment —when we had just quite possibly found a way to our salvation. The pressure of the kiss increased as he tugged on my lower lip with his fangs. I opened up for him, and as his tongue slid over mine, desire rose again, threatening to sweep me under. I wanted to give in to it, to stay right here, in his arms, forever, letting the rest of the world fade away, but we couldn't do that. He knew it, too, because the kiss became less demanding and more sweet—a promise of what would come if we survived. In the next moment, his mouth left mine, trailing soft kisses down the side of my neck.

"What if it doesn't work?" I whispered. "Worse yet, what if it *does* work but it wipes out all supernatural, not just the Dark Witches?"

Henry's kisses on my skin slowed and eventually stopped. He rested his head in the crook of my neck for a moment before lifting his gaze to mine.

"Have hope," he said, looking into my eyes. "I have just found you. I am not ready to lose you yet."

"I don't want to lose *you*," I whispered, gripping his shoulders as if I could hold on to him forever.

We didn't want to lose each other and the future that what had just happened between us promised.

Henry's gaze flicked to the window where the drawn curtains hid the darkness outside, and I knew that the moment we had carved out for ourselves was over.

"We need to go to the border and tell Celeste we found a way to activate the amulet," he said, his gaze returning to me. The rest was left unspoken—hopefully we would know what to do from there.

Do we have to go? almost escaped from my mouth but I held my tongue. I'd come so far, sacrificed so much. I would see this through, even if the future was uncertain.

I nodded, and Henry gently lifted me off him, setting me down as he rose to his feet.

"Sophie…" he said, bringing his hand up and gliding his fingers down my cheek.

"Don't." I stopped him with my hand on his chest. I didn't know what he was going to say, but I had a feeling it was good-bye, and I refused to accept that. "Have hope," I whispered as I covered his hand on my cheek with mine and turned my face to kiss his palm.

Emotions churned in his stormy blue eyes as a ragged breath left him. His other hand went up and fisted in my hair before he gave me another scorching kiss.

"I am in awe of you," he whispered against my lips, making my heart lurch in my chest.

He pulled away abruptly as if he didn't trust himself to linger lest we never leave this room.

"Get dressed. I will come to get you shortly," he said before he pulled on his breeches and swept from my bedroom.

I didn't move for a few seconds, my attention lingering on the door long after it had closed. He'd said he was in awe of me. I was in awe of him, too—of what we'd just shared and of how happy it made me feel. How happy *he* made me feel. I wanted more of that, more of *him*, wondering if I would ever be able to get enough. What we'd shared went beyond the physical. I felt him seeping into my skin and settling in my heart. I wanted to fight for him, for us, stopping at nothing. And fight I would, with my fangs and with my claws if I had to. I hoped it wouldn't come to that, though, as I caught my reflection in the vanity mirror, the amulet still pulsing on my chest.

The power of three. The answer had been right in front of me the whole time. I realized I was glad that I hadn't known about it before now. The past few weeks had been important. I'd needed the time to get to know Henry so I could trust him to turn me and guide me through the change. He'd needed the time to show me that becoming a vampire didn't mean becoming a monster.

Forcing myself out of my thoughts, I willed my numb limbs to move, quickly getting dressed in black pants and a black tunic. I hung the locket with the portrait of my mother back around my neck, tucking it under my collar. I left the Tear over my clothes, and it glowed on my chest like a star, still smeared with my blood. Facing the vanity mirror again, I dragged the brush through my tousled hair before pulling it up and out of my face. My cheeks were still flushed from what Henry and I had done earlier, and a shudder rolled through me when my mind flashed back to what we'd shared, to how his body had felt against mine.

As if I'd conjured him with my mind, the Lord came back to collect me, softly rapping his knuckles on my bedroom door.

When I opened it, he hauled me to his hard chest and kissed me deeply, stealing my breath away.

"It seems I can't stop kissing you," he murmured against my lips.

"If we survive tonight, you'll never have to stop," I breathed.

He pulled away then and looked into my eyes.

"Whatever happens tonight…I want you to know that what we shared earlier was one of the best moments of my entire life," he rasped.

"Mine too," I whispered. I knew that my nineteen years didn't come remotely close to his two hundred, but I still wanted him to know.

He shook his head as if to clear his thoughts before his gaze swept over me.

"You should wear armor, just in case," he said. He was already wearing his.

In case the Tear doesn't work, he didn't say, but his gaze dropped to the amulet pulsing on my chest.

My heart twisted as emotion seized me, and I clasped his face, claiming his mouth, realizing this might be the last time I got to do so. This might be our very last kiss, so soon after we'd had our first. I wanted more firsts with him. I would do *anything* for it.

My mouth moved over his with desperation I felt in my bones, and we were both breathless when I pulled away and rested my forehead on his.

"We have to go," he said low and thick.

"I know," I whispered, inhaling his fresh and woodsy scent before I pulled away. "I'm ready," I said, surprised to find my voice steady.

I *was* ready—ready to find out if my mother's creation truly worked.

Several minutes later, we appeared on the border, hand in hand, both clad in leather and iron. The other clans were already here, and I caught a few curious glances in our direction as Henry and I made our way to the wall. I'd been the first vampire turned to join the clans since the Red War, so I could understand the others' interest in me. I was proud to be a part of the Duval clan and took my new role seriously, planning to help Henry and Isabelle carry on the legacy Vincent and Rosalind had left behind. I would also carry on my mother's legacy. I hoped I would get a chance to learn the magic in my blood and do all the great things my father had spoken about before he'd left.

Henry was still holding my hand when we made our way to the top of the border wall, where we joined the clan leaders. Isabelle was there as well, her black armor blending in with the night. Her nostrils flared as we neared before she smirked, giving me a knowing look. I almost rolled my eyes as a smile tugged at my lips. Camilla stood by her, clad in white armor, the color matching her hair, and she chuckled low as her ice-blue eyes dropped to where Henry held my hand. Thankfully, she chose not to say anything as her expression turned serious, and she trained her eyes on the impenetrable darkness of the Black Forest looming on the other side of the border.

I looked past Camilla and saw Celeste and the other White

Witches, all dressed in blue cloaks. There were only about fifty of them, and my heart broke all over again as I thought about the fate of their kind. *My kind,* I reminded myself. It was truly a miracle that the White Witches were here, joining our fight, even though only so few of them remained.

Celeste was looking at the Black Forest when I found her in the crowd, but then her eyes darted to me as if she could sense I was here. And perhaps she could; perhaps the world whispered it to her. Her gaze fastened on the amulet on my chest before she lifted her eyes to mine, her eyebrows raised in question. I nodded, and the witch moved, walking hurriedly toward me.

"How did you do it?" she asked low when she approached.

"Power of three," I whispered as Henry squeezed my hand in quiet support. "Power of all three species," I explained.

"Which you now possess," Celeste surmised, understanding dawning on her.

Isabelle and Camilla exchanged a look, standing a few feet behind the witch.

"How do I use it?" I asked urgently, not sure how much time we had.

"It should just follow your will," Celeste replied just as horns blared from several locations along the wall.

Everyone spun toward the Black Forest as unearthly silence settled over the border. I gripped the stone ledge with my free hand as darkness poured out of the woods, spilling into the air and onto the ground.

There were hundreds of them. They moved like smoke, creeping toward the border, their shadows thick and murky against the black of the night. Within minutes, they were almost to the border, and the entire stone wall seemed to shudder. My heart dropped as I looked around me. White lighting crackled at the end of Celeste's fingers as she ducked her chin, preparing for battle. Isabelle and Camilla crouched down, their fangs bared in a snarl and their fingers ending in sharp claws.

I looked at Henry then and found him watching me. He wasn't looking in the direction of the Black Forest. He was looking at me, deep sorrow etched into his features. "I have just found you," he'd told me earlier. Now, his look conveyed, "I have just found you, and we are out of time."

Panic flared as my heart lurched in my chest. I whipped my head back to the other side of the border. The Dark Witches halted a few feet from the wall, creating a sea of churning darkness that stretched all the way to the Black Forest. There were so many of them that I knew once they moved, they would swallow New Haven like a tide of pain and destruction. My mind was instantly filled with images of people dying and being captured for sacrifices.

Once New Haven fell, the Dark Witches would spread like a plague until they reached the Northern region where most of our people were, where my father was currently heading. They would consume the entire Empire, plunging it into darkness and suffering. My heart seized as my eyes filled with tears. I blinked them back as I stared at the black mass of Dark Witches, waiting for the attack. The witches stood unmoving at the border, and in a few seconds, I knew why.

"Surrender," Antaris said, her voice full of slithering shadows. She separated from the sea of darkness, stepping closer to the wall and looking up at where Henry and I stood. "Our numbers are too great. You will not prevail," she hissed as wispy tendrils of smoke pulsed all around her.

She was right. We wouldn't win this war. Not unless the amulet worked.

"It is now or never, Sophie," I heard Henry say.

I looked at him and he met my gaze, his features hard with resolve.

"I don't know what's going to happen," I whispered.

"Whatever happens, I am right here with you. I will follow you into the void if that is our fate," Henry said fiercely.

Our fate.

I was the master of my fate, not the other way around, I thought, closing my eyes and bringing my hand up to my chest.

I covered the amulet resting there, letting my fingers curl around it. The pale-blue crystal burned like ice, frostbite branding the skin of my palm. I heard Henry's sharp inhale as his grip on my other hand tightened, letting me know he was here with me, by my side, like he had been in the past few weeks.

Releasing a controlled breath, I let my instincts take over as I concentrated on the Tear in my hand, my brows pinching. I imagined my mother standing behind me, her hand on my shoulder, guiding me. Suddenly, I was engulfed in her love, so deep and unconditional. And love blossomed in my heart. Love for my parents and for my people. For the one standing next to me, holding my hand.

I blinked open my eyes and realized I wasn't on the border anymore. I was at the Mayfair Park with Rory. The sunlight seeping through the twisted tree branches told me all of this was not real. It couldn't be, because I was now a vampire and couldn't be out in the sun. And because Rory was dead. Still, I lifted my face up to the sunlight, reveling in the feeling of it on my face, before I lowered my gaze to Rory.

"What do you hope for?" I asked her, just like I had that day in the park shortly after the Selection.

"A bright future where I feel safe," she replied, her big brown eyes sparkling and bright.

I knew what I needed to do then as I looked down at the amulet in my hand.

It should just follow your will, Celeste's words floated up in my head.

I wanted a future where humanity was safe. A future where Dark Witches were no more, but White Witches still lived, free and out of hiding. I wanted a future…for Henry and me.

I felt it then. My mother's magic. And my grandmother's. The magic of my entire bloodline stored in the amulet. It coursed through me, filling me as if I were an empty vessel.

The white light in the pale-blue crystal was pulsing brighter and brighter, but it wasn't just the amulet glowing—I was glowing with it. The bright light pulsed in my chest until it filled my entire body, saturating my every pore and spilling outward into the world around me. The light kept building inside me, and with it, I felt impossible power, so pure and beautiful it brought tears to my eyes. It built until I knew I couldn't contain it anymore. Squeezing my eyes shut, I released the light and, with it, the power into the night with a shout, burning like the brightest star, illuminating the dark world around me. The outburst was blinding, painting my vision in white even through the closed eyelids, and for a few minutes, I couldn't see anything, but I felt at peace, as if calm, clear waters were pulling me under.

"Sophie," Henry's soft whisper brought me back to the surface. "Look at me."

My eyes fluttered open, and I saw his face. Had he followed me into the void like he'd promised?

"Are you okay?" he asked low, his worried eyes searching my face.

"Yes," I breathed, my gaze wandering to the starry night sky above him.

This didn't feel like the void. I was lying in his lap, staring up at him. Frowning, I sat up slowly, my mind a bit hazy, and looked around. We were surrounded—human guards, White Witches, and vampires all stood around us, watching me with wide eyes.

"What happened?" I turned to Henry.

"You did it," he whispered, his lips curling into a hesitant smile.

With his help, I scrambled to my feet and dashed to the stone ledge of the wall, leaning out. The Dark Witches were no longer on the other side of the border, ebbing and flowing like a sea of churning black water.

"You destroyed them all," Henry said low behind me.

He sounded like he couldn't quite believe it. I couldn't believe it, either, but he was still here, and so was I.

"Is everyone else—"

"Unharmed." I heard Celeste's voice behind my back.

Shocked, I looked down at the amulet on my chest. It no longer pulsed, the pale-blue crystal dull and cold. Closing my eyes, I released the longest exhale of my life, feeling like I'd been holding my breath for eons. Then, I inhaled deeply, filling my lungs with air of a new world. The world where Dark Witches no longer existed.

"What happens now?" Henry asked, and I turned around to face him.

His eyes shone with admiration, affection, and a myriad of other emotions that brought me to tears with their intensity. I also noticed a faint shadow of apprehension, as if he weren't sure what I would say.

"Now, we give the humans their world back and slink back into the shadows where we belong," I told him and held my breath.

Did he want that? He'd said he did in the past, but had that changed? More importantly, did he want that with *me*?

A smile broke across his face, stunning in its warmth and beauty.

"Yes," he breathed, cupping my face. "I don't care where we belong. As long as we're together."

I didn't care, either, I realized, looking into his eyes and seeing my future. As long as I was with Henry and the humans were safe.

EPILOGUE

HENRY

I hungered for her more than blood, as if she were the very essence I needed to survive. I craved her as I had never craved anything before in my long life.

"I don't think the clans will give up control that easily," Sophie said when we returned to the estate.

She had defeated the Dark Witches, giving the humans their world back. I couldn't believe it. Just like I couldn't believe she was mine. She was brave and courageous, and mine.

"That is a problem for another day," I told her, scooping her up in my arms and taking her to my bedroom.

She gave a startled gasp when I tossed her on the bed and began taking off her armor, then her clothes. Even with my supernatural speed, I couldn't get her naked fast enough. I needed to be inside her. Only a couple of hours had passed since I'd had her, but it felt like an eternity. Now that I knew what it felt like to be buried deep inside her, I wondered how I had lived without that for so long.

A shuddering breath left me when I tossed the last piece of clothing aside and looked at Sophie sprawled naked before me.

My own personal feast. The smile she gave me was downright sinful as she tugged down my pants while I took off my armor and tunic. The molten heat in her gaze told me she was as desperate for me as I was for her. We moved at the same time, coming together, our mouths colliding. Catching her lower lip between my teeth, I bit her, drawing blood, and she moaned, the sound taking my desire to new heights. I wanted to drag this out, to take my time—we had it now because Sophie had ensured it— but I couldn't wait.

Curling my arm around her waist, I lowered her down to the mattress, my other hand fisting in her hair. With one mighty thrust, I was where I had wanted to be all along—deep inside her. She wrapped her legs around my hips, taking all of me in as I thrust harder and faster until the only sound was that of our bodies coming together. She was gasping with pleasure as I felt her quivering around me, bringing me to the edge. I had her—all of her—but I wanted more.

Pulling her head back, I exposed her neck as my hunger for her intensified. She panted as my fangs grazed her pulse, and when they pressed in, she cried out and shattered, clenching around me. A harsh groan left me as her blood coated my tongue. The taste of her and the feel of her dragged me over the edge, my body bucking as bolts of intense pleasure rolled through me.

Once the spasms rocking my body slowed, I drew her mouth to mine, kissing her slowly and thoroughly. I could never get enough of this—of her.

"You are mine," I whispered against her lips.

"I am yours," she whispered back.

My heart was bursting with so much emotion, I had to swallow to relieve the dryness in my throat. When I pushed up to look at her, I noticed the amulet she was still wearing had slid off her chest, pooling at her neck. I gently moved it back down to settle between her breasts, my fingers smearing her blood over the pale-blue crystal in the middle. When I lifted my gaze to hers, what I saw in her eyes nearly undid me. Soon, we would be living in the shadows, but the future was still bright because she was by my side. Tears glimmered in her eyes as she smiled at me. I smiled back as my gaze glided down her neck and chest to where the amulet lay, pulsing once again.

ABOUT THE AUTHOR

V.I. is a chocolate-loving coffee enthusiast who enjoys a quiet life in a small town with her husband and two kids. She writes stories with fantasy, romance, and all your favorite tropes. Her journey as an author has only just begun, but she has a feeling it will be a great one. You can sign up for her newsletter or find her on social media platforms if you want to follow along. Happy reading!